THE
Revenge
PACT

Wall Street Journal Bestselling Author

ILSA MADDEN-MILLS

The Revenge Pact
Copyright © 2020 by Ilsa Madden-Mills

Cover Designer: Letitia Hasser, RBA Designs
Editor: Editing by C. Marie
Content Editor: Rebecca, Fairest Reviews Editing Services
Proof Reader: Kara Hildebrand

IMM Publishing
ISBN: 9798572854664

First Edition December 2020.

PROLOGUE

See those three boys over there?

Yeah, the kings of football?

The ones with their heads in their hands, drinking their beers and trying to figure out what the hell happened to their season?

They choked.

That's right. These All-Americans became the biggest upset in college football and a complete embarrassment to their town.

Can it really be that bad?

Yes.

Former national champions, Braxton College was annihilated this year.

No, not just annihilated—completely and utterly destroyed.

Three games.

That's it.

They won three games all season.

Interceptions. Dropped balls. Missed blocks. Fumbles. Name it, they did it.

First, there's River Tate, the popular frat boy. He's supposed to be a superstar wide receiver but dropped more passes than he caught.

Next is Crew Smith, the protective one. Once an NFL hopeful, he now holds the record for the most interceptions in a season for a quarterback.

And rounding out the trifecta of crap is Hollis Hudson, the mysterious tight end who keeps everything locked down. He couldn't run a route to save his life this year.

Guys wanted to be them.

Girls wanted their hearts.

But at this point, not sure anyone would touch them with a ten-foot pole.

The truth is, they've screwed up their prospective NFL careers.

Maybe their entire lives.

There are three stories to be told...

This is River's.

I lie to myself all the time.
    But I never
    believe me.

— *THE OUTSIDERS,* S. E. HINTON

1

River

At half past six, I pop awake, and my first class isn't till nine. Typical. Once my head winds up, there's no shutting off the replay reel. Dark and ugly, our last football game rushes at me and my hands clench the sheets.

The score? Forty-seven to fourteen.

We got decimated.

Screw that.

Jumping up, I stick my earbuds in and listen to "My Own Worst Enemy" by Lit as my fingers wrap around a pull-up bar I have in the doorway. I count out fifty, hop back down, and roll my neck. Blood rushes through my veins, adrenaline kicking in and obliterating the dark thoughts. I check the mirror. My face screams exhaustion and my 'famous' lips are in a thin, hard line.

Good morning, world. River Tate is ready to kick ass.

Yeah. *Keep telling yourself that.*

The older, Craftsman-style off-campus house I share with my teammates, Crew and Hollis, is dead quiet when I walk down the hall to the bathroom. The silence pricks at me, crawling like spiders, reminding me of a funeral home. It brings back unwanted memories of my dad, and I kick those ugly thoughts away. A man can only handle so many losses in his head at once.

After my shower, I rip back the curtain that hangs around the old claw-foot tub. "Dammit!" Forgot my clothes. Again. My brain truly is the Bermuda Triangle. Info comes in and *poof*, it vanishes. I have excellent recall for the oddest things. Mating rituals of animals? Check. Football stats? Locked and loaded. Movie quotes? Branded in my skull. My classes at Braxton? Freaking ghost town with tumbleweeds blowing through it. That plane has flown over the Triangle and disappeared.

My brain goes too fast to focus on small details like underwear.

I wrap a towel around my waist and open the door, water dripping on the hardwood.

You'd lose your head if it wasn't screwed on, Mom says. Then she'll laugh and say, *Now, what the heck was I doing?* An image of her pops into my head, glossy brown hair, blue eyes, and the best smile on this planet. My chest tightens. She's not awake yet or I'd call her. *She sleeps until noon*, my sister Rae told me.

A trip to my closet tells me I haven't done laundry in a while. The only shirt that passes muster is one from sophomore year. It's purple with our mascot on it, a brown badger on the pocket. Screw the haters who want to judge us for a shit season. Badgers forever! I yank it out and slip it on. "At least I have clean underwear," I mutter as I shove my legs into a pair of black skinny jeans and zip them up.

I find the Chucks I'm feeling for today—I have ten different pairs—slap them on, then fish around on the floor for my novel and backpack.

"Yes!" I call out as I find them under a mound of clothes in my closet. Makes sense. I tore into my room like a tornado on Thursday before we flew to Louisiana for the game. I barely recall packing my duffle and running out the door.

My head was in a weird place after seeing *her* on campus. Didn't talk to her—oh no, can't do that—but I saw her in the student center. She was...sad? Fuck if I know. Her head was down as she read a book, not laughing with her roommates as they sat in one of the lounge areas. Inexplicably, she looked up (maybe feeling the intensity of my stare), saw me, then her gaze moved on, not pausing. *That* I can handle. It's the usual. We've done it for a year. But her not smiling? WTF. Girl has the world. Smart. Beautiful. Perfect boyfriend.

I stop at Crew's door and bang on it. "Rise and shine, Hollywood."

Just need to see someone's face before I head out. It's a thing. And he knows.

"Go away," he groans.

I tap on Hollis's door. "Yo, man. You okay in there? Hungry?" Code for *Come talk to me.*

"Asshole" is the low response.

I smirk. We had a few too many drinks last night at our favorite bar, The Truth Is Out There. It's a fitting name for a college dive devoted to *X-Files* memorabilia and newspaper clippings from supposed alien sightings that took place in Walker in the eighties.

Otherwise, Walker, Georgia, is home to Braxton College, a prestigious D1 school with one of the best football programs in the country.

Not anymore.

I swallow down jagged bitterness.

I groan aloud when I see that our cupboards are nearly bare. There's one piece of bread (I don't eat the heel), an empty box of Ritz crackers, and a bag of Funyuns. Those disgusting things belong to Crew and he'll freak if I eat them, not that I would. I have standards.

In the fridge, I find leftover pineapple pizza (Hollis

wrote his name on the box) and a box of pad thai noodles (mine) that have green fuzz on top. Well hell.

"Trip to Big Star today," I mutter as I grab the only thing edible, a half-pack of bacon. I'm nuking it in the microwave when Crew, our quarterback, sticks his head out of his room.

"I just came out so you could see my face. You aren't normal." He grabs a hat off the hook in the hall and puts it on his head backward.

"Completely aware. Morning." I push up a smile, but it's more of a wince.

He grunts his reply as he comes farther into the kitchen. "Jesus. How can you *eat*?"

I smirk. "Bacon is manna from heaven. Besides, grease hits the spot after a hangover. I'll hit the grocery today. It's my turn." I pause. "You remember last night?"

He squints. "Do I want to? Aleve?"

"Maybe not." I toss him the pain meds I grabbed earlier for myself along with a bottled water from the fridge.

We rarely get wasted. Sure, we drink some, but once training camp starts in the summer, we toe the line. Last night was different.

Our season is officially freaking over—before Christmas. Not even a bowl game.

He guzzles the water then drops it and looks at me, a

furrow on his brow. "Wait a damn minute—did Crazy Carl hang out with us?"

"Yep." Crazy Carl is a regular at The Truth Is Out There. He's in his sixties and a bit wacko.

"It's starting to come back...like a nightmare." He plops down on a stool at the kitchen island and rubs his eyes.

I nod. "He said you looked sad and wanted to do karaoke with you, a Lady Gaga duet. You had the sense to say no. Hollis, on the other hand, sang 'Hello' by Adele. Brought down the house. The boy can sing, can't deny that, but that's a cry for help." I grab a piece of bacon and eat it fast. "The bar was packed. I think people just wanted to see if we'd show up to our usual Sunday hangout. Carl was the only one brave enough to say we needed to get our shit together."

I actually dig Carl. He's nutty but says wise things. Does that even make sense? No, it doesn't.

Crew grimaces. "Too late. Football is over, man."

I lean on the counter, needing to talk to let out some energy. "He meant our personal issues. Then he rambled a bit and told me a story about an alien he saw once. People in this town really go crazy about that stuff. Did you know he played for the Badgers when he was at Braxton? Defensive lineman. All-American. I bet he was good. He's big."

He lets out a pained groan. "*We're* All-Americans. Is it really over for us?"

"You don't want me to answer that."

The promising chatter about us storming professional football has tanked.

We're seniors this year, but unlike Crew and Hollis, I'm considering coming back to Braxton for a fifth year (and another season). I was redshirted my freshman year and only played four games, which gives me another year to play.

Hollis, our tight end, stumbles out of his room and rights himself on the wall. He's tall and built with a head of messy dark hair. "Can you assholes *please* stop yelling?"

Crew and I snicker. I sing the first line of "Hello" (my voice not nearly as good as his) and he flips me off. "Guess you remember," I say dryly.

He grunts.

I sigh as I gaze at them, and some of the tension in my chest loosens. We've been best friends since freshman year.

I love the fuck out of them.

The Three Amigos on the field.

I'm the can't-shut-up one, Crew's the mother hen, and Hollis is the mysterious one. We're gods on campus. Huh...well, *former* gods.

Hollis holds up a muscled forearm and blinks at the

lights in the kitchen. "God, it's bright. Water," he croaks. "My head's about to explode."

"Look alive," I say and toss him a cold one from the fridge.

"You'll need this, bro." Crew throws the Aleve to Hollis, but he's juggling the water and misses the pill container. He lets out a juicy curse as he bends and snatches it off the floor.

"Can't even catch a damn underhanded throw," he mutters as he plops down on a stool next to Crew. He heaves out a gusty exhalation. "We suck so hard."

"Yep," I say, my tone grim.

We've let down our school, our team, ourselves. Even Crazy Carl.

My fingers twist the sterling silver snake ring on my index finger that belonged to my dad. He played for the New York Pythons before blowing out his knee five years into his NFL career. When I was fifteen, he died in a car wreck, leaving a giant hole in our family. Then my mom got cancer. Like the kickass fighter she is, she beat it, but...

I rub my chest.

Go away, go away...

I turn away from them and look out the kitchen window. It's getting harder to pretend I'm okay. I'm a domino, on the verge of falling and making the whole pile crash down. The elephant on my chest started when

Mom's cancer came back this spring, then that pressure escalated with every game we lost.

Out the window, a red-tailed hawk lands on a bare tree, looking happy as shit in the dead of winter. His feathers ruffle slightly in the wind as his eyes sweep the area. *You need to fly farther south*, I tell him but he ignores my mental telepathy and stalks along the branch. He's a fighter.

Am I?

I close my eyes briefly.

Just get through this semester.

Come back next year.

Play better next season.

Get your degree.

Do what you *can* control.

Mom's words from Saturday swirl around in my gut. She called me as soon as the game was over, her voice weak but confident. *Slay your demons, River. All is possible. I believe in you.*

I get it, but I'm a ship without a rudder and I'm terrified I'm going to sink to the bottom of the sea. I don't have a future, can't see what's coming, can't get a grasp on what I need to do for the rest of my life.

And Mom, my beautiful, feisty mother...

If she dies...

I kick the dark thought down and think about my

first class. Like it always does, a tingle of electricity zips over me, knowing I'll be close, but not too close.

Can't touch her, but...

Five rows in front of me, *she will be there.*

Rainbow Girl.

Hair like spun silk.

Green eyes.

Lush mouth.

Short skirts.

Banging body.

Not mine.

My unease spikes as I stare down at my copy of *Lady Chatterley's Lover.* The cover is pristine because I've never cracked it open. It's a bunch of mumbo-jumbo, the words all running together.

For the hundredth time this semester, I ask myself...

Why the hell did I take this class?

I have ADHD, dyslexia, and dyscalculia, a trio of pure hell. My attention deficient and hyperactivity make "decoding" even tougher. You know those articles they write about athletes who slip through the cracks academically because they're talented athletically? Hello, I'm River. I catch footballs.

My reading level has been tested at... I can't even say it's so bad. In a weak moment, I told Blair, my ex, and she laughed in my face. She legit thought I was joking. *Yeah, just kidding* was my reply, and I swore to never tell a girl again. Let them think I'm just like them.

Pressing my fingers to the cover, I twirl it on the island. Frustration ripples over me. There are days, like today, when I wish I were like everyone else.

That boy can't sound out words.

Doesn't know numbers.

Talks too much.

My teachers had a lot to say about me in elementary school.

Then, Dad put a football in my hands.

Hollis and Crew move to the den and stretch out on the couch, their legs propped up on the coffee table. I follow them, too antsy to sit, so I pace.

Crew reaches for the remote, sees my face, then eases it back down like it's a grenade.

I sigh. "Not worth seeing our faces all over ESPN."

He closes his eyes and leans his head back on the couch.

Hollis has grabbed a Ding Dong—where did he get that?—and eats it in two bites. "When is this godawful semester over?"

"Two more weeks till winter break," I say tightly as I grab my backpack and a bag of laundry I pulled together to drop off at the Kappa house where there's a washer and dryer.

I'm the president of Kappa and alternate between

spending time here and at the frat house. A huff comes from me. I used to crash in my room there on and off (I get a free one since I'm an officer), but not since *she* appeared on the scene.

Hollis straightens up from his slouch and wipes at the chocolate crumbs around his mouth. "Holy shit..." His voice rises. "Did Crazy Carl...*kiss me?*"

Crew, who was scrolling on his phone, holds up his cell and makes a kissy noise. "A big ol' smooch on the cheek. I have a pic to prove it."

"Post that and you die." Hollis scrubs his face. "I'm never drinking again."

My chest feels tight again as I watch them.

I twist my ring, my head tumbling as Mom's words dance around in my head.

Slay your demons.

The idea's been pricking at me ever since I got in the shower. It's where I do my best thinking. If I get ramped up, I strip down and let the water wash over me. The small space, steam, and being naked help my mind focus. I average about three showers a day, morning, afternoon, and night. My grades might be shit, but I'm quite possibly the cleanest person at Braxton. This is also why I'm constantly out of laundry.

"I've been thinking."

The guys look at me. Part fear, part anticipation.

"Don't look so freaked out," I drawl.

Hollis pops a second Ding Dong in his mouth. "We've seen your thinking. Your ideas can be a lot of work."

"You're still pissy about the pie-throwing contest at the Kappa house," I say. "It raised a shit ton of money. Sorry you took a lot of cream in the face, Hollis."

He groans. "I can't even look at pie without flinching. You know I love sweets."

"You volunteered," Crew reminds him.

Hollis points at me. "He convinced me! He said there'd be hot girls in bikinis throwing pie. You forgot to mention there'd also be a line of Pikes and ATOs who'd want a piece of me. I had black eyes for a week."

Crew smirks. "River could convince a nun to give up her panties."

"Why would I when I have an entire frat to mess with," I say on a laugh as I shift on my feet, adjusting my shoulders, fidgeting. "Anyway...today's Monday, and even though our season is over, it's a fresh start. There's a new year coming, and I need something, not really a resolution, but..." I pause, mulling it over in my head. "I need to figure out my future. I'm at a crossroads."

"Feeling the same," Crew mutters.

"Dude," comes from Hollis. "It's too early to discuss heavy shit."

We laugh.

Later, after telling them bye, I step off the porch and

my fingers jiggle my keys, startling the hawk from his tree. He buzzes past me as he flies across the yard. *Fly on, man.* Find a hot bird babe and have some little bird babies.

Then I'm down a rabbit hole wondering if hawks mate for life.

I get in the truck and crank it.

I know what my monsters are.

I can't wave a magic wand and cure Mom.

I can't go back in time and fix a disastrous football season.

I can't fix my learning issues.

But...

I can pass this class.

I can stop thinking about *that girl* in my class. She makes my skin tighten, the hair on my arms rise. Even my scalp does weird things when I see her.

I hate that feeling. It goes against everything I believe about brotherhood. It's disloyal as shit, and I want to scrub it off my skin.

She doesn't belong to me.

She loves *him.*

My friend. My frat brother.

My hands clench the steering wheel.

"You do not exist, Anastasia Bailey. You. Are. No. One. To. Me."

Yeah.

Been saying that since the moment I saw her.

Fighting the pull of my thoughts, I stare down at the inked letters on both sets of fingers that spell THREE under the knuckles. It's my jersey number and Dad's. It represents the family triad: man, woman, child; it's birth, love, and death.

I focus on three things I'm grateful for: despite my learning issues, my IQ is higher than the norm (shocker); I have the frat; and I have my team.

I don't have her.

But it's enough.

Right?

2

Anastasia

ANA! I got my email acceptance to Harvard! I'm going to the best law school in the country! I had to tell you first!!!!! is the text from Donovan as I trudge up the steps of the Wyler Humanities Building.

Happiness flares bright at my boyfriend's news. I smile at his overuse of exclamations. He must be ecstatic. I come to an abrupt stop and let out a *whoop* as I punch a victorious fist at the sky. *Good for him!*

A tall, muscular guy in a purple shirt bumps into me and mutters something under his breath as his arm brushes against mine. Tingles dance down my spine. Without looking up, I murmur "Sorry" to his back as I let my backpack fall to the steps and type out a response.

I knew you had it from day one! I end it with several heart emojis. I'm about to send another text suggesting we meet up when one comes from him.

Have you gotten your email yet?

Elation for him takes a nosedive as unease curls around me, thick and heavy. My throat tightens as if needles are pricking it. We applied to Harvard Law on the same day, both of our laptops on our knees as we sat on his bed at the Kappa house and simultaneously pushed the button. He made a big production out of it, giving me a kiss for luck afterward. He even bought us matching crimson and black Harvard shirts he ordered online. That shirt now hangs in my closet, taunting me.

My LSAT score is in the top ten percent of the country, but I don't have the volunteer activities, the self-made charity foundations, or the social clubs. Between my classes and waiting tables, I barely have time to date Donovan.

He's been planning for Harvard since he enrolled at Braxton College. His freshman year he established a charity to donate tennis shoes to needy children in Honduras. Genius. He invested five grand into the website, rented a storage facility, hired a small crew to ship them out, all while raising money for sponsors. Shoes for Children has been going strong for three and a half years. There's no telling how much of his own money he's put into it. *Because his family is wealthy*, I remind myself. They're Harvard alumni. That had to have helped his application.

Ana? You there?

A lump of cement swirls in my gut as I stare at his words.

My rejection email came five days ago. Not even waitlisted.

My official letter arrived the next day, like I needed physical confirmation of being a reject. A pit of emptiness pulls at me, and I shove it away before its tentacles can dig too deep.

"You couldn't afford Harvard anyway," I mutter under my breath. With tuition and living expenses, the grand total came to ninety-eight thousand dollars a year. My heart dips at the thought of paying off an almost-half-a-million-dollar degree. If it wasn't for my scholarship at Braxton, I'd never be able to pay the fifty grand a year here.

Ana?

I take a big breath, ignoring the tightening of my chest. Of course I'm happy for Donovan. Harvard is his dream.

No word yet, I reply, adding a thumbs-up emoji.

I should tell him. I really should.

You'll get in. I just know it. Wish I could see you

tonight to celebrate, but I'll be deep in a research paper at the library. Toga party Friday?

I blink. *Really?* That's five days from now. Surely he wants to see me before then? I must be misunderstanding him.

It's just...

We didn't see each other this weekend because he drove to Atlanta to see his family—without me—which is absolutely cool. I had to work at The Truth Is Out There. "And his parents think you're a gold digger," I say to myself.

So. Yeah.

His family has generational wealth, and while I'm not destitute, I didn't grow up with Rembrandts on the wall either. This past summer I was there for his grandparents' fiftieth wedding anniversary gala. The place settings at the table featured countless plates, forks, spoons, and crystal glasses. The flower arrangements were three feet tall. I legit had to look around them to see Donovan—who wasn't sitting next to me but across the table next to an eligible girl from his parents' circle of friends. My retro yellow velvet dress didn't fit in with the black cocktail dresses the other women wore. My black thigh-high heeled boots were cheap pleather. My lavender hair made everyone squint.

His grandmother passed me in the hall before

dinner, raked her eyes over me, and curled her lip. *Dear, the catering staff stays in the kitchen, and shouldn't you pull your hair up and wear something more appropriate?* Then she asked me to refresh her champagne.

The socialite who sat next to me during dinner went on and on about her daughter's debutante ball while the man on the other side of me (her husband) rested his hand on my back every time he mentioned one of his vacation homes or his investment portfolio, which was a lot. Donovan wouldn't meet my gaze across the table, and an anxious feeling began to grow and grow and grow. Short story: I drank a little too much champagne, ate tiramisu with an oyster fork, then asked for A.1. Steak Sauce for my filet.

You'd have thought I murdered someone the way his mom gaped at me.

Cold December wind whips my hair around my face, obscuring my view as I grip my phone. My shoulders slump as my fingers hover over my cell, waiting for a text from him—the one he needs to send *right freaking now*.

I wait a full minute. Crickets.

I jerk up my backpack and walk.

He didn't mention my birthday.

Stomping up the steps, I chew on my bottom lip as I wrestle with my emotions. He *is* forgetful. On top of his classes and volunteer work, he's also the vice president of the Kappa fraternity.

It's fine, I rationalize. He just got in from a weekend out of town, saw he got into Harvard, and that's all he's thinking about.

Maybe he's planning something and wants to surprise me later. I wince. He really isn't a surprise kind of guy—except for our meet cute. I soften as I recall that night in the library.

He was with his fraternity brothers at a table next to mine, his brown eyes behind a pair of modern black frames as he checked me out. When I left my table to find a book, I came back to find a note on my copy of *The Outsiders*.

I have his message memorized.

'YOU SHOULD BE *kissed and often, and by someone who knows how.*'

Let me introduce myself. I'm your next boyfriend. Yeah, let that horrible come-on line sink in, but the sentiment is sincere. Cross my heart and hope to die—not really, but you know what I mean.

There are three things about you that caught my attention. You smell like sunshine, your hair needs my hands in it, and I'll be honest... I dig your kickass shoes. Those sparkly Chucks are a conversation starter.

Where are you from?

Are you new here?

What are you doing after this?

Please tell me you're single.

Also... I'm not a serial killer.

Or an alien. (People in Walker really dig that stuff.)

Or a player.

Or a douchebag.

Or a dick.

Wait? Are those last three kind of all the same thing? Maybe? Anyway...

I'm just the guy in front of you, at a table in the library, baring his soul.

I'll wait for you outside when the library closes. If you pack up and leave now, I'll know it's a no.

Your first reaction to this note may be to run as far away as you can, but you only live once and what do you have to lose?

Fate has a way of bringing people together, and maybe we're meant to be. Give me a chance to prove I'm much better in person than on paper. I haven't seen you smile and I want to.

Kappa Boy (at the table across from you)

WHEN I PICKED up the messily scrawled message to study it, I looked over and two of the three guys at the Kappa table froze.

Had to be from one of them.

The author of the note noticed that I didn't smile. As a transfer student, I *was* down that night, worried about credit card debt and making friends, all while trying to adjust to a big university from online classes.

Was the note cheesy, ridiculous, and over the top? Oh yeah.

But...

It was the *Gone with the Wind* quote that sealed the deal.

A guy who's read one of my favorite books? Hello, handsome.

Plus, it was funny in a charming way that made me laugh, as if he had word vomit and wrote out random thoughts.

My eyes flitted to them. These three guys were hot in different ways, each with hard bodies like they worked out twenty-four seven, their black and gold Kappa shirts tight on their chests.

I'd heard they were the most popular frat on campus, all the rich guys and superstar athletes. But why would one of them be interested in *me*? That night, my pale face was devoid of makeup and my hair was in a disastrous topknot shaped like a tornado. I wore my big white glasses, a pair of gray tie-dyed leggings, and a pink Nirvana hoodie. In other words, a hot mess without the *hot*.

I studied them as covertly as possible with my head

bent, my eyes scanning over them. There was the sandy hair and glasses guy (Donovan), another male with the most devastatingly perfect face I'd ever seen, and a blond-haired fellow who was half-asleep.

I narrowed it down to either Glasses or Perfect Guy. Both of them openly stared as I clutched the note.

My body liked Perfect Guy—he had tattoos and his lips were to die for—but he made my stomach jumpy. Earlier in the night, I'd watched a stream of sorority girls fawn over him when he dropped his pen. He was out of my league. Too hot. Too popular.

In the end, I waited until the bell pinged that the library was closing. The guys stood up and left. Anxious yet excited about which one of them it was, I gave them five minutes.

When I walked out of the library—pepper spray in hand because a girl has to be careful—Glasses (Donovan) was the one sitting at the fountain in the courtyard with a huge smile on his face. He rushed up to me and grabbed my hands. "You are the most beautiful girl I've ever seen."

It was so not true, but I laughed anyway, and we've been together ever since. We became friends first, then lovers.

Funny. I wish he'd leave more notes like that.

"But he doesn't," I mutter loudly. A passing student starts and gives me side-eye.

"Yes, I talk to myself," I say to her back. "It was a lonely childhood."

Warm air hits me as I walk into the lobby and dash for the elevator. I'm late. I groan knowing I'll have to walk into Dr. Whitman's lecture while he's talking. The man is vicious.

I push the button for the elevator then the air changes behind me, crackling. My shoulders stiffen. There's only one person in the world who makes the hair on my nape rise. *Him.* And by him, I mean that egotistical bad boy who thinks he's God's gift. River Tate —AKA Perfect Guy from the night I met Donovan.

Ah! He was the guy who bumped into me on the steps. Should have known. It's happened before, a slight bump here, a brush there. I never see it coming, but oh yeah, I always feel the effects.

Neither of us speaks as the doors slide open, but I can feel the disdain in his gaze right between my shoulder blades. I step in and slowly turn around. Yep! There he is, all six feet four inches of broad-shouldered hot college boy wearing a purple Braxton Badgers shirt that's sculpted to his chest, clinging to his muscled arms. Unfortunately, the color also makes his eyes pop and complements his skin tone. And the hair? Ugh. It's thick and dark and perfectly messy as if he just came from a blowout at the salon. The color is a deep mahogany with pops of gold from the sun, and it frames his face, accentuating high cheekbones and a square chin. His body is built and massive, a gladiator with legs for miles.

He. Is. Devastating.

Yes, I've noticed.

I *can* look.

A person can appreciate art from the heavens.

Sunshine is pretty too. It also burns your eyes.

"Well played, God, well played," I murmur under my breath, barely audible. "He has a fan club devoted entirely to his lips, but you could have made him *kind* to go along with it. Hey, maybe you have a plan for him, I don't know. Whatever. I'm not judging. I leave that to you."

He's talking on his phone, his lips quirked up as his deep voice rumbles. "Yeah. I'll bring you something special, baby girl."

Gag.

Without acknowledging me, he laughs at the reply on the other end, the sound husky and deep. "Mhmm, I got your little gift. I smile every time I look at it."

Probably a mirror.

He smiles into the phone, a dimple popping on the side of his jaw.

It doesn't affect me at all.

Nothing about him makes me swoon.

He tips his head back to stare at the ceiling. "You

want a big one?" He chuckles. "Why am I not surprised? I always deliver what you want, don't I?"

Get a room!

I clear my throat and send him a glare—which he doesn't notice because he isn't looking at me.

His voice lowers. "I've got class. I'll see you soon, baby girl." He makes a kissy noise into the phone, taps end, and tucks it in his jeans.

His eyes flit to me then slide away as he stares at the ground. He whistles to himself, seeming lost in thought and annoyingly happy.

I slap the button for the sixth floor. Lord knows he won't—even though we're going to the same class. Every Monday, Wednesday, and Friday, it's the same scenario. I get on the elevator and he follows. We never speak. But, oh the tension is thick. On my side. He barely notices.

Besides being the star wide receiver for Braxton, he's the Kappa president. You'd think he'd be friendly to me since I date Donovan and he was there for our meet cute, but River goes out of his way to avoid me. On the first day of class, he rushed in late with his head bent as he sat down next to me. He looked over, met my gaze, murmured *Oops, can't do it,* then promptly rose up and walked to another desk five rows behind me. I had to discreetly sniff my pits.

Case in point: this past May when Donovan gave me

his Kappa pin—pretty much pre-engagement if you're Greek—River raised a maddening eyebrow, draped a lazy look over my three-inch high-tops and mini skirt, and sneered. Sneered! The pin made me an honorary little sister, but judging by his face, I didn't rate. It's fine. Totally! Not everyone is an Ana fan.

I'm not in a sorority.

I'm not good enough for one of the gods on campus.

The elevator stops on the second level and three girls get on, all Deltas. I've been to enough parties at the Kappa house over the past year to know their faces. Without even a glance at me, they gush at River as they surround him. I take a step to the back, putting distance between us.

My gaze snags on one in particular, Harper Michaels. She glances over her shoulder, her cool gaze meeting mine.

Oh, no, girl, I won't back down, my face says. *Not today. Bring it.*

I hold her eyes for several seconds until she's the one to look away.

With her white-blonde hair—not out of a bottle— pale blue cardigan, and pink lipstick, she's beautiful in a classic way I can never be. Hailing from the same ritzy prep school in Atlanta as Donovan, they came to Braxton as boyfriend and girlfriend but broke up right before I came along. Her sorority pegged me as the "home-wrecker" of their relationship, which is ridiculous. He was single when I met him and he pursued me. My chest tightens. She's pre-law, and I wonder if she got into Harvard.

I eavesdrop on their conversation. Hard not to in an elevator.

"You're amazing, River, and you know it," comes from one of the Deltas. Mellany Something. Her hair is red and curled in beach waves. She strokes her hand down his arm as if she's done it before. Probably has.

"Appreciate it, Mel, but I dropped five passes," is his reply. "We only won three games all season. Not even a bowl game. It's been the worst year..." His words trail off. He fidgets as he swirls the silver snake ring on his left index finger. The man is constantly moving his body, touching that ring, tapping his legs, or shifting his shoulders.

As a trio, they coo, placating him over the loss this past Saturday.

"God, tell me, *why* do they fall at his feet?" I mouth to myself. "He's gorgeous, I get it, but so damn evil. Oops. Sorry, I cussed." I'm staring at my shoes as I silently grouse, but when I glance up, I *think* he might have been staring at me. I'm not sure. He didn't hear me because it wasn't audible, yet my face heats.

"Aw, don't be sad," the bosomy brunette murmurs in a sexy voice as she leans into him. Audrey Something. "Besides, I can make it up to you."

"That's an invitation if I ever heard one," I whisper to myself. "Poor wittle football player. Let me rub your shoulders and maybe your tiny little dick—"

He swivels his head and looks at me. I freeze mid-sentence, then cough.

"Allergies," I murmur.

He moves his eyes off me and looks at Audrey.

Yep.

He's hooked up with her. I walked in on them upstairs in a bathroom at the Kappa house at the start of the semester. It was a campus-wide mixer, and the line to the bathroom was long, so I slipped up to the top floor where it was quieter. I opened the door, and he had her bent over the vanity, her hair clenched in his fist as he took her from behind—fully clothed with his pants unzipped and hanging around his hips.

Our eyes met in the mirror as he fucked her.

Still as a statue, I stood there entirely too long as our eyes clung. I can recall every nuance of that incident, her *yes, yes, yes,* the loud roar in my head, the wash of heat that flashed over me. With my chest rising rapidly, I was transfixed as he orgasmed, his eyes low and heavy on my face. Then he had the audacity to smile. Yeah. I've seen River Tate's O-face. He bites his bottom lip.

I shove the unwanted image out of my head.

The elevator stops on the fourth level and the girls get off. Audrey gives River a kiss on his cheek and whispers something in his ear.

No doubt what *that* was about.

On her way out, Harper's face is flat as she sniffs at my pink knee socks, black velvet mini skirt, and Eiffel Tower cropped sweater. I push up my glasses in defiance. *Try me, sorority girl.*

She gives me a sly smile and lifts her hand to push a strand of hair out of her face. My breath hitches as I catch the glimmer of the diamond tennis bracelet Donovan gave her for *her* birthday. It's sparkly with two rows of jewels. The total weight is three carats. Not to my taste, but she never misses an opportunity to flash it at every party and have loud conversations about it...

Donovan was the most attentive boyfriend. He buys the best gifts, she'd gush to her Delta sisters as she—once again—flashed her bracelet. *I can't believe he's dating* that *girl.* Then, she'd smirk, giggle, and walk away.

Just like now.

Whatever.

I mostly ignore them, but today—well, today, my patience is shredding as each minute passes, a tightrope walker about to fall.

Why did I have to see her *today*?

Dammit. How could he forget my birthday?

The door slides shut. Finally.

River gets his phone out of his skinny jeans. I guess it was on silent. He laughs softly as he answers. "Baby girl, you gotta stop calling me. Get dressed, okay? Alright, alright, wear the one that has sequins on it. I know, baby girl. Soon. I can't wait to see you. You rock my world too." Another kiss into the phone.

He hangs up and hums under his breath, not a care in the world, and my tightrope walker says *Fuck it* and falls off the high wire.

I huff out a laugh. "Wow. Two girls on the hook, one on the phone and one in the elevator, and it's just a regular day for you—in spite of losing to a cupcake team from nowhere Louisiana this weekend. Your game *sucked*. Your season *sucked*. Furthermore, I'm shocked you didn't call Audrey *baby girl*. Let me educate you: that term is infantilizing. A baby girl is an actual thing and to use it as a term of endearment is gross. What if I called you *baby boy*? Not the same, right?"

He turns to me slowly. His lips part as if I've sprouted two heads.

I want to stomp my foot. He pretends I'm not here—when I can see myself clearly in the mirrored walls.

"Yeah, you see how that doesn't work," I add since he seems speechless. "If you must have a pet name, try *dear* or *love* or, I don't know, *honey* or *darling*. Anything less obnoxious, but hey... You. Are. Obnoxious."

It's deathly quiet in the elevator.

Oh crap, I've crossed a line.

He and I, we don't address the tension between us.

"Anastasia." He says my name as if he's tasting it, lingering and dragging out the four syllables.

"What?" I snap.

"Infantilizing? What a word." He shuts his eyes. "There. Maybe it'll stick." He opens them and gives me a slow once-over, from top to bottom. "This might be the most you've said to me in a while. Having a bad day?"

"My day is freaking perfect."

"Are you jealous of my 'baby girl'?"

I shake my head to clear it. "No! And the most I've ever said—please. I'm at the house constantly. I've been in your class all semester. I'm around you all the time, but..."

"But what?"

"You..." My voice trails off.

"Yes, me? Keep talking."

No, I can't (he's Donovan's frat brother), so instead I look away from him. My shoulders slump as a long exhalation comes from my chest.

What am I doing? This isn't me.

I don't lash out at others to make myself feel better. I'm not hot-headed or sassy like my roommates. I veer to the meek side unless you hurt someone I care about.

I stare at the floor, hoping it swallows me. My life is

just so uncertain, and everything I thought was going to happen isn't. No Harvard next fall. A relationship that's on the verge of ending.

It's not *his* fault I'm having a terrible day.

"Never mind," I say. "I shouldn't have... Just forget it."

"No."

"Yes. Forget we even spoke. Please."

"No."

"Okay, keep saying no, but I'm forgetting it." To further prove this, I stare at my cell phone, pretending to scroll.

"If I'd known all it took to push your buttons was having a conversation with my four-year-old niece, I'd have been talking to her all the time. She's nervous about preschool and keeps calling me. She also wants me to buy her a big stuffed unicorn for Christmas. Every shirt she owns has a horse, a dog, or a unicorn on it. With sequins. She's the sweetest. Unlike you." He pauses. "I've been calling her *baby girl* since the day I held her in my arms at the hospital."

I flick my eyes at him. "Likely story. You've been pushing my buttons for a year."

Quietly. Stealthily. Just enough so that it's not too obvious.

If we're in a group talking at the Kappa house, he pointedly looks at his nails or stares over my shoulder.

Two weeks ago, I walked in the house while he played poker with some of the guys in the basement. They invited me to play the next round, and I said yes since Donovan was taking a nap. River jumped up from the table as soon as I sat down, grabbed a random girl, pulled her into his lap, and sat on the couch. I lost two rounds because I couldn't stop watching her nearly strangle him with her tongue.

My phone pings with a text from Donovan and I tear my eyes off River to read it, holding out hope that he remembered. **Ana? You never replied. Are you coming to the toga party? We can celebrate my acceptance. I thought you might have to work? Btw, I checked out some neighborhoods for apartments near Harvard. What do you think about Longwood? Or Mission Hill? Let me send you some links.**

Celebrate his acceptance?

My chest squeezes as disappointment sharpens to deep hurt.

River says my name again, bringing me back. He stares at me, fingers back to twisting that ring around his finger. He frowns. "I thought the bathroom door was locked that night."

And we're back to *that*. Anger rushes through my veins.

"It wasn't!"

He gives me an incredulous look. "Why are you yelling? I didn't invite you to watch."

"I don't know! I *am* having a bad day. Why is this elevator so slow?" I pinch the bridge of my nose.

He looks at my cell, then me. His voice lowers. "What's wrong?"

I swallow thickly. "Nothing."

"No, it's something. Your face is red and you're clenching your phone. Something has you fired up. It's not me—I've done nothing but be myself."

Precisely.

"You pretend I don't exist. Don't deny it."

"I'm not," he says quietly.

I suck in a breath, feeling a stab right to my chest. I blink rapidly. I mean, I knew this, but today it really stings.

What have I done to him? Why does he hate me?

"Anastasia—"

"It's Ana." I grind my teeth. "You're the only person who calls me Anastasia besides my parents."

"Would you prefer baby girl?"

"It's pointless to talk to you."

The door slides open for the sixth floor, and all I can think about is escaping his proximity. I dash out and he follows me, closer than I anticipated.

He smells like citrus and man and...sex. Not like

actual sex, but in a pheromone-induced *I'm the alpha male your body is craving* kind of way. Gah, that makes no sense. I focus on Donovan. He smells like cinnamon. Good, honest, clean.

Donovan was the most attentive boyfriend echoes in my head.

Yeah? If so, then where's my damn gift?

Don't get me wrong—it's not about the gift. I've never needed pretty, expensive things. They aren't part of my life goals. I just yearn to be happy, to have a home and love.

Is it too much to ask for a simple *Happy Birthday, Ana* from Donovan?

"Anastasia," he says, then mutters under his breath, "Jesus, I said I wasn't going to do this."

"Do what?" I don't know what he's talking about.

I'm almost to the door to the lecture hall when he takes my elbow, his hand wrapping around me as his thumb presses into my inner arm. "Wait," he says huskily, and I flinch.

Wait?

The past tugs at me. I remember the last time he said that word...

THE BEDROOM DOOR *is half open and I push it the rest of the way, halting in the center—just as Perfect Guy comes out of the bathroom. He's wearing a towel around his waist and rubs another one over his damp hair. I see part of a snake tattoo that's wrapped around his right thigh, the golden and black pattern of the skin coiling around the thick muscles then disappearing on his backside. His chest is a work of art, his abs cut like diamonds, deep Vs on his hips.*

He's humming a song with his head down.

Be stealthy. Back away slowly.

He'll never know.

I'm almost out when I glance back up at him. How can I resist one last peek?

He's raised his head and stares at me, eyes draping over me, lingering on my mini skirt, before coming back to my face.

"Wait," comes from him, a purr.

My body buzzes, and I can't even explain the sensation except that he's quite possibly the most beautiful man I've ever seen.

I cough. "Sorry. I was, um, looking for Donovan's room. There are so many doors up here, and I didn't mean to catch you after a shower." I wave my hands at him. "I'll go."

"No. Wait."

I turn back.

He stares at me, frowning as if he's deciphering a puzzle. My hand clings to his doorknob as I feel my face turning pink. Ten seconds go by. Why isn't he saying anything? "Um, we haven't met officially. I mean, I saw you at the library a few days ago—"

"When you met Donovan," he finishes, his gaze hardening. "Yeah. I had to take off." He turns his back to me and stalks over to a dresser. My mouth gapes at the head of the python on his mid-back, its mouth open to strike, fangs dripping venom. It's a massive tattoo and I wonder how long it took to get—and what it signifies. You don't commit to artwork like that unless there's a reason.

He pulls out a pair of black underwear. It's the silky kind, the sort that will cling to his hips and show the outline of his crotch. My mind wanders, picturing it, and when he turns back around, I start and laugh nervously, keeping my gaze firmly on his face. "Sorry. Again. Wrong room. Good to see you again."

"I'm River."

"Donovan mentioned you." Briefly. We've only had one date since the library. Tonight is our second.

"Did he?" he says, his top teeth digging into his bottom lip. "He mentioned you. You're Ana."

"Short for Anastasia actually. A-N-A not A-N-N-A."

His eyes flare.

"Something wrong?"

His chest rises, an incredulous look growing on his face. "Anastasia, you say? Are you sure?"

I tense, uncertainty rising at his reaction. "Yes, I'm sure that's the name my parents gave me."

"Fuck me."

Okayyyy. "Um, it's Greek, actually, and means resurrection. *It's most popular in Russia. My mom spent a summer in Moscow and really got into the story about their famous Anastasia, the daughter of the last czar. People thought the princess escaped the murders, but well, we know now that she didn't..." I stop. His face is super weird right now.*

"It's *the* name," *he says.*

"What? You like Russian history?"

"No."

I blink. "You hate the name. I see."

"No," *he repeats.*

"Then explain—"

"No." *He twists the ring on his finger as he looks away from me.* "Figures," *he mutters to himself.* "Karma really is a bitch."

"Ah, I get it. You have an ex with that name? I'll try to stay out of your way."

"No," *he says as his head swivels back to me.* "Close your eyes."

"No," *I say automatically, an instinct. He's fascinating, and not only visually, plus the name thing reaction is pricking at me. The truth is, deep down, I kind of thought* he was *the one who wrote my note in the library, but he wasn't.*

We stare at each other. A hum dances over my skin.

"You gonna watch me get dressed?" *he says.*

Mortification washes over me. "Oh God. I-I didn't know you wanted to get dressed. I was just being...funny. You kept *saying no before, and I thought if I said it, you know, it would be hilarious and we could bond over it, maybe get past the tension from me seeing you nearly naked..."*

"I get it. Close them."

I don't.

"Anastasia, close your eyes" is dragged from him.

"Right." I do, sounds of clothing rustling reaching my ears.

"I'm decent."

My eyes open and he's put on a black tank and gray drawstring shorts. His muscled arms are crossed over his chest, his face blank. "You and Donovan? How's it going?"

"He's a nice guy..." and I've never had one.

He laughs, but it's not a sound of amusement. "Yeah. That little note was genius."

"It got my attention." *My fingers pluck at my skirt nervously.* "I liked the quote at the beginning—"

"Whatever."

I frown. River is kind of a dick.

He stalks toward me, his arm brushing against mine, and I gasp at the tingles that cause the hair on it to rise. His arm has goose bumps too.

He opens the door all the way with his face shuttered. "We've met and now it's done and over. Word of advice: don't walk into my room again, Anastasia."

I huff. "Like I said, lots of doors up here. My mistake."

"Yeah? Well, now that you know where I am, don't make another mistake."

"Hmmm. Is that because you have a thing about my name, or is it because you're an ass?"

He rakes his eyes over me, from head to toe, then ends on my lips. "You figure it out."

3

Anastasia

I shake off the memory of the day in his bedroom and gape at him.

He's actually *touching* me—on purpose. I'm five eight but have to tip my head up to gaze at him. I stare down at his hand. "What are you doing?"

His forehead furrows. "Did Donovan do something?"

He's eerily close to the truth. I pull out of his grasp.

He drops his hand. "I didn't mean to touch you."

Unsure what to say, I stare at his lavender-colored Chucks. They're worn but clean, the shoestrings white enough to look as if they've been replaced. They're shoes a guy loves. Is it strange that we're wearing almost the same exact pair? Mine have a bit of a heel and his don't.

"Anastasia, look at me." He steeples his hands together as he watches me, calling attention to the letters tattooed there. Written below his knuckles, the letters form the word THREE on both hands, a letter for each finger.

"Did you break up?"

"I don't need relationship advice from you."

"Maybe you need a psychiatrist. You talk to yourself a lot. What was that shit in the elevator?"

"Knew it. You just can't help being a jerk."

"Let me educate *you*. Jerk is unimaginative, not quite *infantilizing*, but close since it insinuates emotional immaturity. You're smart—supposedly. Can't you come up with something, oh, I don't know, more *obnoxious*?"

I can't even. My *even* has just gone boom. "Tool."

"Nope, try again."

"You're more disappointing than an unsalted pretzel."

"Pathetic. I happen to like my pretzels dipped in mustard, salted or not."

"I forgot the world revolves around you. Sorry, how silly of me."

He narrows his gaze. "You've disappointed me. I need you to really let it out, baby girl."

"You're the human version of my cramps."

"Gross, but lacks conviction. Haven't you heard? *Everyone* adores me. I thought you had some fire underneath that purple head of yours."

My fists clench. "It's lavender! Fine! You're an arrogant, bed-hopping asshole."

He smirks. "Ouch, you went to sex—just leaving the door open for me. I guess you're implying I get laid a lot. Oh, wait, you've seen me. You stood there a *really* long time, Anastasia. You caught the best part. Our eyes met. And held. Maybe you should have stuck around for round two—"

"Fuck you forever, River Tate," I snap.

"Fuck me forever—that's a new one. Finally." He lets out a gruff laugh. "Feel better?"

I blink. "Maybe."

"You need to let it out. I use the punching bag in the basement of the Kappa house. And showers. Tell me what happened to ruin your day. The more you talk about it, the easier it will be."

I break our gaze. He has a way about him, a gift for encouraging others and getting them stoked. Not me, of course.

As a football player, he's an unlikely candidate to be president, but he and Donovan work well together. River has big ideas and Donovan loves to execute them. At the beginning of the semester, River brought in several bigwigs from the business world in Atlanta to speak at a campus-wide event. Then, he came up with a dance contest for the Greeks. Every sorority and frat signed up and did an entire show. Costumes, music—

you name it. It raised twenty thousand dollars for a homeless shelter. Donovan typed the event up on his resume with glee.

"Donovan..." I bite my lip, unsure what to say.

"What did he do?"

"He forgot my birthday." I check my phone again, hoping for a birthday text from him. Nothing. "It's not that big of a deal," I lie.

He frowns. "That sucks. It must hurt."

I glance away from him. I don't even bring up my parents and how much I'm missing them lately. They've been in Greece for a year and haven't called me for my birthday yet, which isn't too surprising. My parents are artists who barely keep up with the day of the week.

Growing up, Mom would wake up on a regular day and start packing. *Let's live on a houseboat in Seattle.* A few months there and we'd be off to a new place. I don't have a real home and never attended a real school. I only came to Braxton for my last two years because it would look good on law school applications.

My parents taught me to depend on myself. To be strong.

But, sometimes, Jesus, I just wish they were...here. When I don't get into Harvard. When money is tight. When the guy I love forgets—

I stop the spiral in my head.

"You'll probably see him at the house, but don't tell

him he forgot, okay? I just..." don't want to get River involved.

"Forgetting something that important isn't like him. He's my right-hand man." He pauses, his eyes on my lips. "And a good friend."

"He's overwhelmed this semester. *You* keep him busy."

River's jaw flexes. "What can I say, he's super organized. I couldn't have held office without him. We're opposites but click."

"Everyone clicks with you. Except me."

"You think?" He shifts closer and I take a tiny step back, bumping into the wall. With his height, he towers over me and makes me feel fragile and small, when normally I don't.

"Um..." I say, then stop, taking in the colors in his eyes. Indigo dipped in smoke. Sapphires wrapped in a storm. I swallow thickly, taking in his thick lashes, dark brows, and the sharp angles of his face.

"Would you, um, take a step back, please?"

He doesn't. "How old are you today?"

"Twenty-one."

He nods. "I'm going to be twenty-two. Had to repeat kindergarten. Almost had to repeat seventh and eleventh, but my coach fixed it. They say the odd years in school are the hardest. I thought they all sucked." His lips quirk.

I blink. Besides the fact that he isn't moving back when I asked him to, I'm definitely in a parallel universe where River is sort of *nice* to me. *Don't get used to it,* I remind myself. There's probably a reason. Maybe he got a concussion at the game this weekend. Maybe he's having an aneurysm. Maybe he's—

I hear the professor's voice calling roll. "We should go to class," I say.

Neither of us moves.

He runs a hand through his hair. It looks soft, the top longer than the sides, the back curling around his collar. "You know what I do when my day is shit? I remember three things I'm grateful for. Anything. Could be the fact that the Wi-Fi in the Kappa house is working. Might be clean underwear. Could be a phone call from Callie—that's my niece. What's yours?"

"Does the high and mighty River Tate have a gratitude journal?"

"In my head."

"Is that really who you were talking to on the phone?"

"Come on. Try. Give me one thing you're grateful for." His finger flicks the Kappa pin on my sweatshirt, his touch ghosting over my throat. "This?"

Electricity sparks, and I gasp, pushing the tingles away. Those little shocks don't mean *a thing.* Yes, he's accidentally touched me before, and he always flinches away.

So why is he standing so close to me today?

"I don't know. I told you to fuck off. You've had it coming."

"Maybe I have." He smiles, but it isn't a charming one; no, it's lethal. He really means it. We *are* enemies. His gaze skates over me, coming back to my face then lingering on my Kappa pin. "I tolerate you because you wear his pin. Otherwise, I don't want to be near you."

"Hmmm, you're in my space bubble. Is there a reason?" I snap.

Another dangerous smile. "Torture, isn't it?"

Before I can reply, the classroom door opens.

"Ms. Bailey and Mr. Tate?" Professor Whitman's sharp voice makes me start. "We can hear you talking through the door. Plan on joining us today?"

River's jaw pops, his gaze still on me. "Coming, sir."

The professor looks at him with beady eyes. "I hope so. You and I need to chat after class."

I look at River, searchingly, but he dips his head and brushes past me into the classroom, broad shoulders swaying.

I bump into him when he comes to a halt. Easing up next to him, I see the problem. Our usual seats are taken. Two stadium-style seats are vacant in the front row—where no one wants to sit. I scan the place again, hoping for a spot near the back or any place that isn't near him. I exhale. Nothing is free. It's nearing finals of the winter semester, so everyone is here and present.

I push past him. "Looks like you'll have to sit next to me. Try to endure it, baby boy."

4

Anastasia

"Your research paper counts as your exam grade. I expect topnotch themes and exemplary writing," Dr. Whitman says. He runs through various topics we can choose from, and my heart lifts a little. I'm pre-law but seize every opportunity to take an upper-level lit class.

River sets his phone out on his desk and hits the record button. Does he always record the lecture? I'd never know since we don't sit together, but I find it curious.

I flick my eyes to him. Even unsmiling and looking broody, his face is a work of art. Sunlight from the window creates a shadow on his chiseled face, leaving half in light, the other side in shadow. A fallen angel turned into the devil.

"Some of you," the professor continues as his eyes sweep the room and linger on River, "seem to think you can skate by in my class. I'm not sure why you took it."

River exhales, his leg accidentally pressing against mine before he pulls it away.

I shift around, trying to put space between us. His eyes dart my way, then he inches away as well. I imagine what we must look like, each of us hugging the opposite side of our desk.

"He's talking about me and you, River," a male voice whispers from behind us. "We're the oddballs. This class is wall-to-wall English majors."

I throw a look over my shoulder at Benji Williams, River's little brother. Not an actual brother, but a Kappa one. He's a junior, tall and handsome, with shoulder-length wavy blond hair, and the third guy from the night at the library. He's looking at River, who doesn't turn around. "I took this class because you did, and now we're both screwed," he adds with smirk, then gives me a chin nod. "Hey, Ana. How you doing?"

"Good. Ready to write this paper."

He rolls his eyes. "Nerd. Poker night soon?"

"You always win, but yeah. I will beat you one day."

He waggles his brows. "Good at cards, unlucky in love. You need to hook me up with one of your roomies, Ana. Sweet girls. You and Donovan—man, couple goals."

"I know your rep," I say with a small laugh. "Stay away from Colette and Lila."

"Can you two shut up?" River grouses. "Some of us are trying to listen to the professor."

"Sorry to disturb your concentration, baby boy," I hiss at him as I turn back.

Benji snorts. "Oh, man, I must have missed something out in the hall."

Dr. Whitman's voice slices through the air. "Ms. Bailey? Care to talk to the entire class? What's your topic for the term paper?"

Dang it.

I smooth my hair down as I squirm in my chair and clear my throat. "I chose *Lady Chatterley's Lover*." We started the semester with several famously banned books including *American Psycho* and *Lolita*, but *Lady Chatterley's Lover* was the one I was drawn to.

"Topic?" he asks again.

I pause. "Um, 'The Power of Restorative Sex.'"

A few chuckles come from the other students, ears perking up at the word *sex*. I sigh. It's one of the most common themes of the book, so I don't see the issue. Sex. Everyone does it. Even amoebas. My parents, well, they've made no secret of their penchant for inviting others into their bed. It's fine for them and they *are* devoted to each other, but I long for a guy who wants only *me*.

River's eyes flash over at me as his fingers hover over his notebook, which is covered in doodles and squiggly lines. I admit to an interest in what he's writing.

The professor walks forward. "Explain to the class. They seem to be slightly interested today. In case some of you have forgotten, that particular novel was banned for forty years in the US. It was dubbed as pornographic and it took a Supreme Court case to finally get the book published here. Ms. Bailey? Care to elaborate?"

I nod. "Connie, the female protagonist, is in a love-less marriage in the twenties in England and longs for true passion. When she meets the gamekeeper of her estate, Oliver, in the forest, they have sex, which hints at the premise of baser instincts and nature. The experience awakens her spirit and she heals from her depression, hence *restorative*."

Dr. Whitman purses his lips. "There are explicit sex scenes. What did you think of them?"

I feel my face reddening. I can debate books all day, and normally I wouldn't be embarrassed, but River is next to me. "A bit over the top, yes. Did D.H. Lawrence set out to write a titillating book? Perhaps. He was dying of tuberculosis and couldn't perform sexually. His own marriage was failing."

"Dude," Benji whispers so only River and I can hear. "That would suck."

I ignore him and carry on. "The sex scenes aren't

explicit by today's standards. The book is more a statement about the characters' unhappiness. It was a sexual awakening for both of them, but they aren't together at the end."

"They orgasm at the same time. Pretty sure I read that part a few times. That'll restore my faith in sex," Benji cuts in with a laugh.

"What's your topic, Mr. Williams?" the professor asks, his voice sharpening.

Benji clears his throat. "I went with *American Psycho*. Haven't chosen a topic, sir. Mayhem and serial killers probably. He murders lots of people. Blood and gore. I can get behind that one hundred percent."

"Indeed." Dr. Whitman compresses his lips. "Perhaps focus on the shallowness of capitalism in that novel, hmmm? Not the serial killer aspect. Mr. Tate?" He looks at River.

River straightens in his chair, pauses, then leans in over his desk. There's a coiled tension in him, a storm waiting to erupt. He seems to battle it, his hands fisting. "'The Power of Restorative Sex' from *Lady Chatterley's Lover*."

Benji chuckles.

I gasp.

River looks at me. "We can have the same topic."

I know. Just hearing him say 'sex'—

And now *I'm* immature.

"Of course," Dr. Whitman replies. "Just be sure it's *your* work, Mr. Tate, and not hers."

Whoa. I frown at the professor.

"It's a common theme," I say in a loud voice. The class needs to know. "There are thousands of papers on this topic. I do my own work and don't cheat. Neither does River." I don't know how I know this, just a gut instinct. Our animosity aside, he's an honorable person around his brothers. When Parker, one of the freshman pledges, lost his sister in a car wreck in September, River flew to Arizona to be with him at the funeral. He's the only Kappa who went. I've also seen him sitting with Parker in the basement, their heads huddled as they talk. When Crew lost his Pops this summer, River was there for him too.

"Of course he doesn't cheat. He's failing this class," Whitman says under his breath, yet loud enough for the front row to hear. He moves to another student.

I mutter under my breath.

Dr. Whitman swivels back to me. "Did I miss something you said, Ms. Bailey?"

River moves, his leg pressing against mine, as if to say *Don't do it.*

My hands clutch my novel. "I said, it's not appropriate for you to insinuate that either of us would cheat or announce that he's failing this class."

"You just announced it." His eyes narrow behind

wire-frame glasses. "This is my class—I can say whatever I want. You're paying for my knowledge, and I impart it in the way I see fit. Please keep your comments to yourself. Unless you'd rather give this lecture yourself?"

Truth? I probably could. Books are my jam, the one solid thing I clung to growing up. Blood rushes through my veins, and I open my mouth—

"Let it go, Anastasia," River whispers.

Five seconds pass as Dr. Whitman watches me, daring me, then walks away.

"Holy shit. That was an epic stare-down. You and River *should* work together," whispers Benji.

"No thanks," River says as he bounces his leg. Every brush of his jeans touches my thigh. I ease away.

"Ah, that's right," Benji muses. "You two aren't friends. So weird when you think about it..." His voice trails off. "Makes me wonder..."

River inhales a breath then turns to him. "If you have something to say, say it."

He holds his hands up in a placating manner, but there's a glint of glee in his eyes. "Nothing. Well, okay— since you asked. I think you two have a lot in common. Ana is beloved by the frat. So are you. She's..."—he looks at me and grins—"different, and you, big brother, don't be offended, are kind of a woo-woo dude."

"Woo-woo?" River grinds out as his cheekbones flush. "Seriously?"

I dart my eyes between them, fascinated. Benji clearly knows a side of River I do not. Woo-woo implies believing in unconventional spiritual ideas, and I've never gotten that vibe from River. Although, hmmm. All the guys do go to him for advice...

Benji laughs under his breath and taps his chin as if he's thinking. His lips purse. "All I'm saying is, you're different from the normal frat guy, although you don't let everyone see it—"

"And you're done talking," River snaps.

Benji grins. "Yes, Mr. President."

"River doesn't think I'm good enough for the frat," I say. Yeah, my tightrope walker is back, teetering. "He ignores me, snubs me, and basically pretends I don't exist."

River's eyes fly to me. "I never said you weren't good enough—"

Professor Whitman juts in loudly, "If you three are done chatting, we'd like to hear from the rest of the class."

Caught. Again.

River and I turn back around. He exhales and stares down at his novel, his hands twirling it on top of the desk. His index finger presses hard into the paperback as if he wants to drill a hole in it.

I stare down at mine, thumbing through it, my head tumbling with what Benji said about River and me having things in common. He called me different. I guess talking to myself qualifies. My parents are non-traditional. I don't have many friends. And my hair is unique. It's long and straight and thick, the lavender ends brushing my mid-back. Lila says it's my best asset, even though she wants me to jazz it up with some multi-colored stripes. My dad says my eyes are his favorite: bright green with dark lashes. I don't put much stock into looks. (Although I admit to weak moments around River. It's the artist side of me.) I prefer to look at a person's insides, to the depths of *who* they are. I want the layers within, unfolding and unpacking someone's true nature. I've learned that beauty on the outside doesn't matter if the inside is rotten.

My first taste of masculine beauty was at seventeen. He was thirty and—

I stop that train of thought when Whitman slaps River's character analysis from last week down on his desk. River tucks it inside his notebook, but not before I see his F.

River's jaw tightens, and I see fury on the granite planes of his face. Then, as the moments tick by, resigned acceptance. Oh. My breath catches. It's a defeated expression I've never seen him wear.

Whitman hands me my A, and a few minutes later, the bell chimes for class to be dismissed.

River stays in his seat as students file past us, and I

guess he's waiting to talk to Whitman. My body is hyper-aware of his proximity, and my hands hurry to get out of his space. The strap of my backpack gets tangled on my chair, and when I yank on it, several items spill out while my phone flies under his desk. I bend down and snatch it up, brushing against his thigh. Inwardly, I groan.

Must. Stop. Touching. Him.

Maybe it *was* a good idea he didn't sit next to me that first day.

My cell lights up with several texts, and I scan them. All from Donovan. More info about Harvard. Nothing about my birthday.

Loneliness claws, catching me unexpectedly. Time is running out for law school applications to be accepted. It's not my dream to be a corporate lawyer, tax attorney, or work in the entertainment field like many in my cohort; no, I want to work with people with legal issues who can't pay the fees. The poor and disenfranchised. At this rate, I may be waiting tables for another year until I find a spot.

"And yet morning will come," I say to myself. "And you *will* watch the sunrise."

I tuck my phone away then glance up to meet River's gaze. I think he's been watching me the entire time.

I straighten my shoulders as our eyes cling.

There's not one expression on his face I can identify.

But it's his eyes that give him away.

They burn. Smoky sapphires in flames.

My chest rises. "What? You're pissed? I had to defend you. And me."

"I'm not angry. Not at all."

"Then why the smoldering glare, Snake?"

His lids lower, a little smile curling his full lips. "My tattoo is actually a python."

"Python doesn't have quite the same ring to it."

"I'm flattered by the nickname." His tongue darts out and dips to his bottom lip, sweeping across the skin, and it's a crime against all women that he looks damn hot doing it.

"Don't be," I mutter. "I wasn't being sweet."

I'm walking away when he calls out, "Wait."

I flip around. "Boy, I've heard that before. What do you want?"

He stands up and walks to me, his feet eating up the space between us. He stops and stares down at me as we ignore the jostle of people walking around us.

"Well?"

His lashes lower, hiding his eyes as he reaches out. His thumb traces the line of my jaw from my cheek to my chin, his fingers grazing down my throat. "Happy birthday, Anastasia," he purrs.

My chest tightens, my body buzzing as I sputter and jerk away from him.

He can't...

He can't do *this* to me.

That was not an ordinary birthday wish.

"Stop your games," I snap.

His lashes lower again. "Not even sorry."

My hands clench around my backpack. "There's a thick line between us, River, one you put up a long time ago."

Whitman approaches us, and River stiffens, dropping my gaze as he shifts in the professor's direction. Feeling as if I've been released by a hungry predator, I whip around and jog out of the room, skipping the elevator to take the stairs. My heart pounds as I keep my head down and dash to my next class.

River Tate is a dangerous man.

And the best thing I can do is stay away from him.

5

River

After getting my ass reamed by Whitman, I jog to the parking lot and shove my backpack in my black GMC, scrub my face, and take off running. It's two miles across campus to the athletic administration building, but I need the cold wind in my face. Whitman knows about my issues but doesn't care. He believes I shouldn't be in his class. He isn't wrong. Failure tugs at me, and I run faster.

Doesn't matter that I'm wearing jeans and not workout gear. I need this, the release from anxiety.

I zoom past a group of ATOs. They call out my name, but I keep going.

For months since Mom got her diagnosis, I've been running mentally, from good things that feel fake to bad things that are real. On the outside, I'm cool, the same old River, but sometimes I stop and look hard at people. Don't they know that life is short? Don't they see that this world is a fucking scary place?

People can be yanked away from you in one second.

Dad.

Mom.

Hang in there, please, I say to her in my head.

I reach the building and come to a stop, bending over to breathe.

Once on the elevator, I glance down at the buttons on the panel. Three of them look exactly alike. I've been in this place enough times to know which button will get me to the fifth floor.

As the elevator rises, I drum out "Yeah!" by Usher on the wall with my fingers. My energy is blasting, my body still twitching after running into Anastasia.

Well. I didn't exactly run into her.

I waited, knowing she was coming, right after I said I was going to forget about her.

Just needed a small hit of dopamine.

And I got more than I bargained for.

Yeah.

Got a glimpse of what she looks like fired up.

Her lush mouth, that line she has in the middle of her bottom lip.

Those legs in those short skirts. The girl rarely wears pants. Don't blame her.

With a body like that—

Nope.

What the hell was I thinking, *touching* her.

It was a fuck-up, a mistake I won't make again.

I swirl my ring. Boom. Bye. She's gone. Out of my head.

A text comes in from my boys. It takes me a minute to read because of my dyslexia, but our conversations are usually to the point. My font size, though—man, it's for old people.

Some Pike asshole just said I'm the king of throwing interceptions, Crew sends. **Tell me not to hit him.**

Hollis chimes in. **Not worth the jail time, boo bear. You're a lover not a fighter. Bar? Tonight?**

Thought you were never drinking again, Hollis? I say into my phone, and it sends it as a text.

I lied, he replies, along with a shrugging emoji.

The elevator doors open on the football administration floor and I tuck my phone away. Once we start texting, it can go on and on, and I have to focus.

"River! You sweet boy, come on in here. How are you?" says the older woman sitting behind a desk.

No one calls me *sweet boy* except Mom and Miss Janie. "Hey, Miss Janie. Good. You sure look pretty today. Did you do something different to your hair?"

She blushes, a hand patting her gray curls. "No. You're such a flatterer. What do you need today?"

I saunter her way, tucking my hands into my pockets. "You got a million dollars?"

"Would I be here if I did? No. Would I give it to you? No."

"Hmmm, is there an agent or a scout hanging around today who wants to sign me?"

"Not a one. They're crazy."

I let out a pretend long sigh. "Huh. How about a pretty girl?"

"I do have a distant cousin—"

I slash through the air, a bit dramatically, just to get her going. "I was kidding. No setups. You tried, and it didn't work."

"Your mom said you were lonely." She lifts her hands and smiles.

"She says that to rile you up. How can I be lonely in the frat?" Those brothers keep me going.

She laughs. "Your mom is a meddler."

"You aren't innocent," I say with a grin.

The girl Miss Janie set me up with disliked me on the spot. I only agreed to a coffee date to make Mom and Miss Janie happy.

"Tara didn't like football, Miss Janie. She called me a meathead. We had zilch in common."

"She's pretty."

"Doesn't matter if there's no connection." I wink. "Guess I need to go back to bed, wake up, and try again for that million dollars."

She stands up, straightening her skirt. "You got any new pictures of your niece?"

"Sure do." I cross over to her desk, pull out my phone, and bring up one of Callie holding the dog my sister Rae got her. "She got a poodle. Begged for it, and my sister and Mom can't say no to that face. Rae said he chews shoes and scratches up the couch. Chaos." I chuckle.

She leans in and takes in the photo. "Oh, River, she looks like you in this one."

"Hmmm." I look down at Callie's face, and my heart softens to a pile of mush.

"Any plans for the break? You doing the ski trip?"

Uncertainty rises. I love the feeling of flying over snow, my skis swishing as everything drifts away. The university gives us a discounted rate, and this year's destination is close to my hometown in Vermont. I grew up a few hours from the Adirondack Mountains, and when the campus chose White Face Lodge in January, I was stoked and made my reservation.

But...

My chest tightens, emotion stinging. "I was all in until Mom got sick. She's insisting I still go. We argued about it." I roll my eyes. "Well, she yelled while I held the phone out. She..." *wants life to go on as usual.*

"She wouldn't want you to give up on what you do every year."

I arch a brow. "You've been texting with her again. You two kill me."

"We do Zoom calls and drink margaritas once a week." She grins. "Nina is dear to me and technically I'm your campus mom, so deal with it."

Miss Janie and Mom met my freshman year at a meet and greet for the players and staff, and they immediately hit it off. They're both from the New England area, in their fifties, single, and adore me.

"Go. Enjoy yourself. It's just a three-day trip. Then go see your mom for two weeks."

I exhale. Mom is recovering after several chemo cycles. She didn't make any games this year because she couldn't be around crowds. Chemo weakens her immune system, and any kind of viral or bacterial infection might put her in the hospital.

"We'll see." Code for *I'm not going.*

Miss Janie gives me a side hug, and my throat is raw as I hug her back. She pats my arm then moves to her desk. "Now, who are you here to see today?"

"Edward." My anxiousness ramps up.

She types into her computer. "He's finishing up a call."

"Got it." I plop down in one of the leather seats and bounce my knee.

The elevator pings, and she moves her gaze to the doors behind me.

"Can I help you?" she says.

A man dressed in a polo shirt and khakis walks up to her desk. Late twenties with a red goatee, he's holding a phone in front of him like he's recording.

"Hello! I hope so!" He smiles broadly. "I'm doing a story and was wondering if I could get the administration's reaction to the Badgers' season—"

"That's enough," Miss Janie says, her normally sweet voice sharp as knives. "Put that phone down and stop recording immediately!"

He swivels his phone around the room. "Hello, viewers. Here's where the magic *didn't* happen this year for the Braxton Badgers. A former national championship team, they were supposed to be at the top of their game. What went wrong?"

Miss Janie stalks toward him, all five feet of her.

"Don't get too close," I tell her as I stand and step between them. I've been in the limelight long enough to see reporters trample people to get what they want. Last year after we won the championship, a guy from ESPN mowed down two athletic trainers to stick a mic in my face.

He shoves his phone in my direction. "...and here we

have River Tate, star wide receiver. Not quite a star though, am I right? Is it true you frequently fought with your teammates?"

"No." My fists curl. That is *not* true. My team means everything to me.

"How do you explain five dropped passes?"

Honestly? I played after a rough tackle when I shouldn't have. It wasn't a concussion—the trainers checked—but it was serious, and I went back in anyway.

Miss Janie inches closer to us, hands flapping. "In the state of Georgia, our legal statutes prescribe that if you want to film in this building, you need to have written permission from Braxton. You do not have written permission, and any video you have taken since you parked your car is illegal. If you use any of those recordings, including this one, without blurring the image of every individual associated with this university, we will be forced to sue you and whatever platform on which you broadcast your production. Do you understand what I just explained to you?"

The guy shoves the phone in my face. "Do you think you have a shot at recovering your status as one of the best players in the SEC? Are your hopes for the NFL gone?"

When you're golden, reporters love you, but when you've lost your shine, they dig a hole and throw you in.

"Don't answer that, River!" Miss Janie darts back to

her desk and fiddles with a button I know is hidden under it.

"I got this." I saunter over to him and smile. "Hello, everybody. River Tate here. I assure you Braxton is still one of the best football programs in the country." Then, I snatch the phone out of his hand and scan the screen to see if it was live. Shit, it is. I smile into the camera then wink. "Sorry, folks, this video is unauthorized. Have a great day!" I turn it off and stuff the cell into my pocket.

He shoves at my chest. "Hey! That's mine!"

My teeth grit, but I don't punch him. Sure, I've been known to lose my temper. I'm passionate—but not stupid.

I wait for the ping.

Right on cue, the elevator doors open and two bulky guys in their early thirties appear.

Dressed in black, they wear the campus security logo on their shirts. Stun guns are on their hips. "Denny and Ken. How's it going?" I ask with a grin. They've broken up a few of our frat parties. They usually give us a warning to pipe down then leave.

I point my finger at the reporter. "Red here brought in an unauthorized recording device. Miss Janie explained it, but he didn't listen." I slap the phone in Denny's hands.

He nods, all business. "Thanks, River. Sorry, Miss

Janie. He must have slipped in one of the maintenance doors at the back of the building."

"All I wanted was a story! Everyone wants to know what happened!" the man says as they get on either side and escort him to the elevator.

Ken gives me a chin nod. "Good to see you, River."

I smile. "Later. Stop by the house when you're off duty. Bud Light, right?"

He gives me a thumbs-up as they leave. "Will do."

Miss Janie pulls at her little cardigan, her feathers clearly ruffled.

"You okay?"

She shakes her head. "It's been a while since someone busted in here. I need a margarita. I'm glad you were here, River."

Ah. Yeah. The question is, will I be here for long...

LATER, I stand outside Edward's office. He's my student-athlete academic advisor.

Just get it over with.

I finally knock on the doorframe.

"Come on in, River. How are you doing?"

I reply with a noncommittal answer. He's not Miss Janie. I'm just a number to him.

"Good, good, have a seat," he murmurs as he opens

up a thick folder with my name on it. "We have a few things to talk about. Most importantly, we need to know if you have made your decision about the draft or if you want to return to Braxton next semester?"

Cement lands on my chest. "My mind changes every day, sir. One minute I want to stay, and the next I want to take my chances as a low draft pick."

He frowns. "You don't know?"

"No."

He laughs a little under his breath as he shakes his head. Dude doesn't get how my brain works. "I see. What are you thinking today?"

A long sigh comes from me. "Let's say I want to come back. Are my grades okay, or am I in trouble?"

He types some more on the computer, his expression hardening as he furrows his brow. "Your grades suck in this lit class."

No shit.

"You're cool in *Dances of North America, Beginning Improv*, and *Modern Art*." He looks at me. "I told you not to take this literature class. I had that geology one lined up. Much less reading."

"Right." I sigh. That geology class is known as *Rocks for Jocks*. I'm wary of easy classes people 'like me' take. They're boring—well, except for the dance one—and don't require complex thinking. I *can* analyze content— once I've digested it.

"You don't have enough hours toward graduation and still haven't declared a major. At this point, I can maybe pull you a general studies major next year," he muses as he stares at my transcript. He tilts the computer toward me, and I blink, the small words running together. I can't make sense of it, not in this light. I glance away, an empty feeling in my stomach. Why can't I just be normal?

"I'm majoring in football and everyone knows it," I say grimly. "I want a degree—for my mom."

What would I even do with a degree?

Mom sold Dad's Mercedes dealership to retire, so I can't sell cars. My freshman year, I entertained the idea of being a sports announcer, but if you can't follow the prompter on TV, who would hire you? Sure, the NFL is an option, but after this last season...

"My dad didn't graduate college and regretted it," I add. "I wanted to take that lit class to challenge myself."

Half lie. There's another reason.

"It's challenging you alright—that's apparent. If you fail, we'll have to put you on the academically ineligible list for next semester. That means no spring practice. Death sentence for you if you can't play in the fall."

Not play in the fall?

Shit. *Shit.*

It's worse than I thought. Sure, I knew I was doing

bad, but I was holding out hope that my last paper was decent. Until Whitman slapped that F on my desk.

What's the point of staying at Braxton if I can't play?

My hands shake and I stuff them under my seat. "I get it."

He takes a sip of coffee. "What's your plan to get this up?"

"Whitman says I need an A on my paper to pass the class," I mutter, recalling our conversation.

He winces. "Damn. At this point, is that even possible?"

Thanks for the support, man.

"Is it done yet?" he asks

"Haven't started," I mutter.

"In the past, I had athletic tutors in the study center, but those days are over."

I exhale. Before I came to Braxton, they had a group of 'tutors' in the athletic department—until a few were caught fixing test questions, writing essays, and even showing up to class for superstars. The NCAA fined us; ESPN wrote countless articles about it. Maybe Whitman's prejudice toward athletes is justified, somewhat. Since that happened, athletes use the same tutoring center as the rest of the student body.

I get it. Several of my high school teachers pushed me through just to appease my coaches. Did I like it? Hell no. It was degrading, but I was helpless to stop it.

Accommodations were made for my difficulties, extra time on tests and oral reports, and I did try, but when you *just can't get the written word*, most of them let you slide by. I'm not dogging teachers. Our world needs good people who love kids—and they *did* care about me—but when you have a classroom of rowdy students and there's that *one* kid who can't focus, sit still, or read well, you do what you have to do.

"Ever consider a reading coach? I've heard of those before." He scrolls on his laptop.

I can fucking read. It just takes me being in a quiet place with no distractions—and time. My finger spins the ring on my hand faster and faster. "I listen to the books on audio, but I..." I pause, again bemoaning the fact that I took this class. My eyes go to the window in his office as a bird flies by. A red cardinal. Do they mate for life? I wonder where that hawk is now...

"Your ADHD takes over, right? There are drugs."

The meds make me dizzy. My parents tried them all. "They mess with my equilibrium. Not good for football," I say curtly. He and I have been down this road before, and it ticks me off that I have to refresh him.

"Right. I knew that." He leans back and considers me. "Let's nix the student learning center. It's a busy place, lots of people coming and going. You need quiet. No other people around to distract you. I suggest a private tutor. We have a list of students who do one-on-ones.

They won't do your work, but they'll help. Take a look."
He prints out a list of names and slides it over to me.

Dread inches up my spine that I have to read this in front of him. My throat tightens, and the paper shakes as panic claws at me. Fuck. Focus. I inhale a deep breath and glance through the names, not really reading, then stop. The *A* at the beginning is branded in my brain. I trace my fingers over it. "I know this girl. Anastasia."

"Excellent. She helped one of the tennis players last year when he was flunking biology. Also helped a volleyball player with algebra. She's a natural."

"She isn't a fan of mine."

He huffs out a laugh. "I thought everyone was a fan of yours."

He hasn't seen us...together. It's like throwing water on a grease fire.

"I don't want her to know about..." my issues.

He shrugs. "You want me to email her?"

My face flattens.

He exhales. "River, if you can't get this grade up, you won't be eligible to play next year. You need help with this class. And next time, take the classes I pick out for you."

I sit there quietly, my jaw popping. Me and Anastasia. Working together. Probably in the library in one of those private rooms.

Alone.

Fuck no.

"Sound like a plan?" he says, extending a fist in my direction.

Edward says the same thing at the end of all his meetings. It's his polite way of saying, 'Now get the hell out of my office. I'm busy.'

"I'll talk to her," I say as I stand and return his fist bump.

But I know I won't.

Can't.

Mustn't.

Shouldn't.

6

River

"My brothers, your king has arrived!" I yell as I walk in the back door of the Kappa house a few hours later. I've decompressed from my meeting with Edward and I've talked to Mom. I'm loose and feeling good, especially after a workout with my guys and my second shower.

Music thumps from the speakers overhead, and I hear pledges yelling from various parts of the house as they greet me in the way they've been taught. "Welcome home, Mr. President! May we get you anything?"

"I'm good!" I shout back, smiling. Damn, I love pledges and the bonding experiences. Last week I gave them an exercise. *Bring a stick to the house. Make it special. You decide.* Parker cut down an elm tree in the woods with a chainsaw and paid a delivery truck to bring it to the house. We gave him his own special recliner in the basement.

My freshman year, I was the "backpack pledge" and had to carry a kid's SpongeBob Squarepants bag to class for an entire semester. It had to remain unzipped at all times. My brothers packed it full of condoms, KY jelly, and leaflets about safe sex. When I walked into class, people swarmed me. I probably saved hundreds from STDs and dry intercourse.

Crew was the "fruit pledge." It started with taking grapes everywhere he went, like they were his baby. Oranges were next, then cucumbers, until he ended with carting a watermelon in a wagon. He drew a smiley face on it. We loved that watermelon. Named him Wally.

Hollis was the "weather pledge." Every day at 5 AM, he had to get up and do a Snapchat of the forecast. He also had to jump up and down in place for two minutes any time someone on campus asked about the weather. Everyone did.

I laugh. Good times.

The kitchen is dead except for Benji, who's currently lip-locked with a girl. She's sitting on the table and he's between her legs. His shirt is gone; she's fully dressed. Must have just started.

"Yo. I said, 'I'm home.'" I toss my backpack and laundry on the floor and it makes a loud thump. My gaze catches on our Greek crest painted on the wall. Black and gold with a lion in the middle, the words loyalty and service etched above it. I brush my fingers over them.

True to yourself.

True to your brothers.

Always.

But I could use a reminder today.

"Just pretend I'm not here," I muse as I ease around Benji and the girl.

She moans, her hands curling in his blond hair. He murmurs, "Oh, yeah" and kisses her throat.

I cough. "But, you know, I *am* right here."

Benji pops an eye open, and I read the laughter in his gaze.

My stomach rumbles. "And I'm going to eat dinner because I'm starving. So, if you want to put on a show, I'm willing. But..." I hold up a finger. "First, you have a room. It's across the hall from mine. It's rare for a junior to have a room, and you got that room because I vouched for you. I'm your magical connection." Another finger goes up. "Second, we have a den. And a basement. And plenty of bathrooms. I really want to eat without your moaning as a soundtrack. Third, must I continue, or will you move your ass to a private location?"

He pulls back from the dazed Delta. Dude is a player, and my best friend besides Crew and Hollis. He gives the girl a quick kiss then taps her nose. "Thanks for agreeing to do my paper. I'll text you the theme, something about greed and capitalism. Make it sparkle." He brushes his hand over her cheek and gives her a smile. "You have no idea how much it means to me, babe."

She simpers. "I can read *American Psycho*. Anything for you," she says breathily. "You'll be my date at the toga party, right?"

"You bet."

Good God. He's a genius.

At this point, perhaps I should be considering asking a girl—there are plenty who would jump at the chance—but deep down, I want to do my own work. I have to prove that I *can*. And I'm not a cheater, no matter what Whitman thinks.

Benji straightens her shirt. "Catch you later?"

"Call me." She fixes her hair and flounces out the door.

He watches her go, then gives me a victorious smile as he snatches up his shirt and tugs it back over his head. "My paper is going to be awesome. She's a whiz apparently. Feels good to get that monkey off my back."

"Do you even like this girl?"

He looks offended. "I'm not that much of a douche."

I arch a brow. Both of us are notorious for our brief relationships. Easy come, easy go. No one gets their heart trampled and we all move on. My longest relationship (six months) was with Blair. We met at freshman orientation and I fell hard. We were exclusive—until she screwed Dex, one of my pledge brothers, while I was at a bowl game. They were drunk. Supposedly. Not an excuse. Please.

Everyone knew what Dex and Blair did—they were caught in the basement—and it created major havoc in the house. My lips twist. Yeah, probably because I kicked his ass in the front yard. We had a knock-down drag-out. He ended up with two black eyes and a limp. Someone called the cops and Denny and Ken broke it up.

My own *friend*, the guy who sat next to me at meetings, who ate meals with me, who laughed with me, screwing my girl. It's the kind of pain you never forget— because you never see it coming. He pulled the blinders off my eyes and showed me exactly the kind of person he was. A cheater. A user. A pretender. I couldn't let the betrayal go, and because I was the more promising brother, the officers cut him. The truth is, if you want to be part of *our* frat, loyalty is key.

He left us and joined the Pikes.

So. Yeah. Got stabbed in the back by my friend and had my heart broken freshman year.

I pull a rectangular pan out of the fridge. "Did someone make lasagna over the weekend?" I raise it up to the ceiling like a gift from the gods. "I am fucking starving." I check out the top of the noodles. "No fuzz— nice. Who made this and how old is it?"

These are important questions. Benji likes to cook

but doesn't know salt from sugar. Parker, our "dinner pledge," makes some meals but douses everything in spicy sauces and jalapeños. He nearly killed us last month with chili.

I've already scooped out the last square and have it in the microwave.

Benji watches me, a glint of something in his gaze that I can't decipher.

"What?"

He shrugs. "You're lucky there's any left."

"Oh?" I grab the sizzling dish, plop down on a chair, slice off a bite, then moan as it hits my tongue. "Fuck. Parker did *not* make this. Who?"

"Ana made it Friday while you guys were in Louisiana. Dude, she didn't even boil the noodles. She soaked them in hot water for like ten minutes, then bam, they were ready to go in the pan. Her sauce was legit too. Not out of a bottle. She brought everything over here and made it. It was fun. I may have talked her ear off, but she can keep up."

I pause mid-bite. "She made it for Donovan?"

"Nah. He was in Atlanta with his folks. She made it for whoever was around. I love that girl."

I stiffen as I send him a long look.

"Oh, for fuck's sake. She's like a sister."

I chew. "You're a horndog. Leave her alone is all I'm saying."

It's what I *try* to do. I never want to be the dude who hits on another brother's girl. It's been done to *me*.

Yeah? *What happened today then?*

He sits down. "So...the tension in class today. And I'm not talking about the obvious dislike you and Whitman give off. I mean Ana. Things were weird. You were talking outside the door, then you sat together. Want to tell me about it?"

I wipe my face with a napkin. "No. What was up with that woo-woo shit?"

He watches me shovel in more food. A small smile curls his lips. "Oh, let me see. You mean don't tell her that when your father died and you were in the ICU, he came to you in a vision and told you to 'wait for Anastasia'? No, wait. He didn't just say that, he told you *three* things: take care of your mom, be a good brother, and wait for Anastasia. Do I have it right?"

I toss down my napkin and look over my shoulder to make sure we're alone. "I told you that when I was slightly intoxicated months ago. I was rambling. You can't bring it up now."

He holds up a finger. "First, you were three sheets to the wind. Blitzed. I've never seen you that drunk. It was the night Donovan gave her his pin." Up goes the next finger. "Second, you were as serious as a heart attack." He holds up a third one. "Also, I'm tired of you being a dick to her. I don't think anyone else really notices, but I do. You never talk to her. Never look at her. If she walks in, you leave—or grab a girl."

What the...

His face is serious as he leans in. "You and I both know you believe the vision really happened."

I hold a finger up. "One, stop mimicking my finger thing. It's mine and you're stealing it."

He chuckles. "Just imitating the best."

"And, to be clear, I was in a coma for two days, I was fifteen, and I'd just watched my dad die. Of course I'm going to *dream* about him." I take another bite, pretending he isn't messing with my head. "What is up with you today?"

He rubs his eyes. "I don't know. That class...and Anastasia didn't seem like herself—"

My fork clatters down to my plate. "Must we talk about her?"

He snaps his mouth shut and studies my expression searchingly.

Dammit. "Look, you, Crew, Hollis, and my family are the only ones who know about my dad thing. It makes me sound like a wacko, and I already..." think about it constantly.

My chest tightens and I rub it, an image of my father popping into my head.

We'd been to a football game, just me and him, when our truck skidded on wet pavement, hit an embankment, and slid off into a ravine. The road was notoriously curvy and rural, and he wasn't speeding, but a deer ran across in front of us. I awoke in the car and found him slumped over the steering wheel. I suffered a broken leg, a ruptured spleen and kidney, and a head injury. I was lucky. His side of the truck collided with a boulder, the jagged edges piercing the windshield, and my dad's face. Bones protruding. Blood everywhere. Carnage.

Pinned in by the seatbelt, I begged him to hang on, to not leave me...

My breath hitches and I dip my face away from Benji's prying eyes.

But the dream? Shit.

He walked into my hospital room, sat down next to me, and took my hand. He looked like he always did. Tall, brown hair, hazel eyes. He smelled of his cologne. He smiled and told me everything was going to be okay. He said I was the best son. He told me I was going to make him proud and that he'd always be with me.

In my dream, I wept. And wept. *Please stay, Dad, please don't go.*

Then he faded away.

Defining moment? Hell yeah.

Life is just one breath away from death. Every single motherfucking second counts.

"It was special to you," Benji murmurs quietly.

My fingers pick up my fork, a lump in my throat. "It

doesn't make it real. *Anastasia* was my sister's favorite princess movie. Mom made jokes about it. It. Was. A. Weird. Dream."

He steals a noodle and pops it in his mouth. "Okay, okay, I'll shut up about it. But, let me say this—"

"You just can't let it go."

"I did some googling—"

"Dude. Not everything you read on the internet is true."

"—and found this piece about dreams from dead people, like, it *could* be real. When you're asleep—or in a coma—it shuts down your critical thinking and leaves your brain open—"

"To make believe. You're talking hocus-pocus crap."

"No. Seriously. What if it was his way of comforting you? Like a piece of his soul connected with you. Didn't that experience ease you? Didn't it make you feel better —in that moment?"

"You're the woo-woo one," I say as I go back to eating.

"I'm a psych major. This is possible."

"You should look into mystic mediums. Or one of those call-in places." I mimic making a phone call. "Hello, Mystical Benji, can you let me talk to my dead parakeet?"

"Ah, man, you had to bring up Roscoe. You know I loved that parakeet."

"Who's got a parakeet?" Hollis says as he breezes into

the kitchen from outside with Crew and drops his book bag. "I wanna see it. I want to teach it some bad words." He cocks his head. "Definitely teach it to say *Hollis is a badass motherfucker.*"

"True that. I need some funny," Crew grouses. "If someone brings the game up one more time, I'm going ballistic."

I relay the story about the reporter I saw, and they growl and mutter. The three of us just want to forget this season ever happened.

"Benji wants a new bird," I say a bit later. "His childhood one passed away last month."

Benji grimaces. "I should have been there when Roscoe died. He was alone with my mom and brother, but no Benji." He exhales. "I have an idea: let's get one for the house and name her Adele in honor of Hollis's performance last night in karaoke."

Hollis flips us off then stares at my plate, eyes lighting up. "Who made food and where can I get some?"

"I ate the last of it," I say. "Payback for the Ding Dongs you keep hidden."

Crew eyes me and Benji. "So, did we interrupt a talk? You guys looked serious."

I jump up from the table, rinse my dish, and toss it in the dishwasher. "Nope."

But I can still feel Benji's gaze on me.

Sure. I've analyzed the dream with my mom. She thinks it was real. So does my sister. But it's because we want to cling to the hope that there's an afterlife and Dad's still with us in some way. People die. They don't visit you in dreams. Right?

"Hey guys!" comes a female voice, and I turn to see Harper Michaels standing in the kitchen. She's slipping a blue sweater on and picking up her book bag from where it's hanging on one of the hooks near the door.

Petite, blonde, and pretty, she's Donovan's ex.

She used to spend every free moment here with him when they dated—but not anymore.

"Hey," Benji says cautiously.

Crew and Hollis send her a wave, but they aren't smiling.

Her face is flushed, and she won't meet any of our gazes. "Gotta go. See you Friday at the party," she tells us as she dashes out the back door.

Weird.

I look at Benji. He's been at the house the longest. "How long has she been here?"

He lifts his hands. "I got here an hour ago and no one has come in, so she's been here a while."

There's a silence in the kitchen as the guys look at each other, then at me.

Crew arches a brow, like, *Dude, what are you going to do about* that?

Hollis grimaces. "Is he messing around with her?"

We all know who *he* is.

Anastasia isn't part of the fraternity brotherhood *officially*, but she's wearing his pin, and that makes her one of our little sisters. Not as important as a brother, sure, and girlfriends with pins come and go, but...

A long exhalation comes from my chest. If Donovan—

"Where is he?" I ask.

"His Tesla is parked on the street, so he's definitely here," Hollis says.

"Basement probably," Benji adds as he stands and peeks into the den.

"Later," I tell them and walk through the den, saying hi to the guys there. I make a point to check on them, especially the pledges. I ask how their day is going, though I'm only half-listening, my mind lasered in on Harper and why she was here. After fifteen minutes, my finger is twisting my ring furiously as I take the stairs down to the basement.

I step down into the spacious bottom floor of our four-story house. The walls are dark paneling with photo collages of every year, various awards we've gotten for service work, and candid pictures of the football team. Hollis, Crew, and I are framed in one from last year after we won the national championship, our arms draped around each other. Seeing it reminds me of how fucked this season was, and I turn away.

After I pass the pool table, I find Donovan sitting on one of the theater recliners as he hunches over his laptop. He's tall, about six two, and fit. He's handsome, I guess. Nice guy. Smart. A little oblivious.

I've watched him study for a test with earbuds in while we partied. I've seen him walk right past Anastasia, his head far away, and not notice her. My hands clench.

But he—oh yeah, he knows when to pay attention when it counts.

After all, he noticed her *first*. And dibs count among brothers.

"SEE THAT GIRL? She's in my chemistry class. I've had my eye on her all semester."

I glance up from the textbook I'm pretending to read in the library and follow Donovan's gaze to the babe at a table a few feet away.

I know almost everyone on campus, but—

"She has to be new here. Don't know her name and I'm too shy to just go up to her." He leans in. "You're killer at scoring girls. What do I do?"

I'm barely listening.

Her hair is a soft purple, and a pen is tucked into her updo or whatever you call it. Her eyes—can't see the color—are behind glasses, but I can tell they're expressive and thickly lashed. Her mouth is pouty as she pulls it down in a frown. Her shirt is bright pink, the curve of her tits...definitely a D cup, and her legs are long.

Tall.

Curvy.

Unconventional.

MY TYPE.

"She's hot, right?"

"She's alright," *I murmur.*

She isn't beautiful in a cookie-cutter way like some of the made-up sorority girls who hang at our house; no, she's frighteningly pretty in an ethereal, natural way. Like a wild angel. All that color.

I almost expect rainbow wings to pop out behind her back.

Her face is heart-shaped and delicate, her nose a hair too long, the arch of her dark eyebrows dramatic against her pale skin.

I tear my gaze off her and look at Donovan. "She really isn't your type."

"I hear you, but I need a change from Harper. We keep hooking up since we broke up, and it never goes anywhere."

"Hmmm."

Donovan's eyes practically glow as he stares at the girl. "I mean, look at her. It's hard to look away, am I right? She's so *different from me though. Advice? How do I start? Just walk up and then what? Fuck. I have no game. I'm useless when it comes to girls."*

"No, you're not."

He taps his pen on the table. "I'm a geek and you know it. I'm going over there. Maybe ask her about class? No, that's too generic. I need a good pick-up line." He stands up, a panicked look on his face. "River. Shit. Help."

I laugh and pull him down. "Hold off on storming the castle." My eyes go back to her, and I stand. "Let me do a walk-by."

Her head is down as I slowly walk past her and pretend to look for a book on the nearby shelves. She moves around, uncrossing and crossing her legs. A long sigh comes from her chest.

Being covert, I spy the numerous thick textbooks on her table. Can't read the names of them, but shit, she's way smarter than me.

There's a worn paperback off to the side. I squint at it, mouthing the letters in my head. T-h-e O-u-t-s-i-d-e-r-s. *The Outsiders.*

Never heard of it. Not that I would.

Who. The Fuck. Is. She.

Her lips turn down again, as if something is bugging her, and I keep myself from moving in, sitting down, and saying, Tell me three things that make you happy. Smile for me.

I glance at Donovan, and he gives me a wide-eyed, hopeful look.

I ease closer, pretending to read a book I grabbed as I hold it up to my face. When I reach her table, I drop my pen and keep going.

"Um, excuse me?" comes from behind me, her voice husky and soft. "You dropped something."

"Oh?" I turn back to her, and when our eyes meet, my heart dips. Emeralds with gold around the pupils.

She pushes her glasses up. "A pen. I think it rolled under my table."

"Did it? I was, um, reading, and didn't notice."

"Here, let me grab it." She stands and dips down to check the floor. Her head flips over and her nape is long and creamy, the skin pale and translucent. I bet she doesn't tan well. She probably uses the hell out of sunscreen when she's outside. I wonder what her natural hair color is—

I blink, refocusing my brain when she rises up and holds the pen out for me. "Tada. It's got a unicorn on it. Nice."

Our hands brush when she hands it off. "Yeah, um, yeah. Callie, she, uh, she likes to buy them and when I go home, I end up with one or two, you know, so I can have something magical at Braxton, that's what she says anyway..." I peter off, wincing.

She glances at my book. She's standing close, and I watch as her dark lashes fall against her cheek. Her scent hits me, light and fresh, like summer and sunshine.

Her dark eyebrows arch. "Not My Romeo? Romance lover, huh?"

Shit! I glance down at the shirtless guy on the cover. Leave it to me to grab a chick book. "Ah, no, I was just looking at it."

"You said you were reading." Her lips quirk up on one side, so lush and—

Donovan clears his throat, and I glance over at him. He gives me a What the hell are you doing? look.

Right.

How could I forget?

He's my brother and he saw her first.

She's just a random girl.

He's had his eye on her all semester.

He's lonely.

I'm not.

She smiles shyly. "I love to read. If you ever... I mean, just...ah, the library is a great place for books, duh, and if you need recommendations for a good book to grab, I can help." She bites her lip. "Wow. I'm saying the stupidest things."

Her voice is soft and her accent... I can't place it. Most of the students at Braxton are from the South, but she isn't.

"I'm super awkward around people my own age." She laughs under her breath and tingles go down my spine.

I hold her gaze as goose bumps rise on my arms.

What the hell?

Another smile curls her lips as she sticks out her hand.

"Hi. Let me introduce myself before I say something else weird. My name is—"

"You need a pen?" Audrey says as she appears out of nowhere and crooks her arm in mine, interrupting Rainbow Girl.

I blink down at Audrey. I guess she was hovering nearby and listening to us...

"Ah, no, this one works fine, but thanks," I tell her.

Mellany joins her and they start asking me about the next party at the house.

I feel Rainbow Girl's eyes on me as I give her one last look, pivot away, and leave her there.

After a few moments, I shake the Deltas off and sit down next to Donovan. I take three deep, steadying breaths.

I have the frat, my team, my family.

I have everything.

I'm not hurting for girls.

Donovan has no game and saw her first.

I went over there to get her for him.

But...

Wow...

She's fucking...

"Well?" he asks. "You were over there for a long time. What did you find out?"

Not enough.

"River?"

I come back and focus.

"I've got a great idea," I say. "You're going to write her a note. Say everything I tell you to."

I PUSH the past aside and plop down next to Donovan. "Yo, my man. How's it going?"

He looks up briefly then goes back to typing on his laptop. "Just finalizing the DJ for the party, the usual." He runs a hand through his light brown hair. It's cut in a short style, trimmed over the ears, shaved in the back so it doesn't touch his collar.

"Nice. I've got catering covered with The Truth Is Out There. Marilyn is bringing a taco bar." She's the owner and we use her all the time. "I double-checked with her on Sunday."

He pauses and looks up again. "Sorry about your game."

"I'm considering coming back for my fifth year for another go." A harsh laugh comes from me. "Or I won't come back after Christmas and try my luck in the draft. Who knows?"

"Ah, okay, I see," he muses, a quizzical expression on his face. He's a guy who always has a plan, and I baffle him.

Okay, let's get real—I baffle most people.

"I got my acceptance into Harvard," he adds.

I slap him on the back. "Congrats. That's awesome, man. Proud of you."

He murmurs a confirmation, his concentration back on what's on the screen.

Has he remembered it's her birthday?

I chew on my lip to stop myself from telling him. She told me not to, but—

Taking his glasses off, he rubs his eyes as he stands and stretches. He rolls his neck and rubs the muscles there.

"Long day?" I ask as I watch him, my eyes snagging on the pink lip stain on his throat. Tension flares inside me. That *isn't* Anastasia's color. Her lips are always deep red.

"Yeah. Long weekend."

I flick my finger at him as I fake nonchalance. "You've got lipstick on your throat. Harper's." It's not a question. "I saw her leave."

He heaves out a long sigh. "Um, yeah. She, ah, came over when she got her acceptance to Harvard. We both got our emails today. We're pretty excited." He walks over to a mirror on the wall and rubs at his neck. A sheepish expression crosses his face. "She went a little nuts and kissed me."

A little?

"Uh-huh." I lean back in the recliner, propping my arms behind my head. I lift a brow, still pretending I don't care, just mildly interested. "Something you're not telling me?"

A furrow forms on his forehead as he looks down at his feet. "Maybe. I don't know." A long breath comes from his chest. "Shit. I'm..." He stops and scrubs his face.

Here it comes...

I straighten up and lean in, putting my elbows on my knees. It's my easy face, the *Let it all out* look. "It's been a while since we had a chat. Tell me what's bothering you. I'm a vault. Brother's honor." Using two fingers, I tap my heart twice, our secret Kappa signal.

He taps his heart back. "Kappa forever," he murmurs.

"Let it out, brother."

He sighs. Wearing khakis and a polo shirt, he crosses his arms, a frown on his face. "It's Ana. She's distant, not replying to texts. She should have heard from Harvard by now and hasn't, which makes me wonder if she didn't get in."

Oh. That might explain her unhappiness last week when I saw her in the student center.

"And this is a big deal? There are other schools nearby, yeah?"

"Not according to my family." He winces. "Look, my grandfather is a senator. My dad is on the city council for Atlanta and, well, um, he had her family looked into."

My eyes flare. "Do they always investigate your girl-friends?"

"If they don't know them." He starts pacing around the room, his head tilted down. "Ana...she grew up weird. Her dad used to be a professor at Columbia, which is great, but he quit to travel the world with her mom. This last year, in Greece, he vandalized a building at a political protest, some graffiti stuff. He got arrested and spent a month in jail. Her mom was charged with shoplifting once in the States, nothing serious, but they're like, hippie liberals."

"Hmmm," I say.

He exhales, scowling. "They're not even married. Ana says they don't believe in getting married just to make it legal, but—get this: at one point, Ana's mom had another guy she was with. They were, like, *all* together for a few months. I'm sure there are other things going on, and trust me, my parents will dig it up."

"Like a throuple?" My lips quirk.

"Yeah. And don't say I'm uptight. People can have any kind of consensual relationship they want, but it's not normal. What if all that comes out, you know, if we get married?" He blows out a breath. "She doesn't know we've had her looked into. Vault." He taps his heart, and I do the same.

"Of course."

"Right. You aren't close with her. It's just we have a lot of political status in Georgia, and my family doesn't want to jeopardize their reputation."

"Her parents don't define her. She's her own person."

He nods, his jaw working. "I know, I know, but..."

My eyes narrow. "Your parents want Harper—or someone like her. For status." Harper's family owns half of Atlanta, most of it in commercial real estate.

He lifts his hands. "You nailed it. Advice?"

"Do you want a political career?" I ask, trying to hammer out a solution in my head.

"No, but my dad might make a run for governor soon. He has a strong, conservative base. You know how they dig into your family once you run for office. Every skeleton gets plastered all over. Even if it's not true, the media twists it up and makes it work for them."

Ah.

Well.

He isn't wrong.

I take a deep breath. *Be objective, don't let emotion get in the way, don't steer him in the wrong direction because of ulterior motives.*

I shove the image of Anastasia in the library far, far away.

"You've been with Anastasia for a year. She has your pin. You *are* in love with her, right?" I tense as I wait for his reply. It's a cheesy question for dudes, but...

He nods.

"Are you sure?"

I need to know, Donovan.

"Yes," he says. "We enjoy the same things. We both want to work with needy people. With my money, we can open our own firm someday. We have fun."

Vague. I need concrete shit, like, I dig how she doesn't care what people think, the way she arches her dark eyebrows when she's surprised, the way she yells *Boo-yah!* when she wins at poker, or the way she gasps for air when Benji twirls her around in the kitchen.

I stare down at my hands.

Oh, I heard their *fun* from his room last year. After several nights of hearing him call her name out during sex or whatever, I asked for a different floor and found someone who'd switch rooms with me. Then, I quit sleeping here altogether after seeing them together at the house, the soft look on her face when she gazed at him.

"She's going to be a lawyer and that's a huge thing to have in common," I say. "She's smart and beautiful."

"So is Harper." He darts his eyes at me.

I blink. Say what?

"Real talk here, Donovan: are you using your parents as an excuse to fuck with Harper?"

He takes a step back, a wild look on his face. "No! You know how she is. She's never gotten over me. She came over here uninvited—"

"Do you still have feelings for her?"

He pauses and licks his lips. "We're friends. We have coffee periodically—off campus. We text."

I laugh, a little bitterly. "Dude, you can't be friends with your ex. First rule of having a girlfriend. She trumps the ex."

He groans. "It's just...our families are friends. We see each other at gatherings and holidays. She's always there, you know. It's hard to let go of a childhood friend."

"Harper doesn't want to be your friend. She wants a ring. She hates Anastasia and now you're... Does Anastasia know you still talk to her?"

He scrubs his hair. "No."

"So, you're lying to your girl?"

"No!" He rushes over and sits down. "I haven't told her, but I don't think she'd care."

Dude...

"I can't think," he mutters as he hangs his head. "My parents think she's low class. She came to stay this past summer, and it was uncomfortable. They hate how she dresses, her hair. My grandmother called her a floozy behind her back."

"She isn't that," I say curtly.

"I know." His gaze pleads with me to understand. "Do I need to tell Ana what happened with Harper?"

I give him a look that says *yes*. I'd be calling my girl right now and laying out that Harper came to the house and got handsy. I'd cop to the coffee meetups. In real life,

I never would have *done* the coffee dates. Sure, I haven't been in a committed relationship in a while and my experience is lacking, but if I had a girl like Anastasia, I'd want to protect it.

He reads my face and groans. "You're right. I haven't been upfront. It's going to hurt her."

My throat tightens as I remember Anastasia's face outside class. She was devastated because he didn't mention her birthday, and if she also knew he got into Harvard and she didn't...double whammy.

If he tells her about Harper, damn...

I heave out a breath. "Look, your parents will always be on your side. They care about you. You're wondering if Anastasia will fit in with them? She won't." I hold a finger up. "She's not a debutante." Second finger. "She's a real girl with a messy upbringing." Third finger. "If you love her, why the fuck does it matter?"

He shuts his eyes briefly. "You make it sound so easy. You don't know how persuasive my family can be. They hinted they may not pay for Harvard." His throat bobs as he looks away from me.

"Get a loan."

"That's crazy."

"Is she worth it?"

"Of course! When I..." He stops, a soft, dreamy look flashing on his face. "When I kiss her, man, the whole world disappears."

My body tenses, and I do my best to hide it, to pretend I don't care, but, shit...

He loves her. I mean, that *expression* on his face...

A long exhalation comes from my chest as I realize *this* is my reminder that *I* shouldn't be fucking with her like I did in class today.

And right now, I'm managing to stay fair, but underneath, the manipulative side of me is itching to pull strings and orchestrate their—

No.

I stand.

An alarm on his phone goes off and he checks it. "I have to get to the library. I've got a paper due tomorrow."

He rushes to gather up his laptop and backpack.

"Have you seen her today?" I say as he takes off for the stairs.

He stops, a furrow on his brow. "No. Maybe she'll pop by, but she's working tonight. I'll catch her tomorrow for dinner probably. Toga party for sure. Oh, wait—you saw her in class."

"Yeah."

He fiddles with his book bag, worry on his face. "Did she seem off?"

It's her *birthday*.

"Um, we don't talk much."

He pauses, lingering on the steps, then turns back to me. "River? Why do you call her Anastasia?"

Tingles ghost over my skin and into my scalp. *Wait for Anastasia.*

"No reason."

He chews on his lip. "Huh."

I stick my hands into my pockets as my uneasiness rises. At least next fall, if I come back, neither of them will be at Braxton. I'll be here. Alone.

"Thanks for letting me vent. And Harper... Nothing has ever happened between us. I want you to know that. She's offered, yeah, plenty of times, but I haven't done anything wrong."

"So you say" slips out.

He narrows his eyes, his lids lowering. "Ana *is* the one I love, River. She's the *one* for me. I'll figure out my parents."

I keep my face completely blank.

She. Does. Not. Exist.

I force a smile. "Right."

7

Anastasia

"You smell like grease and French fries," I say to myself as I climb out of my white Honda Civic. "With a dash of beer."

Grabbing the bags off of the passenger seat, I walk to the alley between my building and the next one, a rambling old factory where they make shoes. My apartment complex is old, built in the fifties, but well-maintained with a clean manicured lawn. The area isn't the best, but it's near campus. And it's cheap.

Steam rises and floats in the air from the exhaust vent in the basement. Thank goodness for that old furnace. An old striped blanket is pitched over the vent between two milk crates, making a tent of sorts. Two legs stick out.

A small brown dog, a mutt, sits near the feet and

glances up at me as I approach. His tail wags. He's old, bits of gray in his fur. Sweet little Oscar.

"Hey, handsome." I break off half of a hamburger patty, toss it down, and he sniffs then pounces on it. "I brought dog food, but you need a treat."

"Who's there?" June peeks out of her tent. "Oh. You." She folds the top over so she can see me better. Her eyes glint from the streetlights. "You're like a roach. Can't get rid of you."

"Were you expecting anyone else?"

"Holding out hope for Bruce Willis."

"Hmmm. Have you seen *The Sixth Sense*? Very tense. A psychological thriller. 'I see dead people,'" I quote in a breathy voice like the kid in the movie.

I tug my coat around me in the cold night then find a piece of an old box near the dumpster and drag it over to where she is. Setting it down, I plop down on it. My back leans against the building.

"Nah, I don't do scary. *Die Hard*, now that's his best," she replies. "If you could kindly bring him with you next time, I'd appreciate it."

"I'll call his agent first thing tomorrow. How's it going?"

She eases out farther and throws me a wary glance. She's in her sixties, I think, has a small pixie face, brown eyes, and wears an Atlanta Falcons beanie on her head. Her pale face is surprisingly clean, and I wonder if she has a place where she washes up. Maybe a gas station?

There's a heavy coat and a fuzzy blanket around her shoulders, and she tugs them closer. "Cut the small talk. What you got?" she asks.

I grin widely and hand over the first bag, a baked potato and fried chicken from the bar. It's not the healthiest meal, but she won't eat salads. I've tried. I hand over two bottles of water and a container of Gatorade I grabbed at the gas station. "There are chips, some baby wipes, dog food, and a few candy bars in the bag. Snickers and Heath."

"I hate Heath bars."

I laugh. I can't help it. She reminds me of the cantankerous grandmother I never had. "I can see you from my den window, you know. You devoured the last one."

"You imagined that. And stop spying on me. Weirdo." She props the takeout box in her lap and eats the food slowly, almost delicately. She's not starving, that's clear. She isn't an alcoholic or a druggie either. I've looked for the signs, bloodshot eyes and shakes. Her voice is always clear and steady, her thoughts sharp.

I gaze up at the stars. I don't know June's story or why she's here, but my protective instincts are high. My heart squeezes every time I see her here.

I find the Orion constellation, see his belt then the hazy glow of the Milky Way behind him. I glance back at her. "It's going to get down to forty tonight and the wind is cold. The shelter is ten minutes from here. Just saying," I murmur casually.

She glares at me, and I glare right back. I'm used to her little dirty looks. There's no menace in them. Maybe confusion at my nightly appearances.

Perhaps relief.

Is she lonely?

"No shelters." Her voice is husky and gravelly with a slight Southern accent. She's from the area, I suspect. "I hate crowds. Plus, they come in while you're sleeping and put tracking devices in your ears. They won't let Oscar in, and it's not that cold. I grew up playing outside all the time. We didn't come home until we wanted to."

I start at the tidbit of personal information she's given me.

She swallows down a bite. "Don't get excited. I don't want you in my business."

"Too late. You can't get rid of me."

"Maybe I'll move to another apartment building."

"You better not. I sort of like you."

She stands and stretches, then tosses her trash in the dumpster a few feet away. She gets around well, and I'm thankful she seems to be in good health.

I ease up. "Let me see that scrape on your arm. Does it hurt?" Last night, she had blood on her sweatshirt, a cut she got from a lamppost she walked by.

She huffs. "Will you go away if I show it to you?"

"Swear. Let me have a peek, check it out, and I'm gone."

She takes off her coat, pulls up her sleeve, and exposes the two-inch gash above her elbow. Dousing my hands in sanitizer, I remove the bandage I put on last night.

"Well, doc? Is it terminal?"

"You may not recover," I deadpan.

"Knew it. I'm dying." She places a hand over her brow and wilts.

My lips twitch. She's in a good mood. "Let's do more antibiotic ointment and a new covering. I bought Garfield Band-Aids." I pat my backpack.

"Pain in my ass. Fine." She pauses and says softly, "Thank you, Ana."

I smile. "How was your day?"

She purses her lips. "Same. Walked to Walmart. Walked to Big Star. Some guy gave me twenty bucks and I didn't even ask for it. Went to the park. Ate. Took a nap. Oscar chased a squirrel. You?"

"I went to class. Saw a boy." I pause on the memory of River, my hands stopping for a moment as I work on her arm. He's under my skin, always has been, and I don't know what to do about it. "Went to work. Came home."

"Is the boy nice?"

"He's a bit of a bad boy on campus, but there's something different about him. He likes to pretend I don't exist, and I suspect there's a reason why."

She mulls that over as I help straighten her coat back around her shoulders, and she *lets* me. She has boundaries with people, I've learned. The first night I ventured into the alley to see who she was, she told me to fuck off and leave. But I know pain when I see it and couldn't walk away. I sat down next to her and talked about books. She ignored me, refused to answer any of my questions about her, but I kept it up, and finally, on the fifth night, she was out of her tent and waiting for me. Sure, she replied in one-word answers, but she didn't run me off. I get it. Her walls are built from self-preservation.

That way, when someone lets you down, it doesn't hurt as much.

Been there.

Her eyes squint. "Is he handsome?"

"Crazy hot. Kind of cruel," I murmur as I re-sanitize my hands, then pick up Oscar for snuggles. Not sure what good it does to be clean when I'm holding him. He licks my face, and I giggle.

She sips her water. "Bad boys are the devil. When I was young, that was all I wanted. I used to sing at this bar—" She abruptly stops and glares at me. "I see what you're doing. Trying to get me to talk."

"What was the name of the bar?"

"Never you mind."

"Do you have any family?" I ask softly. "You know, someone who might be worried—"

"No." She pauses, and her fingerless woolen gloves clench into fists. "I had a son, but he's dead. Fire. They say he never woke up."

My heart dips and tears prick in my throat. Was it her house? Is that why she's homeless?

Oh, June. What must it feel like to be *this* alone? "I'm sorry for your loss. I can't imagine."

She grunts and looks away, frowning.

I gaze into Oscar's big brown eyes, but my words are directed to her. "They have private rooms at the shelter for women."

Part of me wonders if she's been harassed at shelters before or if she really believes they put tracking devices in her head. I believe she just says that stuff because she wants me to shut up about it. But, if there *are* mental issues going on, she needs help I can't give. "They serve three meals a day and have counseling services, a staff of nurses and doctors. This boy I was telling you about? His frat just donated a lot of money to one and—"

"You can go now."

A long sigh comes from me as I set the dog down. Maybe I pushed too hard this time. "You know I'm in 3B if you need anything. My roommates are a handful, but sweet. I've talked to them and you're welcome to stay on the couch until I can find you a place—"

Her voice rises. "This is my place. It's home."

I stand my ground. "The weather's going to get colder. It's December."

"The heat from the furnace works."

But being out here...it can't be good for her. It just can't. "June..."

She ducks back into her tent, and Oscar follows.

I stand there considering throwing her in my car and driving to the shelter, but I know she'd fight me the whole way, and in the end, it has to be her decision. She *is* her own person. I kick at a pebble, my head tumbling. She refused my offer of giving her an extra key to the basement, which could totally get me kicked out of the building if the landlord found out, but at least it's heated. The Walker Police Department doesn't have any missing persons. I checked. I want to help her, want her to be okay. If I just keep coming, keep talking, keep checking on her, maybe one day—

Her head pops back out, her eyes glittering in the streetlights. "Go home, girl. Oh, and happy birthday. You're legal. Drink one for me. Get crazy, but not too crazy. Use a condom if you do the dirty dance."

She remembered.

Warmth sinks into my bones, soft and easy.

"Thank you," I murmur.

"Don't think I like you."

"You adore me."

"See you tomorrow night." She disappears.

Five minutes later, I'm getting the mail in the lobby of our building when I see Sam exiting his office. Our maintenance man, he's of medium height with brown hair and a short beard. A tool belt hangs around his waist and he hitches it up, then crosses his arms when he sees me. He frowns. "I saw you pull up and go back there. You gotta stop feeding her, Ana. She'll just keep coming back."

Unease curls around me. It's more than just giving her food. I'm a person to her when I don't think she has anyone. "Sam, come on. She doesn't make a mess and cleans up after Oscar. No one sees her. It's dark out there."

His round face scrunches, and his hand goes to his jeans, his thumb hooking into his waistband. "Mr. Winston is a stickler for vagrants. You know how meticulous he is about this place. This can't keep on. She's been here for a month and I haven't said a word—"

"How was the lasagna? How's the new baby?"

He huffs. "Tiff loved the casserole, and the baby sleeps like a log. She said to tell you thanks for the food and the baby outfit." He grimaces. "You're too damn nice. June needs to get gone."

He said her name, which means she's a person to him too.

"Just let her be," I say softly. I don't ask Sam for much, even when the sink gets clogged or the lights go out. I buy Drano or dash to the basement and flip the breaker.

"She's harmless," I add. "I can guarantee another casserole. I'll even babysit—for free. Wouldn't you love a night out just you two?"

"Hmmm, yeah." He rubs a hand through his beard. "June's always gone in the mornings."

"No one even sees her. She only sleeps here."

"I should call Mr. Winston though. Right?" He blows out a gust of air, an uncertain look on his face.

"Not tonight. It's late. Get some sleep and kiss the baby for me." *Please, Sam.*

I hear him grumbling behind me as I walk up the stairs to my apartment.

I put my key in and open the door.

"Happy birthday!" comes from my two roomies, Lila and Colette, as I walk in the front door of our three-bedroom apartment.

Before I can even set down my bags and the mail, Lila jumps at me with a tight hug and Colette follows. We make a circle, squeal, and jump up and down.

Blonde and petite, Lila's wearing booty shorts and a sleep shirt, while dark-haired Colette sports a PJ flannel set with yellow rubber ducks on it. They're fraternal twins.

"Pajama party?" I say on a laugh.

Lila pumps the air as they yell in unison, "Hell yeah!"

They whoop and I join them, emotion tugging at me as I take in the mylar balloons in the den. Amongst the *Happy Birthday!* ones, a few say *Get Well Soon*, *Happy Graduation*, and *Happy Mother's Day*.

"We wanted a festive look. Bought all the balloons they had," Lila says with a giggle. Pink and purple streamers crisscross the den. It's a mess, no rhyme or reason, and I smile broadly.

The three of us met last spring at The Truth Is Out There. Lila works there with me, and Colette is a regular. Still finding my footing at Braxton, I was renting a room in a drafty old boarding house. They had an extra bedroom and asked me to move in.

Lila tosses her blonde hair over her shoulder. "I've got the good stuff tonight." She twirls around, grabs a box off the media center, and opens it. She preens as if it's the Hope Diamond. "It's your birthday, bitch. We're getting high."

Colette grabs a jar of peanut butter off the coffee table, picks up the spoon stuck inside the container, and sticks it in her mouth. Her eyebrows waggle. She talks around the spoon. "We smoked one already."

I laugh. Of course they have.

On Lila's birthday, a few months ago, we got high. It was my first time, and I ended up with a terrible case of paranoia. I convinced them the police were after us with K9 drug dogs. We hid in our basement with the washers and dryers.

"Please, join us," Colette begs as she drags me into the kitchen. "Look, I made nachos for your birthday, your favorite, and I have cupcakes from the Busy Bakery!" She waves her hands in a flourish around purple cupcakes. *Ana* is written in white icing on the tops. My throat tightens, my stomach pitching at the emotion.

"Don't you dare cry!" she says.

"I'm not!" I say on a laugh as I wipe my face.

"Liar!" She opens the fridge and pulls out the prosecco. "This is a throwdown! Screw Donovan. You got us, babe!"

I laugh. Typically, recreational drugs don't hold much appeal, but well, today...

Lila hums as she sets to work at the table, rolling the joint. Colette murmurs that she needs talking points for our conversations and grabs a notebook in case we forget our 'revelations.'

I dash to my room and change into black leggings and a cropped *Queen of Naps* shirt. I scour my backpack for my copy of *Lady Chatterley's Lover*, thinking we might discuss it during a high chat, but I can't find it. Weird.

An hour later, our buzz hits.

I'm singing "Wonderwall" by Oasis on top of the coffee table. "I sound *great*," I tell them, but Colette laughs at me from the floor. Lila goes to the front door then reappears with Chinese takeout that no one recalls ordering, but I suspect she's messing with me.

We head to the kitchen. Leftover nachos and cupcakes litter the counters as we dig into the Chinese food.

Colette chomps on a tube of frozen chocolate chip cookie dough as I eat an egg roll. The mix of crispy flour and lettuce is freaking amazing. I dunk it in the sweet sauce and decide the color of the egg roll shell is the same as Donovan's hair.

F him.

"Even birthday fiasco aside, Donovan and I are off," I say. "It's like, we're circling this awful thing and don't want to acknowledge it."

"He's stuck up. Let's go beat his stupid Tesla with a baseball bat," Lila says with quiet venom, looking fierce. "We'll call an Uber, do the deed, maybe swing by Pizza Hut for a supreme on the way back." She's already grabbing the metal bat we keep in the corner for intruders.

"We have plenty of food," I remind her calmly.

She swings the bat over her shoulder, and I giggle and take it away from her. "Simmer down, Lila. I know you're pissed at him, but we aren't going anywhere while we're stoned—"

My words are interrupted by a deep voice.

"Anastasia Bailey is high. My, my, my," a man says, dragging out the words in a low tone. He makes a tsking noise. "I need evidence. Haven't blackmailed anyone in a while."

8

Anastasia

W e freeze at the masculine voice and collectively turn to the doorway that leads to the den. Lila squeaks, Colette blinks—and my mouth drops open. A piece of lettuce tickles my lip and I swipe at it, then shake my head to clear it.

Doesn't work.

A massive, tattooed hottie is in our kitchen.

He holds up his phone. "Say cheese. Or egg roll. Whatever works." Finished, he tucks his cell back in his pocket and leans against the doorjamb. One maddening eyebrow goes up as he smirks at me. "Hey, you."

"Hey?" is my reply.

Lila clutches my arm. "Is that River Tate or am I hallucinating?"

"Can we have the same hallucination?" Colette asks as she slaps her hand on the counter and picks up the cookie dough—all without taking her eyes off River.

"He's not real," I say with conviction, the idea simple. "I manifested him because he wished me happy birthday. He's been on my mind—very irritating, if you must know. Somehow my brain is a movie projector and there he is. It's science."

"Makes sense," Lila agrees. "He's a hologram. So cool."

I inch forward. "Ever noticed his eyes? What is *up* with that color? It's not blue, not gray, but something in between. Like dove feathers touching the sky. They darken to molten silver when he's emotional."

"You noticed?" the vision asks.

"Like I wouldn't," I say.

"You're quite poetic, Anastasia," Fake River says.

"You noticed?"

"Like I wouldn't," he replies.

A tingle dances down my spine.

He smiles then bites his bottom lip and rakes a hand through his messy hair, and I swallow. It's not often his visage is happy to see me, and Fake River *is* strangely happy as he looks at me.

I close my eyes. *Disappear!* I say in my head.

Still here.

"Lila, was there acid in that weed?" I ask warily.

"No. I get my stuff from Mason, the motocross guy. He's topnotch—in bed and with the weed."

"I know him," Fake River murmurs. "Nice guy."

Around her chews, Colette says, "You think you can project his pants off so I can see the snake?"

"Snake?" Fake River asks.

"It's what we call your penis," I admit with a shrug as I wave my hands at him. "Because of your tattoo."

"You called me Snake today," he says. "Were you actually talking to my dick?"

"No!" I huff. "It's confusing, okay?"

Lila taps her chin. "Is he circumcised? I've never seen one that isn't. Show us, please, Ana. Purely for the research of course."

"No," I say adamantly. "It's sexualizing him, and demeaning. He's a person."

"Use your magic mind and take his shirt off at least," Colette says. "I wanna see that six-pack."

"I wanna see his snake!" Lila declares. She emits a hissing sound, *sssssss*.

I slap an egg roll in her hands. "Here. Eat this."

She stares at it. "Not what I wanted. But. Okay." She takes a bite.

I look back at the mirage in the doorway. "Go away. You're messing with our mojo."

"He's still here," Colette whispers. "Should we get the bat?"

"He's not *really* here," I insist. "Why would River Tate walk into our house uninvited?"

The hologram rolls his eyes. "Your door was cracked. I heard the giggling and came in when no one answered. It smells like reefer in here, by the way. Imagine my surprise when I catch you being naughty. Breaking the law. Always knew you had a wicked streak."

"The law!" Lila grasps my arm. "Basement, Ana! You get the nachos. I'll get Colette."

"You're being paranoid. Fight it. He's not real!" I exclaim.

"Chill. I won't tell the cops," Fake River says on a chuckle. "I'm River Lucius Tate. Going to be a fifth-year senior next fall. Maybe. Who knows if I'll come back? Even I don't know. My dream is to play in the NFL, but nobody wants a loser, so I need a year to straighten my life out. Oh, and I'm in class with Anastasia. I ride the elevator with her every Monday, Wednesday, and Friday. It's an experience. She talks to herself, and I can't read lips."

"The mirage is trying to convince us by giving personal details, but it's my subconscious creating him. Has to be." I lean into the girls. "Donovan is weird about him."

"You don't say," Lila says. "Because of his snake? It's big and he's jealous?"

I choke. "No."

Fake River gives me a squint. "Why?"

I shrug. "He says you stare at me when no one else is looking. I find it highly unlikely." I wave my hands in front of him. "Go away. Poof. Disappear."

"Still here," he says dryly.

I walk over to him and stop about a foot away. It's close, too close for us in real life, but he's *not* real, so it's cool. I inhale a deep breath. "He smells like when you eat coconuts and mangoes. And sex, but not actual sex, like semen and woman, gross, but more like an alpha male. Is that weird? Don't answer. It's freaking strange. He must be using some kind of citrusy body wash with sex pheromones."

"Took a shower before I came over."

"His voice even sounds like his!" I touch his diamond-cut jawline, rubbing my fingers over the prickly dark shadow there. "His scruff tickles."

"He can tickle between my legs," Lila says as she chews.

"Hussy," I say on a laugh. "But, mmm, yeah."

"We can make that happen," Vision River murmurs as he gazes at me.

"Don't talk," I tell him sternly. "Technically, you should only say things I *want* you to say." My thumb ghosts over his pouty bottom lip. The skin is soft, the color a dusky pink. "Mind. Blown. I've created him just from memory. Maybe I *did* get some of the artist gene from my parents."

Lila scrunches her nose. "But, don't you think it's weird that all three of us see him? I mean, I understand *you* seeing him, but how are you getting in *our* heads at the same time? Is it telepathy?"

"Pot makes us powerful." My fingers go to his hair, tugging on the longer strands on top as I twirl them around. Like spun silk, the golden highlights sparkle under the kitchen lights.

I run my hands over his scalp and dig in, and he lets out a small groan, leaning into my touch. "You're gonna regret this tomorrow," he murmurs.

"In the end, we only regret the things we *didn't* do," I tell him.

"Amen!" Colette says.

"Gonna get that tattooed on my ass!" Lila calls out. "Tattoo parlor! Let's go!"

"Next time, Lila," I say absently, not really paying attention, not with Fake River in front of me.

His chest rises as he leans closer and our eyes cling. "You hate me, baby girl, but it's hard to tell you no when you're like this," he murmurs. "I could get used to high Anastasia."

"I hate you?"

"Mhmm. I'm a tool. And cramps. And an unsalted

pretzel. That one made me laugh about ten times today. I went to the snack spot in the student center and bought one in honor of you."

My hands land on his broad shoulders, kneading into the muscles there. "He's solid and hard."

"So many jokes there," Fake River murmurs.

"Can I touch the vision?" Lila asks.

"No. He's mine," I reply.

She snorts. "You've got a thing for him. Your eyes linger on him a *little too long*, Ana!"

"No, I don't! I'm merely checking out the awesomeness of my mind's abilities. Some scientists believe we only use about ten percent of our brain, so it's possible we're accessing the creative side that isn't used much."

His eyes lower as I brush my fingers over the strong column of his throat then go back up. I trace the outline of his patrician nose, the straight bridge, the slight bump at the top where he might have broken it, the shape of his dark brows, then I'm back to his lips.

"Well played, God," I whisper.

I inch closer, wondering—

His teeth nip at me, and I scream and jump back, nearly tripping as I grasp the edge of the counter. He gives me his lethal smile and his eyes roam over me, lingering on my exposed stomach before coming back to my face. "You're skating on thin ice, Anastasia. If you were in your right mind, you'd never get that close to me."

Three seconds pass, then...

"He's real, Ana," Lila says breathlessly, wonder in her tone. "You don't have a photographic memory, and he is the exact replica. But...why is he here? Oh my God, I can see the headlines now: *Three girls murdered by football player*. It's Ted Bundy all over again! I changed my mind about the cops! Someone call 911!"

He laughs. "Lila, right? Ted Bundy was *not* a football player. He was a psychopath. Mom calls me deranged sometimes, but she's only teasing because I can't sit still."

My gaze narrows, a tendril of sobriety brushing through my mind. "We know his middle name and now he's talking about his mom," I say, frowning as I cross my arms. "Okay, Vision River, who were you *really* calling baby girl in the elevator?"

"Callie, my niece, although I'll admit I can never call her that again. That's all yours now. And, the last phone conversation was entirely fake, just to rile you up. I didn't realize you were already on the verge of a breakdown." He moves farther inside, picks up a cupcake, and devours it in two bites. He leans against the counter. "You left your copy of *Lady Chatterley's Lover* in class today. I brought it back, plus the pan from the house."

I gasp. "I lost my book. And I took a pan to the Kappa house."

"The book fell out of your backpack. Remember? You sat next to me."

"Not on purpose!"

He has my book!

Don't be high, don't be high.

I sputter, my hand clutching my throat. "Oh my god. Is this happening? For real? Kill me now."

"No killing!" Lila yells as she edges around him and darts for the den. "I need more pot."

"Wait for me, sis," Colette says. "Roll a fat one."

River and I stare at each other.

HE IS HERE.

"No," I gasp.

"I see you've caught up," he murmurs with amusement as he puts coffee grounds in the machine, fills it with water, then pushes the button to let it brew.

"You mind if I get a drink?" He pulls a water out of the fridge.

"No."

He guzzles it, the strong lines of his throat moving. He wipes his mouth with his wrist, an action that's masculine and confident and downright sexy—

"How did you know where I live?"

He opens the cabinet, grabs a plate, and puts nachos on it. He dips the chip in the sour cream sitting on the counter and takes a huge bite. "I know things. Sometimes they don't always stick, but I filed you away in the private safe in my head. Only I have the combination."

I scrunch my nose. "Stop talking in riddles. Why am I in a safe?"

"No reason."

"You think I'm weird," I mutter.

"I never said that."

"You think I'm boring."

"You haven't been boring a day in your life."

"You think I'm not good enough."

"Let that go," he says. "You're perfect the way you are. You are loyal though. Like me, I guess. It's a real bitch, isn't it?"

"You're not nice to me. Ever. Maybe once."

"Ever wonder why?" he drawls.

"I don't like you!" I say.

"Liar."

I sputter.

He takes down a cup and pours coffee in, then sends me a glance. "Lots of cream? About half?"

When has he noticed I like my coffee with fifty percent creamer?

I nod. "Pumpkin spice creamer. It's in the fridge, on the side, near the middle."

He turns and opens it. He's wearing the same lavender Chucks but a different shirt, short-sleeved with his Greek letters on the back. His forearms are tightly roped and muscled as he grasps the door of the fridge, and his backside is tight and, well, magnificent. He's got one of those bubble asses you want to put your hands on and—

"Don't touch!" I yell, and he flips around.

"What? No creamer?"

I rub my face, pleading with myself to be straight. "No, no, creamer is fine. Just... What do you want?" I look around. "Where did Lila and Colette go?"

He smirks. "Den. From the noise, it sounds like they're playing Fortnite."

"Oh." I take a seat at the table. "Hey, don't tell Donovan I was high. He's not a fan of Lila. Or Colette, really." I pause. "I keep asking you to not tell him stuff. Is that against your bro code?"

"Yeah." He brings me the coffee and sits across from me. He doesn't get too close or touch me, his movements made intentionally to avoid contact. I might be stoned, but I haven't stopped analyzing him. He leans back in his seat and studies me. "Why doesn't he like them?"

"They're misfits and rebels, I guess. Lila's going to Hollywood to be a screenwriter when she graduates. Colette's a sculptor. Donovan doesn't understand being *different*, but it's how I grew up. I moved all over. My parents left me with friends sometimes, mostly scholars who taught me. I mean, I learned physics from a real physicist in Switzerland and literature from a professor in London. I don't have any siblings or grandparents. It was hard, always bouncing around, and we never had much money. Is that revealing? Yeah. Shut up, Ana. Anyway, my parents adored me. They're just different, you know? Free spirits who care for others—like Lila and Colette. They don't judge. Why does he have an issue with pot? It's legal in some places. I trust my gut, and those girls are awesome. Also, there's a homeless woman I kind of want to be my grandma. Am I talking too much?"

"Oh yes, definitely."

I take a long sip of my coffee. "Question: is it the S or the C that's silent in the word *scent*?"

His lips quirk. "I have no idea. Drink up."

I run my finger over the rim. "You want me sober. Today, I don't want to be. What about *sand*? Do you think they called it that because it's between the sea and the land?"

He gets me a refill then sits back down. "My body wash is mangoes. You notice a lot, Anastasia."

Gingerly, I take a sip. "You say my name weird."

He wipes at the crumbs on the table. "How's that?"

"You linger over it, like you're about to take its clothes off and fuck it."

"Weed is truth serum for you."

"You ever been high?"

"Once by accident when I ate something at the frat

house. Football is front and center. Drugs are a no-go for me. I can't even take—" He stops.

"What?"

He spins a nacho chip around on his plate. "I have ADHD. The drugs don't work on me."

"That explains your energy, always twisting that ring. Honestly?"

"Mhmm."

"Your vivacity is part of your appeal. Women see the electricity you emit and want to grab hold of it. Ride the bull. Get electrocuted."

"I kill girls with my snake?"

"Shut up."

"*Vivacity*," he says with a smirk. "Another big word. Actually, I'm pretty chill—right now. You're like..." He sighs. "The calm before a storm."

"Hurricane Ana."

"Hurricane Anastasia," he says softly.

My breath hitches. "There it is. Sex—you're dripping in it."

He straightens his shoulders and gives me a deadpan look then repeats my name in a monotone. "Better?"

"No. You look like..." a walking, talking god. I wave my hands at him. "You."

"I can't help that you're attracted to me."

Oh. He went there.

My buzz flattens, and I grow silent as the tension in

the room thickens. I lift my cup and drink coffee. I picture Donovan in my head. "I'm not. At all. You're the total opposite of what I look for in a guy. I don't do bad boys."

"I'm a bad boy?"

I arch a brow. "Seriously?"

His tattooed fingers tap the table. "Hmmm. Have you ever wondered what would have happened if I'd been the one waiting for you that night after the library?"

My heart dips.

Part of me *wanted* it to be him. I swallow and don't speak—afraid of what I might say.

"I don't think you'll remember this conversation tomorrow or else I wouldn't have mentioned it," he murmurs, playing with his water bottle.

"I won't?"

"I hope you don't." He reaches behind him, pulls my book out of his back pocket, and slides it over to me. "I came to see if you'd help me with my paper in this class. *This* I want you to remember."

My heart kicks up as I recall the tension between us today outside the elevator. How close he stood to me, the tingles when he touched my face and wished me happy birthday. "I can't." It's wrong.

"Why? No, don't answer that." A long exhalation comes from his chest. "Why did I come here? Shit."

"You're impetuous," I say.

"I'm an electrical hazard plus impulsive. I see."

"You're dangerous..." *to me.*

And I lied before.

He's exactly the kind of guy I go for: tattooed and sexy AF. He reminds me a little of Bryson, my great love at seventeen, but only in how they look. Deep down, I suspect they are vastly different, which is a good thing.

But I have Donovan.

From the den, the girls crank up "Low" by Flo Rida, and I jump up from the table. I need out of this conversation!

"That's my theme song! Let's go, Real River!"

He follows me into the den. Lila sways her hips to the beat, a teddy bear in her hands, and Colette sits on the floor, playing video games with streamers wrapped around her neck. Lila gives me a lopsided high five then moves the coffee table against the wall to give us more room. "Shake it, girl!" she calls out.

I spin in circles and whoop with my arms raised. Stopping in the center of the den, I bend my knees and twerk, the thump of the bass syncing with the pounding of my heart.

I can get down with a good beat.

When I was seventeen, my parents traveled to Vancouver and left me in New York City with one of the many friends they collected. His name was Bryson, a thirty-year-old musician with tattoos and dreamy eyes. I was there to study music with him and his sister. He'd crank up the speakers in his loft and we'd dance. Older people were all I'd ever known, and the thirteen years between us felt like a small, inconsequential thing. My mom is ten years younger than my dad, so it felt normal. I was young and looking for love in all the wrong places, and boy, did he ever woo me: long walks in Central Park, candlelit dinners, and poetry. He took my virginity—and my heart. Darker memories of him pull at me, recollections of the hurtful secrets he kept.

I shove them away, burying them deep down.

Then I think about Donovan, wondering where he is right now...

"Not here!" I say aloud to no one in particular.

River watches me, that eyebrow raised.

"Dance with me! It's my birthday!" I tell him over the music.

He blows out a breath, makes a move toward me, then stops and shakes his head. "I can't."

"You can't dance? I've seen you!"

"Rainbow, I can fucking dance, just not with you."

I sway my hips toward him and shove him down on the couch. "Then sit and stop hovering."

I'll recall 'Rainbow' much later.

The music booms, and I let it out: the hurt of today, the worry about law school, my parents, June. I dance like a madwoman, smiling as I bend and go low, low, low with the lyrics. River sits back and laughs, wiping his eyes as I give my 'big booty a smack'—

"What the hell is going on?" comes a man's voice.

I stop and flip around.

Oh shit.

9

Anastasia

Lila turns the music down as Donovan marches into the den. His hair is disheveled, and he rakes a hand through it, his brow furrowing as he lands on River. "River? What are you doing here?"

River stands, his face blank. "I dropped off her book and pan."

"You've been here before?" Donovan's eyes narrow.

"No."

The five of us stare at each other, only I can't look at River. I feel guilty for shaking my ass in front of him, and we can't forget me running my hands over him in the kitchen. My stomach drops.

I blame it on the pot. Never again!

My body tenses as Donovan's eyes flit to Lila holding her joint. He opens his mouth, then shuts it, an incredulous look on his face as he shifts his focus from River to me. "You're high?" Disappointment settles on his face. "You aren't a stoner, Ana."

Right now, my high has plummeted.

His lips compress. "Pot impairs your judgment and kills brain cells."

Actually, it doesn't kill brain cells. Those studies have been debunked.

"Don't patronize me," I mutter. "This makes twice in my life."

"You're killing my buzz, Donny," Lila grouses as she splays out on the floor.

My jaw tightens. "It's a birthday party. You'd think my boyfriend would have taken me to dinner. Or somewhere. Oh, wait—you forgot I turned twenty-one today! All I got were texts about Harvard and apartments and how happy you are!"

Panic flashes on his face. "Ana! Calm down! That's why I'm here! I just remembered at the library! And you're getting high to get back at me." His face scrunches.

"Wanna play Fortnite, Donny?" Lila asks. "Oh, and you don't really *know* her. Girl is lit. She is fire."

"Lila, don't..." I say. We've had plenty of conversations about how different Donovan and I are, but it works.

Or it did.

Donovan stiffens. "This is..." He looks at Lila, then me. "...not what I want for you."

"This isn't about you, Donovan," I say, my eyes narrowing, anger rising higher at his holier-than-thou attitude. "My *friends* remembered."

"Burn," Lila says smugly.

Several moments tick by, maybe not that many, but time feels stretched.

"You forgot," I say softly. At least my parents called me earlier. They didn't forget.

Donovan shuts his eyes, his face sliding into remorse. "Jesus. I'm sorry. You're right. Totally. I should have said something this weekend or today..." He lets out a long sigh. "Life is crazy right now. That isn't an excuse, okay, it's just the truth. Things are happening with my parents..." He stops and pinches the bridge of his nose.

Nervous and antsy, my hands twist my long hair up in a messy topknot. I go through the checklist in my head. He's distant, walls up, is always busy or on edge, and he hasn't even confirmed our holiday plans. My parents won't be around, and I need to know what I'm doing, only every time I bring it up, he changes the topic. I don't want to spend the holidays alone.

Lila and Colette are doing the ski trip, and while the deadline has passed for me to sign up, they assured me I can still tag along, just not on Braxton's reservation.

My resolve builds. "Lila and Colette, give us a

moment, please. River, thank you for dropping off my book."

"You sure?" Lila pinches off the joint she has in her hands and tucks it inside her little box. "This party was just getting good. I hadn't even brought out Jenga yet. That's always fun when I'm high."

"Yes," I say.

Colette takes her arm. "Come on. Let's go drink some of the coffee Fake River made."

"Is it real coffee?" Lila asks seriously.

"I don't know," is her reply. "I bought some shrimp cocktail today. Want some?"

"Question: is that black stuff on the shrimp poop?" Lila asks.

Colette frowns. "Let's say *no.*"

"Hell yeah, then. Let's eat 'em," Lila shouts as they disappear into the kitchen.

"Is everything okay?" River says as he approaches me.

I bite my lip. No, it isn't, but—

Donovan frowns at River. "Why did you drop by again?"

I grab my novel off the coffee table—I brought it with me from the kitchen—and wave it at him. "I left my novel in class. He brought it. In case you've forgotten, it's a hard class." I'm certain River doesn't want Donovan to know he asked me for help.

Donovan fidgets, his eyes darting around the room, taking in the mylar balloons, the streamers on the floor. He studies my countenance, no doubt reading my hurt. His face crumples as he rushes toward me. "Okay, I'm an asshole. I swear I have a gift for you, a beautiful one at the house. All day, something's been niggling at me, and I couldn't..." His voice trails off as he grimaces. "No wonder you never replied to my texts."

He takes my hands that are at my sides. He unlaces my fists and tangles our fingers together as he pulls me against him. "This is bad, I know, I know. I got derailed. You know how my head works. I get consumed. Just forgive me. Please."

My throat tightens as prickles of unease wash over me. I want to let it go, I do, but it's the other things...

"I love you, Ana, and you love me," he says in my ear, but it's loud enough for River to hear. "You feel me?"

He embraces me, one hand kneading the muscles in my back, the other on my ass. A long sigh slips from my lips as I inhale his cinnamon smell.

Donovan's the guy I've been with the longest. He brought me flowers every week for the first six months we dated. He moved me into this apartment, even though he didn't approve of the neighborhood. He laughs at my jokes. He tells me I'm beautiful, that he needs me with him at Harvard...

"I'm out of here." River brushes past us, and my eyes

follow him over Donovan's shoulders. His right hand taps his leg over and over. ADHD.

Or emotion? I wish I could see his face—

"Later," Donovan tells him as his arms tighten around me.

The door slams as I call out a goodbye.

Donovan tugs me to the couch and sets me in his lap. My back presses to his chest, and when I try to pull away, he buries his face in my hair. "Just listen to me, okay? Hear me out. You're hurt and angry. I would be too. I came in and acted self-righteous. Of course you're your own person. I don't like seeing you high because it's bad for you." He groans under his breath. "Fuck. I-I can't believe I forgot. It was a tough weekend, horrible. I kept wishing you were there. My parents drove me crazy—" He stops and exhales a long breath.

"Over me," I state.

He grows silent, the air thickening. He moves my hair to the side and presses a kiss to my shoulder. "Let's not talk about them. Let's talk about what a dick I am. Talking about getting into Harvard, asking for advice on neighborhoods—"

"I didn't get in."

He freezes, an incredulous sound in his tone. "What? When?"

I untangle his arms from around me, stand, and face him. "I knew last week. Columbia, Boston College,

Boston University, Suffolk—they all rejected me. I don't have a school next year."

He rubs his eyes with the heels of his palms. "All of them? Why wouldn't you tell me?"

I shrug.

"We can fix this. I'll get my parents to talk to the dean of admissions..." He stops, frowning.

A wan smile crosses my face. "Your parents aren't going to help me, and I don't want them to. There are other universities. I haven't heard from some of them, but I think Brooklyn Law will take me..." It's the closest to Harvard, but still three hours away.

He grimaces. "Harvard is the best, Ana. It's the volunteer stuff, the extracurriculars. If you could find some time to polish up your application—"

"It's too late now. You know I work a lot of hours."

He stands and tries to pull me into his arms, but I step away. "Ana. Come on." He gives me a baleful look. "I can't go to Brooklyn with you. You know that. Don't blame *me* because you didn't get into Harvard. If you'd let me help you with money, you wouldn't have to work—"

"I'm *not* blaming you," I say curtly.

And him give me money? Ha.

I carve my own way. Always have.

He checks his watch, smugness on his face. "Hey, it's

still your birthday so I didn't entirely miss it. Let's get out of here and go back to the house."

Sounds so romantic.

"I need to study."

"High?" His lips compress. "I'm not staying here. This place reeks."

"Go home then," I say as I step away and nod my head. "There's the door."

"Come with me."

"I need to stay here in case Lila and Colette end up in the basement or at a tattoo parlor." True.

He drops his hands. "Why can't you give me some slack here? I'm sorry I forgot."

"Oh, I'm being very understanding, Donovan."

He narrows his eyes. "Are you? Really? You know how important this semester has been, the work I've done for the frat. My charity. My classes. I'm allowed to forget things."

We're going in circles. "It's not just my birthday and you know it."

His jaw pops.

"Did you talk to your parents about the holidays?"

An uneasy look flashes before he shuts it down. "No. I will. I promise."

I inhale a sharp breath. I can *feel* his lie.

Why hasn't he settled things with them?

He just saw them! Winter break is right around the corner!

"Don't. I'm going skiing with Lila and Colette. We'll fly back afterward, and I'll stay in Ellijay with them for the holidays." It's better than spending Christmas alone in the apartment. I chew on my lip. Gah. June! I need to find her a home before I leave!

He fidgets, mulling my words over, then, "If that's what you want to do, I'm cool." He sighs. "Look, Ellijay isn't far from Atlanta. It's a redneck town with nothing to do, but I'll drive to you. We'll be together on Christmas and New Year's. I can stay at a hotel. We'll get a room."

Of course he doesn't want to stay with my friends, and technically, he hasn't been invited to their house. Yeah, that wouldn't go over well, but me and him, alone, with just each other in a hotel? Anxiety tugs at me. I don't know. I mean, shouldn't I want that? Somehow it feels...bleak. I guess it's the distance we've had these past weeks. There's an empty black pit in front of us, and it's either fall in and lose each other or hold each other and jump over it.

"What about your parents? Won't they be upset? You mentioned they have a huge party on Christmas with your extended family." I bet their tree is fifty feet tall. I bet there'll be oyster forks at dinner. I bet his mom wears the perfect little black dress. I bet his grandmother will be glad I'm not there.

He avoids my gaze. "I'll talk to them and figure it out."

Oh, Donovan.

You've had every chance since this past summer to figure us out, and you haven't...

Tick tock.

Time is running out for us.

I know it, can feel it, and it hurts.

10

River

"**I**f you don't go on that ski trip, I'm going to invite Carrie Longmore over for the holidays," my mom says. "You know she never got over you—"

"She had a crush on me in high school. She's four years younger than me. There is nothing to get over—"

"—and you know how cute and perky she is. She'll be sitting across from you as you eat your stuffing. She'll flirt and rush to get your pecan pie. She'll insist you watch TV with her, probably some terrible Christmas movie, then she'll finagle you outside for a walk in the snow. How's that?"

The scenario sounds suspiciously like last Christmas when Carrie suddenly showed up with her parents at Mom's invitation. They might be our nearest neighbors, but I begged her to never do it again.

I make a groan as I sit inside my black truck outside Ana's apartment. It's late, but Mom was up and called me just as I got in. "You are a cruel woman."

"Will you go skiing? Please?"

I lean my head back against the headrest, emotion clawing at me. I *need* to see her. "Mom, I haven't seen you since fall break, and that was only for one day because of football—"

"You need this, River. Finish your semester, ski for a few days, then come home. I just..." Her voice stops, and she exhales.

I picture her at our house in Barley, a two-story colonial on twenty acres in rural Vermont. It's an older home she and Dad loved renovating. She's probably wearing her blue fuzzy robe and a pair of slippers. I can hear the crackle of the fireplace roaring in the den. On the wall is a framed picture of me and her and Rae and Dad. It was taken a week before he died, and every time I look at it, my gut clenches.

She sniffs. Rather dramatically. Several times.

I huff out a laugh. "If you were really crying, you'd hang up on me and pretend everything's okay."

She blows out a breath. "Fine. I was faking it. But! But! I am serious about skiing! If you don't go..."

"I want to see you."

"Grrrr. Look, you need to be normal. *I* need you to be normal. I am alive. I am here. I want it to be just a regular holiday when we do the things we always do. You ski, I bake a dry, nasty turkey that everyone says is good, Rae bitches about the snow, and Callie squeals when she opens her gifts. Just like always. I don't want people acting like it's the end of the world. I know how much you love that mountain."

I let her words settle over me. My hands trace the steering wheel. I would love to ski the same slopes Dad and I went down.

"I'll think about it."

"I know what that means—no. You're stubborn, just like your father. You're a terrible child. Never listens. Carrie would make a good girlfriend for you. Local. Pretty. Likes me. Likes Rae. Likes Callie. Yeah, she talks too much and she's not the brightest, but so what? Ugh. How is that class?"

I chuckle. Hearing her give me a hard time is the perfect way to ease my tension after seeing Donovan and Anastasia. "Never mind the class. How are *you* feeling?"

"Better today. My hair is coming back. I have a little stubble on top. My nails are weird though. I have no eyelashes, but Callie says I look badass. Four-year-old little girls are brilliant. Let me text you a picture."

A photo comes through, an image of her in her robe, a yellow headwrap on her scalp, a big smile on her face.

Her face is thin and drawn, her eyes haunted.

I love the daily photos she sends me, but fear spears

me. It's as if she's disappearing a little at a time. You know that feeling you get, the one that makes your soul shrivel, the one that tells you what's happening is out of your control. There's nothing I can do to save her.

I do a selfie of me sticking my tongue out and send it. "I love you," I say.

"If you did, you'd go skiing." She sighs. "You've never once brought a girl home for me to decide if she's good enough. If you're gay, it's okay."

"Stop messing around." I laugh. "I'm not—"

"One of my doctors is gay. So is one of the firemen in town. Super masculine and quite the hottie. Rae had a little crush on him until she met Jason." She pauses. "Jason is moving to Manhattan in January. He got a job at a financial company, and it's a great opportunity. Did she tell you?"

Jason is my sister's fiancé, and they're getting married in May. I like him a lot, especially the way he treats Callie. When Rae got pregnant, Callie's bio dad moved to Florida and has nothing to do with them. Rae and Callie have been living with Mom ever since. I just assumed they'd live close to Mom after they were married—but Manhattan is five hours away.

Uneasiness hits. "No, she didn't. Who's going to be there to help take care of—"

"Well, it just came about, so don't give her a hard time about it. She's worried and I don't want her to be.

She wants to commute between here and New York and that's just crazy. She needs to get on with her life, and I don't need someone here twenty-four seven, River. I'm okay! You, however, are on my bad list. No gifts for you. I'm putting dead goldfish in your stocking."

I bark out a laugh. "I didn't mean to kill Rae's goldfish, Mom. I was five and thought they needed a bath."

"With dish soap. Ten dead fish I had to replace before your sister saw it."

I laugh. "You're the best mom in the world."

She really is.

"God, I love you," she says as she exhales. "I do have bad moments, but I also have great ones. It's a mixed bag, okay? Every breath is a gift. I want to see you happy, River. Sometimes, I feel like I'm losing out on memories that I used to have. Which is why I want you to walk in my door after going down that mountain. I need to see that look of serenity in your eyes. Just go fucking skiing. See, you made me say the F word." She sighs. "I'm feisty tonight."

My eyes shut, my heart torn.

It's just a three-day trip, plus she's only a few hours away... "I'll go, Mom."

She shrieks her reply, and I chuckle.

After getting off the phone with her, I crank my truck, just as Donovan walks out of the apartment lobby and heads to his Tesla. I wait for him to pull out, then follow. He's going to the Kappa house, and I still need to pick up my laundry before I head to my house.

Humming "Low," I tap my fingers on my knee. A smile flits over my face at the memory of Anastasia dancing. Then, I remember how I let things slide by showing up at her door. It felt like fate meant for me to see her. She left her book and then there was the pan at the house. It made perfect sense to drive to her place and ask her to help me with the paper.

Right, keep telling yourself that.

Donovan turns on Greek Row but doesn't pull in at the Kappa house, instead driving slowly down to the Delta house. Frowning, I ease back on the accelerator and follow him. He parks and I do a loop and come back, pulling in at the Theta house next door.

I watch as he exits the car, his head down, the streetlight accentuating the harried look on his face. He takes the steps and knocks. Audrey answers and widens the door for him, but he shakes his head. She leaves and he paces the porch, then Harper appears at the door and rushes out to him. She encircles him in a hug, but he disentangles her and picks back up pacing.

His arms move excitedly as he talks, and when I catch a flash of his face, he's frowning. Okay, okay, this is good. He's cutting her off, doing the whole *No more coffee dates* and *Leave me alone so I can focus on my girlfriend* thing.

Right?

I heard him loud and clear in the basement. *The world disappears when I kiss her.*

Harper walks toward him, her face beseeching. She puts her arms around his shoulders. He pushes her away and scrubs his face.

Harper pounces at him and presses her lips to his— and my stomach rolls. His arms flail around, unsure what to do. She grabs his ass, and he leans into her, his arms going around her as they kiss.

And kiss.

And kiss.

Fuck, no, Donovan. Don't do it, don't do it. Don't hurt Anastasia.

DO IT. DO IT.

Hurt your *Ana*, break her heart, let go of the best girl you've ever held, let her slip right through your fingers—

Donovan jerks away, his chest rising and falling rapidly. He says loud words I can't hear, then flips around and fast-walks to his car, gets inside. He looks pissed. I sit there, watching Harper, the defiant set of her shoulders, the determined expression on her face.

I know that look. It says, *I'll do whatever it takes to get him.*

Why did he come here?

What the hell is he trying to prove?

Why isn't he with Anastasia?

Another thought sneaks in. What am *I* willing to do to get what *I* want?

"You can't," I snarl into the night. "Let. Her. Go."

Yeah? Yeah? the dark side of me whispers.

Aren't you sick of waiting?

ON WEDNESDAY, I follow her to the elevator. We don't speak. She walks into class ahead of me and takes her regular seat. I take my seat behind her and watch like I always do. I stare hard, wondering if she feels it. When she talks in class, I hang on every word. When she plays with her hair, twisting the strands, my fingers twitch. As soon as class is over, without a glance over her shoulder at me or Benji, she dashes out of the lecture hall.

Thank fuck. I don't want to be near her.

I hate how she makes me feel.

By the time Friday rolls around, my resolve has stalled and rolled off a cliff. I dreamed about her. Nothing sexual (thank you for small mercies), but a replay of our conversation in her kitchen, her hands touching my lips, her goofy questions, the way she rambled about her childhood.

I wait in the lobby for her to arrive then trail her to the elevator.

There's nothing wrong with it. *Just don't touch.*

She gets on and I follow, my eyes on my phone.

Pretending.

I'm cool.

I'm cool.

She's wearing a tight green dress that hugs her curves and hits a few inches below her ass. Black tights are on her legs. Heeled thigh-high boots on her feet. Her lavender hair is down, long and straight as it brushes her back.

My throat dries.

I shift around in the small space, easing the thickness in my jeans.

Her lips are a deep red, a hint that she's in a 'mood.' I recall one of her moods. She and Donovan had a tiff at the house once because she brought Lila and Colette to a party. I happened to overhear it when I walked past his room. I watched her storm out, slam his door, then jerk out her lipstick and roll it on her full lips. Then, she stomped away. Lipstick is her armor when things are going to hell.

She huffs and slaps the button for our floor then sends me a long look, or I think she does, based on the reflection in the mirrored walls. She picks up her phone. "Hey, you." She laughs low and husky, the sound skating down my spine. "You did? Oh, stop it, you're making me blush. Oh? A big one? You're teasing me." Her voice lowers. "You should get dressed. I know,

I know, it's hard. Okay, I have to go. Class. Bye, *baby boy*."

A silence settles in the elevator as she hums "Low."

My eyes narrow. "Who was that?"

"Hmmm? Sorry. Are you *talking* to me?" She checks her chipped nail polish.

"Who's baby boy?"

"My nephew." She brushes unseen lint off her dress.

"You don't have siblings."

"Don't I?" She shrugs. "Family can be anyone."

"You said you have no real family but your parents."

"Oh, that. I barely recall you being at my house." Her green eyes finally meet mine and my body tightens.

"Don't believe you, Anastasia."

"Am I a hurricane today? Do you feel calm...right now?"

"As it happens, I do not." My hands clench. "I have a lot on my mind."

The doors open on the second floor, and Audrey, Mellany, and Harper get on as a wave of perfume drifts in. They rush around me, but my eyes are on *her*.

She smirks and sticks her tongue out at me. Then she mouths something inaudible, and dammit, I can't read lips. She makes a gagging expression as Audrey plasters herself against me and hangs on my arm.

That little... My lips twitch. She's fucking with me.

Audrey's talking about the party and *What should I*

wear, River? like I care, and I nod in all the right places but can't stop glancing at Anastasia. What will she do next? She's a little unpredictable, to be honest.

The girls bombard me with compliments I barely hear (I don't buy it, never have) then with questions. Do I have a date for the party? *No.* Do I want to go with them as a group? *Sorry, I'm hanging with my guys.* Am I going on the ski trip? *Yeah.* They make a plan for us to hang out on the slopes. I give a noncommittal reply, my fingers twisting my ring like crazy.

They get off on their floor, and I don't miss when Harper flashes her bracelet at us. Just before the door shuts, I hear her say, "Girls, Ana didn't get into Harvard and I did." She lets out a tinkling laugh and says more, but the sound disappears as the doors snick closed.

Anastasia dips her head, her hair hiding her face as a long exhalation comes from her. Her hands clench her backpack straps, the tips of her fingers whitening.

I'm in front of her before I know what's happening. "It's okay. I'm here. Three things, three things, Anastasia. Tell me."

Her chin tilts up, a slight mist in her eyes. "River…"

"Don't let her get to you."

She blinks rapidly. "I've heard worse from her. Sly digs, little comments at parties. But how does she know?"

My chest tightens. I have an idea. "Harvard hurts you."

"Like a knife in my back. Did Donovan tell her?"

"Three things, Anastasia. Tell me."

She chews on her red lips. "You tell me three things today. Maybe if I can live vicariously through the most popular guy on campus..." Her voice trails off, her jaw popping as if she's holding back emotion.

"Alright." I count them down on my fingers. "I found Hollis's secret stash of Ding Dongs—they were under his bed, so typical—I remembered underwear this morning, and Crew made omelets for breakfast." I pause. "Your turn."

"Why?"

"Why not?"

"Why is the elevator so slow?" she mutters.

"Tell me three things. Please."

She does a double take. "Is this where I'm like your... pet project? Don't feel sorry for me."

Rainbow, sorry is the *last* thing I feel for you.

I want you under me.

Deep and hard.

There aren't enough minutes in the day for how long I want to fuck you.

She blows out a breath. "Fine. I can see you aren't going to budge. One, June is still around. Sam is keeping her low key. Two, I finished my paper, and three, I got off work to go on the ski trip."

I get hung up on the last one. "You're going?"

"Mhmm. I'm not on the same flight as you guys, but yeah."

"You ski?"

"I plan to sit in the hot tub and drink. Kidding—I can ski."

"How are things with Donovan?"

Her throat bobs. "I-I can't talk to you about him. I mean, yeah, um, it...doesn't feel right, you know, to him." A sigh escapes her lips.

The door opens and she slips out, her arm brushing against my chest. I follow, sucking down the electricity between us. "Right. I just wanted to check in—"

"I know what this is, why you're being nice to me—"

"Yeah? Tell me, because I can't figure it out," I snap, annoyed she won't open up while the other side is pissed at myself for asking. "Trust me, I wish I didn't..." I stop, my jaw clenching.

She stops at the door to class and turns to face me. Her expression torn, she takes a deep breath. "Your paper. I'm sorry I can't help you, I really am. I love helping others, but I don't think it's a good idea for us..." She licks her lips, her gaze avoiding mine. "There's something about you and me—" She halts and looks down at her feet. "Anyway, I know a few students who tutor athletes. Let me give you their names—"

"No one but you, Anastasia."

"What? Why?"

Instinct takes over and I back her against the wall, towering over her. I tilt her chin up, and she doesn't speak or move, just breathing fast, as my hand slides around to her nape. A hum of heat goes through my body as my hands tangle in her hair.

"River...what..." Pink rises on her cheeks as her lashes flutter.

Fuck.

Every time, I'm pushing a little more, the dark side of me winning. Monday. Her apartment. Now.

I could kiss her right now, but it's wrong, immensely so, I'm being bad, so bad, but one touch and my dick is a steel pipe, damn, what would it be like to have her in my arms...

She gazes up at me, her eyes flaring, the gold around her pupils darkening. She swallows as goose bumps appear on her neck.

A primal sound builds in my throat.

Anger.

Frustration.

Loyalty.

Dammit. I shouldn't be this close, shouldn't touch her—

"I'll wait." I grind my teeth and step back.

Her lips part, a small puff of air coming out. She looks at my mouth. "For what?"

The lethal side of me, the one itching to play this game no matter the consequences, tries to take over and speak the truth. I shove it down.

You, I say in my head.

Leaving her there, I sweep past her and go to my seat.

Five fucking rows back.

11

Anastasia

"**A**re you sure this is okay? Donny won't flip out?" Colette asks as she straightens the ducky toga she made from a sheet. Yes, she has a thing for ducks. She's sculpted at least twenty, and they litter our apartment.

"It's the biggest party of the year. He won't even notice us," Lila snarks as she adjusts the cream-colored Grecian-style dress she ordered online. "Kappas have the *best* parties, and Ana is our hookup."

"You're welcome," I say dryly. "And don't worry, there are plenty of non-Greeks here tonight. Donovan will be fine." I made it clear months ago that I don't enjoy parties where my besties aren't with me.

I lead them around the sidewalk to the kitchen

entrance of the house. We parked three blocks over since the street and parking lot were full. We're late. Big time. I worked a five-to-ten shift at the bar, flew home, saw June, then threw my outfit together. Donovan sent several texts asking when I was coming, even though he *knows* I work on Fridays.

"Love the mini toga. Strapless works with your boobs. And you're wearing your red lipstick. Shit is about to go down," Lila murmurs as she takes in the outfit I shortened with my sewing machine. Made from a white sheet, the bodice is gathered, and a silver chain belt dangles around my waist, cinching it. My hair is pulled up on the sides with silver leaf-shaped combs, the strands cascading down my bare back. Wide metal cuffs wrap around my upper arms, and the silver stilettos on my feet put me close to six feet.

We walk in the door, and the kitchen is wall-to-wall with people. Music thumps from speakers in the ceiling and people pour into the hallway, waiting in line to get down to the basement where the majority congregates.

"I'm going on a Mason hunt," Lila calls out as she grabs a Solo cup of punch from the bar and dashes down the hall.

"Stay safe!" I yell.

"I think I see a guy from class," Colette says as she peers out the window to the pool.

"Go on," I say. "I'm going to find Donovan."

She gives me an arm squeeze then takes off.

I exhale a long breath as I look around the kitchen. I debated even coming tonight, but I didn't want to disappoint my roomies, and I need to talk to Donovan.

Benji swoops in and swings me around, cutting off my thoughts. "Ana! Where you been this week? This party is LIT! Every house representing. You drinking? What can I get you?"

His toga is black satin (fitting), his blond hair messy. There's a giant lizard thing curled on his shoulder. How it didn't fall off when he twirled me, I have no idea.

I laugh. "I'm the DD tonight. What the heck is that monster?"

He smirks. "River nixed my wish for a parakeet, said it would be loud, but he bought me a bearded dragon this week. Dude—I have the best big bro." The dragon twitches his tail and looks at me with beady pale brown eyes. His throat puffs up. "He's fucking awesome. Full grown. Named him Spike. See the prickly things on his head?"

"Um, yeah."

The creature licks at the air then tucks his head into Benji's throat.

"Sweet boy," he croons at the dragon. "We've bonded. I've got a tank for him in my room, but he likes people."

"Does he?" I laugh.

"He's an honorary Kappa. I'm calling him my emotional support animal. For real. He calms me. Go on and pet him, but not near his mouth—his teeth are sharp. Their venom is similar to a rattlesnake, but they're only lethal to mice and stuff."

I laugh. "I'll pass."

"Chicken. He slept on my pillow last night, all curled up under a fleece blanket. You have to keep them warm. Oh, he eats crickets. Live ones. Holy shit, you put them in his cage, and he pounces. He doesn't look like he can move fast, but he does. Funny. He only eats like five crickets at once, and the rest of them just walk around the cage all terrified, waiting for their death sentence. Dead cricket walking. It's a riot."

"Murder and mayhem in the Kappa house."

"True dat."

A random girl walks by and is about to give Benji a kiss on the cheek, then rears back and walks away.

"Not a chick magnet," I muse.

"Maybe he's not great for mojo, but he's great, not slimy at all," he says, clearly excited. "I miss all the animals I grew up with. Roscoe died. I had him for fifteen years." He sighs.

"I'm sorry." Benji moped around the house for a week after his mom told him.

"Bearded dragons live a long time too. Come on, hold him." He eases him up and offers, and I squeak. He chuckles and puts him back on his shoulder as he rubs his head. "Don't let it hurt your feelings, Spike." He glances at me. "Where did your roomies go?"

"Off to see people they know."

He hands me a water from the island as my eyes search the kitchen. It's hard to see everyone with the press of students, and I frown.

"Looking for Donovan?"

A guilty pang flits through my head. Actually, I was checking for River's dark hair, but I nod. Today before class, things went a little haywire between us.

I've seen Donovan twice since our showdown in the apartment. We met for quick dinners on Tuesday and Wednesday before I went to work. He was apologetic, sweet, and attentive. We discussed nothing important, avoiding the hard topics.

Yesterday, he spent his free time studying and finalizing the toga party. This morning I texted him after what Harper said outside the elevator. He vehemently denied telling her. The thing is, only a handful of people knew: June, Crazy Carl from the bar, Lila and Colette, a girl in one of my classes who also got rejected, and a few professors. He mentioned that Harper and I have the same advisor, so perhaps he told her, but that feels unlikely and unprofessional.

A hollow feeling gnaws at my gut.

It's not like word isn't going to get out, I get that, but still...

Water in hand, I tell Benji bye and head to the basement. It's a madhouse and takes me at least ten minutes to get through the throng of people. "Hot in Herre" by Nelly blasts from the speakers. Students dance near the stage where the DJ is set up.

Just as I reach the edge of the dancers, my neck tingles. I turn my head and meet River's gaze. He's leaned against a support column near the back.

Wearing a white toga tied on his shoulder, he looks hot AF, tall and muscled, the guns on his arms flexing under the strobe lights as he rakes a hand through his hair. Small gold leaves form a laurel around his head.

I stick my tongue out like I did in the elevator; it's childish and involuntary, and I smile.

He raises an eyebrow, his stoic expression cracking *just* a little. I'm not sure exactly what we are right now... not friends, but not the enemies from before either. Audrey sidles up to him, beckoning him out to the dance floor. He says no as she trails her hands over his broad shoulders.

A sharp breath escapes me. Jealousy? Yes. Oh, yes.

Completely irrational.

Someone shoot me.

Ignoring Audrey, his eyes roam over me, pausing on

my cleavage, then my legs, before coming back to my face. Even in the dim light, his gaze is a physical touch. Hot and slick. Stroking me.

Heat washes over me. It's not often he checks me out so blatantly.

I remember the last time his eyes glittered with that kind of emotion.

"PUT *some damn clothes on in this house," comes a terse voice. "I don't need pledges panting over a little sister."*

I flip around from the fridge, an unopened beer in my hand as I tug my cover-up around my white bikini. It's skimpy, yes, with cutouts that I love, but—Jesus, I have a mid-thigh-length terrycloth robe on over it.

Asshole!

Nervously, I grab my paperback of The Outsiders *off the table and tuck it under my arm. "Your pledges know how to control themselves. It's May and hot. No one ever uses the pool, and everyone is in class—"*

"Taking advantage of the benefits of your pin, I see. Did you know he was going to give it to you? You looked surprised." A sneer curls his lips. "So romantic."

My jaw clenches. I had no clue Donovan was going to make his big gesture last night. He didn't even discuss the idea of "pinning" with me, and because I'm not Greek, I was confused when he invited me to their weekly frat meeting.

Sure, I knew what pinning meant, but I was fine with our exclusive arrangement. He'd told me he loved me, but this felt different.

He presented me at the meeting then nervously asked if I wanted to be serious.

I love the sense of family the frat has, and I'd have been crazy to not take the best relationship I've ever had to the next level.

He pinned my blouse while his brothers looked on. Then we partied.

I lift my chin. "How's that hangover? You look like shit." Lie. He's wearing gym shorts and a sleeveless football practice shirt, his muscles taut and misty with sweat. "Which girl did you end up with last night?" I open my beer and take a swig of the longneck.

His eyes are stormy as he watches me swallow.

"Hello? River? Which girl? Audrey?" I sneer, just like he did.

"Not the one I wanted."

"Poor little frat boy," I say dryly.

Honestly, I live for these brief "interactions" with him. They're infrequent—but intoxicating. My pulse hammers even now, my breathing increasing.

"Where. Is. Donovan?"

I take another sip. "Ever speak in long sentences, River? You. Should. Try. It."

"Don't come here if he isn't here."

I slam the bottle down on the table then whip off my cover-up and throw it at him. It bounces off his magnificent chest and hits the floor. "Eat a bag of dicks."

His eyes glitter like stars. "I don't fucking like you."

"'I lie to myself all the time. I never believe me,'" I reply as I shove the paperback into his chest. Hard.

He takes it without looking at it, his lashes fluttering.

"That quote is from The Outsiders. *It's like...you're a wealthy West-Side Soc and I'm a poor East-Side Greaser and we fight all the time, even without provocation, for no reason at all except that we come from different worlds. The moral is, we all watch the same sunrise and sunset. Ponyboy, he's the outsider, a Greaser just living his best life and telling the story of what happened to him. It's a hard lesson he learns, and I'm him—right now. I'm fighting my way through life, trying to be more than what I came from. And you? Oh, you're the bad guy, maybe not Bob, the one who tried to drown Ponyboy, but yeah, you're a total rich prick. Ever read the Robert Frost poem about how 'Nothing Gold Can Stay'? Ponyboy struggles to understand its meaning. He's hanging on to innocence with a tight grip. Like me. Maybe like you. I don't know because you don't have real conversations with me. Why do you hate me?" I pause, sucking in air. My mouth is out of control, but I can't stop. "The book's been banned, which I love. I'm taking a lit class about those types of books in the fall. This book is a gift, from me to you. Read it and learn to treat me better, asshole."*

It's a great exit line.

I bend down, snatch my cover-up off the floor, and—

He jerks it away from my hands before I can slip it on, his chest heaving as he balls it up in his fist. His eyes burn as they drift over my body, the triangle bikini top that hugs my breasts, the tiny white bottoms on my hips.

The muscles in his jaw pop.

I count the seconds that stretch between us.

Twenty.

Then thirty.

Then forty.

Fifty.

Sixty.

The kitchen heats, the air thick as smoke.

I gasp. Needing to breathe.

He takes a step toward me, his eyes dilating, the black filling up the blue-gray of his irises.

The cover-up drops from his hands to the floor.

Neither of us notices.

"Anastasia."

Is that...

Is that longing in his voice?

Sweat breaks out all over me and my body leans into him. The heat of his skin burns from just inches away. I tremble, his name on the tip of my tongue, tempted to ask him, please, God, what the hell is this between us—

"River," I say breathlessly. "What—"

His lashes flutter against his cheeks. "Don't say it."

"I-I-I'm so confused—" *My hand reaches out.*

"Stop! Just..." *He clenches his fists.* "Get the hell out of this kitchen."

12

Anastasia

Donovan appears at my side. Kicking down the memory of River, I inhale a cleansing breath and turn to him, a forced smile on my face.

"...are you listening to me, Ana?"

"Sorry, the music is loud."

"You're late."

"I had to work. Like always."

"You should have asked off. We're supposed to be celebrating Harvard and your birthday." Wearing a cream-colored toga, he pats himself then wobbles a bit. "I have your gift—no wait, no pockets. Oops. I left it on the stage."

He could have given it to me when we met for dinner this week but insisted we wait for tonight to celebrate.

"Are you drunk?" I ask when he sways again. Normally, he's a moderate drinker.

"What if I am?" he grouses. "You were high."

And here we go...

"Are we back to this? Already? And I wasn't judging you, just surprised."

"Donovan, you're supposed to announce the costume winners. It's past time," comes from River as he appears next to Donovan, never glancing at me. "The DJ will finish up this song then you're up. I left the list behind the stage for you." He pauses, studying him. "You okay?"

"Yep! On it," Donovan replies as he takes a drink from his Solo cup, his eyes peering at me over the rim, an odd look in his gaze. He looks away and punches River in the arm. "She's hot, right, man?"

I don't like his tone.

River looks away from us, his mouth tight. "Yeah. Whatever."

Donovan's road-map eyes come back to me and rake over me, lingering on my bodice. I resist the urge to tug it up.

"You sure know how to make a man crazy," he murmurs. "Best I ever had."

"Donovan!" My lips part as color floods my face. I'm acutely aware of River, his head lowered like he doesn't hear us.

"What the hell is up with you?" I hiss at Donovan. "I'm going upstairs."

I flip around and he grabs my arm.

"Wait. Ana. Shit." He closes his eyes briefly.

"What's gotten into you?" I snap.

"Ana...my life is falling apart." Turmoil swirls in his words.

Before I can say anything, he clasps my hand and drags me away from River and toward the stage, tugging me through a throng of dancers as we head over. We bump into several as he plows through, and I keep apologizing to people we jostle.

"I need to do the announcements." He pulls me up the steps and behind the curtains, which are partly opened for the DJ but still leave about six feet of private area that's not seen by the partiers. There are electrical cords and music equipment and speakers sitting on the floor. He drops my hand and reaches for one of the wireless mics on a shelf, clips it to the rope around his waist where he's tied his toga. He squints as he tries to adjust the microphone part, and I take it from his fumbling hands and help him secure it to the top of his shoulder.

"Where are your glasses?" I ask.

"Don't know," he slurs as he turns to pat the top shelf.

I sigh. "Are you okay? You said your life is falling apart and—"

"I'm fine," he mutters. "Or I will be."

Okaayy. "Why did you bring me back here?"

"It's where I put your gift!"

"Enough," I mutter. "I don't want a gift. I'm going to find the girls. We can talk when you're sober—"

"Found it!" He flips around and shows me a rectangular black box with a pink bow on it. A jewelry store logo is on the top. He pushes it into my hands.

I slide the bow off, open the box, and take several deep breaths, hoping I'm not seeing—

A diamond tennis bracelet inside.

Yep.

I cringe, not even daring to take it out of the box.

"Beautiful, right?"

I'm dimly aware of the music stopping, the DJ announcing a short break, the low hum of voices a few feet away on the other side of the curtain.

"We've been together a while. Figured you deserved a great gift."

"It's just like Harper's," I push out.

"Actually, it's bigger than hers."

"I can't..." ever wear it.

I place it back on the shelf and turn to him. I know what I need to do...

"Donovan, it was never about a gift. Material things don't matter to me. I was never with you for your money, but since this past summer, we've been off—"

His head snaps up. "I'll tell you what's jacked up. It's not that I bought you a gift similar to Harper's. No, it's the fact that you were arrested for stealing a car in Manhattan—and other things!"

Grimacing, I draw back at his raised tone.

How does he...

What is going on?

"Who told you that? I was seventeen when that happened and never charged. Are you crazy?" The theft claim was dropped almost immediately, and the details should be private.

He paces around the small space, eyes shining with wildness. "My family told me today. A two-hour phone call with them and our lawyer breaking down your past. They had you investigated. I know all about you, Ana." A bitter laugh comes from him. "They aren't going to pay for Harvard if we're together. They were very clear about that today—"

"Donovan—"

"No, let me finish. This is why I wanted you to come early, so we could talk. They told me *many* things. How you traipsed across the world, living with different men—"

I gasp. "Not true. My parents lived with all sorts of people, and I went where they did. Sometimes they left me—"

"—and then you stole your *married* lover's car. He

was thirty years old, Ana. He says you seduced him, some sort of Lolita. I don't even know you!"

Oh my God. I stagger back as my past rushes at me like a tidal wave, sucking and dragging me under. I can't breathe.

"You don't know what you're talking about." My chest rises. "I wasn't the adult in that situation. He never told my parents he was married. She didn't live with him."

"His wife divorced him—over you."

A whimper of shock comes from me. "I-I didn't know that."

"Explain why the girl I love isn't who I thought she was!"

"Stop yelling," I say, raising my hands and trying to infuse calm in my tone. "You don't know the details—"

"Just thinking about you with some old guy makes me sick."

I frown and glance away from him, emotion tugging at me as those needles prick at my throat.

I was a kid, a stupid, stupid kid. Bryson never wore a ring, and my parents felt good about his apartment situation. It was roomy, next to Central Park, and his younger sister and her friend also lived there, all of them musicians. A few weeks after I moved in, they left, leaving me alone with him. He owned a home in Connecticut too, and looking back, I suppose his wife lived there. I stayed with him in his loft, yes, and I slept with him (after I fell for him). I also cleaned and cooked our meals. I basked in his adoring attention, his embraces, his kisses, his music. I thought it was *love*.

While he was out one day, I borrowed his Porsche to drive out of the city. I pulled into his parking spot when I returned and a woman glowered there, waiting, her face angry. When she confronted me about what I was doing with his car, I haltingly admitted I was his girlfriend, not knowing *who* she was. She said she was his wife, and with her toddler crying on her hip, she called the cops. It wasn't until Bryson showed up and explained that I was his unofficial 'ward' that they let me go.

The age of consent for consensual sex in New York is seventeen, and, boy, did Bryson hammer that in as he shoved my duffle into the back of his car. *I'm sorry. How could I resist you? You'll find someone else. Please don't come back to my place again.* He drove me to a hotel, paid for a week's stay, and walked out of my life.

My parents rushed back to New York. My normally laidback dad was furious that he was married and about how he handled it, but I begged him to let it go. Mom suggested we try Italy, so we packed up and left.

My chest clenches at the painful memory.

"I didn't know he was married. I was young—"

"Ana, just stop." A torn expression flits over his face as he lowers his voice. He tries to take my hands, and I jerk them away. "Look, maybe he took advantage of you, okay, okay, but can't you see that I can't keep finding out these secrets? My family members are important people—"

"I never told you because I knew you wouldn't get it," I snap.

He shuts his eyes. "Look, I've known since we met that we didn't go together, and I was drawn to that, but I can't help wondering what else is going to pop up. Your family, your past, you not getting into Harvard, your friends, the pot—it's too much. And I want to go to Harvard. It's all I've ever wanted—until you. I can't let you distract me." He sways on his feet and braces himself against the wall. "We need a break from each other."

And there it is. Finally. Confirmation.

"You don't deserve me," I say, my voice low and thick.

A hesitant expression ripples over his face as he stares at the floor.

"What else, Donovan?" My hands fist. Waiting. I know there's more.

He slowly raises his head, and when they come, his words are slurred. "Ana... I'm sorry, I'm really sorry, but I've seen Harper a few times for coffee. I haven't cheated on you, I wouldn't do that, but I was confused and didn't know which way to turn and she's always been my friend and understood how my family is..." His voice trails off as he takes a deep breath. "I-I kissed her."

I blink. "When? Tonight?"

"Monday. After I left your place." The words are dragged from him.

Hurt lances straight through my heart. I sensed the breakup was coming, but to be with *her* on my birthday.

It slices deep.

"Kissing is cheating!" I exclaim. "You *did* tell her I didn't get into Harvard. Screw your—what, parting gift? Please. I don't want a *thing* from you—"

"What the hell?" River whisper-yells as he appears backstage like a storm and rushes to Donovan. "Your mic is on." He reaches for the wireless box, fiddles with the buttons, removes it, then plucks the mic off his toga.

Benji shoves inside the space and gives me a long look. "Ana? You okay?"

I stare at him blankly, then it dawns on me...the eerie silence out in the basement. My head shakes, realization hitting me. "Wait, wait—did people hear us?"

Benji grimaces. "It was blasted over the speakers in the kitchen, mostly his voice. I could barely hear you. Pool area, too, I'd guess. I ran all the way down here."

My eyes close.

All these people.

Students I have classes with.

The fraternity brothers.

Humiliation rises as the blood leaves my face. Stomach jumping, I slide the curtain aside the tiniest bit. Harper and her sorority sisters are gathered a few feet away. Mellany has her phone out as she takes pictures or records. Harper smiles like it's the best day of her life, her face animated as she murmurs to Audrey.

Donovan rubs his forehead. "What's going on? Was... was my mic on?"

"Yeah, catch up. All the party rooms have speakers," Benji mutters.

River grunts his agreement as he puts the mic on Benji then presses a piece of paper into his hands and slaps him on the back. "Here's the list. Read the winners, be cool, and act like nothing happened."

"Wait a minute! *I* was going to do that," Donovan mutters, jostling around to stand in front of Benji.

River pulls him away from the stage entrance. "No. You walk out of here and clear your head. Maybe stick to your room until this blows over."

Donovan frowns. "Come on. It's not that big of a deal. I'll make a joke—"

"You're not taking the stage," River says firmly through gritted teeth.

"Yeah, then why don't *you* do it, President! Oh, wait. You never want to read—"

"Shut up, Donovan," Benji mutters, scowling. "You've already dug a hole."

"Go on out there," River tells Benji, ignoring Donovan's protests.

Benji leaves, the spotlight hitting him as he spreads

his hands and grins broadly at the crowd. The lizard is still on his shoulder. "PARTY PEOPLE! Who's ready to hear who won the toga contest? We've got one boy and one girl to crown King and Queen of the Greeks!" A spattering of applause and hoots come from the partiers.

"What happened back there?" a male voice from the audience yells out. "Y'all filming *Days of Our Lives at the Kappa House*?"

Benji laughs. "Hey, every day is a party with the Kappas. And the winners are..." He rattles off the names then—

"Who stole a car?" a voice cries out.

"Who had an affair with a married man?" another person asks. "Was it Ana?"

"Did Donovan break up with Ana?" comes from a girl near the front of the stage. "Tell us what happened, Benji!"

This is what happens when you date a guy from the most popular frat on campus. Everyone knows your business; they're always watching.

They heard Donovan.

It sinks in, hard and sure, and Benji's reply is lost as a roaring noise fills up the space in my ears. I press back against the wall. My stomach pitches, the dinner I had earlier rumbling.

Donovan scowls at River. "You had no right to send

him out there! This is my house, my party, my last year here—"

River grabs his arm and gives him a shake. "You publicly broke up with a little sister. You ripped her apart in front of everyone. Have some fucking respect."

"I didn't mean to do it like that." Tense moments pass as Donovan's face compresses. He sends me a desperate look. "Ana, look, I'm sorry—"

"No," I say tightly. Hasn't he said everything already?

He looks uncertain and takes a step toward me but stops just as Crew and Hollis appear at the door. He blinks at them.

Great. The whole frat is coming back here to see what's going on. They all know!

Donovan scoops up the jewelry box then tucks it under his arm. "I'm taking this, then. Just thought since I bought it months ago, I might as well give it to you..." He sways on his feet.

Crew and Hollis get on either side of Donovan.

"Hey, buddy, let's get you off the stage," Crew says, his tone even and calm.

Hollis nods. "Yeah, bro, let's sober you up."

He walks out with them and disappears.

Benji has a couple on stage and is putting laurel wreaths on their heads, but most everyone is watching the stage door. As soon as Donovan walks out, he shakes off Crew and Hollis and shoulders his way to the Deltas

—to Harper. Unable to look away from the small break in the curtains, I watch as she grabs his hand and leads him through the throng of people.

Every eye is on them.

Heads turn as they whisper.

My chest pings as a riot of emotions spiral through my head. Hurt and frustration are first. As Donovan and Harper disappear from my view, heading up the stairs to the main floor, white-hot anger shoves down the hurt. My scalp prickles with rage and I want to scream. Okay, I knew we were teetering on the edge, but...

He judged me with a list of crimes—then announced them for everyone to *hear*?

My fists clench as the incredulity rises, the ramifications settling in. They think I'm an awful person—and he dumped me because of it!

"How could he say those things to me?" I say mostly to myself, my voice low. "I knew we were different, but we were always friends first. Deep down, though, he doesn't get me, does he? He needs black cocktail dresses and a perfect pedigree and hair that isn't lavender, because that would be a travesty!" I stop, my voice cracking. I'm not making sense, but I can't...

"Let it out," River says.

"He—he used my past against me! Who I am, where I came from! He should have ended it after they put their stamp of disapproval on me this past summer, the sonofabitch!" I picture the baseball bat from the apartment in my hands, going at his Tesla. "Sneaking around and kissing her? That's cheating, it is, it is, and he told her about Harvard, and God, what else has he told her..." My voice trails off as I squeeze my hands even tighter.

He touches my arm, and I start. He's ripped a piece of his toga off and hands it to me. "You're crying."

I take it from him and press it to my eyes, seeing mascara on the fabric. My chest hitches.

"He's drunk."

"People say what they really think when they're trashed, and you know it. I can't change who I am or who my parents are for him. I don't want to. I like who I am. I'm me, just *me*." I hit my chest.

"You're special, Anastasia. Don't let what he said sink in. I don't think he meant for everyone to hear—"

"Don't defend him!"

River nods, his face shuttered. "You're right. It's not my place."

"Yet here you are. You got here before anyone else," I say.

He opens his mouth, then shuts it as Benji comes back.

The DJ takes the stage and cranks up the music.

"New king and queen crowned—check," Benji says. "Where did Donovan go? I couldn't see with that spotlight."

"He ran straight to Harper," I say bitterly. "Has she been here, at the house?" My head fires off in a million directions, wondering how deep the betrayal goes. The Kappa house has felt like *home* to me, and to think he might have been with her here is...

"Yes. Once," River tells me grudgingly. "On Monday, but that's the only time I've seen her here."

My hands clench. "I need to get out of here, but I don't..." I swallow, trying to push down the anger so I can think. "...have my purse. I can't recall where I put it, maybe the pantry in the kitchen..." I pinch my nose. "My roommates... I'm the designated driver—"

"I've got them if you want to leave," Benji says as he gives Spike a pet.

"I'm going to kill that bastard!" It's Lila's voice as she wrestles with a few Kappa pledges who are guarding the door to the stage. "Let me in! She's my friend!" Thank goodness the music is loud and no one hears her.

Did River put the guards there on his way to the stage?

She gets past the pledge and rushes to me. "Where did he go? I'm going to rip his nuts off. And his nipples!"

"You heard?" I ask.

She bites her lip. "Yeah. I was playing pool. Not gonna lie, it was loud and clear on the PA system, more his side." She continues, "I can't find Colette. I'll get her and we'll—"

"No," River says, interrupting her. "I've got Anastasia. I'm taking her home."

Our gazes cling. He's unreadable, his face like granite, his eyes shuttered. I get the sense of a barely leashed tiger about to pounce.

"I thought you wanted to stay out of this," I say.

His jaw pops. "I can take you home. You are a little sister."

Am I? Still?

Lila gives me a surprised arch of her brow then squints at River. "No, football player. I don't really know you, okay? Sure, you appeared like magic when I was high, and you have a notorious playboy rep that kind of fascinates me, but *I'll* take her home, then come back and kill Donovan. Slowly." She chugs the rest of the drink in her Solo cup then tosses it over her shoulder.

A wan smile crosses my face. She had several shots of Fireball before we left the apartment. Explains the temper—Fireball always makes her want to fight. Okay, any alcohol makes her want to fight. No way is she driving me anywhere. Sure, Colette could take me home, but where the heck is she? I need to go. Now.

"No, stay at the party, please. I-I need to be alone for a minute." To figure this out in my head. To cry in private. "I'll need you tomorrow, but right now, just find Mason or let Benji bring you home."

She mulls that over, reading my expression. "You're

sure you want him to take you home?" she asks, tilting her head at River.

I nod. Yes, we've shared plenty of barbs, but he's being protective, and I... I don't know. Part of me needs him, and I can't explain it.

"Okay. Tomorrow, we'll make a plan," she tells me as she crosses her arms. "I've got some ideas on how to eviscerate the bastard. Leave it to Mama Lila." She eyes Benji, her eyes flaring at Spike. "Benji, if you're my DD, that better be a non-threatening animal on your shoulder."

"He's a reptile. I guess, technically, he's an animal?"

She rolls her eyes. "You really are a true blond. Look, if you're in charge of me, you must not drink. I love to party but also want to live. You must get me home in one piece. If you get frisky, I'll throat-punch."

"Oh, I'll take good care of you," he drawls, draping his eyes over her. "One thing: there's a Delta who's technically my date, but that's only because she's writing my paper. If she's all over me, just let it be, baby. You're my number one."

She slaps him on the arm. "You're awful. I kind of like it, frat boy."

They continue to banter, and I tune them out and stare at my hands as my head replays the conversation with Donovan. I cringe.

"I know where your head is. You didn't do anything wrong," River says quietly.

"Okay, if you've got Ana covered, I'm going to start a beer pong contest," Benji says to River as he takes Lila's hand. "Come on, baby, let's see how well you can bounce a ball in a cup."

Lila breaks away and gives me a hug. "You sure you're okay?"

No.

"Yeah." I just need distance from the Kappa house.

After they leave, I glance at River. "I'm sorry this happened at your party—"

His fists clench. "No. *I'm* sorry he broke up with you like that."

My eyes narrow. "He's with *her* right now. They walked away in front of everyone. They probably went to his room, and—TMI—I haven't had sex with him in weeks, so he's probably up there *getting laid*—"

"Don't. Let's get you out of here." He approaches, settling himself next to me. "Okay, here's the plan..."

13

River

The moment she stepped in the basement and found me staring, I knew shit was going to be bad.

Her. Him.

They love each other.

And *me*?

This triangle (that only I'm aware of) is chewing me up and spitting me out.

Guilt hangs over me.

The secrets I keep.

She's off limits.

Even if they *did* just break up.

Yeah, yeah, I know what I just heard, what everyone heard, but he's trashed, totally blindsided by his parents; he's going to wake up and freak out. Harper *isn't* Anastasia. She's a blank piece of paper; Anastasia is *poetry* on the paper.

He chose Harvard over her. A day or a week or a month from now, he's going to open his eyes and have a breakdown, wondering what the fuck happened when he let her slip away.

The chaos started this afternoon when Donovan stormed out of his room and came into the kitchen. He'd been on the phone with his family for a couple of hours. With a grim face and bleary eyes, he grabbed the tequila and took one shot after another. He hung his head and laid it out for me, everything his parents said.

He asked for advice...

The pledge comes back with Anastasia's purse and my letterman jacket from my room (I wondered where that was and took a stab). He hands them to her, and she slips her arms inside and tugs it around her, her nose dipping to the collar as she inhales the smell.

My chest tightens as she turns, and I see the 3 on the back under my last name. I murmur under my breath.

She adjusts her crossbody-style purse over it. "What did you say?"

I blink. "Three. It's the magic number."

She gives me a half-smile. "Right."

"Ready?"

She nods, hiding her face. "Yeah. Let's get out of this place."

I throw an arm around her, being casual, yet aware of the press of her against me, that sweet scent of hers that stirs the air.

I guide her out the door, my hand at the small of her back. It's a sizzle to my skin, but I shove it down. A row of pledges are lined up (on my orders), blocking the view from the dance floor. I give them a nod as we dash for the exit to the right and step out into the cold air.

I nod my head at the parking lot to the side of the house. "My truck's over here."

She looks around the property, a furrow on her brow. "I'm leaving when he's the one who should be embarrassed for being such a dick," she mutters. "But it's his house, and *I'm* embarrassed. Ugh."

Several partiers are standing in the front yard, dancing, laughing, drinking, but no one seems to notice us.

I pop the lock on my truck, and she crawls in the passenger side. I slide in and give her a long look, then glance back to the road as I crank the vehicle.

Lost. She looks lost.

"Audrey will be disappointed when she can't find you," she says quietly as I drive down the street and make the turn that takes us off Greek Row.

"I haven't been with her in months..." My words taper off. I don't want to talk about *that*. Would she want to know that when I fucked, she was the one in my head? Probably not. The night she opened the door and saw me, shame washed over me, deep and thick, which was crazy because I had every right to fuck whoever I wanted. She had Donovan! But she...

Her eyes. Her face.

I can't be with anyone like that again.

She's gotten her phone out and gasps.

"What?"

I glance over at her, and she shows me a post on IG, a picture of Donovan and Harper on a couch in the den of the house, snuggled up. "Wow. That didn't take long. Mellany posted it. *True love always wins over skanks* is the caption." Her hands tremble. "She also posted the audio of the breakup, it seems. I can't..."—her head shakes—

"...listen to it. Not yet."

A long exhalation leaves my chest. I figured this was coming. That conversation behind the curtain went on way too long for people not to jump on it.

She squeezes her hands into fists. "I lost your toga piece. Do you have something I can clean my face with? Tissues or a napkin—" She fumbles with the glove box, opens it, and stops.

She pulls out the copy of *The Outsiders*, her lips parting. "River? You *kept* this?" Her eyes widen as she looks at me.

I shift around, tensing. "Yeah."

She lets out a long breath. "It's my copy from when I was thirteen, a childhood treasure. I met the author, my parents arranged it, and I got to talk to her about the characters. Normally, I wouldn't have loaned it out, but that day...wow, I wasn't myself..." Her lips tremble. "I assumed you set fire to it and did a victory dance around it. Did you read it?"

Tension rolls over me at the memory of that day in the kitchen with her.

Her in that bathing suit. My loss of control.

Did I read it?

A harsh laugh comes from me and I clench the steering wheel. "Yeah. It took me"—a month of reading every night—"a while, but yeah. Every single word..." is etched on my soul. "'Stay gold, Ponyboy.' That's what Johnny told Ponyboy. He begged him to fight against the odds, to always hold his breath right before the sunrise and to watch every sunset," I say. "My favorite quote is, 'You still have a lot of time to make yourself be what you want.'"

Wonder colors her voice as she clutches the book to her heart. "You read it. My God. You get it, you get it. Out of all this...debacle tonight...to discover this? You have no idea what it means to me. Yeah, I know it's a young adult novel, but I never dreamed you'd really read it and...and I-I feel better for some reason, knowing you *know* a quote...thank you." A tear slips down her face, and the thing is, she isn't making a sound, and I don't think she realizes she's crying. I'm not sure why she's thanking me, but maybe it's for getting her out of there, then the book.

Maybe everything is crashing down on her.

I swallow thickly. I wrote her name in it, too, slowly, with painstaking care, being sure. My handwriting is crazy messy, and I prefer typing. I highlighted passages. I held it so much the color rubbed off the cover. I'm thankful the cab of the truck's dark and she doesn't notice as she sticks it back in the glove box.

I turn on my playlist. "Iris" by The Goo Goo Dolls croons from the speakers, a song about a guy who wants a girl to know who he is, where the truth meets the lies.

She leans her head back on the seat. "My favorite quote from *The Outsiders* is, 'Greasers grew up on the outside. They weren't looking for a fight. They were looking to belong.' I don't have it as bad as the Greasers, but I've never fit in. Donovan's right about his family. They never would have accepted me."

"Everything is relative. Sometimes a person can be your home."

She chews on her lips. "I have to tell you something..." She stops and looks out the window.

"What?"

"Forget it."

"Tell me."

She continues to stare out at the passing buildings. A long breath comes from her chest. "That night, in the library, I'd have bet a hundred bucks you'd be the one waiting for me. I know, it's weird, but when you came over and dropped your pen, I don't know, I thought we had this *moment...*" She stares down at her lap. "Obviously, I was wrong."

Silence reigns in the truck.

My jaw clenches.

She's quiet as I approach her apartment and pull into an empty parking spot.

Her hand goes to the door handle, then she stops and glances back at me. "River, I lied. I-I don't want to be alone."

I draw in a sharp breath as her stark emotion spears me, those big green eyes.

Don't leave me, they plead.

I put my vehicle in park. "I don't think it's a good idea..." to be alone with you in your apartment.

She gives me a jerky nod. "No, no, I totally get it—that's not what I meant. Of course not. You and I...we aren't even friends. You're Donovan's friend. I meant, I should have brought my roommates. I wasn't thinking straight. They'd know what to do. My head is jumbled." She runs her finger down the leather of the seat. "Being alone is the worst."

Fuck.

Taking her home is one thing. Spending time with her is another.

"Where do you want to go? Are you hungry? We can hit a drive-through—"

"No, I can't eat. I'll throw up. Just drive?"

"Drive?"

A faint smile flits over her face. "Yeah. Ever been to Henning Park at sunrise?"

I start. "You want to stay out all night at a park?"

"Well, from the look on your face, you hate the idea."

"I didn't say I hate it."

"Your right eye twitched. You do that when you're emotional. It's a tell. You twitched."

"No, I didn't."

"You did. You do it when you play poker or when one of the pledges is getting on your nerves. Once you did it in the elevator with me. Truth? I was kinda enraptured, gleeful almost, hoping it was me and I was irritating you. Was I?"

"It's dark in here. You got X-ray vision?" I ask.

"You didn't answer my question."

"No, I didn't."

"Are you a good liar, River?"

"Excellent."

"No! You twitch when you lie. It just happened! The skin right under your eye moved."

"If, and I say *if* I'm twitching, it's because you're a diabolical woman! You really don't want to get out of this truck, do you?"

"Diabolical? Me? You're the literal devil, so we're even. Your middle name is Lucius, which is oddly close to Lucifer. Bring up one little nervous tic, and you have a meltdown—"

"I'm not melting down!"

She arches her brows. "I know. We're bantering."

"No, we're arguing."

"You twitched!"

I cover my eyes with my hands then slowly let them fall. "If I'm the twitching devil, you're his crazy henchman."

She smiles, a sad one. "Sure, whatever you say. I have an idea: let's drive around and talk about *The Outsiders*. We'll compare notes. It's the only thing we have in common. I enjoy football, but honestly, it's mostly for the warrior attitude, and the tight pants. I wish one of the players would have a crush on an opposing player. I've imagined them throwing off their helmets and kissing... Okay, okay, I can see by your face, you aren't on board. I never pictured *you* doing that, so...yeah, I'll shut up now."

"You daydream about footballers getting it on?"

"Just once. Two defensive players. Big guys. Very masculine." She shrugs. "I read MM sometimes."

No clue what MM is and I'm afraid to ask. "I can't stay out all night. I have girls at the party to go bang."

Her eyes narrow. "You twitched!"

I huff out a wondering laugh.

"Alright, Anastasia. I'll just *drive*."

A victorious half-smile crosses her lips. "Just let me check on June."

"You mentioned her today. Who is she?"

She leans forward to peer through the windshield. "My pretend grandma. She's ornery. I can't get her to stay in a shelter, and...just hang on, let me go say hi." She bolts out of the truck and dashes to the alley, disappearing.

I grab my phone. **I'm with Anastasia. May not be home till late,** I say into my cell, and it sends to the guys.

Crew sends, **Dude. Glad you got her out. Donovan is trashed. He's always been crazy about her. WTF happened?**

Harvard happened. His parents happened. *I* happened.

Keep your dick under control, River, all two inches of it, Hollis replies with an eggplant emoji.

I smirk. **Bigger than yours.**

Yeah. They know I need a reminder when it comes to her.

I'm trying, I'm trying...

She's been gone for several minutes, and I'm about to get out when she jogs back, opens the door, and settles into her seat, some of the tension gone from her face.

"She okay? Do we need to get her anything?"

"She's good. Half-asleep. I brought her dinner earlier, but..."

"Yeah?"

She bites her lip. "I'm terrified she's going to disappear."

It dawns on me. How did I miss it? Donovan mentioned she hasn't seen her parents in a year, and they left her periodically growing up...

People *leave* Anastasia.

"Crank the heat up, roll down the windows, and go really fast," she murmurs.

I give her an incredulous look.

"What? I'm depressed and irrational. My boyfriend just broke up with me. He told the whole world what a pot-smoking slut I am—"

"You are *not*."

"Whatever. You know what people will say. The truth is, I'm feeling crazy. I'm talking way more than I should. You're lucky I'm not asking for cupcakes, ice cream, *and* a chick flick. Go with it. Please."

I roll down the windows and turn up the heat.

I glance over at her, taking in the soft curve of her face.

This is just *one* night. I can be a...friend.

I pull out onto the street and gun it, and she laughs as she jerks her hair out of its updo. She puts her arm out the window, hands riding the airstream. "That's what I'm talking about!"

It feels a little forced, her sadness lingering just under the surface, but I'm here.

With her.

Waiting.

SEVERAL HOURS LATER, we've hashed out *The Outsiders* to the point where I feel like I lived the damn story myself. I didn't tell her how I had to take notes on every chapter or that I listened to the audio *and* watched the movie version. We discussed the themes as we drove down every backroad in Walker, Georgia.

We ended up in the neighboring county, got lost once and had to pull up Google, almost ran over a raccoon, stopped to let her pee in the woods, had a debate about cats versus dogs (she's pro-cat and I'm not), discussed how freaky Santa and the Easter Bunny really are, touched on *Twilight* versus *Vampire Dairies*. I had no skin in that game, but she laid it out for me for about an hour. The girl can talk. A lot. She wasn't an Edward fan. Team Jacob all the way. I hung on every word she uttered but made a mental note to never watch either.

"Romance—bah," I said, and she pretended to be mad.

She showcased her British accent, which sucks, and I did my interpretation of Rhett Butler's "Frankly, my dear, I don't give a damn." (Mom's favorite movie is *Gone with the Wind*.)

She begged for more.

"Bond. James Bond."

She hooted.

"E.T. phone home," I said in my best raspy alien voice.

"My precious," was her Gollum from *The Lord of the Rings*.

"I'm the king of the world," I shouted with my free hand out the window.

Then I looked at her and did, "Show me the money," and she countered with "You had me at hello."

She's more random than I realized.

Maybe it's the late night, maybe it's her heart breaking.

"We have more than just *The Outsiders* in common," I told her.

I see you, Rainbow.

We got quiet during the last hour, one of those easy silences where you don't have to say anything at all. I don't have a lot of those. I talk to keep the world turning, and sometimes my head never shuts off, but with her, it's different. She stills the erratic side of me, and I'm not sure why that is.

Maybe I do, but...

It was me and her and the dark road.

Now we're parked at Henning Park, a rundown place near campus with old swings, rusted monkey bars, and seesaws that are falling apart. I glance around. This place needs to be cleaned up, new equipment and a fence, some landscaping. The frat needs a new project, and this is perfect for the pledges.

"This place needs some love," she says, and I glance at her, taking in the tangles in her hair, and smirk.

"I was thinking the same thing."

She tilts the rearview mirror at herself and gasps. "Holy shit. I'm shocked you didn't chuck me out on the side of the road hours ago. Sorry I got us lost. Those backroads all look the same."

"Mhmm." It might have been one of the best nights I've had in a while.

She sighs and looks out the windshield to the park. "The east is that way. Up on the hill—that's where we'll go to watch the sun come up."

"It's kind of cold. You sure?" I ask, bemused at her idea.

"Heck yeah, Snake. Let's go. Race you to the top."

She dashes out of the truck and runs in her heels across the playground.

I hang back and let her win, then join her at the top. I

slide in next to her as she looks out over the rolling hills and trees. "How are we gonna do this?"

She checks her phone. "The weather app says it should come up any minute. We'll do what Ponyboy did. We're going to hold our breaths and wait for the sun to come up. You're an athlete, right? You can go for, what, thirty seconds?"

"Baby girl, I can go way longer."

She sends me a smirk. "You act all *I'm a bad boy* when you're deflecting your emotions. You're not fooling me. There's depth to you."

I hide my face and smile.

She sighs. "Thank you for doing this with me."

"Yeah. No problem." I stick my hands in the pockets of my jeans, not sure what else to say. There's an intimacy between us that wasn't there before, a fragile thread that feels as if it might disappear at any moment.

A red-tailed hawk swoops past us and lands on a tree. "They mate for life," I say. "Crows too. Weird, right? Swans, bald eagles, barn owls, beavers, gray wolves, coyotes—now that's an interesting one. There's this website with videos of coyotes, showing them nuzzling each other..." I stop at her expression. "What? I watch *Animal Planet*." I twist my ring. "Why are you staring at me like I just grew an extra head?"

"I like you. *Who* you are."

"It's the weird stuff that sticks in my mind."

She hums. "Did you not try hard in high school and now it's catching up with you?"

"Yeah." I sway on my feet, part loopy exhaustion, part *No, that's a lie.*

"Thank you, you know, for indulging me. I needed this."

Any time is on the tip of my tongue, but I shut it down.

She points at the horizon. "It's coming! Go!" She takes a breath in, her cheeks puffing out as she faces the east.

I suck in air, and she startles me when she clasps my hand and laces our fingers together. We face the sunrise as it peeks over the horizon, a soft gleam of orange illuminating the dimness, slowly brightening the day. I count out thirty seconds in my head.

She lets out a long exhalation and we stand there for another minute or two, not speaking as we hold hands and watch as the glow inches higher. She faces me, too close, and I stare down at the smudges of black under her eyes, the delicate slope of her shoulders, the rise of her breasts in her dress.

My jacket that engulfs her.

Neither of us speaks for several moments.

Ten.

Twenty.

Thirty.

Forty.

Fifty.

Sixty.

Her voice is soft. "New day. New beginning. Life's full of possibilities in this moment. It's a fresh start. It's like a book when you open it to page one. Can you feel it?"

Rainbow... I *feel* everything.

"Be a football star. Live your best life. Take chances and have no regrets. Those are my three things for you on this new day," she says, her face tilting up to me. Her hand squeezes mine.

My voice is husky. "*You* stay gold, Anastasia, breathe every breath, read all the books, get into law school, fuck the haters, and stay beautiful. Six things for you because you deserve them all."

She smiles tremulously, a mist appearing in her eyes.

"What?" I ask.

"River...your words." She bites her bottom lip.

"Yeah? Tell me."

"No. I shouldn't say it. I..." She swallows thickly and looks at the ground.

I can't resist tipping her chin up. "What?"

Her eyes cling to mine. "I need someone to tell me that every day of my life. Just like this. In person. Looking into my eyes."

Fuck.

Fuck.

Anastasia.

Drawn inexplicably, I take a step toward her and almost wrap my arms around her. *Almost.*

But I can't do it.

Shouldn't.

Mustn't.

14

Anastasia

"Order up, Ana!" comes the cook's voice as he sets a burger and fries up on the kitchen window.

Lila elbows me out of the way and takes it. "You stick to the bar. The prick and Harper are in the back. I'll take this out to Carl."

I tuck my hands in my green apron. I can't keep on avoiding him. It's been two days, and at some point, we're going to come face to face. "I'm surprised he had the nerve to show up here tonight," I mutter.

The Kappas always come in on Sunday evenings. There's a twenty-top near the back, and it's an unwritten rule that it belongs to them. They came in an hour ago, filing past me, most of them giving me uneasy glances when they waved.

"No," I say and take the plate out of her hands. "This is for Carl. I'm fine."

"Are you?" she asks. "You didn't look fine yesterday."

I'm doing okay, considering.

But my rage, it's simmering under the surface. For the past two mornings, I've awoken to a sharp sense of shame over his words, his accusations that I was a Lolita type, and I hate it—which feeds my anger, stoking it higher and higher.

Lila takes the plate back. "I'm doing it—"

"Somebody needs to take it while it's still hot," Derek, our cook, grouses. "The fries will get cold."

Marilyn gives me an eyebrow arch as she pours draft beer in a pitcher. "Ana, it's your table and Carl adores you. Go."

"On it." I flip around and head past the bar, just as Parker, one of the pledges, meets me at the corner. "Hey, Ana."

"Hey, Lila or Marilyn will take your order. I don't have your table—"

"No, um..." He sighs. "Geeze. Uh, how do I say this? Um, Donovan wants his pin back." He grimaces. "That's all I came to say. Had to, you know. They make us do shit, I mean, I love the frat, and you're like the sweetest person ever, so yeah, I didn't want to come up here and say that. I'm sorry."

My voice is incredulous. "He sent you?"

He nods and winces.

"What a fucking coward," I mutter vehemently.

Parker's eyes flare. "Right, right. I delivered the message. Just don't hurt the messenger." He looks down at his shoes. "He said you can drop it off in an envelope in the Kappa mailbox. As soon as possible," he whispers.

Hurt crawls up my throat.

"How convenient—for him. Tell him he'll have to pry it out of my cold, dead hands when I'm eighty." A fake, wry smile flashes. "Kidding. I burned the pin along with the books and shirts he left at my place. It melted in the flames. It was *so* pretty. Okay, kidding again, chill. You look pale. I'll take care of it, Parker. Bye."

He shuffles away.

Lila has heard and follows me as I head to Carl's table. He's a regular, our unofficial bar mascot.

Her voice is low. "Ana, you can't keep ignoring that he's ruined your rep, he's *here* flaunting that girl, and now he's sending a poor pledge to do his dirty work. What are you going to do about it? You haven't called him, texted him, or said anything. You're just *taking* it. Make some drama, girl."

I ignore her and stop at Carl's table. He's in his late sixties with frizzy gray hair and a paunch. He's an outsider, like me. If June is the grandma I never had, Carl's my grandfather.

218 | THE REVENGE PACT

A bubble of laughter comes out of me. "I'm losing it," I muse to myself as I set his food down.

"No, darling. We're all a little wacko." He squints up at me. "You don't look right. Tell ol' Crazy Carl what's happening."

Lila plops down in the booth seat across from him and steals a fry off his plate. "Frat boy broke her heart."

Carl's eyes swivel to me as he takes a sip from his beer mug. He's only had the one, but if he overdrinks, I'll drive him home and he'll catch a ride back the next day to get his truck.

"Donovan?" he asks.

"He's here—with another girl," Lila says, twisting her lips. "He dumped her at the toga party! And he did it in front of everyone!" She proceeds to lay out exactly what happened on Friday.

"Let me at him," he mutters when she's done, making as if he's going to stand, but I ease him back down with a hand on his shoulder.

"He's forty years younger than you, and fighting doesn't solve problems."

He scoffs. "The aliens would disagree. I've met them, you know. They haven't annihilated us because we don't have the resources they need."

"Did they put probes inside you, like in the movies? Did they, um, penetrate your parts?" Lila asks in a serious voice.

He chokes. "No."

"Good," she says. "I've wondered, you know, even thought of writing some intergalactic porn. I have a strange mind." She taps the side of her head.

Carl loves talking about aliens; it makes him happy. I don't know if it's true. Don't care. He just *is* who he is.

He swallows down a bite of his burger. "It's funny... they *really* are like you see on TV. Green. Giant head. Big eyeballs. Tiny mouth. The leader wore a silver cape like he was a male model, swishing around like a supervillain. My theory? The government has one of them in Area 51 out west. I keep waiting for Zen—that's the leader's name—to come back."

"Let's circle back to the real villain tonight," Lila mutters as she watches the Kappa table. "Donovan."

Carl gives me a rueful glance. "I'd give Donovan a piece of my mind, but my right hook ain't what it used to be, darling. Got a pacemaker. Gotta protect it."

I pat his shoulder. "You're fine. I'm fine. Eat up." I slap Lila's hand when she goes in for another fry.

She rolls her eyes and leans forward. "Carl, you've been witness to their relationship for a year. You've seen him in here with her. He was never good enough for *her*. She needs to get *revenge*. I've been talking my head off but she won't listen—"

"I'm an adult," I say, letting out an exhalation as I sit down next to her.

Can't beat them, join them.

Carl takes a sip of beer. "If it were me, I'd get him back where it cuts the most."

I shrug. "That would be Harvard, and no hope there."

"That's it! You'll get even by getting into Harvard," Lila gasps. "You'll show up, all pretty and smart, sit in his class on the first day, and Harper will be like, *What is she doing here?* and Donovan will be like, *Oh my god, what did I do, I need Ana!* and you can be like, *Who are you, asshole?*" She fist-pumps the air.

Carl freezes mid-bite of a fry. "That's the plot of *Legally Blonde*."

"No. Elle Woods got dumped by her popular frat boyfriend. Then he got into Harvard and took up with his prep school sweetheart—" Lila stops, her mouth flapping open.

"*Legally Blonde*," Carl says with a smirk.

I laugh. "To be clear, I'm not an Elle Woods. I take some of the toughest classes on campus, and I support myself. And no way would I go to Harvard just to get him back."

"*Legally Lavender*," Lila whispers as she moves her hand in a sweeping motion. "I could write a satire. A screenplay. Down-on-her-luck girl gets dumped by her rich boyfriend for being *herself*, then rises above, goes to Harvard, becomes a kickass lawyer to rival him, and then makes him cry like a baby when she marries some hot lawyer with a big dick—"

"Language, Lila," Carl says sternly. "And, no, not a fancy hero. Make him an athlete with a heart of gold." He puffs out his chest. "I was a football player back in the day. All the ladies wanted a piece of me."

She tilts her head. "A jock? Hmmm. I don't know. She needs—"

"*She* is right here," I say dryly.

"She needs a man with a *soul*," Carl says. "A man who cares for others. A man who walks in the room and other men look up to him. A man who looks at her and the whole world stops spinning. The more nuanced a man's soul, the deeper he loves. It's a forever kind of thing, the kind that's written in the stars."

I blink. "Dang, Carl. Where's this guy when I need him?"

He shrugs. "Donovan isn't yours. Always knew it."

"Really?" I ask.

He nods gravely. "But he'll regret losing you."

"Too bad," I mutter. "I wouldn't have him for a thousand diamond tennis bracelets piled on a silver platter. I wouldn't have him if he dropped to his knees and begged. I wouldn't have him if he cut off contact with his parents and dropped out of Harvard for me!"

"Yes," Lila says victoriously. "I like you fired up! You're getting it now, baby!"

Carl smirks. "I predict he'll marry three times, have no children, and get a venereal disease at some point."

"From Harper!" Lila calls out as she high-fives Carl.

"I adore you, Carl. Lila, stop yelling." I glance over my shoulder to check out the Kappa table. Several have gotten up to play pool, but Donovan and Harper sit, their heads bent as they talk. As if he can sense me looking, he rises up and darts his gaze at me. His lips part, a frown furrowing his brow. His eyes are bloodshot as they meet mine. His face crumples—

I flip around.

I don't want his sadness!

"No," I mutter under my breath. He kissed her on my birthday, told her about my rejection, and judged me in front of everyone.

Lila filches another fry from Carl. "I'm desperate. She's already nixed my idea of egging his car and wrapping it in plastic wrap—"

"Not a twelve-year-old," I toss in.

She waves me off. "Come on, Carl. How can Ana get her groove back and save face?" She leans closer. "Everyone knows what he said about her."

Mellany's audio recording has been shared hundreds of times. Lila and Colette went on a campaign to "report" the post, texting all their friends to help, but...whatever. It's too late.

I come back to the present as Lila continues talking.

"...all I'm saying is, if you won't retaliate in a physical way, at least man up and show him you aren't *down*. He is with *her*. At your place of work. He sent a pledge to get his pin." She presses her lips together. "I propose the best way to get back at him is to get a new hottie and post that crap all over social. Rub it in his face. Let him know some sexy man is banging his ex. We have the ski trip coming up—baseball players, Pikes, ATOs, those grizzly agriculture guys, even the tennis players are going. Mecca of men! Yes, yes, yes!" she groans.

"I'll have what she's having," Carl says.

I smile. "*When Harry Met Sally.*"

He winks. "Love the rom-coms."

I turn to Lila. "Back to your grand idea...who would want a piece of me after what he said? Not that I'd use sex to manipulate Donovan."

Carl leans in, pushing his plate to the side. "Okay, I may not look it, but I'm the smartest guy in this room... and I have an idea."

"You do?" I ask.

"He just walked in." His eyes move past me to the front door, and a slow smile spreads over his face.

I turn to see who's come in.

River. Freaking. Tate.

"*Legally Lavender,*" Lila whispers in awe, following our gazes. "An athlete with a heart of gold—well, in his case, a black heart when it comes to you—but still, I can see it."

His heart isn't so black.

I haven't told Lila about sharing the sunrise with him...

"Nope," I say.

It doesn't matter how hot River is; he is *way, way, way* off limits.

15

Anastasia

He stalks into the bar, his head down as he checks his cell. Wearing skinny jeans that cling to his thighs and a black leather jacket, he looks like a bad boy rock star. His hair is messy, the longer strands on top brushing against his forehead. His hand sweeps them back, his ring glinting under the light.

A long breath slips through my lips, anticipation rising. Is it odd that I've thought about him hundreds of times this weekend? Any time Donovan's harsh words crept into my head, I'd squash them down and replay my time with River, our movie quote exchanges, the way he steered his truck, for God's sake, and the most frequent thought? I'd recall the way he looked at me after the sun rose. The words he said...

Stop being silly, Ana.

He's here to be with the Kappas, not see you.

Yet...

Friday night our walls crashed down, and I got a peek at a side he's never shown me. Watching that sunrise with him, seeing a new day being born, it meant something.

To me.

I chew on my lip.

Okay, alright, let's be truthful. My body has some heady chemistry with his—

"Hmmm. A bad boy can be magical for a good girl," Lila says. "Come on. You'd like to lick his snake tattoo."

"No licking," I mutter.

"Just trail your tongue around that thigh, up his hip, to his ass—bite that, it's juicy—then circle back to his big—"

"Lila..." Carl warns. "Save that for your writing."

She grins. "Fine. I'll stop."

Carl looks at me. "Ana. I've seen you...how do y'all say it...checking him out."

I shake my head. "I only look, like everyone else. Don't rope him into this, Carl. We're just now getting to know each other and—"

He pats my hand. "Leave it to me, darling."

Ugh.

I look at the door again, and River looks up and catches me staring. Coughing, I flip back around.

Carl throws up a hand and beckons him over. "Yo, over here, bro!"

He reverts to being twenty when he sees River. I see it every Sunday.

"Got a question for you, my man," Carl says as River arrives at the booth. "You're a man of big ideas, right?"

"That's what they say." River does a scan of the bar, pausing on the Kappas. His jaw pops when he sees Donovan and Harper.

With a sigh, he looks back at us.

"Have a seat, then. We need some input. It's an emergency," Carl says.

I cringe. "No, it's not—"

"And very confidential," Carl adds in a conspiratorial tone, ignoring me. "Therefore, no real names will be used. Cone of silence is now in progress." He waves his arms around the booth.

River taps his fingers against his leg as his eyes drift over me. My face flushes as I catch my reflection in the metal napkin dispenser. My hair is up in a messy knot, I'm wearing deep red lipstick, and I didn't wear my contacts, picking my big white glasses instead.

"This is vital, River," Lila declares.

"Your brothers can wait," Carl says.

"Alright." He folds his tall frame into the booth next to Carl and across from me.

Marilyn brings him a Guinness, and he takes a sip of it. "What's up?"

Carl props an elbow on the table. "Let's say, hypothetically, there's a girl. She has her own personal demon to slay. You know how that is, right?"

River nods. "Indeed."

"She's been dumped in a nasty way and wants to get back at her ex. Let's also say, hypothetically, this girl is thinking the best way to get back at him is to find a 'hottie'—"

"To bang," Lila throws in.

"—thus making Donovan regret everything," Carl continues after a glare at Lila. "River, in your opinion, is this a good idea, or do you have other suggestions?"

"Kill me now," I whisper.

River's shoulder twitches. "Hypothetically, of course, assuming the relationship is truly over—"

"Oh, it's over. He's kicked to the curb. She ain't ever hitting that again," interjects Lila. Everyone stares at her. "Hypothetically," she mutters.

River continues, "I'd say she'd be well within her rights." He holds a finger up. "However, it would be wrong to pursue a member of her ex's fraternity...you know, if he's in one."

"The hypothetical ass sure is," I mutter as I lean in

over the table. "So, what do you think of this..." My voice trails off.

"Revenge plan?" River raises an eyebrow.

"Such a strong word," I say. "Any thoughts on *who* she should—"

"Screw," Lila finishes in a loud whisper.

I sigh. "Can't you be good?"

She shrugs.

River peels at the label on his bottle, his gaze lowered. "I'd suggest she find a hottie"—his lips tighten —"at a rival fraternity, *or* a super-smart guy. I'm assuming this hypothetical ex is smart?"

"Yes," I say.

Carl taps his chin. "Someone he'd be envious of! The plot thickens."

"No plot," I say. "This is all conjecture."

"A pre-med, pre-law, or physics major," Lila exclaims. "Genius. The Phi Beta Kappas are doing the ski trip—all brains, skinny arms, and geeky, but you like that, Ana."

Do I?

My eyes brush over the leather jacket on River, the slope of his broad shoulders, the color of his gaze. Tonight, the gray of his irises hints at smoke and his lashes flutter against his cheeks as he breaks our gaze.

"If I Can't Have You" by Shawn Mendes plays on the speakers, a song about keeping your distance, about hating to admit how you really *feel* about someone you can't have.

Goose bumps skate over my arms.

Why does that song make me think of him?

He twists his ring. "Let's say there's a third guy in this scenario. He's a good friend of her ex. He's a popular athlete—hypothetically. If this girl wanted, he could help her find the *right* guy. He knows everyone, could help by introducing her to the perfect rebound."

My chest rises, nerves flying. "What does this third person want in return?"

He takes a sip of his beer and sets it down gingerly, eyes downcast. "This guy needs a favor."

"What?" I ask, my voice lowering.

"He has four days to write a paper. He needs this girl to tutor him. It will mean a lot of work on her part, but he'll make it worthwhile on the ski trip he's going on."

Lila looks between all of us. "I'm hypothetically confused. There're too many fake people in this conversation." She rolls her eyes. "River, will you help Ana find the right booty call that will make Donovan jealous if she helps you in that lit class?"

There's a tense silence, then, "Sounds good to me," he says in a tight voice. He rubs a circle on the table with his finger.

Lila faces me. "Ana, will you help River so he will set you up with some fine-ass man you can diddle, which will ensure Donavon knows you are better than him in every way?"

I glance over and see Harper trailing her fingers down Donovan's arm.

My jaw sets.

"Are you for real?" I ask River, a tremor in my voice.

He looks up at me, and my breath snags at the uncertainty I see in his eyes.

"Yes."

Five seconds pass as we stare at each other.

Revenge *would* be sweet.

Me showing Donovan I've moved on. With someone he'd be envious of...

"Then let's rock this." I breathe out and extend my hand for a handshake.

He exhales and takes my hand, his thumb skating over my palm, lingering. Fire goes up my arm.

"Hell yeah!" Lila calls. "Progress! My girl's got balls!"

I barely notice her, and River doesn't acknowledge her either. He drops my hand, picks up his beer, and takes a swig, never dropping his eyes. I see emotion there, hot and fierce.

Heat builds on my face.

Carl clears his throat, a little laugh coming from him as he watches us. "Alright, then. Crazy Carl saves the day! By the power vested in me by the aliens, I pronounce you participants in this hypothetical revenge pact. You may now drink up."

I don't have a drink, but I lower my lashes and watch River take another swig. I take in his muscled arms, the way his broad shoulders flex, the way his eyes drape over me.

Um, we made a pact for a rebound, but...

Come on, let's be real.

The ultimate revenge would be to bang River. His frat brother.

I can't do that.

Right?

16

River

I burst through the front door of the house I share with Crew and Hollis. Tossing my jacket on the coat rack, I take in the place and storm to the kitchen, throwing dirty dishes in the sink then throwing a dishtowel over them. Darting to the den, I pick up cups and plates and an empty Funyun bag—disgusting—and run them to the kitchen.

"Whoa. Who's coming over this late?" Hollis asks as he looks back at me from the couch. "I'm getting ready to watch the game."

"Anastasia." I throw shoes into our basket near the door. Doesn't anyone pick up in this house? Okay, most of them are mine.

There's a quizzical expression on his face. "Really?"

"Yeah."

"Dude. I thought you were gonna wait, like your dad said."

"It's a study thing. The library closes early on Sundays, so it's my place or the Kappa house and, well, we all know we can't go there. Our house is the only option. I don't want to go to her place. That feels worse. Right? At least I'm in control here. I don't know. Dammit. She's going to be here any minute. She gets off at ten..." I jerk up a damp towel someone left on the ground. (It was me.)

"I can help you write it," he offers.

"You suck at lit."

"True." He props his feet on the coffee table, scratches his abs, and picks up the remote to click the TV on.

"Put a shirt on. Geeze. No one wants to see your six-pack but you."

He waves a hand at his chest. "You're just jealous 'cause I'm cut like diamonds. How did this study thing come about?"

"I saw her at the bar," I explain. Crew and Hollis weren't there tonight. "She wants a rebound, and Crazy Carl was there. I wasn't even going to sit down with them, but I did, and now I made a deal for her help with my paper. She's going on the ski trip with me, and I said I'd find her a guy." I pause. "Basically, I'm insane."

He nods. "The best people are. Guess you aren't telling Donovan about the study thing?"

"Not sure why he would need to know. He wouldn't like it, I'm sure. It's too late now. I mean, my mouth was saying crap while my brain was yelling *What are you doing?*, and holy shit, *It was my idea.* I couldn't stop, and what if she figures out I can't understand these books and thinks I'm stupid—"

Crew comes out of his room, frowning. At least he has a shirt on. "Ana's coming over?"

"Yeah," I say.

He checks me out. "You look sober."

"It's a class thing," I mutter. "Nothing else."

"You're wound tight, bro. You okay?" he adds as I spin my ring.

"We're on your side" comes from Hollis as he stands. "One hundred fucking percent. If you wanna take a shot at her, it will cause some strife with the brothers, can't lie, but we support *you.* I said to keep it in your pants, but I was joking. You do you."

It's not anything they haven't said before.

But I *am* the president.

He *is* my friend.

"We're just studying," I say, stalking into the kitchen. Everything is piling up in my head. Her. This class. My future at Braxton. *Mom.*

It makes it hard to figure out what to do.

I wipe off the counters with a paper towel then head to my bedroom and shut the door, my eyes darting from one mess to another.

In record time, I make my bed, straighten my desk, and shove all the dirty clothes in the closet or under the bed, whichever is closest—just as the doorbell rings.

I dash to the bathroom and check my hair, fingers rearranging it. I toss on some cologne—then stop. No attracting the hot girl.

I hear her voice out in the den, and I step out and walk that way.

She's talking to Hollis—who's put a shirt on—and Crew.

There's a hesitant look on her face, as if she doesn't quite know what to say to them, and I hate it. Normally she'd be laughing with them. They're nice to her, asking how she is and what her plans are for exams and Christmas.

Her green eyes find mine and she pushes her glasses up nervously. She's gone home to grab her laptop and has changed into black leggings and a gray Braxton sweatshirt with a Badger on it.

"How was June?" I ask, infusing my voice with nonchalance.

She smiles. "Changed her bandages. Took her dinner. She's good. It's colder tonight, but, ah, yeah, she refuses any help. Thank you for asking."

"Who's June?" Crew asks.

She pauses. "Family."

I nod, not able to take my eyes off her.

She's in my fucking house.

"No trouble finding our place?" I ask.

"I've known where you live for a while." She taps her temple. "Locked in my safe."

I huff out a laugh. "Touché."

"You didn't think I'd remember you being at my apartment, but I do. I can't believe I thought you were a mirage projected by my brain." A blush steals up her face. "I really can't believe I danced—"

"You went low, low, low..." I grin. Oh, I recall it very well. Her heart-shaped, perfect ass, the bare skin of her waist, the press of her full breasts against her shirt, the way her hair fell around her face, the teasing glint in her eyes when she begged me to dance—

Pause that thought. Shit. Right. No flirting. Was I flirting? Nah, I was being nice. Just nice. That's it. I swear.

We all stare at each other in silence. No one seems to know what to say.

"This isn't weird at all," Hollis murmurs under his breath with a smirk as he passes me to head into the kitchen to grab a drink.

She fidgets as she toys with the strap on her backpack. "Um, what now? I brought my notes and the book. Where do you want to do this?"

"Hollis and Crew usually watch Sunday night football, so I thought we'd go to my room. It's down the hall on the left."

She says bye to the guys and follows me to my room.

I shut the bedroom door behind me. "Um, I only have one chair, so if you want to sit on the bed, I'll take the desk."

She nods, slips off her Chucks, and sits cross-legged on my navy comforter. Her eyes sweep my room, snagging on a framed picture of me, Mom, Rae, and Callie. Snow-capped hills are behind us as we pose outside our house last Christmas. My throat tightens. Mom probably had cancer in that picture, but we wouldn't know it for months.

Beautiful, tall, and statuesque, she met my dad his first year in the NFL. Her story is, *I took one look at that fine piece of ass and said, I'm going to make him mine.* Since he died, she's never dated. *Real love, true and beautiful, comes only one time, River. And someday, we'll be together. The universe wouldn't be so cruel as to deny me another chance to see him. Heaven or hell, I don't care.*

Anastasia fluffs up a pillow and props her laptop on it, then opens it. Her eyes drift over the queen-sized bed and she waves her arms around. "So, this is where the magic happens."

"Magic?"

"You know what I mean."

"No girls come back here."

"Oh. You just get your freak on at the Kappa house, huh?"

I drop my gaze from her face and take the seat at my desk. Not touching that. "We can use the library next go-round. Sorry my room is a wreck. Don't open the closet or look under the bed. Health hazard. It's mostly clothes and shoes. I have a slight addiction to showers and things pile up like crazy. I'm up to three a day..." I stop, realizing I'm rambling.

She dips her head and smiles. "So, how much do you have written? I can take a look—"

I stiffen as I open my laptop. "I've got some notes down, but no paper." I pause. "I used speech-to-text dictation, and it's accurate about seventy percent of the time, so it's kind of messy." Understatement!

"Interesting. Never used that. Our paper is due Friday. It's going to be tight, River."

Tell me about it. "I've been procrastinating. I'm not a book lover," I say stiffly.

"Why did you take this class?"

I ignore that.

"Here. What do you think?" I hand over the notes, and she takes the paper, her forehead furrowing. Based on previous experiences, it's a jumbled mess. Usually I spend hours going over papers I have to write, which aren't many. Hello, easy classes.

She's quiet for way too long, and dread grows, beating at me. My head races with a hundred thoughts at once: *how many words are misspelled, is the punctuation screwy, how wonky is the layout, does any of it make sense?*

What's she thinking?

Why doesn't she say *something*?

"I listened to the book," I say warily. "Twice. Audio is better for me. Otherwise, it's hard to focus and..." the vocabulary in those books is ridiculous.

Her eyes come up. "This is a start." She taps her chin. "Let's talk about the theme and narrow down the points you want to make."

"Restorative sex. I totally stole that from you."

"Well, it's the most common theme, so we're good. Whitman is a jerk, so ignore him. He knows we'll all focus on the sex." She huffs out a laugh. "What did you think about the intercourse in the book, you know, how it develops the characters?"

My chest rises. This I can do. I *can* talk.

"It was wordy, flowery. Sure, they fuck a lot. Outside, inside, everywhere, but it's not a happy story. I prefer suspense like *American Psycho*, but that book spent chapters describing every character's clothing and accessories. It was insane. *Lolita*? Creeped me out and was downright bizarre, even though he tried to write it beautifully, I guess? The main character abused a teenage girl and called it love."

She pales, and I realize what I've said and lean forward. "Wait. Don't let your head go there, please, Anastasia, I'm sorry I even brought that book up to you—"

"No, it's fine. I want to address it." She bites her lip. "The connotation of the term *Lolita* means a sexually precocious young girl who seduces, and I know Donovan said that about me, but I didn't seduce Bryson."

Bryson. So that's his name. I twist my ring.

"Never in a million years would I believe you did." I'd like to pay a visit to this douchebag. "He was a grown-ass man and shouldn't have touched you."

She stares at my comforter. "I was—*am*—surprisingly naïve even though my parents encouraged me to be a free spirit." She touches her throat, rubbing it. "I never went to a real school, never got to spend time with people my own age. If my parents got the urge to go anywhere alone, they went and left me with friends, usually artists, writers, scholars. Most of the people I stayed with were wonderful. I learned some cool things, you know? I saw Mount Everest, the Great Wall of China, the pyramids in Egypt, the Colosseum in Rome..." She breathes in deep. "It sounds weird, me and Bryson, but just... I want you to know that I loved him, as much as a seventeen-year-old girl can, and I thought it was normal, because I didn't *know* any different." She lets her breath out slowly.

He hurt you.

"Talk to me, Anastasia." I prop my elbows on my knees.

She dips her face and stares at my comforter. Her shoulders hunch. "Did he take advantage of me? Yes. He was thirty, and I was inexperienced." She bites her bottom lip. "I didn't know he was married. My parents didn't know. His sister and another girl lived there at the beginning, otherwise my parents wouldn't have left me. I could have called and told them I was alone with him, but I didn't. The day I met his wife, my whole world fell apart. We never had any contact after he dropped me off..." She sighs. "Anyway, Donovan's parents managed to dig all that up. It's crazy. I didn't steal his car, either. He let me have the keys. I thought I was his girlfriend." A rough sound comes from her throat. "I didn't know he got a divorce." Her brow furrows. "He had a toddler. Maybe more kids, I don't know. There's a family out there that I messed up—"

"*He* messed up his family," I say firmly. "And if I ever see him, I'm going to punch him." My jaw pops.

She inhales a deep breath. "Wow," she says softly as she stares at the floor. "Underneath your exterior, you aren't what I thought at all. Just layers and layers." Her eyes find mine. "You're making me like you too much, Snake."

"It's impossible to resist me."

"Hmmm, enough of that." She glances back at the notes in her hands. "Let's chat about *Lady Chatterley's Lover.*"

Do we have to?

"Right. The book."

That *is* why she's here.

"I get that they used sex. Their passion covered up their problems." I pause. "The issue is..." I can't read these books fast enough *and* comprehend them. A long exhalation comes from my chest. "I struggle to put my ideas on paper."

"What's your reading comprehension level?"

Anxiety ripples over me. "Why?"

"It's a difficult book, River. I just want to get an idea —" She stops, her eyes squinting at me. "Is there more than just the ADHD going on?"

My heartrate spikes. I jerk up from my seat. "You want a drink? I need water."

She blinks. "Sure. Water is great."

I leave the room and stop in front of the fridge. Unfocused, I open the door and peer inside. The football game plays in the background, and I'm not sure how long I stand there, my head tumbling. She and I... It feels as if we're speeding closer and closer to *something*, and I'm on the edge of my seat with anxiety.

She's so fucking smart. And I'm not.

She's going to figure me out and—

"Everything good?" Hollis calls out.

"Perfect," I mutter.

I grab two waters and head back.

She's moved on my bed, propped up against the headboard as she gazes down at the notes. She glances up. "Just a guess—you're dyslexic? It would explain your reluctance to read, the audio, and speech-to-text notes."

My eyes flare as my mouth opens but nothing comes out.

"Judging by your face, I'm right, which means you didn't tell me because you're worried about what I think. You can trust me, River. I've done tutoring for athletes, and it's not uncommon. Everything we discuss is confidential."

My breathing escalates.

The silence in the room builds, and I'm aware, *totally aware*, that I'm backed into a corner.

She crawls to the edge of the bed and stands in front of me. "Wait—do you think I'd think less of you? If anything, I think *more* of you. Look at everything you've accomplished."

"I don't want pity."

"It's not pity. Your differences don't define you. It

makes reading harder, and probably a host of other things I can't even imagine. It means you're different, yes, but in a good way. You see things with a unique viewpoint, and honestly, the world needs more of that. I know we haven't been...close, but I-I see a side of you that's amazing and sort of beautiful. There's a softness under your evil smile." Her hands flutter in front of her, an uncertain look on her face.

I realize two things: she's as nervous as I am, and she *sees* me.

I set the water bottles on the desk. "You're the first person to say that besides my mom. Not the evil smile part—the beautiful part. Keep talking."

She rolls her eyes, huffing out a laugh. "You do things for others, especially Benji—you bought him that lizard. You talk to Parker about his sister when everyone else is afraid to bring it up. You're more in tune to emotions than facts. You're one of the most creative people I've ever met. You dream up fun things for the pledges. The dance contest was brilliant. Others before you have taken dyslexia combined with ADHD and accomplished great things. Whoopi, Justin Timberlake, Michael Phelps, Tim Tebow. I'm sure there are more—"

"And dyscalculia. Tack that on too." I pause, unsure how to continue, not sure if I want to. This is too revealing!

"No judgment. The more you open up to me, the

better." Her tone is soft. "I know you're intelligent. Your IQ is off the charts, I bet."

I swallow, and something that's been buried deep loosens. What if, what if with her, I can just let go?

Then I remember my ex laughing at me.

I stalk around the room, pacing.

"Talk to me, River."

I stop, my chest heaving as I rake a hand through my hair.

"Truth? My brain is wired like a crazy funhouse at a carnival. You walk in and don't know what to fix first, so instead you hop on the rollercoaster that happens to be there and enjoy the ride. There are colors everywhere, dangling wires, uneven floors, and wacky staircases. That's just my ADHD. The other stuff...I think in pictures rather than words." A sigh escapes my chest. "I'm messy and disorganized. It's the Bermuda Triangle, no shit, in my head. Reading out loud? Insanity. It will give me a panic attack. I can't breathe, like someone has their hands around my throat. It feels like everyone is looking at me, waiting, waiting to see *if* I can read. I will run from the room. I did once in middle school. It took an entire day for my dad to find me hiding under the bleachers. Menus? I rely on pictures or order the same thing over and over. Overheads and PowerPoints? Forget it. They move too fast for me to keep up. Computer screens? A hassle. Elevator buttons? Hate them. Algebra? The numbers dance on the page, getting jumbled, and I can't focus enough to make them stop. Road signs? I use GPS. Hospitals and big buildings here at school? I want to scream until, finally, I can make them stick in my head. I memorize football plays. I make these big flashcards and know them by heart. I just...fuck! These banned books are a goddamn nightmare—"

She's moved closer and takes my hands.

I freeze, realizing my voice had risen toward the end.

Then, I'm acutely aware of the feel of her skin against mine. Sparks zing along my nerve endings.

I stare down at our intertwined hands, my big ones and her small, delicate ones. My frustration crashes and dies, snuffed out by her touch.

"It's okay to vent. Anger builds inside of us, especially with things we can't control. Breathe. Tell me your three things."

A small laugh escapes me. Oh, oh, she thinks I froze because I'm upset about my issues. Rainbow, that may have been it at first, but now...

She's a River-whisperer runs through my head as I lean into her. She feels so good. Hesitant and unsure, her arms wrap around my waist and her forehead presses to my chest. She exhales, her face moving as her cheek rests against me.

Can she hear the fast beat of my heart?

I exhale a deep breath as I rest my chin on the top of her head and hold her against me.

It's not a sexual touch; it's accepting and real, and fucking alright. I'm not making any moves on her. This is legit friendship stuff. A hug. A comforting hold. One I wanted to do at the sunrise but resisted.

I'm totally okay, totally fine.

I'm not doing a damn thing wrong.

You are!

A bolt of pain shoots through my skull. "Dammit," I groan.

"What's wrong?" She looks up at me.

With reluctance, I shake my head and ease away from her to drop down to sitting on the bed.

"Headache. Tension. I reached my limit. At the worst possible time when I need to get this paper done. I get them on and off. This whole week is catching up with me..." My voice trails off and I grimace.

"What helps your head?"

I huff out a laugh as I rub my temples. "Ha. Not going there."

She sits down next to me on the bed, her leg against mine. "Huh?"

"Sex helps, Anastasia. And it's been a long time."

She blinks rapidly. "Can I get you an Aleve?"

"I'm kidding." Not. "It's just... I need to relax to make

it disappear. I go and go and go and then my body is like, *Stop thinking so much.*"

"Ah." Her arm brushes against mine, and the blood rushes to my groin. Trying to be discreet, I shift my jeans around. That hug wasn't just a friendly one... Jesus! What am I doing with her?

"I get it. You need your own restorative sex. Funny. One of the best quotes in *Lady Chatterley's Lover* is from Oliver, 'We fucked a flame into being.' You think we can fuck your headache away?" She throws me a look.

"What?"

"Kidding. Seems to be the theme of the day. Look, I can leave, and you can call a girl—"

"No," I mutter.

"Okay."

I lie back and sprawl out on the bed.

She lies down next to me, and my breath stutters in my chest. She's pushing me, pushing me...

We both stare at the ceiling of my room, which is pretty damn unremarkable. But it is clean.

And I'm not looking at her.

Because it's dangerous.

Winning.

She props her arms behind her head. "Since you brought up sex—"

"Hello, it's the topic of our paper—"

"—have you thought about us?" She pauses. "It's

just...that day in the kitchen was intense, right? Did I dream that?"

Damn. She went there.

"Never thought of us together," I lie to the ceiling.

There's a pause. "Oh. Well. That's good. We're total opposites."

Are we?

I have my doubts. We're both a little rudderless, both of us on the cusp of an uncertain future. She's random as hell. So am I. She looks at people like she needs them, like she cares, and I hope I do too.

I turn my head and gaze at her. There's a foot between us, but it feels like less. She's gazing at me, a glint in her eye, and I wonder how long that's been going on.

"You put on fresh lipstick," I say softly. My eyes linger on her mouth, that full bottom lip, the little V in the upper part. Deep red. Soft.

I want to crush it.

"So what?" she asks.

"To come over here. To see me."

"To *help* you. I didn't put it on for *you*."

"You looked to the left when you said that. That's *your* tell when you lie. FYI, people generally look to the left when they lie."

She props her head up with her palm. "Don't

comment on my lipstick—unless you plan on kissing me. It's a rule. I just made it."

I ease up and prop my head up like she did. "Serious talk: I guess we need rules. No kissing. We both know what will happen if I kiss you."

"Hold on. You said you'd never thought about it."

"I'm a dude—now I'm thinking about it."

She curls her lips. "Huh. I can guess what would happen. You'd get grossed out and puke or die from the poison on my tongue. I'd faint from bliss because you are so awesome. Right?"

"If you're trying to hit on me, mentioning puke is not the way to go—"

"Like I'd hit on you! *Please.* You're the last man on earth I'd ever consider—"

"As I was saying, if we kissed, it would lead to us doing more, and that can never happen..." My voice trails off.

Her eyes search mine. "Donovan is your friend."

"Not like Crew and Hollis and Benji, but yeah. We pledged together. He was there for me when one of the other pledges slept with my girlfriend. He supported me in getting him kicked out. We've spent over three years hanging out together as brothers."

"He broke up with me in a horrible way," she says with a defiant tilt of her chin.

"It just happened, and you're hurting. Right now, you

want to lash out at him, and I get that—I would too—but you can't use me."

"Jesus, get over yourself. I wasn't going to! I made one little comment and you can't let it go." She jumps up off the bed and prowls around my room. She picks up the picture of my family and sighs. "Beautiful," she murmurs, then heads to the closet, opens it, and gapes. I don't even try to stop her. It's not *that* bad.

"What are you thinking?" I ask as she walks back to the end of the bed.

"What I think, what I think...hmmm, you really want to know?"

"Yeah?" I say uneasily. I know I'm saying all the wrong shit, but I can't seem to stop. Why did I bring up her lipstick? Why did I insinuate that she was hitting on me?

It's me. *Me.* I'm poking the tiger, seeing where she is...

A hesitant expression crosses her face. "I'm not sure you can handle it. I'm not sure my ego can."

"You can't be vague like that. I think we've come a long way, so lay it out."

She takes a deep breath. "Alright. You asked for it. I think we have some kind of connection. Like, I know this is crazy, but since day one in the library, there was something between us. Insta-hate? Insta-attraction?"

My heart pounds.

Not hate, Rainbow.

"You can deny all you want, but it's there. If you kissed me, hate or attraction, yeah, we'd probably hook up just to get it out of our systems, and that has *nothing* to do with my ex." She sighs.

I stand up, uncertain how to reply.

"How's your head?" she asks.

"Better. Strange...they usually last hours. You think we have a connection?" I can't let it go.

"Yes, but..." A frustrated expression flits over her face. "I guess we *do* need ground rules. First, no talking about my lips. And stop saying my name like you want to fuck it."

"Hmmm. Anastasia," I murmur, dragging out the syllables. "Sounds totally normal to me."

"It's not!" She inhales.

"Sorry." Not.

"Moving on, tomorrow, we'll meet in the library at eight. Don't be late, and don't have any of your hangers-on with you—"

"Who?"

Her eyes spear me. "Don't act like you don't have girls all over you."

"Anything else?"

"Yeah, I'm rearranging my schedule at the bar to fit you in this week. Don't waste my time. Bring your book and your notes. Keep up the work in the meantime. Also,

Lila mentioned a possible candidate for this revenge thing—"

"What? Already?"

"—and he just so happens to be in a study group at the library during the week. Don't ask how Lila knows these things. She just does."

My voice lowers and I cross my arms. "I thought you were waiting until the ski trip." I don't want to think about this part of our revenge pact yet.

"No time like the present. Might as well get my rebound in, check it off, post the hell out of it, then continue at the ski trip. Yeah, he's going."

"Who is this guy?" I mutter, a tight feeling growing in my chest.

She fiddles around in her backpack, pulls out her phone, and shows me a picture Lila texted her. I lean into her space and check him out. He's handsome, I guess, dark hair, olive skin, and a blinding white smile. Prick.

"You know him?"

My lips compress. "Kian Brewster. Top of his class, going to Cal Tech for grad school, not Greek but popular, comes to parties we host, not a great people person, in my opinion, but also not a good friend with Donovan. He's considered a genius."

"Wow. In awe."

"Again, I recall details that don't matter."

"Still. No wonder people love you. You *know* them."

"Mhmm."

"Anyway, Lila says his ex cheated on him with her ex, so we have similar situations. I've seen him but haven't talked to him, but we can mosey past their study group and you can do the intros. *Here, meet Ana, she's awesome, hey you two should hang out, and maybe get in her pants on the ski trip* kind of thing. But not too obvious. I'm trusting you to handle that aspect. You're the social butterfly and I'm the shy moth in this scenario. He's perfect, and not bad to look at. Yes?" She pushes it at me again, and my nose flares.

Okay, I lied about him being a prick. He's an alright dude.

So why do I want to rip the phone out of her hand and stomp on it?

"You're really going to do this?"

"Did you doubt me? *Please.* I'm a woman of my word. We made a pact. I help you, I get a rebound fuck. Revenge is oh so sweet." She purses her lush lips, her attitude fiery.

At the sound of that dirty word on her lips, jealousy and lust slam into me. Every atom in my body buzzes. I want to push her against the wall, wrap her legs around my waist, and show her exactly how I fuck, hard and fast, her hair clenched in my hands, my name on her lips—

Whoa.

She tells me some things to work on for my paper then she's out the door. She said bye, but I didn't reply.

I suck in a deep breath and fall back on the bed. I stare up at the ceiling, replaying everything in my head, from the moment she entered the house to the words she uttered.

She thinks my differences make me *better*.

A smile ghosts over my face—before I shut it down.

How the hell am I going to walk away when she finds her guy?

17

River

I stuff the last of an unsalted pretzel into my mouth as I come out of the student center on Tuesday afternoon. Damn, it tastes pretty good. Who knew? I smile at nothing, probably looking like an idiot as I think about Anastasia's lame comebacks outside the elevator.

I laugh, and a guy walking past gives me a long look.

I'm not crazy, my glance tells him. Just high on life, and those moments have been few and far between lately.

"Good day," I murmur to myself. I checked off a study session with her in the library last night and kept my cool. Even though we sat side by side, I kept myself in line and got work done. It *was* hard, the proximity, can't say it wasn't, but we focused on the book. Just being around her soothes me in a way I can't explain.

My phone rings.

"Mom!" I hitch my backpack up on my shoulder and head across campus.

"Hey, honey," she says.

Frowning, I stop in front of one of the giant oak trees on the quad. "You only call me honey when you sit me down and impart wisdom you think I need to hear."

"Ha. Funny. Trust me, you always needed it. Remember that time you thought it was a good idea to ski down a diamond slope at thirteen, then ended up in a new town on the other side of the mountain? Or the time you let a skunk in the house because you thought it was a stray cat? The house was covered in skunk spray and your father and I had to move us to a hotel for five days. I won't even mention the day you shaved off your sister's eyebrows."

"I was ten and she asked me to," I say on a small chuckle.

"Never a dull moment with you." She sighs.

"How was your doctor's appointment? The tests?"

"Some of my exhaustion has abated. I went to the grocery store today after my visit. I can smell food without gagging. Life is good."

"You didn't answer my question."

I hear Callie in the background. "Nana, color

with me!"

My hand grips the phone as my voice lowers. "Is it gone? Did the chemo work?" She beat it once. She beat it once...

There's a long pause.

"Progression." Her words are soft. "It's okay, I promise. This is something I prepared for mentally. Been there, checked out the library book. My spirit is stronger than cancer. You know it, *I* know it..." She stops, her breath hitching.

My world crashes. "Mom..."

She clears her throat. "We can cry. We can shake our fist at God. We can scream if we want, we can, and trust me, I have, but we don't give up."

"I'm not," I say, closing my eyes. "Never."

"I know you aren't, but I need to remind you. And myself." She pauses, and I picture her face, see her in our kitchen, battling to be strong for me.

"Was Rae with you? You weren't alone?"

"She was with me." She pauses. "Sometimes certain drugs work and sometimes they don't. Our bodies are all different. Not all treatments are the same, and they're monitoring me closely. It doesn't mean all is lost. It means a new way of fighting." A small laugh comes from her. "We hoped for a partial remission or just a stable prognosis, but I've got this, River. I'm a survivor. I'm the luckiest mom in the world. The best grandma ever."

Everything she says is the right thing, but...

"What happens next? Did they say?"

"Hmmm. I'm going to forget about the ugly C word. We'll figure out next steps after Christmas. These things take time."

Time? *Time?*

What's wrong with those doctors?

She needs to be surrounded by a team of people. Now.

I grapple with the tight feeling in my chest. "Shouldn't we be working on a plan?"

"I need to enjoy my holidays," she says softly. "I'm not giving up. I'm not. Not when I have so much to live for. You and Rae and Callie... I can't die. Just can't."

Emotion slams into me and I can't get air. My throat feels like it's going to close up.

She never says *die*. Never.

A group of Kappa pledges call my name and wave from about fifty feet away. They look as if they're going to come over, and I hold my hand up and shake my head.

"How do you feel?" I ask gruffly.

"Good."

I sigh at the lie in her words. "Hmmm, really?"

"I. Am. Fine. Some nerve damage I hadn't expected has set in. Neuropathy. I keep dropping shit. My hairbrush, a bowl of blueberries, a can of green beans on my big toe. That wasn't pretty. Can't wear button-up shirts anymore because of the tingles in my fingers. There's therapy to help with that, so it's fine. One more hill to conquer. My liver is acting up from the chemo, but hey, it's still there."

She talks to Callie for a moment—*Hey lovely, your flower is gorgeous*—then comes back to me. Her voice has a strange brightness to it. "I'm going to Callie's Christmas show at the preschool tonight. She's going to be an elf, can you believe it? You should see the costume: pointed green shoes, red stockings, and the most adorable little dress. Rae has whipped up some amazing chicken soup for me, and there's a new episode of *Schitt's Creek* waiting for me later. And I got to hear your voice. Those are my three, well four, things today. I love you, son, to the moon and back. When I close my eyes at night, I see your face and I swear, it makes everything okay. I'm so proud of the man you are. I know your father would be too. You keep up the good work. I should go."

"Mom, not yet."

The pledges call my name again and I turn my back to them. They don't get it; no one knows, no one, how much it hurts to imagine an existence without my mom, how deep that fear is inside me.

She inhales a sharp breath. "Oh, River. Don't. It's going to be okay." She pauses and I hear her rustling around, the sound of Callie's voice closer. "I dreamed about your father last night. Six years and I can still conjure his face in my head, down to the birthmark shaped like Tennessee on his shoulder and the amber glints in his eyes."

My hand clenches the phone. "Was the dream...was it like mine?"

A long breath comes from her. "I long for yours, River, to have him visit me, to have him hold my hand and tell me it's going to be okay. This one... It was our first wedding anniversary and he took me to that terrible Italian place in Manhattan..."

"Romano's?"

"Yeah. You remember." She laughs. "Anyway, the piped-in music was horrendous, our table was stuck next to the kitchen, the pasta was cold, the wine was too sweet, but we didn't care. He whispered in my ear how much he loved me, told me he couldn't wait to spend the rest of his life with me, and it wasn't nearly long enough, it wasn't..." She sucks in a breath.

"Mom?"

A cough comes from her. "I have some advice for you, about your Anastasia. And life, I guess."

Yeah, she knows about her.

"What?"

"If you never say the things you should, you might never. People can go away."

"I know."

"If you never get your degree, you might never. And

that's okay. It is. Maybe I've pushed you too much for the education. I believe in you and know what you're capable of. I wanted you to show everyone how very smart you are, but my concentration is shit, just muddled lately, and maybe I put too much on you."

"Mom..."

"I suppose what I'm trying to say is something has to give. Your semester ends Friday. Look out for yourself. Take what's yours. Just put your mighty hands on it and *take* it. Maybe it's your Anastasia. Maybe it's school. Maybe it's football. You decide what your dreams are."

I exhale.

She pushes out a laugh as Callie says hi to me through the phone. I talk to her for a few minutes, then she gives it back to Mom. Her voice is stronger. "Ah, yeah, Callie and I, we're going to color, then get her ready for the play. We'll talk more tomorrow?"

"Send me a picture," I say.

"Always. Bye. I love you."

She clicks off and sends an image through.

It's a selfie of her and Callie, their heads pressed together as they sit at the kitchen table. In the den, I see the Christmas tree with the gifts under it, the silver garland they put up on the staircase. Life keeps going, the world keeps spinning, Christmas still comes, even when she's sick.

My heart clenches as I look at her. She has a huge

smile on her face, but her eyes... I see a woman barely hanging on.

I drop my backpack and send her one of me smiling. It hurts, *it hurts* to smile, but I do it.

I've walked for five minutes, my head churning, before I glance up and notice people. The pledges have wandered off, but Harper, Mellany, and Audrey stand near the steps of the big fountain in the center of the quad, a hangout spot. They have their phones out, laughing, as I stalk over.

I'm in their space before they notice.

"River!" Audrey squeals and latches onto me.

"Don't touch me." I peel her off and look at Mellany. "Did you take down that post like I asked?" It wasn't really asking. I went to the Delta house Sunday night before Anastasia came over, got in Mellany's face, and told her to take it down. I actually went to their house on Saturday morning after I dropped Anastasia off, but she'd left town for the rest of the weekend. Otherwise, it would have been taken down earlier.

Mellany shrugs, a guarded look on her face. "I did what you said."

"Good. I'd hate to blacklist you from my frat, but I will if I see anything about Anastasia or Donovan posted, feel me?"

Harper laughs nervously. "Of course. It was the heat of the moment, River. It's over, done, and gone."

Yeah, but not before they made sure everyone had a chance to save it or screenshot it or whatever these drama queens do.

I flip around but then turn back. "One more thing, it would be super great if you three could not take the elevator in Wyler anymore. Stairs are good for cardio. In fact, now that I think about it, if you see Anastasia coming, just turn around and walk the other way. And be polite about it. Harper, stop flashing your bracelet in front of her. Nobody gives a shit. Oh, and in case you missed it over the PA system, he tried to give her one and it was bigger than yours."

They gape at me. Yeah.

On Monday, when they got on the elevator with us, I plastered myself next to Anastasia, a line of defense against them.

I'm on *her* side.

"What's up with you?" Audrey asks.

My nerves are stretched thin is what's up. "I take care of my people. She's one of them."

"We get it, River. She was a little sister, and you're trying to smooth things over for the frat," Harper says, her eyes hard. "But she never fit in with the Kappas—"

"He's done with you, isn't he?" I say curtly. "He ran to you, but it didn't mean jack. He used you to cut her off." I'm not sure if it's true, but it's what I suspect.

Her lips tighten as she tugs her sweater around her shoulders. "Stay out of it."

Ha. Too fucking late for that.

If she only knew the dark strings I pulled at the party...

My finger twists my ring, pushing that guilt away.

And Donovan?

He found me at the house on Monday afternoon, right before I met Anastasia in the library for the first time—which I didn't tell him about.

I said horrible things to her, River. I hate it. So much. Did I make a mistake, did I, what if I did? How can I fix this—

I kick down those thoughts.

"Yo! River!" comes Benji's voice as I pivot in the opposite direction of the Deltas. Donovan is with him and they jog over to me. Tension rolls over me and I clench my fists.

Jesus! Not now.

Donovan looks like crap, face drawn, his eyes flitting between me and the Deltas as they walk past us. Harper acts as if she might join us, even taking a step toward us, but he frowns, and she doesn't.

Called it.

After they've gone, he licks his lips and looks at me. "I meant to ask...did you see Anastasia in class yesterday? How was she?"

My jaw tightens.

Yeah. I sat next to her. I smiled at her. Then, I walked her to her next class.

"The usual." Lie.

"She didn't seem...upset?"

"I don't know, I didn't pay attention." Second lie. I barely noticed anything *but* her.

He rubs his forehead. "I've tried to call. She won't pick up."

"Hmmm." I look away. I'm going to see her tonight, and you don't even know.

Benji slaps me on the back, clearly trying to change the topic. "You headed home, to the house, or to work out?"

A long breath comes from me. "I'm taking a shower then working out."

Benji laughs. "Most people would reverse that order."

"Most people aren't me." I start walking.

"True that. You're one of a kind," Donovan says as he matches his steps with mine. He blows out a breath and sticks his hands in his pockets. "Hey, um, I've been kind of all over the place for the past few days. Just trying to figure it all out..."

"Mhmm."

He dips his head and stares at the ground as we walk. "I'm sorry I got up in your face backstage. You were right. I was trashed and didn't know what I was doing. I'm glad you came back there and stopped me from getting on stage. You're the best, man. Really. You always jump in when things go sideways."

Remorse gnaws at me. I am *not* the best. He has no clue the things I've done.

"I wish none of it had happened, wish I hadn't announced our drama for everyone to hear..." His voice trails off, a frown furrowing his forehead.

My teeth grit.

"Hey, you'll see her in class tomorrow. Could you, ah, maybe test the waters, see where she is?"

I sigh. "No, man. I need to stay out of it."

Donovan grimaces. "But you kind of *are* in it. You took her home after the party so you must have a feel for her thoughts." There's a hopeful look on his face, and my jaw pops. "Just maybe talk to her? Tell her I..." Donovan swallows, not finishing.

"You saw her at the bar Sunday. Why didn't you talk to her then?" I say tightly.

"I wasn't ready. It felt too fresh. Wasn't sure she'd let me."

"You asked for your pin back. And Harper was with you."

"I asked to get a reaction, but it didn't work. She ignored me. And Harper tagged along. I'm not with her," he adds vehemently. "*You*, though, *you* talked to Ana."

"I visited with Carl," I snap. "And then I went home. I didn't stick around. Don't drag me into this."

He lets out a heavy breath. "Right. Sorry. It's just... you're easy to talk to, and she might open up to you. I'm just trying to figure out if I can get a loan for Harvard or maybe, um, I don't know, apply to Brooklyn Law at the last minute."

What?

I mean I knew his revelation was coming, but fuck me, it feels fast.

"You don't sound sure, Donovan."

He chews on his lips. "Hard to give up a dream, man, but I love her—"

"I need to call my sister," I growl, stopping on the sidewalk.

"Okay," Benji says as they stop with me. His eyes dart between us. "Come on, let's hit the student center," he says to Donovan.

"Hey. Are you okay?" Donovan grabs my arm, studying my face.

No.

My mom is sick.

I don't know my future.

And guilt eats at me for what I *did* to them.

Without answering, I turn around and walk in the opposite direction. "Catch you guys later."

And then I'm gone, running, running...

18

Anastasia

How's it going? I write in my text to River as I come out of the shower. I'm going to see him in a few hours, but a yearning is there to check in and see how he is. It's Tuesday and we've already checked off two sessions, one in the library and the one in his room.

Where he rejected me. Kind of.

Yeah, I was testing the waters.

He wouldn't stop staring at my lips.

What else was I supposed to think?

Something *is* there.

It's just...

A tiny thread was born at the sunrise, something real and tangible, and I want to see where it leads.

He sat next to me in class Monday, his leg pressed

against mine, his hands tapping out a beat only he could hear. I watched the flash of his ring, taking in the silver, wondering what it would feel like to have those hands on my skin, sliding into my hair, up my thighs, parting my legs, then I was down a rabbit hole of him kissing me.

Heat washed over me, and I had to look away from the visceral pull of him, his magnetic aura that sucks me into his orbit. I brushed my arm against his more than I should have. I smiled at him. I honest to God have no clue what Whitman talked about. It's like we have a secret, a little thing between us that only we know—or maybe it's just me.

We left class and he walked me to my next one. I couldn't tell you one person we passed or saw. We talked about *Lady Chatterley's Lover*, his football season, his mom, his sister, his niece, and Crazy Carl. Turns out, he digs him as much as I do. I explained how anxious I was when I first came to Braxton, my first foray into a true campus with people my own age. It's like... I wanted to tell him a whole year's worth of things about me, trying to catch him up.

We walked slow, dragging out the minutes, and he stared at my lips when we said goodbye. And when I got inside my building, I looked out the window, and he was still standing at the bottom of the steps.

I wasn't kidding about that connection.

Five minutes pass, then another before a ping comes in on my phone, and I wonder if he's checking his spelling or using speech-to-text to reply. Dyslexia might make texting difficult.

Wrote intro. Stayed up late after our session. Be amazed when I meet you tonight.

A long sigh comes from me as I tighten the sash on my robe. A smile curls my lips as I sprawl back on my bed. *You wow me already, River.* You're kind in small ways I don't think others see, and you're intelligent, not only intellectually, but emotionally. He's tuned in, and when he talks about his three things, it makes my heart skip. I want to reply with all of that, but, well, I shouldn't.

I prop my pillows up against the bed and impulsively FaceTime him. He doesn't answer.

Where are you? I send.

Home.

Then why can't he answer his phone?

Five more minutes pass.

Are you ignoring me because you're "getting rid of a headache"?

Crickets.

I have some questions. How do you feel about sex on the first date? You know, for my rebound. Personally, I've never had a one-night stand, but my life is a little wacky right now. I could be persuaded.

Since the party, my filter has gone up in smoke.

He's skating a razor's edge too.

Monday in the elevator with River, when the Deltas got on, he plastered himself to my side like a guard. We leaned against the back wall and he ignored the girls, even Audrey, who kept looking over her shoulder at him with her come-hither glances. When Harper flashed her tennis bracelet, he slipped his arm around me and pressed his hand to the small of my back as if to say *Steady now*.

He FaceTimes me and I squeak. My hair is in a towel and I have a robe on. What was I thinking wanting to see his face? Obviously, I wasn't.

WTF. Answer your phone, he sends when I don't pick up.

I call him, no FaceTime, and he answers. "Anastasia, do you have a guy with you?" he snaps into the phone.

"No! I was just..."

"What?"

"Curious. About what you think, I guess, about dating..." I roll my eyes at my own lameness.

There's a brief silence. "You want to chat about dating?" His tone is dry.

"I don't have a lot of experience. Who have you dated? I mean, there's Audrey, of course, but that's not what I mean." There's a long silence and my fingers pluck at my comforter, feeling antsy. "I told you about

Bryson. Who broke your heart, or is it made of fire and brimstone?"

He exhales and I hear rustling sounds, like fabric.

"Are you in your bed?" I ask. "It's four in the afternoon. I can't imagine you napping."

"Mhmm, no. Just got out of the shower."

"Me too," I say.

"What are you wearing?"

"Nothing."

"Nothing?" His breath catches.

"That's what I said. What are you wearing?"

"Nothing."

My voice lowers. "Nothing?"

"That's what I said."

Jumping up, I take my robe off, make sure the bedroom door is locked, then lie back down. Not telling tales now.

"Who was she? The girl who broke your heart?" I don't know the whole story, but I've heard of an incident at the house.

"Blair. Freshman year. My pledge brother screwed her. He got kicked out of the frat."

"You loved her," I say with wonder in my voice.

"She made an impression."

I imagine a brokenhearted River and anger washes over me. I picture a goddess of a girl, sorority type, a tinkling laugh, a lush body. Another Audrey, only sexier.

Longer legs and giant boobs. Probably has a magical vagina.

I glance down at my boobs. They're perky. Full. I've had no complaints. I blow out a breath. *Blair, Blair,* I rack my head for a girl to put with the name, but I don't know enough of the popular crowd, and I imagine she doesn't come to their parties.

"Was she beautiful?" My voice is sullen. And I can't even stop it. Ugh.

"Yes."

"Do you still love her?"

"Came to my senses pretty quick."

"Like you had an epiphany. A come-to-Jesus."

"Just woke up one day and wondered what I ever saw in her. She wasn't who I thought. Integrity and faithfulness mean something to me."

"What helped you realize she wasn't the one? Was it another girl?"

"Why do you want to know?"

Because I'm figuring you out, delving into those layers, seeing the man underneath.

"Just wondering how fast *I* can bounce back. I guess getting my revenge will bring some satisfaction."

"You think it'll be worth it?"

"I think it will feel good temporarily, a new pair of hands on my body, learning my secrets. Making me come. Yes."

There's a ragged sound to his voice. "You went there..." He makes a muffled, groaning sound, and butterflies flutter in my stomach.

"I've seen your face when you come. I wonder what mine looks like. Does this mean I need to have sex in front of a mirror? Could do the video thing, but that always seems to come back and bite people in the ass." My heart beats double-time. "Have you ever wondered what my O-face looks like?" It's official. My filter has gone kaput.

"No" is dragged from him.

"Did your eye just tick?"

"No."

A sudden urge to see his face hits me. Explains the FaceTime impulse. "Send me a picture of you." I pause. "Just your face. No dick, please."

"Like I would!" he growls.

I chuckle, feeling a sense of rightness. Man, I love getting him riled up. "Guess we should limit our talk to books and sunrises. Sad."

"I didn't say that. We can discuss more. Hang on..." I hear him moving around, then a photo comes through. He's propped up against his headboard, sans shirt, the rippling muscles of his upper body on display. There's barely any hair on his chest, and his nipples are a dusky color. His hair is wet and slicked back, his face shaven, his eyes lowered as he shields his gaze. A smirk is on his lips.

"Did you use the mango body wash?"

"Are you writing a book?"

"No, but question, since you said we can discuss more things, who was your first?" I stare up at my ceiling but barely notice anything. I want to know everything about him, and I don't know why.

Or do I?

He huffs. "Has anyone ever told you you're a very single-minded person?"

"I'm determined, yes. Now stop trying to change the topic and give me the scoop."

He lets out a husky laugh. "Her name was Jenny. I was a freshman in high school, and she was a senior. A cheerleader. She wanted to toy with the star wide receiver and I wanted to pop my cherry. It happened on a dirt road during the middle of the day. May, I think."

"Sounds super romantic. Was it good?" My hands grip the phone. I want to smack Jenny in the face wherever she is right now.

"We were in her car, a convertible Mustang. The top was down, it was hot as hell outside, and I lasted for ten —okay, five seconds. She laughed and we did it again." He pauses, his voice lowering. "And again."

"Are you thinking about her right now?"

"No," he says breathily.

I swallow thickly. "You're thinking about someone. Who?"

Silence greets me as his breathing changes, the sound of more rustling...

Heat flashes over my skin as my hand draws a line down my chest to my navel. "What are you doing?" I ask.

"Nothing."

"Who were you thinking about, River?"

Still no reply, just the sound of his breathing.

My eyes flutter. I've jumped into the deep end, and I don't know how to swim. I clear my throat. "What would you want a girl to do? To turn you on?"

"You're pushing boundaries, Anastasia. Do we need another rule in our revenge thing?"

I ignore that. "I've only been with two guys, Bryson and Donovan. Truth? I dated Donovan for four months before we went all the way. We were friends long before we became lovers. So—I need assistance, and you said you'd help. I think tips should be involved in that."

"Four months?" He sounds incredulous. "You spent the night with him several times, early on."

"Hmmm, didn't know you were counting. Doesn't mean we had sex."

"What did you do in his room?"

I laugh. "Seriously?"

"Yeah."

"Okay," I say carefully. "We talked a lot about why we

want to go to law school. We watched TV and studied together, I guess, got to know each other. We hung out with the brothers. We partied together. Sounds lame, but it's the usual college hangout stuff."

"You've barely spent any time with me."

Nerves fly at me, and I realize I'm clutching my phone. "Sometimes it only takes one sunrise to know someone."

"Hmmm."

"What of it?"

"Nothing," he mutters.

"No."

"No?" I hear amusement.

"Yeah, no," I say.

"Huh. You just say no and I'm supposed to give in?"

"Snake, I won't let you push me around—"

"Jesus, Rainbow. I'm not—"

I smile at the Rainbow but tuck it away for later as I interrupt him. "You want to clam up on me. Admit it. Why does it matter if we haven't spent time together? *You* never let me."

"I see your point. Let's move on."

"Fine, but as you can see, obviously, I need a guide for my revenge—"

He lets out another gusty exhalation, and I smile. He's riled up again.

"You could share your *vast* experience..." I add.

"Hold up. First, quantity doesn't mean quality. I don't recommend following in my footsteps. It's empty and doesn't make you happy. Sex is better when it's with someone you have feelings for."

"You had feelings for all those sorority girls you banged at the Kappa house?"

"No, but it's because I'm..."

"What?"

"I can't have the one I want."

"Blair."

"No."

"Ah, and here we are again, full circle. Who is she?"

"Moving on," he declares adamantly. "My suggestion is you ditch this revenge idea and wait for the right guy. Maybe you'll meet him at some book event or at law school, or maybe you'll be at the grocery store one day and he'll bump your cart with his and it will be love at first sight. Don't rush it."

"My, my, don't you sound like a little goody-goody. Who are you? And no, I'm definitely going to find a guy, and he doesn't have to be Mr. Right."

Do you want a taste of my revenge, River? Just a little nibble?

"What's your ultimate fantasy?" I ask.

"Have you smoked a joint?"

I giggle. "No. I've only done that twice in my life.

Growing up, I saw drugs. My parents have, um, experimental friends."

"Yet you remain sweet."

"Sometimes sugar looks like salt, and I'm feeling salty. I need pointers, and I won't let you try to change the subject. Help me, River."

"You are relentless." A huff comes from him. "Fine. Fantasy: I walk into a room and my girl, she's there waiting for me, wearing nothing but my hoodie or a shirt. 'Iris' by The Goo Goo Dolls plays in the background. She takes it off real slow, makes a striptease out of it—"

"Not much to strip with one piece of clothing."

"My fantasy, so shut it. She doesn't need much. She's different and beautiful with no makeup, and her hair... it's like silk, long and straight and thick, down her back. I want to wrap my hands in it—" He stops abruptly.

"That's it?" I say softly. "Where's the glitz and glam? Where's the handcuffs and whips and lacey underthings? Or even some whipped cream? Are all dudes this basic?"

He growls into the phone and a shiver goes through me.

I laugh. "Details. Must. Have. Them."

"Diabolical."

"Spill your secrets. Please." In my mind, it's me in River's varsity jacket, and I take it off slowly, revealing my nakedness. His hand curls in my hair and pulls me to my knees in front of him...

"Did you just groan?" he asks.

"Did I?"

"You did."

"You're mistaken. Finish the fantasy. It's a rule. I just made it. Getting my revenge requires you telling me how to be sexy."

"You don't need any help in that department."

I touch my nipples and my thighs clench.

"You're breathing hard, Anastasia."

"Were you touching yourself before?"

"No."

"Eye twitch, I bet. Look, I haven't had..." sex in a while. Didn't want to.

"Haven't had what?" he asks.

Wait.

I stop and frown as I sit up on the bed and think about my relationship with Donovan. I can point fingers at him all day long, and I have—he pushed me away because of his parents, he was too busy, I had work—but...

Clarity trickles in and I gasp. It was *me* too. I helped dig our grave. Since the summer at his parents' place, I avoided sex, recoiled from intimacy, took extra shifts, spent more time studying. I never protested when he drove to Atlanta to see his family on the weekends, never protested when he spent time with the frat, never confided about Bryson, didn't tell him about Harvard until I had to, and deep down I *dreaded* the idea of spending the holidays with his family *or* him.

Yet he was that little piece of security I didn't want to let go of. I loved the frat house, the home it represented...

"I..." My voice trails off.

"What?"

I don't want to say Donovan's name. It's a wall between us, and River—he's slowly stacking more bricks onto it.

"Never mind."

"Were you thinking about Donovan?"

I bite my lip. "Not like you think."

"Are you okay? I mean, are you sad?"

Am I sad? I was betrayed by a friend, by a man I thought I might share a future with, so yes. But there's part of me that feels relief. I know his true colors now.

"It's a weird kind of feeling, I guess," I say, toying with the quilt on my bed.

"You miss him."

My jaw tightens. "Hard to miss him when he did what he did."

There's a long silence. "Fine. What's *your* fantasy?"

I lean back on the pillows. "Shower sex. I've never done it."

"So. Basic."

"Shut up." I laugh.

"Well, tell me already, woman."

I smile. "He's taking a shower and doesn't know I'm there. I get in and get on my knees for him. His hands are on my head, guiding me. He says my name over and over, but he doesn't come. Not yet. He wants me for that. I've never had sex without a condom, but with him, it's bareback. He picks me up, presses me against the tile. He can't stop looking at my face. He tells me he's never wanted anyone like he does me, that I complete him. His irises are a furnace of need. They say the eyes are the windows to the soul, and I see his. I am his everything."

His breathing is labored.

"Finish yours," I say softly.

"She drops the hoodie and watches me take my clothes off. Slow. We stare at each other. I like looking at her. It reminds me of how lucky I am. Finally, we kiss, and I want to go slow, but part of me doesn't. She comes on my fingers and I steal her gasps with my mouth. Then I go down on her. Then I fuck her. Face to face, my eyes on hers, sweat on our skin—"

I'm panting. "Stop."

His breath hitches. "You're right. Too far."

Not far enough.

I bite my lip and try to ignore the goose bumps on my skin, the heat in my core.

His voice is raspy when it comes. "Have dinner with me."

I sit up on the bed, body on alert. "Really? Like a..." date?

"We both have to eat, right? Then, we work on the paper."

"Okay, where? I can meet you there."

"Paulo's? It's a pizza dive on Second Ave?"

"Yeah. Off campus. Mostly townies." Which means no one will see us.

"Yeah."

I check the clock. "See you in an hour?"

"It's a date," he says as he clicks off.

I stare down at the phone.

I know he didn't mean it, that it's a date.

"Freud says slips of the tongue reveal unconscious thoughts," I murmur to myself as I dash to my closet to find something to wear.

Later, as I'm about to head out, my phone pings with a text.

Ana. I'm sorry, so sorry I hurt you. Can we talk? Can I see you? I don't want to do this over the phone. Please.

My hands tighten around the cell and I tuck it into my purse. He's called and texted me on and off since Monday, but still, the humiliation from Friday rears its ugly head.

"No, Donovan. Not now."

And then I'm out the door.

I'M DRIVING DOWN HIGHLAND, about five minutes away from Paulo's when my phone rings and I glance down, anxious that it's Donovan, but it's not.

I see my dad's name and immediately pull over. They called on my birthday, but it was rushed since I was at work.

"Anastasia!" they both sing into the phone as I answer.

My mom takes over, a smile in her voice. "We miss you!"

"Miss you too," I say. "It's late there."

"Ah, you know us—we're just getting started," she says. I hear people in the background, low voices, the soft sounds of music. I picture the house they share in Santorini with a few people. The photos they've sent are breathtaking, a small, white-washed, blue-domed villa that overlooks the Aegean Sea with stucco walls and rustic furniture.

She asks how school is, how Donovan is, how the law school applications are going, and I tell her about us breaking up, leaving out the hurtful things he said about me and them. Maybe I'll tell them someday. They still feel guilty about Bryson, extremely, and I don't want to dig that up.

She gives her condolences about everything. "You'll do great things someday, sunshine," she tells me. "What you feel, you attract. What you imagine, you create. A jug fills drop by drop."

I smile. "Buddha."

She laughs, and I sigh at the sound. I. Miss. Them.

My mom is forty-five, beautiful and leggy with long jet-black hair and a vivaciousness that sucks you in. My dad is tall and handsome, older, with a craggy face and a shy smile. He fell for her in college when he was her art professor. Sucked into her orbit, she coaxed him into leaving his job and living a bohemian lifestyle.

"We decided to come home for the holidays," Dad tells me when he gets on. "Can we see you?"

Oh! The last time we spoke, they didn't have the money.

"I-I didn't think I'd see you. I actually made plans." I briefly catch them up about the ski trip then Ellijay with Lila and Colette.

"Your mom's jewelry is selling like crazy in the boutiques, and I sold a big painting this weekend, a few thousand bucks, so we have extra cash. We don't want to intrude on your plans with your friends, but it would be perfect to see you since school is out. We miss you, and

288 | THE REVENGE PACT

it's time to connect. Think you can work us in, sunshine?"

I need to see them. Maybe they can help me figure out a plan for the fall.

"Of course! Lila and Colette would totally understand. They invited me because I didn't have plans. I hate to miss the ski trip, but... Where were you thinking of staying?"

"We can work around the ski trip. We have access to a beach house in Malibu. There's also a place on Nantucket someone offered. Or we could go to the houseboat in Seattle. It's vacant. You decide. You know we're easy."

They are.

An idea hits. "How about my apartment? I don't have the money to fly to you." I spent my savings on the ski trip. "You've never seen it and my roommates won't be there, so we'll have the place to ourselves, and then there's June..." I go into an explanation about her.

"Tell me about this grandma," Mom says as she gets back on the phone. I laugh and repeat everything. She listens intently, offering suggestions on how to help her. It's not anything I haven't tried, but I appreciate her interest.

"Um, I actually need to go. I have a date," I say later as I check the time.

"What? Already? Which is good! Who?" Mom asks.

"Long story. I'll be back from the ski trip on the 22nd, so if you could fly into Atlanta that day or after, that would be great. Just text me when you book your flight, and I'll pick you up."

They tell me they love me and will see me soon. Clicking off with them, I pull back onto the road, my mind already focused on River.

On our date.

I smile at nothing, then laugh out loud.

There's something *real* between us...

The question is, what am I willing to do about it?

19

River

She's ten minutes late and I'm antsy, twitching, fiddling with the menu and tapping the tabletop.

My pulse spikes as I see her pull into the lot. From inside Paulo's, I watch as she parks her car next to my truck, gets out, and dashes for the door. She breezes in and stops at the hostess stand, and I take the few seconds to take her in. Her hair is down and shines under the lights, her face bare of makeup, her lips a deep red. She's wearing black leggings, royal blue high-top Chucks, and a pale blue sweater, cropped. That one slice of skin is enough to make my hands clench, to picture my fingers encircling her waist and—

She turns and sees me, and I start.

Must. Not. Lust. For. My. Friend's. Ex.

She smiles the entire way to the table I got for us in the back. The place is packed tonight, and there's a band playing on the small stage several feet away. Country music. Not something I listen to a lot, but it fits the ramshackle bar. I scanned the place when I came in. Mostly older crowd. No one from Braxton.

Who cares? the voice in my head says. *She's not with him anymore.*

Yet...

It *does* matter. It's been four days since they broke up. What kind of friend and frat brother would I be to move in on her? A shitty one.

I stand when she reaches the table and catch my reflection in the mirror. There's a stupid smile on my face and shit, shit, shit. I shut it down as I pull out the chair across from me.

She sits. "Sorry I'm late. My parents called while I was driving. You look great," she murmurs as she settles in, her gaze lingering on my Badgers shirt.

I grunt.

Her mouth curls up. "Angsty River tonight—got it."

I huff out a laugh. "Do you always say what you're thinking?"

"Um, it's a little worse lately." She stares down at the menu, her fingers twirling a piece of hair. Another tell of hers. When Harper and company get in the elevator, she touches her hair. When Whitman calls on her in class, she does the same. She's nervous.

My eyes drift over the menu, the words jumbling together in the dim light. I blink and focus but it doesn't help. Whatever. Pizza is easy. I always get the same thing.

Our waitress appears. She's in her mid-twenties and wears a broad smile. She flicks a glance at Anastasia then lingers on me.

Her face brightens. "Hey. River Tate, right?"

"Yeah," I murmur.

She lets out a little squeal, her hands fluttering. "My family are huge Pythons fans and loved your dad. I went to Braxton, and when I heard you came here instead of one of the bigger schools, my family went nuts. You coming back? I heard you haven't decided."

Anastasia raises her head and looks at me, then her.

I shrug. "Maybe."

"Can I get your autograph? And a picture?" Before I can respond, she pulls out her phone, sits down next to me, and snaps a photo. She gets back up, her hand landing on my arm as she gives me a squeeze and a blinding smile. "Oh my God, I can't wait to send this to my roomie. She's crazy about you too. You're the hottest player. You're fast on the field, of course, that counts—"

Anastasia juts in, "I'll have a Coke to drink to start and some breadsticks with marinara."

I dip my head and hide my smile. Oh, Anastasia, you little firecracker.

"I'll have a water," I add. "And double the breadstick order."

The waitress—her name tag says *Sissy*—grimaces. "Sure. On it." She leaves, then turns back around. "Um, are you two, ah, together?" She titters. "I mean, just wondering."

"Yes, he's taken," Anastasia says with a flick of her hair.

After a little harrumph, Sissy walks off, her spine straight.

"Why are you laughing?" Anastasia says, eyeing me. "She was flirting with you. I saved you from further flirting, although I bet she slips you her phone number."

She's jealous.

I lean in, elbows on the table. "What color is your hair underneath that lavender?"

She props her elbows on the table as well, mimicking me. "Black like my mom's. It takes bleach and a great stylist to get this pastel hue. Like it?"

Love it.

"It's alright." The color suits her.

She gives me a half-grin. "You think Sissy will spit in my Coke?"

"Nah. You can drink my water if you want. We'll switch."

A sheepish smile crosses her face. "Maybe I was rude? It's just...she touched you."

I dip my head to hide my smile. "When you have a public image, people don't have boundaries." Random fans do swarm, but I don't let myself get caught up in the hype. Football has never been about the attention; it's about the game, the feel of that pigskin in my hands. It makes me feel powerful, the one thing I'm good at.

Afterward, we order pizza. Turns out we like the same kind: pepperoni and cheese only. Honestly, the food tastes like cardboard, but neither of us comment on it. We can't stop talking. She puts in a to-go order for June that she's going to pick up on our way out.

She pushes her plate to the side and sets a small rectangular box on the table.

"What's this?" I ask.

Pink rises up her face. "Nothing much. I mean, I saw it in the bookstore today and thought you'd like it."

"Oh."

"Don't get your hopes up. It's not like, a diamond tennis bracelet or anything."

I laugh.

She inches it toward me. "Go on. It won't bite."

I take the box, my fingers lingering over the notebook paper she wrapped it in. *For River* is printed in large letters. I untie the little ribbon, open the box, then glance up at her animated expression.

"Tada! It's a pencil!" she exclaims, as if it's a million dollars.

"Thank you."

She cocks her head. "It's not *just* a pencil. It has a unicorn head as an eraser—with sparkles in its mane. I looked for a pen, but all they had were just the regular kind..."

Oh, I *get* it. It makes my heart skip.

She looks down. "Is it silly that I remember you dropping your pen that night?"

"No." I take it out of the box and gaze down at it. "A little piece of magic, which I actually really need right now. Thank you."

She clears her throat. "Ah, yeah. We both need it, right? Neither of us have a clue what's next. 'We still have time to be what we want to be,' remember?"

"*The Outsiders.*"

"I want to fight for people who can't fight for themselves. You want to wow people with football. And you will." She smiles, then fidgets. "You're staring."

Because you believe in me.

Because you're beautiful.

She's the center of a hurricane, a calm that lulls you, then makes your world fucking amazing.

"I have to tell you something," I say.

She leans in. "Yeah?"

I tap my fingers on the table. "About the ski thing...

I'm only staying one night. You wanted me to help with your"—I wince—"revenge, but it looks like I won't be able to do much."

"Your mom?" she asks.

I nod. "Yeah. Um, my sister... I called her today. She's engaged to Jason, this really great guy. They had a big wedding planned for this spring, but, ah, after we talked, she thinks they should move it up and have it on the 23rd at our house. They're leaving for their honeymoon soon after..." I stare down at the table. "Mom got bad news today, and my sister is worried that by the time May gets here, she may not be around..." I stop and take a breath. "Anyway, and all of this is happening kind of fast, like Rae is literally planning it right now, and I need to be around. Get a tux or flowers or call people or whatever my sister wants. She says she's got it under control, but I know she needs me..." I look up. "I really want to be there and help out. I promised my dad I'd be good to her, you know? My mom will flip if I don't ski at least once, so I will, but then..." I need to see her.

Her hand takes mine, her eyes soft. "Of course, River. Be with your family. Nothing else matters. Forget about our thing. It's so unimportant."

It's that easy with her. So damn easy.

The band takes a break, and someone starts up the jukebox. A wistful expression crosses her face.

"What?" I ask.

"It's your song, 'Iris.'"

My lashes shield my gaze as I watch her hum the opening lines about a man who'd give up forever to touch his girl, how she's the closest thing to heaven he'll ever feel—

She's standing and takes my hand.

"What are we doing?" I ask, following her, my eyes drinking in the sway of her hips, the swish of her hair.

"You owe me a dance. You laughed at me in my apartment when I went low, low, low, refused to participate—"

"You know why," I say as we stop in the center of a small dance area. We're the only ones out here.

Her arms curl around my neck, her tits against my chest. "And you called me Rainbow—cute. Why?"

"You're color." I am so fucking lame.

"Color?"

"And beginnings."

"Oh."

"Yeah."

My legs go weak as I pull her against me, my arms wrapping around her waist. My hands linger at her sides, then go behind her back and settle there. She's pressed against me, and it's more than the friendly hug in my room. My hands drift and graze her ass. She melts against me and my heart pounds.

This. Her. The song.

Can't touch her ass. Can't.

My hands shift back to that slice of skin at her waist, my thumbs digging into her sides as my breathing escalates. Her skin is like silk. I dip my head and breathe in the smell of her hair.

She rests her head on my chest, right over my heart.

We're too close. Too close for study buddies.

Fuck it.

Just.

Fuck it.

One song bleeds into another, then another, some faster, not slow songs, but we don't let go.

I can't.

I try to keep my body under control, but I'm in Anastasia overload.

That's what happens when you keep denying yourself.

My lips touch her hair as my cock brushes against her.

She knows I'm hard. She has to.

My throat tightens as she curls her fingers in my hair, a long sigh coming from her lips. "River..."

I pull away from her in the middle of a song and clear my throat. "It's getting late."

A pink flush rises up her throat to her cheeks. "Maybe we should skip the library and go to your house—"

"We shouldn't." I walk back to the table, my chest rising and falling rapidly.

I fish out several twenties and toss them on the table as she joins me. "I didn't bring my laptop. Going to get it back at the house and I'll meet you there." It's an inane thing to say, but I can't focus. With nervous hands, I pick up the pencil and put it in my coat pocket.

She watches me, her face carefully blank, but I think I see hurt there.

Fuck.

"Right." She checks her phone. "I'm going to see June, then I'll be there."

She grabs her purse and the to-go box and we leave together, our bodies side by side, but it feels like a universe between us.

I'm still standing in the parking lot, watching her tail-lights disappear five minutes later.

I had her in my arms.

She's too much. Too soon.

She isn't over him. She still thinks about him.

20

Anastasia

I saunter up and plop my books down. It's Wednesday, our third session in the library.

From the disarray on the table and the harried look on his face, he's been here a while. My gaze sweeps over him, taking in his tall fame, the long legs stretched out under the table, the distressed black hoodie over his shirt. His hair is messy, eyes glinting with sparks.

Last night after pizza was kind of a mess. We both showed up at the library and barely talked to each other except to discuss the book.

Our chemistry sizzles, enough to singe my hair, and I *like* him, the person he is. It's more than just how he looks. Yes, we can all agree he is the hottest man on campus, but I'm more entranced by his soul, by his strength and perseverance in dealing with his learning issues. His armor is falling away piece by piece in front of me, and I... I want to see all of him.

But...

He's got a titanium shield up.

I stare at his Chucks, worn but loved, and wish for mine. I flash my pink stilettos.

"Don't fall in those," he quips.

"Too much?" I peer down at my magenta velvet mini skirt and fuzzy pink cropped sweater. "On Wednesdays we wear pink," I say.

"*Mean Girls* quote."

"I'm so fetch."

"Stop trying to make fetch happen. It's not going to happen."

"You blow my mind." I laugh.

He nods as his gaze lingers on my legs. "You're in full makeup, your hair is down, you have contacts in, and your lipstick—"

"Watch it. Control yourself."

"I have massive self-control when it comes to you."

"Knew it! How much time did you spend *not* looking at me? Hmmm?" I'm half-teasing, but serious. "Or maybe you're holding yourself back from throttling me?"

"All the time."

"What happened to getting a private study room for us?" I thought it would help his ADHD, and we discussed it, again, after class today. He said he'd call the library and reserve one. Yet here we are in the open.

"They're all booked. Exam time. We have to hang out with everyone else. Let's get started, woman." He kicks out the chair next to him, and I take it gingerly as I laugh under my breath. I love how we mess with each other.

He glances up. "I don't see Kian here. This makes three times he's a no-show. Lila's intel must be wrong."

"You checked?"

"Did recon when I walked in. I feel bad about the ski trip. I'm getting your help, and you probably won't get mine—"

"Whoa. No. Me helping you? I would have done that anyway—because I like you. I said no at first, but that was because I was still with Donovan and it felt wrong. And you helping your sister is important. Plus, your mom needs you. I totally get it."

"Right." He sighs.

I smile to lighten the mood. "So, *intel* and *recon*—like it. We should come up with a code. 'Alpha alert' for when you see Kian, then I'll say 'locked and loaded' when I make my move, then you can tell me how I'm doing, maybe 'retreat'—obvious meaning there—or 'advance'?"

His lips twitch. "You. Are. Strange."

"Roger that."

The library is packed with students studying for

finals, the low hum of voices in the air. We get a few surprised looks—*What are they doing together?*—like we did on Monday and Tuesday, and sure enough, within ten minutes, a few sorority girls amble over to chat with River. I don't know their names, only that they aren't Deltas. *Oh, River, how are you, you are so amazing, oh I am so sorry about your season, oh I love your IG, your party last weekend was off the chain and where did you disappear to—blah, blah, blah.*

He replies politely, not being flirty...

I accidentally-on-purpose kick him with my heel.

He pivots his body toward mine, our eyes clinging as he leans in and whispers, "You want my full attention?"

"If you're not serious about this, pack up and go," I say. I'm insanely jealous. For no reason. He's only being nice and speaking in short sentences, but they are determined.

"I don't want them here," he whispers as he grazes his finger over my throat, oh so briefly, then lets his hand drop.

Unbidden, heat washes over me, at the image of me under him, and I lean into him until our noses are inches apart. I'm getting braver, testing his walls. "If you were mine, I'd kick those girls' asses all the way out the library door. If you were mine, it'd be so damn hot you'd never want another girl. But...you're not, and this is my own time, and I expect you to be free of entanglements."

"You didn't say a word to Harper," he says in a low voice.

"Maybe it wasn't worth it."

"Hey, River, are you two, like, together?" is the slightly shrill female voice that breaks into our tête-à-tête. "I mean, I've seen you here a couple of times."

In our own world, we both start and turn to face her.

It's just one girl. Her two friends have deserted her and moved on. She's pretty, long blonde hair, pert nose.

River straightens up in his chair. "Just studying for a class."

Sorority Girl gives him a quizzical look. "Okay, 'cause I thought it would be weird for the president of the Kappas to be *with* Ana." A titter comes from her, but she's looking at River, not me. I don't exist in her world except as a tidbit of gossip. "I was at the party, you know. Heard everything. Then Mellany posted the audio, and wow, now everyone—"

My pen sails through the air, hits her sweater, and falls to the floor. "Keep talking, sorority girl, and I'm going to pluck out your eyeballs—"

"Easy now, I don't want to bail you out of jail," River murmurs as he tosses an arm around me casually. His chest shakes, and I think he murmurs *Eyeballs? Really?*

Her face reddens as she glares at me then flips a strand of hair over her shoulder. "You're really rude. I was just making conversation—"

"Bye," I say.

She glances at River.

"Anastasia has spoken," he says very seriously.

She flounces off while he chuckles, the sound low and husky.

"That felt good," I murmur.

"Hmmm. I like you throwing pens at random girls in the library. Epic."

We laugh.

A while later, we've gone over his notes, picked out quotes to support his theme, and organized his paragraphs. Articulating his ideas is where he shines; it's the writing that slows him down. We talk about how to wrap up his conclusion. He's almost there.

"We've been going at this for two hours. I can't believe I sat still that long," he says later as he jiggles his leg under the table.

He whips off his hoodie, the smell of mangoes drifting around us as he tosses it on the table. His muscles flex as he moves his arms back behind his neck and stretches. My eyes drape over him, the perfect body, the bulky arms, his taut forearms, dang how can you have muscles *there*. Even the dark hair on his arms is attractive. I wish I could go back to that night in the library. If I had a do-over—

I rip my eyes away from the perfection of River.

He's a guy with principles and a deep sense of loyalty. He said integrity means something to him.

Another thought sneaks in: he read *The Outsiders* because of *me*, and normally that wouldn't be a big deal —I recommend books to people all the time—but for *him*, it means he spent a lot of time reading it. I influenced him—

My train of thought gets interrupted when my eyes roam the library and snag on a table that's filled up with guys. I straighten my shoulders. "Whiskey, tango, foxtrot, alpha alert in the green zone, repeat, target is in the basket—or the periodicals. Engage, engage." I ease out of my seat while rummaging through my purse, snatching my lipstick and sliding on fresh color.

River watches me, not moving.

"What's the holdup, private?"

His gaze goes behind me, seeing the group, and his eyes narrow. He glances back at me.

"What? Operation Rebound is on."

He lets out a long-suffering groan and stands. "Stop with the military speak in front of them. That's just for me."

"Like it?"

"A little." He grins.

"It's new. You bring it out of me."

"Why?"

I shrug. "Don't know. It's like... I've known you forever."

"Yeah," he says softly as he twists his ring, looks down at the table, then back up at me. "Anastasia?"

The word ripples over my skin like a caress. I swallow. "What?"

"I..." He stops. Several moments tick by.

"I?"

"Are you sure? I don't want you to make a mistake..."

We stare at each other, my body hyperaware of the intensity of his gaze. I'm vaguely aware of the sound of papers shuffling, the low hum of students, but all I see is him.

No, I'm not sure.

I clear my throat. "Worth a shot. It's a good hair day. I had my teeth cleaned recently. I haven't had many carbs today. Lila gave me fancy gold earrings. I showered. Put me in, coach."

His fingers brush my neck, straightening my sweater. He takes a piece of hair and lays it over my shoulder, his hands lingering near my throat as he steps away. "There. Perfect."

All. These. Touches.

Us dancing last night.

I'm going to snap.

I give him a jerky nod.

"Green Zone it is," he murmurs, then takes off for the periodicals.

He walks like a predator, slow and stealthy, looking for his next kill. Kian.

I follow behind him as he stops a few feet away from the table.

"What's the plan?" I whisper as I slide up next to him.

"We need a meet cute."

I glance at him in surprise, roaming over his chiseled cheekbones, the proud line of his forehead, the Roman nose, his broad shoulders—

Another memory resurfaces, clawing to the top. "You like meet cutes?"

"No. I'm a dude. But we want to make an impression. Make him remember you, maybe something funny."

"Huh. My meet cute with Donovan was different. Did you have anything to do with it?"

"No."

"Your eye twitched," I whisper. "Did you have a hand in writing my note?"

He starts, his eyes searching mine. Five seconds tick by as our gazes cling.

"I didn't."

I make a *hmmm* noise and think back to the letter, currently tucked in my bedside drawer along with cards Donovan sent me. I haven't had time to burn them. Yet.

At the beginning of it, there's a quote from *Gone with the Wind*, and River said that was his mom's favorite movie—

He waves his hands in my face. "Are you ready?"

I sigh. "No, they're engrossed in a discussion about hydrogen atoms. It sounds super boring. Maybe we should abort."

"But he's *smart*," he mutters. "He checks your boxes."

I glance away from River to the guy in question. Nice teeth, nice hair, nice stuff. He's no River, but who is?

"Had a 'smart guy' before." I use air quotes. "And, as you know, that didn't turn out so great. Maybe I need to hop in my car, drive down to the local MC bar, pick up a biker, post some pics, and call it a day."

"There are no MC clubs in Walker."

"Too bad," I say.

He rocks on his heels as we linger behind a rack of magazines. Honestly, I could just stand right here all night, basking in River's electricity—

"But duty calls," I mutter.

He mulls something over. "I have an idea, and you won't need me for this. Just walk past him, drop your pen next to his chair, stop, look around, and wait for him to get a look at you, then boom, he'll see you, rush to help you—"

My chest expands. "Wow. This sounds suspiciously

familiar to how you met me. Was that all a ploy to talk to me?"

"No."

"Eye twitch," I mutter.

He turns away, not looking at me. He frowns, his jaw popping.

I huff and glance away. What's up with him?

I push it aside and look at Kian.

Now that it's time to meet this guy, I just…

Don't. Want. To.

My get-up-and-go has gone.

I shrug, itching to extricate myself from this situation and go back to our table. Anxiousness washes over me. "I don't have a pen in my purse. Left my stuff back at the table."

River lets out an exhalation. "I could play 'Low' on my phone and you could break out in dance."

"Funny." My tone is low and unfocused. My head is hung up on the earlier question about how *we* met and the note. There was a definite eye twitch. Did he lie to me? *Why* would he lie?

I'm distracted from my thoughts when he reaches for me, his fingers going to my earlobe, a soft touch, as he removes the dangly gold earring then places it in my palm. "Here. Drop this."

My hands tighten around the piece of jewelry. "What happened to you introducing us?"

His jaw tightens, a closed-off look on his face. "You try on your own first."

I swallow thickly. He wants no part of introducing me to Kian...

"Why?"

"I'd rather not."

I could argue with him. *This* was the deal, but his face looks almost pained.

I blink and look away.

Fine.

I suck in my resolve.

Am I *this* awkward around the opposite sex? No, yet the stakes feel high and there's a strange, hollow feeling in my stomach that has nada to do with Kian.

"Locked and loaded." I flip around and walk toward the table of three guys. I recognize their faces from campus and parties. Their heads are lowered as they discuss science things.

Kian says, "...obtained the energy levels and spectral frequencies of the hydrogen atom after making a number of simple assumptions in order to correct the failed classical model..."

I stop next to him and drop the earring as slyly as I can—which is to say, not very. The gold hoop—*geeze, it's huge*—bounces off the floor, sails a foot away, and pings into a metal bookshelf, then a student walks by and kicks it underneath. A shimmer of gold peeks out.

312 | THE REVENGE PACT

That was crazy, and not one male at the table noticed.

"The assumptions included..." Kian stops and glances up when I clear my throat. His forehead furrows. "Hi?"

I bite my lip. What to say, what to say...

The other guys raise their faces from their laptops and stare at me.

"You need something?" Kian asks.

Here's the part where I'm supposed to say something super witty, but...

"I lost my earring. Somewhere around here, I think?" I say weakly, keeping my eyes on his face and not on the bookshelf where said jewelry is currently hiding.

He glances at the floor for a few seconds. "Oh. Don't see it. Good luck finding it."

"Um, yeah..." thanks for offering to help.

I don't budge.

This sucks.

It really sucks.

My heart thumps in my chest. I feel strangely lightheaded.

"There you are!" River says as he comes up next to me. "Couldn't find you, Ana."

My eyes widen and my stomach does this weird pitch at his use of *Ana*. I don't like it.

He gives me a smile then elbows me (to wake me

from my trance). He focuses on Kian. "Hey, man. How's it going? Finals, huh? Killer." They fist-bump, briefly touch on football, run down how tough exam time is, the ski trip, then… "You know Ana, Kian?"

Don't say my name like that, my eyes say as I look at River.

He gives my shoulder a squeeze. "Usually, she's chatty. In fact, she never shuts up."

"Don't think we've ever officially met. Great to meet you," Kian murmurs, his eyes sweeping over me and stopping on my stilettos. He pops an eyebrow.

Dammit. Too showy. Too—

F that.

"Sorry, hi, yeah, I was distracted." I force a laugh. "You were discussing the theoretical analysis of the hydrogen atom? The Bohr–Sommerfeld model? Very cumbersome."

Kian gives me a surprised look. "Ah, you don't look like the type to keep up with physics."

I smile tightly. "You mean, like a woman? The Bohr–Sommerfeld theory failed to explain many electron systems, such as the hydrogen molecule. Not a physics fan, but I spent a summer with a *lady* physicist who researched quantum mechanics."

Silence hangs over the group as Kian checks me out, eyes lingering on my boobs this time. Guess he's making his way up. Look at my face, Kian.

"I see." He searches for words. "Hey, you're the Ana that Donovan broke up with at the toga party, right?"

And here we go...

River stiffens. "Let's not talk—"

I interrupt with, "Yes, he did. I'm a pothead, a car thief, a Harvard reject, and a teenage homewrecker—not necessarily in that order. I'm quite notorious. Every-where I go, people whisper. All. Week. Long." My shoulders tighten.

"I know Lila. She's your roommate, right? I had a class with her last year," Kian murmurs.

Interest glints in his brown eyes. For me? For Lila?

Just power through, Ana.

A gusty breath comes out from me. It's ten at night, and I really just want to go home, check on June, eat some ice cream, and go to bed.

I grimace. "Yeah, Lila's great. Let's cut to the chase: I'm looking for a rebound, a brainy guy for some fun." I rake my eyes over Kian, my tone flat. "You qualify. Interested?"

Kian gapes at me, his eyes darting from me to River. "Oh. I assumed you, ah, were with River."

I cock my head. "But I just broke up with Donovan—wouldn't that be too soon to jump on his frat brother?" I say it lightly, as a joke. *But really, is it too soon, Kian? What do you think?*

He shrugs as he eyes River. "I'm not in a frat, but um, all's fair in love and war, I guess?"

"We aren't a thing," I say crisply. Because River has a forcefield around himself, and then I'm recounting our conversation, *again*, about meet cutes and notes. Something wasn't right about that. He didn't tell the whole truth. My neck tingles and sweat breaks out on my face. He. Lied. I *feel* it. My head goes back to that night, trying to piece it together—

"Well, *I'm* interested," Guy One says, interrupting my thought. He shuts his book. "I'm a chemistry major. Way smarter than Kian."

"I'm in," Guy Two adds. "You free right now? There's a party at the ATO house. I'm done studying—"

"Hey, I believe she's talking to me," Kian says with a small laugh directed at his friends.

My eyes sweep over them. "That seriously worked? A random girl you've never met just shows up, one the whole campus has gossiped about, and you're eager to jump on the Ana train?"

"Um, yeah," Kian murmurs, his eyes lingering on my tits again. "You're hot. I'm in, baby."

River flinches as if someone slapped him.

I straighten my spine. "Enlightening—really. Fascinating. Ever say *baby girl*?"

He blinks. "If you want me to?"

"I will," comes from Guy One, then, "Baby girl."

"I'll call you whatever you want," Guy Two says, murmuring his agreement.

A huff comes from me. "Wow. The dating pool at Braxton is crap—"

"Whiskey, tango, foxtrot," River mutters in my ear. "Abort." He takes my elbow, murmurs a *Good to see you, we have to go,* then turns me around and stalks away with me in tow. He stops to grab the earring and sticks it in my hand.

His body is wired and tense, and I exhale as he leads me past our table and to the stairwell.

"First, Kian didn't like my shoes. Second, he assumed I didn't understand physics. Third, he stared at my breasts more than my face." My voice rises.

He walks faster. "We're getting off this floor."

"I admit, it didn't go smoothly."

"You're shaking, Anastasia."

Am I?

"You shook the whole time. It's why I came over."

I stare down at my hands, grimacing at how they tremble. My legs feel weak, and I swallow down emotion that's been building for the past few days. From the looks on campus to the whispers...

My emotional state got worse when I sat down with River...

His personality, his mercurial eyes, his beautiful soul...he's a hum in my heart. Truth, it's been pricking at me for a *year*, and now, it's flaring right to the surface, aching to be acknowledged. Not only that, but there's *something* nudging me in the back of my head, a truth I can't grasp hold of as it dances just out of reach—

"Are you okay?" He takes my hands in his.

I swallow down the thickness in my throat. "I did not enjoy that."

"Neither did I," he mutters. "Kian *is* a prick. He called you *baby*, and he doesn't even *know* you. I wanted to pull his tongue out."

"He is out. Marked off the list. Not even for revenge. Want to know what's worse? A girl in my philosophy class asked me if I needed drug counseling today."

"Who was it? I'll have a talk with her."

I smirk. "You're intimidating people for me?"

"Maybe."

I sigh. "Honestly? I can deal with the fallout from Donovan. I made a stupid mistake with Bryson, yes, but I'm happy with *who* I am. I like me, but what I don't have is a school next fall, and it's scary..."

"You have me."

"Do I?"

"Yes, I'm your friend." He studies my face, then flings open the door and we go up the stairs.

Friend.

I firmly disagree, River.

And I'm sick of pretending.

Anastasia

I take the steps with him, our hands brushing in the stairwell. He opens the door to the fifth floor, and we step out into the space.

I take in the lobby area for the administrative offices, currently closed. A twenty-foot badger statue is in the center, a water fountain at his feet. His triangular-shaped face is striped along his snout, his mouth open with sharp fangs, his body thick, his claws raised as if he's about to burrow into something tasty. "I like the silence," I murmur. "But that badger is hideous."

"Agreed. Follow me past the monster." He leads me down a darkened hallway that opens to a spiral staircase. He goes ahead and opens a door at the top, draping his hoodie over my shoulders as we walk out to the center of the rooftop. I pull it against me, sticking my hands in his pockets. It smells like him and I sigh.

See-through partitions block the wind on the sides, but the stars gleam down at us, the muted lights of campus glowing off in the distance. A fire pit crackles in the middle of a lounge area.

"Wow," I murmur as I do a spin. "This is beautiful. I never come up here. And it's empty."

He shrugs, glancing up. "You took me to the sunrise. I bring you the stars."

I crane my neck and find the Milky Way. "They remind me that I shouldn't dwell on small things I can't change. The school thing will work out."

"They make me think of my dad. He's somewhere out there watching me. Listening. He would have liked you."

I stop spinning and *look* at him. I knew his dad passed when he was in high school—that's common knowledge—but I've never heard him talk about it. "There's an Eskimo legend that says they aren't stars at all, but openings where our loved ones watch us."

"I like that," he says softly.

"What happened...wait...can I ask that? I'm sorry. I never know what to say..."

He tucks his hands in his jeans. "Car wreck after a game. We went down a ravine and hit rocks. I couldn't get to him, couldn't move or call 911, and then his chest just stopped..." He trails off, a hesitant look on his face.

"Tell me about him. Who was he to have a son as beautiful as you?" I say. "And I don't mean your appearance. I mean *you*. That piece of you inside that shines."

He dips his head and smiles sheepishly. "Everyone loved him—teachers, cops, shop owners. They asked him to run for mayor one year, but he laughed and said he couldn't be away from his family. He believed in me, no matter the shitty grades or how rambunctious I got. I gave him a run for his money too, fighting in school and being a pill, lashing out because of my issues. He was patient and loving. He adored my mom, always kissing her in front of people." A small laugh comes from him. "He loved to tell the story of how they met. He was on a date with some model, one of those glamorous types, and Mom marched up to him at the bar while his date was in the restroom and said, *I'm the girl you want*, then tucked her number in his shirt pocket and walked away. He called her that night and they were married six months later. He loved hard, with everything he had, always planning things for us to do together. Family trips, crazy themed dinners. Every Christmas we did this mystery dinner where one of us was the bad person trying to mess up Christmas and the rest of us had to figure it out. He wrote the script for it and coached the bad guy. Whoever guessed it right got an old football trophy of his from when he was a kid. It was dumb and silly, but the best. I spent Sundays in our basement with him watching football and playing darts from the age of five to fifteen. He laughed all the time. He told horrible jokes, never could remember the punch lines right. He was so easy to love, so damn easy. He came to every single football game I ever played. He made me feel important, and you could tell him anything and he wouldn't judge, he really listened..." He pauses, grimacing. "God. I miss him, Anastasia, and my mom...I'm terrified she's next."

The pain in his words make tears prick my eyelids. I hold myself back from hugging him. I'm sad for him and his mom, and I dig deep to look for something positive to say that doesn't sound trite. I can't say *She'll be okay* or *You'll be okay* because the truth is, I don't know that.

"Someday you can pass those traditions to your own family. Family is a precious gift."

"You think I'll be like him?" He looks at me uncertainly. "I'm kind of a mess."

Oh, River. A beautiful mess.

"Yes. You will. You're too beautiful for words, River, and again, I don't mean how you look."

I glance at him and he's watching me, his eyes lowered as he stalks closer. His face is open, a glint in his eyes that makes me gasp.

I see pain there.

And *need*. Sharp and visceral. He shields his gaze from me, so often, but now...

My heart pounds as the delicate thread between us tightens. I take a breath.

He's in front of me, our bodies almost touching. "I love the things you say. You're a dreamer, Anastasia. Like me. I'm glad I met you a year ago."

"Even though you hated me?"

"I never hated you. I can't stay away from you."

My heart dips and his eyes widen as the silence builds, stretching.

Ah. He didn't mean to say that.

Then.

Oh. *Oh.*

Everything clicks together.

His eye twitch, his evasiveness earlier.

Clarity hits me, the *real reason* I was shaking downstairs. My brain was slowly putting it together.

How did I miss this?

He frowns. "What's wrong?"

I gaze up at him, my stomach jumpy. "Let me take you back to a night a year ago. In the library, you *did* drop your pen to talk to me. It was your way in, to feel me out. Recon. Then you went back to Donovan, and you may not have written the note that night—it was in his handwriting, I'll give you that—but you dictated it, coached him on what to say. You give advice to all the guys."

"Anastasia—"

I hold my hand up, cutting him off as an exhalation comes from my chest. *"You should be kissed and often, and by someone who knows how.* He never once mentioned that quote to me when we dated, and it's from *Gone with the Wind*. He's never seen the movie and never wrote me any more notes like that. He never wanted to talk about that letter. Never. He'd just laugh and change the subject when I brought it up, even though it meant so much to me—that someone saw that I wasn't smiling, that someone was looking at me hard enough to see under the surface. The note talked about three things he liked about me, things Donovan *never* mentions, and now, it makes perfect sense!"

He sighs.

"Three is your thing, not his," I say, speaking softer as I look at the letters on his fingers, then his face. "River...why?"

His lashes flutter against his cheek. "Anastasia, you shouldn't—"

"It *was* you," I say, feeling the certainty, and the ramifications. "You wrote that letter. Is that why you didn't want to introduce me to Kian...because you'd already sort of fixed me up with Donovan?" I shake my head, trying to line everything up.

"Yes."

"River! I walked out of the library and *he* was there, and that was supposed to be you, and it's just wrong, wrong, wrong—"

He shuts his eyes. "I'm sorry."

"This whole time... Donovan and I started out with a lie. That you built. It's not right!" It feels like a betrayal, another one from Donovan, and a new one from River.

"Don't say that." Frustration colors his words as he pulls me fully into his arms, his grasp strong, the heat of his body engulfing mine.

"I wasted a year on him and it wasn't even real—"

"You fell in love with him, Anastasia. It wasn't just the note," he counters.

"Was it just a game to you?" I look up at him.

"No. Never. I-I just somehow *knew* what to say to you..." He swallows and glances away from me, then drops his arms and takes a step back.

My chest rises. *He* wrote my note. He's the one I should have been with.

"You told me at the sunrise to live each moment. Well, here and now, I'm living it. We've been dancing around each other for days. I want *you*."

"We can't."

I shake my head. "We can. Since the moment we met, the world has been put on pause, waiting for us to figure it out, maybe, I don't know, at least that's how it feels for me. In the library when we met, that night in your bedroom at the Kappa house, in the kitchen in May— you wanted *me*. You've built a fortress around yourself, trying to keep me out, am I right?"

"Anastasia, we can't talk about—"

"Stop," I tell him. "We want each other—"

He sucks in a breath. "Don't say it. Don't."

Oh, I'm going to say it.

I'm done with him pushing me away.

And this *thing* feels like it's going to unravel at any moment if I don't hang on tight. I take the one step that puts me back in his arms and press my cheek to his chest.

His arms go around me. "We can't do this," he says, a catch in his voice. "He's my friend."

My voice is muffled, and I can't look at him when I say the vulnerable words. "Listen to me. We're here. We're under the stars. You can't lie to the stars. We have a connection and you know it. Life doesn't give out a lot of moments like this. Just kiss me, just *kiss me* or walk away."

Long moments pass, and I look up at him.

"Anastasia..." A wild light grows in his eyes.

My hands clench the material of his shirt. "Do you think I've ever begged a man to kiss me? I haven't! River, just—"

His lips swoop down and claim me.

He slants his mouth across mine, and the first taste of him is like a drug. Blood rushes through my veins.

We kiss.

And kiss.

He groans as he nips at my bottom lip, tugging on it, then delving back inside my mouth. My hands slide up his chest, mapping him, tracing the muscles there before caressing his shoulders, circling around his neck. My fingers carve through his hair as our tongues tangle.

His hand drops to my waist, to the bare skin of my midriff, then slides to my ass, his fingers pressing into my skin like a hot brand. Heat sinks into my bones, lust and need rising like a wave. His tongue lashes at me as he picks me up and puts me against one of the partitions. I sit on the ledge as my legs wrap around his waist.

He moves up and cups my face, his hands pushing my head back as he owns my mouth. His kisses are different from Donovan's, vicious, steeped in urgency, a hot flame that incinerates.

He's desperate.

A man on the verge.

We go rocket fast, kissing, tasting, eating at each other, our breaths heavy and fast, our hands roaming over skin, to take it all in.

It's not pretty.

It's dirty and ugly and so fucking good.

A primal sound comes from his throat as he comes

up for air. "Tell me to stop, Anastasia, please," he says breathlessly as his teeth graze my throat. He sucks at the skin, hard.

"Don't stop," I gasp.

"I can't..." He kisses me again, savagely, frustration and anger in his touch, a well of emotion seeping from every erotic stroke of his tongue against mine, as if I'm his torment and his salvation.

Warmth pools deeper in my pelvis. I'm hot for him. My body arches into him, my hips grinding against his hard length. He hisses, his fingers going underneath my panties and finding bare skin. He kneads my ass until I know I'll have handprints there tomorrow.

He rips the hoodie off my arms, his lips never leaving mine. With frantic movements, his hands skate up my stomach, shoving my sweater up. My nipples bead inside my bra, aching. His mouth closes over one, his teeth scraping the lace. He pushes the flimsy material aside and his lips latch onto my breast.

His head tilts as his dilated eyes meet mine. He sticks his thumb in my mouth and I suck it, rolling it around with my tongue. He groans against my nipple, his cock pressing into me.

A ringing sound comes from somewhere, going on and on, and I ignore it and kiss him harder. I unsnap his jeans, undo the zipper, and slip my hands inside. He's hard and thick and long, just like I knew he'd be. I palm him from his root to his mushroom-shaped crown, rubbing the wetness at the tip. An urge to taste him hits me, to wrap my tongue around him and suck him down. He groans, his body tightening, his breathing ragged as he pumps into my hand, his mouth open on my neck.

He picks me up and carries me to one of the couches around the fire. Our mouths cling as he lands on top of me, and finally, finally, I'm under him. He ravages me with his mouth, and it hurts in the best way, the scrape of his jaw, the pull of his teeth as he bites my lips, my throat, my shoulder. My sweater disappears. My bra vanishes.

I rip his shirt off and gasp, my fingers shaking as I trace the perfection of his skin, the hallowed hills and valleys of his muscles.

And when his skin touches mine...we groan at the same time.

"Anastasia..." He slides down and pulls up my skirt. He tears my panties to the side, impatiently, and exposes my slick center. He growls, his chest rumbling as he glances at me, his eyes black. He's lost, he's gone, and he's with me, *he's with me*.

"Stop me," he says, his voice like gravel. "Fucking stop me."

"No."

He bends his head and licks me, his hands clenching and unclenching on my thighs. I grip his scalp as he lashes at me like a man starved. His lips and fingers and tongue and breath become my master. He devours me, a ferocious lover.

One finger, then two are inside me as he flicks my clit with his tongue. He fingers me and grinds his hips into the seat and murmurs filthy things against my skin: how wet I am, how hot I am, how he wants to fuck me hard, how he wants his cock inside me so bad, how he's never going to let me get away from him.

That ringing sound comes again.

It's a phone. His.

It's on the ground next to my sweater.

I grab his shoulders, kneading them, encouraging him. He says my name with reverence, with such longing, and I can't breathe, tensing, as tingles build at my spine, my hips moving with him. When we fuck, it's going to be insane, over the top, and then he does something with his fingers, fast and hard on my clit, I shout, and I'm coming, coming, my core clenching around him, spasming as my legs tighten around his head.

"River, River..." I pull him up and kiss him. My hands go to his ass, palming him, then his waist as I shove his jeans to his hips. I took things slow with Donovan, but this—this is something else entirely. This is *us*. "Now, please."

He lets out a shuddering breath, his head in my neck as he gasps. "Anastasia. Help me. I lov—" His phone rings, and he looks away from me to the ground, his eyes shutting. "Fuck me."

I know the name on the screen.

He pulls back, chest heaving as he sits on his haunches. He scrubs his face as storm clouds color his eyes. "Anastasia," he says in a tortured voice. "That's him."

"I know."

"This can't... We have to stop..."—he sucks in air—"...this insanity. Jesus. I'm sorry." He grimaces as he stands and sweeps his shirt over his head then zips his jeans.

I sit up, watching as he paces the rooftop. I snap up my sweater and slip it on. My hands shake. A bad feeling grows in my gut as I stand.

He doesn't look at me, his feet eating up the ground. "Fuck. *Fuck.* Yes, okay, okay, I told Donovan what to say in the note that night. I did, I did, and I'm sorry I can't go back and fix it. I dropped my pen to get a feel for you, to find an angle, and then, you, God, I don't know, you were so perfect *for me*, but—"

"It doesn't matter. You're the author of my note, and I won't burn it like I planned. We'll start fresh—"

"No." He shakes his head. "We shouldn't have come up here. Don't you see? Donovan is calling me *right now*." He snatches up the phone and scrolls through the messages, his lips compressing in a hard line.

"Maybe he just wants you to pick up some beer on the way to the house." My words are sharp.

River shakes his head, *still* not looking at me. "He wants to talk about you. He's been asking me if he made a mistake—shit, he wants me to talk to you for him..." He pulls at his hair. "You're what he really wants, and I can't *believe* he broke up with you, and how it happened haunts me—"

"We were over this past summer—"

It's like he doesn't hear me. "You love him!"

"Then why am I here? With you?"

His eyes widen.

"And his parents? The bracelet? Harper? The pin? You think I can accept that kind of treatment from someone? I have pride, River."

He groans. "If you love people, you work it out! I'm the bad guy who's messing around with you! I'm the friend moving in on his girl!" He heaves out a breath then scrubs his face. "Ana. God. Ana, I have to tell you something."

He called me Ana! Again.

"What?" I snap.

He covers his face for a moment, drops his hands. "I told him to end it with you on Friday before the party. When he came downstairs and started spewing all this shit about your past, something came over me, and... I told him to let you go. I told him to break it off, said

Harper was meant to be his and he just needed space to try. I told him..." He takes a breath. "...that you'd never make him happy."

Shock washes over me. I blink rapidly.

Silence builds as he stares at me, willing me to reply. My mouth opens. I don't know what to say. River influenced Donovan.

I shake my head, trying to wrap my head around it.

"I'm sorry he... I didn't think he'd do it the way he did. I didn't even know if he would. I never dreamed it would go down like that. I'm sorry."

I struggle to figure out how I feel about this. Am I angry? Surprised for sure. It means...it means River has high stakes in us. "Did you tell him I was a Lolita type?"

"Never, but I encouraged him to dump you. I said he was dragging out the inevitable."

"Wow." My mind races, trying to piece it together. "Did you somehow know about Harvard and tell Harper I didn't get in?"

"I would never hurt you like that. I know how it is, to feel less than." A lost look appears on his face. "He's going to give up Harvard for you, he will, I can feel it coming." He pauses. "I shouldn't have brought you up here, but you and Kian, just the idea, my jealousy is out of control...fuck, fuck, fuck, *I* messed up. This ends here—"

"That was not the end of something." I slip my arms

into his hoodie. Not giving that up. No way, no how. It's mine.

"The things you say... I can't..." He stops, a muscle in his jaw clenching. "You're too much, too soon for me. Can't you see that what I did was wrong? Donovan *listens* to me."

A harsh laugh comes from me. "Honestly? You gave him good advice. Did you have an ulterior motive? Yes," I say.

He closes his eyes briefly, then spears me with a tormented look. "The frat is important. I'm the *president*. There's a code. I can't—"

My hands fist. I'm laying everything out, bare for him to see, and he still doesn't get it. "I've always wanted you, River. You wanted me too, even though you gave me up to him—"

"He picked you, he fucking picked you, he saw you first, he wanted you, and you may think that's stupid, but he was lonely, and I wasn't. *Then.* I didn't realize in that moment how much you'd come to mean..." He heaves out a long breath, regret lacing his words. "I helped him get *you*. And you fell in love with him."

I cross my arms. He keeps bringing that up.

"Yes, it's true," is dragged from him. "I've seen you two together. I've seen how you look at him, how he looks at you."

"I did. You're right. There are all kinds of love, River.

It's different for every person. I couldn't have spent a year with him if I didn't. What was I supposed to do? You orchestrated our relationship!"

"I don't know what to do anymore! I fucked up! I can't think!"

All's fair in love and war plays in my head, but I can't say that, can't go there. This is so new, and he's deeply torn, what if I'm pushing him too much, putting more pressure on him...

You're too soon for me.

He backs away toward the door.

"River. Wait."

A sound comes from his throat, part frustration, part longing. "I'm *always* waiting." He shuts his eyes. "He's my friend and a brother, Ana. I can't be your revenge."

Then he's gone before I can tell him that this, *this* was never about revenge...

Oh no. It's something else entirely.

22

River

The next day the sky is dreary as I run around the track outside the training center. The harsh, cold air cleans my lungs and makes me feel alive. I need it.

Benji is a few laps behind me today, and I glance back at him. During the offseason, Coach Taylor lets us bring close friends to work out as long as they don't do anything stupid. He's been my workout partner for two years now. He's not a football player, but he's a competitive shit.

"I thought we were taking it easy," he pants as I pass him for another lap.

"Need my head cleared," I call out.

"A lot on your mind, yeah?" he yells from behind me. "Wanna cry on your little bro's shoulder?"

"Suck it," I shout as my thoughts circle back to last night.

Jesus, what was I thinking? The way she felt in my arms. The scent of her skin. The electricity between us. The taste of her on my lips. My hands clench.

I've *been* the guy who lost a girl to another brother. Yeah, this situation is different—they're broken up—but the loyal part of me feels like I'm doing something wrong.

That guilt grew this afternoon at the Kappa house when I stopped by to check in and see some faces.

Last night, that sorority girl called Donovan and told him about us at the library. I mean, I knew it was coming. Eventually someone was going to tell him. I was just hoping I could get to winter break first.

This afternoon, he looked like shit, his face haggard, dark smudges under his eyes as he cornered me in the kitchen. *What is going on, why were you studying with her, you didn't mention it, you don't even like Ana, did you talk to her about me? Did you? Come on, River, tell me you put in a good word...*

His pain lashed at me.

I stood there stoic. I'm sure I said something, but I can barely recall my responses. Guilt coursed through me.

Everything *is* my fault. I started their relationship; I helped end it.

I've been a shit brother to him.

I went to her apartment the night of her birthday and I've been telling myself it was for the class, to return her book, but it wasn't, it wasn't. I walked into her place with need in my heart. I knew he'd forgotten her birthday and was at the library. I knew she'd be hurt by it, and maybe, just maybe it was a way in. Hell, I've known where she lives for months. I've driven by her place a hundred times. I watched her dance on her birthday with images of her riding my cock playing in my mind.

It gets worse.

I hang out at the bar where she works. On purpose. She walks by and my eyes follow. She laughs and I commit it to memory. She frowns and I want to know what the hell is wrong.

I ride the elevator with her, and my hands fight to hold her.

I've touched her, *before they were over*, little brushes before class that made her gasp. That was wrong. Fucking wrong.

I knew what I was doing. I manipulated her, knowing there was something there between us, a delicate string. I dipped my toe across the line and tested the boundary, part of me excited, the other side terrified she'd jump across to grab me.

He was getting trashed on tequila, and I told him to dump her. *Anastasia will never make you happy.*

My eyes shut. I lied to push him over a cliff and then he went and did it all wrong!

Deep down, she *would* make him happy. Sure, he'd be sad about Harvard, but he loves her. That kiss with Harper? It bothered him. I saw his face when he turned away from her that night at the Delta house—and he told Anastasia the truth about it. He admitted to it. Dude *is* in love with her, but I tinkered with it, playing on his insecurities about his future and his parents, shoving Harper at him, encouraging him to tap that. *Don't you want to see if something's there, man?* I told him. *She's perfect for you. She's hot.* (She's not.) *You have so much in common. Your family loves her.*

Jesus. I don't know if he fucked her, but...

I. Fucked. With. Them.

I run faster.

When she kisses me, the world disappears.

Yeah?

When *I* kiss her, the world explodes.

As I round the turn to finish my last lap, I see Crew and Hollis talking to Benji at the bench. I jog their way and snap up a towel to rub the sweat off my face.

"You're running like someone's chasing you," Hollis murmurs, giving me a long look. Not surprised. I came home from the library last night, ignoring Donovan's texts, and went straight to my room. Then this morning, I didn't knock on their doors to see their faces. I got up, got dressed, and left.

I slap the towel down. "The question isn't why am I running so hard, it's why your lazy ass isn't."

Hollis stretches his arms out wide. "There ain't no lazy on me, boo bear. I'm below ten percent body fat like always."

"Showoff." Benji looks down at his body, then at the three of us. "I don't know why I work out with you guys. I go to the student center gym and I'm a god—here I'm a peasant."

"You remind us of what we could become if we stopped playing sports. You're the cautionary tale," Crew says with a smirk.

We head inside to the weight room.

"What up, River?" asks Chris, a sophomore wide receiver. He's gifted, but most of his freshman year, he acted like a scared puppy on the field. The transition from high school to college is tough.

I wave and walk over to him.

"There he goes," I hear Benji murmur as I leave our group. "Talking to his fan club."

"Why do people adore him?" Hollis says. "He's a terrible roommate. Messy. Needy. Thinks he's prettier than me."

"I can hear you, and I am." I flip him off behind my back.

"You playing with us next fall or getting paid in the NFL?" Chris asks with a grin as I reach him. He's about six one with dark skin and hands the size of dinner plates.

"Lots of factors in play. I promise, you'll be the last to know." I chuckle.

"Once you're gone, I'm gonna make all those fans forget you were ever here."

"Not with skinny little arms like that you won't," I say, flexing my bicep and comparing it to his.

"Yo, that's why I'm here. I gotta get in that River shape. Be Tate 2.0."

We bump both elbows, a thing I started with the wide receivers after any of us scored a touchdown.

"These young guns. They can't wait for us to get out of here," Crew says when I return.

Benji slides his gloves on and starts his first set on the bench press.

"Put some more weight on that," Hollis calls out, and Benji glares at him. He gets up and slides two more weight plates on the bar, muttering the entire time.

"Chris is a good kid," I murmur. "He's like the rest of us, doesn't know what he wants."

"Speak for yourself," pants Benji. "I know I want to stop working out with you assholes."

We laugh and do a few sets of arm curls before working on our legs.

"Coach Taylor, you gonna work out with us? Show us what you got if you still got anything," Chris calls out as our coach enters the room.

Coach gives off a subtle chuckle as he eyes the young wide receiver up and down. At six five, he's built like a tractor.

My chest tightens, a feeling of loss hitting me. I let him down this season.

Coach puts a hand on Chris's shoulder and replies in a deep gravelly voice. "Kid, there ain't enough weight in this room for me to waste my time on. Get your shit done then get in the film room and figure out why you can't get off the line against press coverage. Speaking of someone who *does* know how to get off the line—Tate, there's a man who wants to see you." Coach swivels his head toward me. "My office."

I start.

"Who's here to see you?" Benji asks.

"No clue," I tell them then call out, "Coming, sir," to Coach as I grab my towel off the bench and wipe my face. "See you guys later."

"Pizza at the house tonight," Benji says as I leave. "Spike misses you. Wants you to hold him."

I roll my eyes.

Coach is waiting for me and we walk down the hall

together. He asks me about classes and my mom. I answer automatically. *Fine* and *fine*. That's me: living a lie. At first when people would ask about her, I'd go into detail, her treatments, her day-to-day, but not anymore.

Her cancer is progressing...

She keeps telling me everything is okay...

I lie to myself all the time. I never believe me.

My pulse ramps up.

In Coach's office is a man with his hands in the pockets of his khakis as he looks out the window. He turns as we enter: older, white hair, nicely dressed. He narrows his gaze and checks me out, assessing. I straighten my shoulders, recognizing that look.

Are you worth it? it says. *Show me what you got.*

Men with an eye for talent have been assessing me since I caught my first football.

"River, I'd like you to meet an old teammate, Dan Simmons. He never got much time on the field, but he practiced a lot and got paid for it."

They chuckle.

The man moves forward and stretches out his hand to shake mine in a firm grasp. "Don't listen to this old man," he says in a smooth voice full of energy. "I started three years with him in Philly, and he knows it. Most people feel like our '87 line was the best in history."

I rack my brain, and surprisingly find what I'm looking for. "That was the year Philly had Jack Smith and Savage Carter. I can never remember who that other guy was."

The man scoffs. "Exactly. I was the 'other guy' on the greatest defensive line in history. Nice to meet you. Heard a lot about you from Taylor."

I glance back at Coach. "Hope it was good."

Coach nods. "Dan's a scout for Houston."

I let those words sink in.

A small kernel of hope unfurls. Nervous, I nod and murmur a greeting as I take a seat.

Coach says, "He knows you're leaning toward coming back but wanted to talk. We good?"

"Absolutely." I try to sit still in the chair but end up tapping my fingers on my knee like a madman.

Coach leaves, and the room fills with silence as Dan sits across from me and takes out a pad of paper. He chuckles. "You would think I'd take notes with my phone like everyone else, but I'm old school. You mind if I write some things down?"

"Sure." Just don't ask me to take any. There's no way I could write a damn thing right now. My ADHD has spiked with *Holy shit, NFL scout!* bouncing around my head. "Feel free."

He leans back and crosses his legs. His eyes hold a hint of calculation. "I hear you've already received your score from the NFL, and it wasn't what you were hoping for."

344 | THE REVENGE PACT

I twist my ring. "Yeah, second to fourth round is what they said. We won a national championship last year. I wanted first."

"Every player hopes for first." He pauses. "I've been watching you play the last few years, and I see what you can do on the field. Taylor has told me about you as a person. He says you're special, a good motivator, a real hard worker. Back in Houston, we've had some discussions about you."

My eyes flare and I swallow.

"Someone can always beat us to your pick—if you go out—but the way things are going for us, we'll probably have a top pick in the draft. Our team is struggling. No secret there."

One of the worst in the league. "My stats from this year aren't a factor?"

He frowns. "It's concerning. We want to see the production on the field, but we feel we can help you improve. I'm not saying first-round pick—that isn't going to happen for you and you know it—but top of the third round or maybe bottom of the second depending on how you perform at the combine in March. We might scoop you up then."

Might.

I haven't planned on going to the combine. I planned on coming back. Sorta.

"In fact, if I were you..." He leans forward. "I'd finish

this semester, unenroll for the spring, and spend your time prepping for the combine. There'll be scouts and teams everywhere, checking out the new talent. You could really shine, River."

I lean forward. "The truth is, sir, my mom really wants me to get a degree because..." she believes in me "...my dad never got his. Then, he blew out his knee. Football wasn't important anymore."

"Ah, we love those moms. I heard about your dad a few years back. I never met him, and I'm sorry for your loss. I'm sure he'd be proud of you."

I glance out the window and up at the sky searchingly. I rub my chest. Yeah, I hope so.

"You have a good talent. It was a hard year. Your defense had some big holes. It wasn't just your offense. Your last game—fuck, son, I don't know what happened there..." He smirks.

I glance back at him. Life happened.

You only regret the things you didn't do.

Jesus! Anastasia won't get out of my head!

"Right, but I thought it might make more sense to grow here as a player, then go out for the draft after. Be a first-round pick."

"What do you want, River?"

I rub my forehead, that anxious pit growing deeper in my gut. I'm afraid to leave the security of this place behind, and I hate to disappoint Mom, yet part of me yearns to release this pretense of getting an education, say *Fuck it* and go play pro, even if it is for lower pay.

I could build with them. I have the talent, the determination, the leadership skills.

He actually *wants* me.

I glance back to the window as I frown and let that sink in. It's not my dream, to be a low draft pick, but...

"River? You okay?"

"Yeah." I rub my face. I'm fucking this up. I need to show confidence, but shit, my head is all over the place. "I have a lot on my mind. I really want..." to see my mom. Hold her. Ask her if she's okay. I want to see Anastasia. Hold her. Ask her if she's okay.

"I'm kind of in a holding pattern."

He studies me. "I know about your learning issues, and you wouldn't be alone. Several players deal with difficulties. We have special playbooks, flashcards, videos, and one-on-one mentoring. I can pair you up with a veteran who's been down the road you have."

"Ah." Wow.

"Taylor also told me about your mama's cancer. Houston is home to MD Anderson, one of the best cancer centers in the world. I'm sure she's getting great care, but if you end up in Houston, she can get that same care or better. Would love to meet her."

I dip my head and stare at the ground. He makes it sound so easy. Has he met my mom? She'd tell him her care *is* top-notch and he's using emotional manipulation like a pro. "I appreciate that, sir."

He clears his throat. "Look, it's a big decision." He stands up and straightens his sport coat. "I was in the area and thought I'd stop by to let you know your options and what we're thinking."

I stand. "Right. This isn't a promise from you. I get it, and I appreciate the candor."

He gives me a smooth smile. "We're strategizing, yes. I'm checking out Justin Fowler tomorrow. Great wide receiver for Alabama. Guess you know him?" A brow arches.

I wince. Yeah, I *know* him. They beat our asses.

He gives me his card and we say our goodbyes.

After he leaves, I close Coach's door and plop back down in the seat. I need silence. To think.

If I pick the draft, that lit class doesn't even matter. I can flunk every course, knowing I'm not coming back. I can spend time with Mom, help take her to the doctor, help Rae move in with Jason after the wedding, work out, hit the combine in March, the draft in April, then summer camp with whatever team I end up with. I'd never have to sit in a classroom again. On the other hand, I'd be giving up another year to improve my stats, get a possible degree, spend time with the brothers—

My eyes close as my heart clenches.

I wouldn't see Anastasia again.

THE KAPPA KITCHEN table is surrounded by brothers as we sit and tear up the pizzas Parker ordered for dinner. Most of us are headed off in different directions tomorrow, and it's the last time we'll see each other until January.

I've got a slice in my mouth when Anastasia walks in the back door. I choke and grab my water, take a swig, my eyes lasered on her face, devouring her, taking in the long hair, the mini skirt. This one is velvet and red. Black thigh-high boots are on her legs. Her hair is down and frames her face.

Crimson is on her lips.

Benji nudges me under the table with his knee, but I can't stop looking at her anymore. I've passed a point of no return, and if this is all I deserve, then why not?

I texted her earlier and told her my paper is good, said we didn't need to meet tonight. Hollis kind of looked at it. Crew ran his eyes over it. Even Crazy Carl got a peek when I stopped by the bar after class. No reason, just seeing if she was working. She wasn't.

I'm set to turn it in tomorrow. Over. Finished.

She didn't reply to my text.

Her hair catches wind through the open door, fluttering around her oval face. She smiles with a sweeping glance, warm and sweet, as if she never left our house on Friday, devastated.

It's silent for about five seconds, the guys pausing, until Benji calls out her name, jumps up, and runs to her. He picks her up and twirls her around. She beats at his back and giggles, the sound a little forced. He pulls Spike off his shoulder and offers to let her hold him. She gives him a pet and says hi to everyone, chatting with the pledges—*How are exams? How is your girlfriend? Are you excited for the break?*—even giving Parker a big hug. He blushes and offers her pizza.

She's sunshine and light.

Angel.

Mine, the dark side of me insists.

She brushes her gaze over our group at the end of the table, then over me, not stopping, as if I'm no one, quickly moving on to the next person. Her eyes land somewhere out the kitchen window.

"Is Donovan around?" she asks, and I flinch.

"Ana. Here I am," he says as he walks in the kitchen. His face is hopeful as he stops in front of her, eating up her face. "You..." He swallows. "...look great. Thanks for coming. My room?"

Her spine straightens, her voice low as she replies. I strain to hear it over the guys. Shit, I can't.

"Alright," he murmurs, then lets out an exhalation and turns to us. They stand next to each other, not touching, but his hand searches for hers. She doesn't take it.

His words come, halting and unsure, as he looks at us. "Brothers, ah, hate to interrupt your dinner, and I realize not everyone is here, but I wanted this to be public..." His face softens as he glances at her. "I'm deeply sorry for what happened at the toga party. Ana didn't deserve that. My brothers didn't need to hear it. It was messed up, and..." He inhales a breath and seems to search for words, his face grimacing as he reaches out and *takes* her hands. "I'm sorry, Ana. For the embarrassment. For the hurt, the gossip, everything. I just wanted the guys to know where I stand—on your side. You are always welcome in this house. No matter what," he finishes, his eyes glued to her face.

She gives him one of her jerky nods, her throat bobbing.

He says something else, just to her, and I can't hear it. My chest rises as my adrenaline spikes.

A half-smile crosses her lips as she turns from him and gazes around the room. "Later, guys." She gives a little wave.

They murmur their goodbyes.

He walks to the door to the kitchen, clearly waiting for her. She hitches up her purse, takes a breath, and they leave the room.

Where are they going?

I'm up before I know what's going on, shoving my chair until a hand lands on my shoulder. Benji. "River, wait—"

Tension rolls over me. "She's back. She came to see him," I hiss under my breath as my fists tighten.

He shakes his head, and I push his hand off and stalk out of the kitchen and into the den. My heart jumps as I hear their voices echoing up from the staircase. They didn't go to his room...

Good.

I start pacing.

But...

The basement is empty.

They'll be alone.

"River," Benji hisses as he joins me then looks over his shoulder to the kitchen as if to make sure no one notices us. "Look, he must have called her. They're going to talk, probably about the party, and we should stay out of it—"

"Why?" I snap.

He watches me, a concerned expression on his face. "Dude. You aren't hiding it anymore. You're teetering on the edge, man, that's all I'm saying. Let them work out whatever they need to, and focus on you, then circle back and see—"

Right. Of course. Makes perfect sense. Do the right thing.

"No."

Something has snapped and I can't pull it back. She's here. With him.

There are all kinds of love, River. I couldn't have spent a year with him if I didn't.

I close my eyes, wishing I could forget those words. You want to know what kills me, what I try my best to *not* think about? I pushed them together a year ago and she *stayed*. She stayed, loved him, fucked him. Thoughts race in my head. I mean, I have questions, things I could have stuck around and asked last night but didn't. Did she always want me like I wanted her? Did she? How could she pretend with him?

I stop pacing.

No, she isn't like that. She did love him, right, right, and it cuts, it cuts.

I fucked them up.

My hands rake through my hair and I let out a juicy curse.

He grabs my shoulder. "One brother to another— they need to talk, and you know it. They didn't have a proper chat Friday."

"Maybe I don't give a shit anymore."

His grip tightens. "Wanna know what I admire about you? When anyone is stressed, you calm them. When a brother is out of gas, you put in fuel. You drop your ego and put yourself second. It's what makes us the best. Guys are begging to be part of Kappa."

It's not enough.

Not anymore.

I may not be back.

I might not see her again except for the ski trip.

Her *Kiss me, River.*

Her breathy gasps.

The sound she makes when she comes...

"Let me go, Benji."

He drops his hand as I take the stairs, and I'm halfway there when I groan out my frustration and stop.

What if I see something I don't want to?

What if she never really wanted me at all?

She wanted revenge. Payback.

Maybe the rooftop was enough to tide her over, to throw in his face and say, *Hey, look what I did with your frat brother*—

Stop.

Fucking.

Stop.

She isn't like that. Kian was a joke to her. She didn't even want to do it; I saw that dread on her face. Regardless of why she dreaded it, payback mentality isn't who she is. She didn't care that I wasn't going to be around on the ski trip to help. She cares about herself too much as a person to give revenge that much power. I know it, I know it. On the rooftop, I told her I didn't want to be her revenge, but I knew as soon as the words came out it was wrong. She's full of love, inside and out, and she doesn't use people.

I grab the handrail, my chest heaving as I plop down on one of the steps.

If I barge in on them, what kind of trouble would it start?

What would I say when I don't even know how she feels about me?

Why is she here?

Do I want a knock-down, drag-out fight like I had with Dex?

Cops coming?

A big upheaval in my own house?

A divided frat?

I have responsibilities, a band of brothers who respect me. I'm their leader and they look up to me. That pressure eats at me, reminding me that they haven't even been broken up for a week, and here I am, jonesing to cause trouble.

Can't I wait?

Give her space?

So many thoughts bounce in my head and I can't focus on any single one enough to calm myself. I twist my ring over and over.

I'm vaguely aware of Benji sitting next to me on the stairs.

He hands Spike over, and I hold him in my lap. Ugliest lizard ever, but he settles in and clings to my shirt. He glances at me, not quite an evil eye, but it's debatable. "Does he bite?"

"Only if he doesn't like you, and he loves everyone. Don't kiss him though."

"Wasn't planning on it."

"He might carry salmonella or strange bacteria, I don't know. He likes Guns N' Roses. Shuts his eyes and goes right to sleep."

"Has he eaten today?"

"Three crickets. Took a video. When you watch it in slow-mo, his tongue is creepy, and the cricket's legs are like *Save me, save me!* It's hilarious. I'll text it to you."

A few moments of silence pass and I take several deep breaths, willing my coiled muscles to relax.

"Thanks for coming after me," I say. "Guess I lost it for a second."

There's a pause, then, "Yeah. I've seen how you stare at her in class. You love her."

I push down the lump in my throat and keep my gaze on Spike. "Crazy. I barely know her," I murmur.

"You *know* her. You've been around her for a year." A huff comes from his chest. "Been thinking about our conversation last week, and you're right—I *am* the woo-woo dude. Laugh all you want, but I think your dad wanted one last talk with you, his only son. Maybe to make sure you survived. Who knows how the afterlife works? Maybe he needed to see you, to comfort himself and share his love. I don't know. I think these experiences happen to people, but we don't hear about it because we think it makes us sound crazy or deranged. I think he was there with you before he passed on to somewhere else."

"Been on the internet, huh?"

"Dude. Near-death experiences are fascinating."

A smile ghosts over my lips. "He was dead, and I wasn't near death. They put me in a coma to help me heal." I pause, my mind on the image of my dad next to my bed in the hospital. I play back the memory, the way he held my hand. "But it was a goodbye. He wanted to see me one last time...yeah, I believe that."

"Always knew you did. You've discussed it with me, more than once, three times if you count this, and that's the magic number. I'm your best friend. Crew and Hollis can suck it."

I huff out a small laugh. "Best little bro ever." My two fingers tap my heart twice.

He does the same.

"Ana... You've held yourself in check with her for a long time. That kind of tension eats at you, man, gets under your skin and never leaves. Your mom is sick, football is up in the air, and you don't know what to do next. It's okay to have moments where you freak out." He nods. "I saw you running today. Like the devil was after you."

"She calls me Snake."

"What do you call her?"

My chest clenches. "Rainbow." I sigh. "The what-ifs and should-haves are eating me up. She knows I authored that note."

"You messed up. I was there. You wanted her."

"I shoulda made my move, shoulda told him—"

"But you didn't."

"She loves him."

"Does she?"

"She wouldn't have stayed if she didn't."

"So? You never made your move. What did you want her to do?"

"Is this your method of talking me down? Hope you don't become a therapist or some shit."

"I'd make a fine psychologist."

I pet Spike on his head. "She's too smart for me."

"Some people have other kinds of smarts."

"She's coming back to school, and I don't know if I am."

"Fate may have other plans."

"She's kind."

"I'm pretty sweet, too." He grins.

"She says I'm beautiful. Inside. Who says that shit?"

"Get over yourself. You're an asshole." He pats my shoulder. "Look, at the end of the day, if *she's* what you want, I support it. I like Donovan. He's a decent guy and he cares about the frat. But you, my friend, are our leader, and warriors deserve to have their glory. Who am I to stand in your way? Now, if you just wanted to bang her, I'd beat the shit out of you."

My throat feels thick. "That's not what this is."

He shrugs. "Well, I'm a player. I don't know jack about feelings, so I can't really help, but..."

"My dad said to wait."

"I get it, but who knows what that means? How do you know when the waiting is over?"

"I've thought maybe he meant to give her space, to let her find her way without me interfering, let her get over him, let some distance build up between her and Donovan, but I haven't been doing that lately, obviously, and I feel like time is running out..." My voice trails off.

"You've had a shit year. Things were bound to snap."

I nod. "Anastasia gets me, Benji. She doesn't care about this revenge thing. I mean, maybe she did at first, but that's not why she's helping me. She's solid and doesn't pretend to be something she isn't. She likes *who* she is, and so do I. Like I could see me and her..." together forever. "I've told her everything, my issues, about Mom. She sees *me*, likes how...messed up I am."

"Not messed up."

"You know what I mean. I never should have walked away from her last night. I should have manned up and laid it out for Donovan. But, now she's here, with him. Dude. I don't know what they're saying down there and it's..." killing me. I roll my neck, trying to ease the pressure.

He slaps me on the back. "Guinness? The Truth Is Out There? Where are your boys tonight?"

"Home. Packing for the break. What I should be doing." With a long breath out, I rise up and hand Spike back. "Yeah. Let's get out of here."

THERE'S sleet falling by the time Benji and I leave the bar and head to my truck. It's not bad, but I give the road an extra look over. People in the South tend to overreact when it spits snow, running out and buying milk and bread like a blizzard apocalypse is imminent. There's hardly any traffic though. I check my watch. It's ten. Is she home yet?

A text comes in from my boys, asking where I am and confirming their travel plans for tomorrow. Crew is flying to California and Hollis is going to Savannah for the break. I pause next to my truck to scan them.

Hollis sends, **River, you wanna talk?**

Um... I can talk about anything, this is known, but ??? I say and hit send.

One of the pledges came by and mentioned Ana was at the house with Donovan, he replies. **They back on?**

Damn. People love to gossip. Even dudes.

Crew sends, **You alright, River?**

Not really, but I picture Crew and Hollis sitting in the den next to each other texting me, and I push up a smile.

I'm okay. She came to the house, yes, but *we* aren't over.

I might be late, I send. **I'll knock on your doors in the morning.**

Weirdo, Crew sends.

I laugh. **You love me, Hollywood.**

Wake me. I'll share my Ding Dongs with you, boo bear, Hollis adds.

There's a joke here somewhere, Crew sends.

They say bye and I stick my phone back in my jeans.

"We could hit the ATO party. They're having one every night this week," Benji muses as he hums "Sweet Child O' Mine" to Spike on his shoulder. He's buzzing, but I only had one drink. My head doesn't need alcohol muddling it up.

"Nah." I'm not in the mood to party.

Benji hops in the passenger side and Spike never

flinches. I shake my head, a rueful laugh coming from me. "I can't believe Marilyn let you bring him in."

"He doesn't bark. He smiles. It's kind of weird, but he does. He doesn't pee—much."

"He pissed on your shirt. And I think he was trying to hump a beer mug."

"No, he was just looking at himself in the reflection of the glass. He's a sexy beast." He tugs at the flannel he's wearing. "Good thing Crazy Carl had an extra in his truck. Dude's alright, isn't he?"

I nod. "Carl's the shit."

"I'm gonna get Spike a collar. Engraved. Something poetic. *Spike, you horny lizard, I love the fuck out of you.*"

We go down a rabbit hole of possible messages to engrave on the lizard's collar.

I crank the truck.

"Where we going?" Benji asks as I miss the turn for Greek Row and head farther into Walker.

"Drive-by."

"Who? Oh, Ana. Cool. I'm down."

My hands tighten on the wheel. Maybe she's still at the Kappa house, and I guess I'll know if her car isn't at her apartment. I'll know to prepare myself when I drop Benji off.

When we pull in, Anastasia is outside her complex with a guy wearing a tool belt around his waist. She's tugging on his arm.

"Something's wrong," I say as I park and get out. Benji follows.

"What happened, Sam! Start from the beginning," comes Anastasia's voice, raised and layered in urgency. "Here. Give me Oscar."

"Please." He heaves out a long exhalation and hands a dog to her, a small one, and she takes it.

"What's going on?" I ask.

She flips around, her face wet from tears.

My adrenaline spikes. "Are you okay?"

Her throat bobs as she wipes at her face with one hand. "No. June... I came home, and she wasn't here. Sam said she was hurt!"

Sam fidgets as I fix my gaze on him. "What happened?"

He blows out a breath, a harried look on his face. "The furnace blew out and a repairman came out to fix it. He saw June, and I guess he's buddies with the landlord. He must have called him, then Mr. Winston showed up and tried to run her off. She threw some stuff at him then Oscar acted like a big dog and nipped at him. Poor dog is old and can barely move, but he gave him a good run. Then he started asking me questions." He looks at Anastasia. "Ana, I had to tell him the truth. She's been here too long." He sighs. "He called the cops, said he was attacked by a dog and had a vagrant on the premises he wanted removed."

Anastasia shakes her head. "Oscar would never hurt anyone, and neither would June!"

Sam nods. "Cops showed up, blue lights blazing. She started running, slipped on the pavement and fell, damn sleet, then jumped up and ran down the road. I didn't see Oscar till they left. He was hiding behind one of her crates."

Anastasia exhales. "I should have found her somewhere to stay. This is my fault. I should have made her stay with us—"

"You can't do that," Sam says. "Her name isn't on the lease, Ana—"

"Forget that. It's sleeting tonight!" She gives him a pleading look. "Which direction did she go, Sam?"

He grimaces. "She ran off down the street toward Highland. The cops took a look around and said to call them if she comes back. I'll have to, Ana."

She blinks rapidly. "She's not a criminal. No one cares about her. People don't *see* her. They don't get that she's a person! We aren't all the same, we aren't, and it's okay if she's different, it's okay..." Her voice trails off, her face crumpling.

"Anastasia," I say and pull her against me, my arms going around her. "Shhh, I got you, I got you." Oscar squirms between us, and I give her some space as I tip her chin up. "We'll figure this out."

"I'm here for this!" Benji announces jovially. "Let's

find this June chick. She hot?" No one replies, and he shrugs. "Tough crowd. Maybe she likes lizards."

Sam sighs. "I'm worried too, Ana. I'm sorry I couldn't stop her or do anything. Don't be mad at me."

She leans on me. "I'm not mad at you, Sam, just terrified for her. I'm sorry I yelled. It's just... She left her coat, her blankets. Even Oscar. It's freezing out here and..." She stops, swallowing as she focuses back on me. "There are only a few places she goes. I have to find her."

"I'll drive my truck. You come with us," I say. I whip off my varsity jacket and help her into it, pulling the collar around her neck. My lips graze hers. I don't give a fuck what happened with her and Donovan in the basement. She's my rainbow.

She nods, her hold tightening around the shivering mutt. "Oscar's coming too."

"Of course."

23

Anastasia

Worry gnaws at my gut as we get in River's truck. I take the front and Benji gets in the back. He's got Oscar in his lap and a lizard on his shoulder. It should be funny, but my head isn't processing humor.

River has my hand tight in his, his left one on the steering wheel as he drives to Walmart. We circle the parking lot three times, driving to the back where the loading docks and semi-trucks are parked. We get out and peek behind a couple of dumpsters. Nothing.

We get back in the truck and sleet beats against the windshield, harder and faster than it was before, and I shiver. He throws a look at me and cranks up the heat then reaches for my hand again, lacing our fingers together.

"She's not here," I say dismally.

Benji leans in between us. "So, this lady? Tell me about her."

"She's in her sixties, horndog," I say.

He grins. "Just trying to lighten the mood. I may have had a few too many."

I exhale. "I appreciate it. I'm just rattled." Another long breath comes from me. "She wears an Atlanta Falcons beanie. She's petite and small..." I stop, dread building in my stomach. What if she's disoriented? What if she's in someone's back yard, slowly freezing to death? What if—

River brings our clasped hands to his lips. "We'll find her."

He makes one more circle around the parking lot, driving slow past the front of the store. We scan over the people coming and going then I hop out and dash inside to talk to the employee greeter. I ask if she's seen her and she says yes, she's seen her before, but not tonight.

"Try Big Star," I murmur as I get back in the truck.

We leave and drive the two miles to the grocery store, my eyes scouring the sidewalks and businesses along the way, wishing it weren't so late.

Big Star is closed with no cars in the parking lot. River drives up and down the front of the building, then goes to the back. He stops and parks and I'm out of the car, checking behind a dumpster and under the loading docks. He helps me, running from one place to the other. He slips once on the ice and I wince, but he rights himself and sends me a smile. "Can't catch a ball this year, but I've got great balance."

We're on our way back to the truck when he throws an arm around me and pulls me underneath one of the overhangs from the store. "Don't worry, I know this town inside out."

"I can't go on the ski trip until she's safe."

He nods. "We'll look all day tomorrow if we don't find her. I'll skip the trip and fly home from here. I won't rest until she's safe, Anastasia."

A wave of emotion slams into me as I look at him.

He doesn't have to know June; he just cares.

Tears prick at my eyes.

"What?" he asks softly.

I swallow thickly. "Aren't you going to ask me why I came to the Kappa house?"

A hesitant look crosses his face. "I was waiting until we found June."

I crane my neck to take him in, the chiseled jawline, those sapphire eyes dipped in smoke. "He called me to apologize. He wanted it public, and those guys are important to me. I wanted them to hear. That house has felt like home to me for a year. It does me no good to dwell on how he broke up with me." I pause. "He offered to go to Brooklyn Law. He said he'd go against his parents and work on us..."

"How do you feel about that?" He studies me intently.

The answer is automatic. "Bad for him. I never considered it, River, not even a little. He isn't mine." I hold his eyes, wanting to be sure he understands where I stand on this. "He and I, we never would have lasted, with or without your interference. You gave him good advice. You feel guilty because you had a motive."

A few seconds pass.

"Did you touch him?" he growls.

"No. We said goodbye, and I gave him his pin."

He breathes out slowly. "I see."

Do you?

I don't think River really *gets* how I feel.

Even now, I'm terrified of the strong emotions I'm experiencing.

From the moment I met him, something shifted in my heart—and never left.

"He isn't the person I'm meant to be with."

He looks away from me for a moment then comes back to me. "Okay."

"It's *you*, River, it's you," I say softly.

"Okay."

"If you say *okay* one more time—"

He kisses me, ravaging my mouth, rough and hard.

His lips are rough, his tongue stroking, sucking, and taking. His mouth slants over mine, slick and hot, and I groan, my hands snaking around his neck. His go under my skirt and pull me up as my legs go around his waist. His lips, his scent, his strong arms, his every touch...it's home, home, home.

Benji lays on the horn and we pull apart. River presses a kiss to my forehead. "It's cold out here. Come on. Let's find your grandma."

By the time midnight arrives and we still haven't found her, I'm biting my nails.

I look out the window as we pull up at Henning Park. "She mentioned coming here with Oscar," I tell them.

Benji is still animal-sitting, so River and I bundle up and split up as we walk the park. The streetlights don't illuminate the area well, so River pulls out two flashlights from a tool chest in the back of his truck. I head for the monkey bars to the right side while he goes left toward the hill we climbed last week. I call out June's name and hear him doing the same.

A few minutes later, he shouts my name, and I take off running through the wet grass.

He's next to a snack area. It's a small building, obviously locked up, but there's a bit of an overhang and a small form is huddled there, her head bent down as she clutches her knees to her chest.

Relief comes so swiftly I have to grasp my chest.

"June," I say breathlessly, kneeling down next to her as River takes a step back to give us room.

She's missing her shoes, her beanie is gone, and she shivers in the cold air. Her pants are ripped at the knees, blood caked from a scrape. Even her gloves are gone. I take River's jacket off and drape it over her shoulders.

"June, it's me, Ana. I've been looking for you. Are you okay?"

I touch her shoulders, her arms, her hands, wincing at the chill.

Her head is still bent to her knees when she speaks. "They came to get me. They came and I had to fight back. I fell down."

"I see that. I'm sorry for it." Ignoring the cold, I sit on the cement sidewalk next to her. "I'm here now."

"You aren't alone." She rises up and her eyes dart past me, squinting at River. Her teeth chatter from the cold. "Is that Bruce Willis?"

I squeeze her hand. "His agent said he was busy. Can you believe it? The nerve. Movie stars these days."

"He's probably on location," she says as a lone tear eases down her face. "Oscar?"

I squeeze her shoulder. "In the truck. He misses you. Let me help you up to go see him." She clings to my hands as I tug her up to standing. Her hair is tangled, and I brush my hand over it. "I want to look at your knees when we get in the truck. Did you hit your head? Does anything feel broken?"

She shakes her head. "No, just scraped up..." She leans back against the building and takes River in, giving him a once-over. "This the bad boy?"

"Yeah. He wants to help you too."

"He isn't going to try to put me in a shelter? People steal your stuff there. You wake up and your shoes are gone. And the last place had lice."

"And they put tracking devices in your ears," I add with a small smile.

She sniffs. "No, they don't. That's silly. I said that so you'd let it go."

I huff out a laugh. "I told you there are private rooms at the shelter in Walker. Maybe—"

"Ana. I don't like them." She plucks at her baggy sweater and her throat bobs. "There was a shelter in Atlanta, a while back. It burned down and three people never got out."

Chills ghost over me.

She sighs. "One of them was my son."

My eyes well with tears and I fight to hold them in. My voice is strangled. "I'm so sorry, June."

She wipes her nose with her hand. "He...he had learning issues since he was born. Not enough oxygen. He was forty, different, and all I had. He was asleep, and I went out to check on Oscar when it happened..." Her breath catches. "I couldn't get to him."

I wrap her up in my arms and pat her back. "I'm sorry, so much. We won't do anything you don't want. You can stay in a motel. I'll stay in a room next to you for a couple of days if you want." I can get her a room on my credit card, pay it up for a week or so, then figure out the future when Mom and Dad get here.

She winces. "You're too nice to me. I can't do that."

"You can't come back to the complex," I tell her gently. "They'll know. I can get your things for you, your blankets and whatever you had in the tent, but the landlord is not happy."

River steps closer, his movements slow and easy. "June, you don't know me, but I have an idea of where you can stay. It's quiet and sort of out of the way from people."

She rubs her arms and gives him a wary look.

"Let's get you in the truck and talk about it there," he continues.

She bites her lip. "Alright, but I'm only listening to you because you wished Ana happy birthday. And you gave me twenty bucks at Big Star."

I start as I look over at River, who's smiling.

"Didn't think you recognized me," he says softly.

"You aren't Bruce, but you'll do."

He smiles, a gentle one. "May I carry you?"

She nods, another tear escaping as her chest hitches. "Yeah."

"WHAT DO YOU THINK ABOUT ALIENS?" Carl asks June. "Real or fake?"

She ponders it as she sips on her coffee, her eyes darting around the den, landing on me as I stand next to the counter then coming back to Carl. She's trying to figure him out as they sit at his kitchen table. "Never met one, but who am I to say what's true. Half the town believes it. There's even some kind of museum downtown."

"The truth is out there," Carl says in a serious voice.

"Brings in tourists, I guess," she says, and the conversation is so mundane that I can't stop staring. "I'm from Atlanta but ended up here to get away."

Oh, June. Her son...

My throat tightens. It's not a topic for now, but I make a note to talk to her about her son later. I'll have to ease into it; I know she has boundaries. Talking doesn't make the pain go away, but it gives the person who died a name in the universe and makes them important. I want her whole story someday. I want her to let me love her.

She nibbles on a piece of toast Benji made earlier. He

slathered strawberry jelly all over it and gave it to her like it was a filet. She looks at Carl from underneath her lashes. "I think you might be crazy though."

He grins. "All the best people are."

She cocks her head.

He gives her another smile.

She blinks rapidly and pets Oscar, who's curled up in her lap.

River drove us to Carl's house about an hour ago, a small brick place on the outside of town. He knocked on Carl's door while we sat in the truck, waiting as River talked to him. I'm not sure what he said, but Carl listened, then opened his door and called out, *Come on in, friends.*

Her knees have been bandaged, and there's a new hat on her head, one Carl offered, an old Braxton beanie. Since her clothes were soaked, she changed into some gray joggers, fuzzy socks, and one of Carl's flannel shirts.

River and I linger in the kitchen, drinking coffee. It's two in the morning, but neither of us seem in a hurry. Benji is slumped in the recliner in the den, snoring, Spike attached to him like a tick.

River has a hand behind my neck, his fingers playing with the hair on the back of my head. I sigh and lean against him as I listen to them. Carl and June seemed to see something in each other from the moment she walked in, a kinship, two people who aren't like everyone else. Once you've experienced loneliness, you see it in others.

Carl tells June about the RV camper he has in his back yard, how it has electric and water and would she like to stay there.

"I don't know," she says slowly.

"There's a skylight," he adds. "I mean it's probably dusty and stuff, but we can clean it up. Might help you feel like you're outside and such. And I don't mind if Oscar stays with you." His voice is gruff, and I think he's feeling her sense of helplessness. Maybe he's been there.

River massages my scalp, his fingers digging in as if sensing my tension.

June swallows thickly, then a long sigh leaves her chest. "I'd like to look at it. And if Oscar likes it..."

Carl grins. "Excellent."

"She's okay," River promises me softly, his voice low in my ear. "Carl wouldn't hurt a flea, and she'll have her space. You can come see your family whenever you want."

I gaze up at him, the strong face, those broad shoulders.

My heart tightens. He's my family, too.

I grab his face and kiss him long and hard right there in Carl's shabby kitchen.

"Thank you for helping," I murmur as I rub my thumb down his jawline.

"I didn't do anything."

He is so wrong.

He was incredibly strong and supportive, all while wondering what happened between me and Donovan. "I wish we were somewhere cool, like a rooftop with the stars looking at us, so I could tell you everything I need to say. I wish you hadn't left me last night, River. Is... I mean, are we okay?"

"You're mine, Anastasia. I can't let you go. I did once."

"I should have ended things with Donovan after this summer, but part of that was not wanting to give up being at the house, seeing everyone, seeing *you*..." I stop, uncertainty tugging at me, at how he'll take my words. "I did love him, but it's nothing like..." this. "Am I a terrible person?"

"Never." He pulls me into him, spreading his legs so I can fit there. He gazes down at me.

"What?" I say when he hasn't said anything, just searching my face.

"Rainbow, I love you," he says in a quiet voice. "Crazy. Insane. Like can't get you out of my head since that night in the library. It all happened so fast, and I was looking out for Donovan...then you showed up in my bedroom, and I figured out your name, and I knew I'd fucked up. Watching you with him nearly killed me, it did, and I pushed through, but that's done. You, you...slay me, baby girl."

Emotion whips at me, sneaking in and wrapping around my heart. A tear slips down my face, and he wipes it away.

"Ah, don't cry."

I fell for him a long time ago, the feeling born that moment in the library when he dropped his pen. The way he gazed at me, like he couldn't take his eyes off me, the way he pretended to be reading a book. Oh, I tried to push him to the back of my mind, to forget him, because it was the right thing to do for Donovan, but I couldn't. He's always been part of my thoughts, lying in wait, itching to bubble to the surface. That feeling blossomed and grew solid the morning he shared the sunrise with me.

You stay gold, Anastasia, breathe every breath, read all the books, get into law school, fuck the haters, and stay beautiful.

Who says things like that? HE DOES.

He believes in me. Accepts me the way I am.

I'm in love with his random personality, the tender way he talks about his mom, his three things that guide him...

The truth is, I never had *these* feelings for Donovan. This consuming need. This feeling of being connected by something bigger than me.

"I love you, Snake." Another tear escapes and I bite my lip. "Sorry. It's just..." I pause, circling back to some of what I think has been worrying him. "I know we haven't spent a lot of time one on one, but we didn't have to. Sometimes big moments happen in a heartbeat, like the library. I believe in destiny and fate, I do. Even when you pretended to hate me and wouldn't look at me, my body knew the exact moment you got on the elevator behind me. I'm saying stuff that feels too soon, I know, and I don't want to put pressure on you. I know you have enough, you do, and I do too, but things are moving fast, it's the end of the term, and we feel so fragile, but..."

"But?"

"You and me? We're going to stay gold—together. Can you see it?" My breath catches.

A slow smile curls his lips. "When all this is over, I'm going to tell you about a dream I had once about my dad —maybe not a dream, whatever—but yeah, I see it. Gold. It feels good, baby girl." He kisses me soft and easy, taking his time, his tongue tangling with mine as my hands curl around his neck.

24

River

The next day, I head up the steps to class. I can't stop smiling. There's a girl in front of me, lingering on the steps. She's wearing a mini skirt and heeled Chucks that match her hair. I slide in next to her, feeling the tingles at her proximity. We don't speak, our hands brushing as we walk inside and head to the elevator.

I let her get on first, then follow. She slaps the button for our floor. I drop my bag, back her against the wall, and tilt her face up. We kiss, my lips eating at hers, my hunger ratcheting up, to feel all of her, to consume her. I want to take it slow, to savor us, but it's hard.

We didn't leave Carl's until after three in the morning, all of us loopy with exhaustion. Anastasia was hesitant to go, but June was exhausted after a tour of the RV.

Carl had it parked on the back of his property surrounded by trees. I knew about it because he'd told me about how he's always wanted to drive it out west to find Area 51. It had been vacant for a while. Anastasia changed the sheets on the bed and shook out rugs while Carl, Benji, and I moved some of the comic books he'd stuck in there to his garage.

June was quiet, always watching, but I saw hope in her eyes, that look of *It's going to be okay.* She worked out a deal with Carl for 'rent.' She said she'd keep a watch out for spaceships, and he said that would work. Is it a permanent place for her? Time will tell. It's a good start, and maybe Carl needs somebody too. Loneliness has followed them both. Friends are a definite possibility.

Afterward, I drove Anastasia home, then Benji, then I went back to her place and crawled into her bed. We didn't have sex—I'm waiting for something special—but I held her as we talked about nothing, and everything. I told her about my dad's 'visit' to me when I was fifteen. She wept, part sorrow for me, part happiness that I experienced seeing him, part amazement that he said her name. At seven, I went home, worked out, showered, then woke up Crew and Hollis so I could see their faces and tell them goodbye. I also told them my decision about school. I'm not coming back. Talking to my mom and sister on Thursday and then the scout? It made everything crystal clear.

And Anastasia? Leaving her?

I can't think about it without freaking out, so I've shoved it way down.

"I wonder if a Delta will get on the elevator today?" she murmurs as we pull away, her lips swollen from my kisses.

I push a strand of hair out of her eyes. "They'll be taking the stairs."

She smirks. "I can't believe you threatened to black-list them. Got your paper?"

I nod. "You?"

"Mhmm."

We walk into class and wait in line to hand in our essays. There's no lecture today, just turn it in and it's over and done. It's anticlimactic after the turmoil this class gave me for four months.

"You never told me why you took this class," she says with a searching look.

"Because you did."

A small smile curls her lips, her eyes dancing. "And it took you all semester."

"Baby girl, now, you know you wanted me from day one—"

She punches me in the arm, and I laugh.

Whitman sits at his desk, his head lowered as I hand mine over. His beady eyes sharpen as he looks from me to Anastasia.

"Your work, Mr. Tate?"

"Always," I mutter.

He takes it with a grunt. "We'll see."

"What's it worth if I don't do it myself?"

He raises an eyebrow. "You've had things handed to you. I'm not the professor who passes you because you're a famous jock."

Huh. Maybe I've had a few things handed to me. I grew up with two amazing parents who loved me. We had money. On the other hand, I lost my dad and I might lose my mom.

"Life is tough, Mr. Tate. You'll figure it out once college is over."

Oh, man, he went there.

"Agreed, life is rarely fair." I nod as I stick my hands into my pockets. "But the next time you know a kid has issues in your class, maybe try some understanding. I'm not talking about an athlete like me. They might be a regular person, the kind who's talented in other ways, but if someone asks them to read, their throat closes up. This class was a mountain to me, Dr. Whitman. I climbed it. Fair and square."

He frowns. "Mr. Tate..."

You can't change assholes. Usually. But I tried.

"Think about it. Have a great Christmas."

He sputters and I keep walking, letting the next person up to his desk.

I walk to where Anastasia waits. She bites her lip. "You didn't toss a pen at him, but still epic."

I grin, feeling confident. She read my paper last night. She said it's good. Do you know what it means to know I wrote something and she thinks it's good? It makes me feel like I can take on anything.

Benji practically runs into the room, his shirt on inside out, his hair a mess. He slaps his paper on Whitman's desk then saunters over to us like he's cool.

I laugh and Anastasia joins me. I think we're both running on a strange energy, but clearly, Benji is not.

"Morning," we say at the same time.

He groans. "I barely made it. What a night, but hey, today's the end of the term. What time's your flight, Ana? Ours is at five in the morning. Shit. Y'all wanna hit the bar for a few hours after classes?"

Anastasia tells him hers is at six at night. "Um, I'm busy. Got to pack and check on June."

Benji looks at me. "Plans today? I need a buddy."

"Packing and...stuff," I say vaguely.

He squints as he darts his eyes between us. "Ah, I get it. Packing is code."

"No, I have to pack," I insist.

"Uh-huh." He blows out a breath. "Guess the days of me and you running game are gone, and that's cool, I approve. I can rope Parker into going to the bar with me. He's a good time."

I slap him on the back, we say goodbye, then Anastasia and I head out and get in the elevator.

She's in my arms before the door shuts. She kisses me like crazy and my heart pounds. I want more of her, so fucking much...

The elevator opens and we separate. We leave the building, bracing ourselves for the cold wind as we walk to her next exam. Before she goes in, I take her hand and lace our fingers together.

"I'm going to tell him. Before he leaves for Atlanta."

She nods, relief on her face. Like me, she wants this over so we can really begin.

He's in his room at his desk typing when I knock on his door and step inside. There's an open suitcase on the bed, clothes draped around the room, books everywhere.

"Hey," I say. "What's up?"

"Hey." He straightens up in his seat, shuts his laptop, and grimaces. "Not much. Checking out Harvard, still looking for a place to live next fall. The good places fill up fast. All my exams are done, 'bout to head out. You?"

My eyes bounce around the room, taking in the framed picture he has of him and Anastasia on his nightstand. It was taken the night he pinned her. Part of me wants to pick it up and look at her face, but the other part wants to burn it to ashes.

He follows my gaze and runs a hand through his hair. "Yeah. Still haven't put that away." A long exhalation comes from his chest.

I brace myself, my voice stilted as I tell him the decision I came to. "This is it. My last day. My mom needs me. She won't say it out loud, but she does."

His eyes flare, and he stands, reading the serious vibe in my voice. "No way. I mean, I knew you were waffling, but I always figured you'd..."

"Come back to Braxton?"

"Yeah, at least next semester. Here take a seat. What about football?" He goes to move clothes to make room on his bed, and I shake my head and wave off his offer to sit. I'm too twitchy.

"Yeah, going to take my chances in the draft. Can we talk a minute?" Get in, say it, and get out.

"Sure."

I look out his window and search for words. I leave my arms loose at my sides, pretending to be relaxed. I exhale. "You're going to be president. The guys look up to you, you have leadership skills, and you'll carry us through the spring. I might be able to get away and visit but..." it's going to be hard. There's a thousand miles between Vermont and Braxton. "...I'll be focused on Mom, getting in shape for the combine, then the draft."

He pushes his glasses up. "I'll do a good job. I mean, you'll be missed." His mouth pulls down and an uncertain expression flashes on his face. "It feels like you're building up to something." He gets strangely still, then glances back at the photo. "Is this about Anastasia?"

I start at the name he uses, and he sees it, a hard expression growing on his face as he gives me a *look*.

"Like I didn't notice. You never took your eyes off her."

I tuck my hands into the pockets of my jeans. "Donovan, yeah."

He swallows, his chest rising rapidly. "Just say it."

Shit, here it comes. "I'm with her. I wanted you to know before people see us on the ski trip."

His jaw pops, a flush rising on his cheeks. His brown eyes harden, his fists clenching. Ten long seconds pass. His eyebrows draw together. "So, this whole time...that night you were at her apartment, the time we talked about her in the basement, then the day of the party?" He stops and scrubs his face. "You told me to break up with her. *You* told me I needed space. Every conversation we had... Fuck me."

"If you really needed her..." like I do "...it wouldn't have mattered what *I* said. You would have ignored me." My voice hardens.

He gets in my face, his finger jabbing me in the chest. "You've wanted her since day one."

And I should have taken her!

Towering over him, I shove his shoulders with both hands, and he stumbles back. "Back off."

He straightens up. "Or what? You'll beat the shit out of me? Nice way to end us, River."

"I'm not here to fight," I tell him curtly. "I waited until it was over, *and it is over.*"

"It's been a week! You're not coming back and she's staying!" he shouts. "How's that going to work? I mean, are you serious about her?" Disbelief colors his words. Something he reads on my face makes his mouth open. "I don't believe you. You're a slut, River, and she'll figure it out. You can't keep it in your pants!"

"I did with her!" Barely.

He shakes his head. "So you're like, what...in love with her?"

"Yes."

The first time I saw her, *before I even knew her name,* something was born. I'm in love with the dreamer side of her, her quirky randomness, the way her eyebrows arch, her passion for books, her intelligence, the way she cares for others, no matter who they are. She's a beginning for me, a future I want.

He paces around the room, stopping periodically to look at me and shake his head. An incredulous sound comes from his throat. "Jesus, you're a joke as president.

You two deserve each other. Enjoy. Just know I was there first and it was fucking spectacular."

I slam my fist into his face and he falls back on the bed, holding his eye.

He grunts. "You're a bastard, the worst kind of brother. You put a girl before us. Disloyal as hell."

Maybe I was...

"It was worth it."

"She'll be here. You'll be there. You can't hang on to a girl like her."

He's hit a nerve, and my hands fist, longing to pound into him, all the pent-up worries I don't want to think about flaring.

I think about my three things for myself, then I give him his.

"Do great at Harvard. Be a lawyer and help others. And leave us alone. One word to Anastasia, one thing, just one, and I'll come back and fuck you up."

I didn't want this to be ugly, I didn't, because he was my friend, but when it comes to matters of the heart, ties get severed, and I'm ripping this one right down the middle.

"Get out of my room," he says as he stands.

"Gladly." A long breath comes from me as I walk away and leave him there.

He doesn't follow, and I hear the slam of his door as I hit the staircase.

Wrestling with my emotions for control, I take a seat on a step, my chest rising as I think about Anastasia. That ring of gold around her irises. The way she feels in my arms. Calm settles over me slowly, sinking into my bones.

After grabbing my things from my room and putting them in a duffle, I hit the basement and say hi to the pledges and a few brothers who are hanging around. I tell Benji I'm not coming back, but I can't tell anyone else. If I make it public now, the media will catch on, then all hell will break loose. I give them hugs that signify *This might be the last time I see you.* Will Donovan drag my name through the mud? Probably, and it's okay. The ones who know me, who see me for who I am, will get it.

She isn't temporary.

She's the ultimate goal.

Yeah, I'm leaving her, and I know it cuts her, it has to, but *I have to.*

An hour later, I walk out and stand in the front yard to look at the house, sadness tugging at me.

I came.

I saw.

I didn't conquer.

But it's time to move on.

Getting a degree was never my dream. Playing football and Anastasia are, and I'm going to do what Mom said: put my hands on it and take it, *take it.*

THAT AFTERNOON, I pace around my house, my head tumbling. I've talked to Mom and Rae on the phone. I've touched base with Coach Taylor and we've made a plan to make an announcement to the press after the holidays. I've made some tweaks to my reservation at the ski lodge, and now I'm jonesing to see her. We only have a couple of days left.

When she shows up at my door, serenity replaces the nerves. Her cheeks are flushed as she beams and shows me the flat boxes and packing tape. She's got a grocery bag looped over her arm. "I have supplies for last-minute packing and food for us tonight."

"Great. I picked up some boxes too."

She studies my face as she comes in the door and I help her with the bags. "You okay?"

"Yeah. It feels good to have it done with him." I set the groceries on the kitchen counter.

She doesn't ask how it went. I'll tell her later. He's irrelevant now.

She moves to stand next to me and takes my hand. "How much stuff do you have to ship home?"

"Not much: my clothes, shoes, trophies, gifts I picked

up for Callie. My bedroom furniture is cheap, and I'll leave it. I have to warn you—my shit is everywhere. My closet...you might need a hazmat suit. I own more shoes and clothes than most girls." I pause, feeling off-kilter. "Thank you for helping me pack up three and a half years."

She stares at me, seeming to read my mood. "No regrets, River. I'd take one day with you over a million days with anyone else."

Unease rises and I sigh.

"I see the worry on your face. We don't know how this will end," she finishes softly.

I pull her to me.

I don't know what the future holds, but she holds it.

"It will always end with you," I reply, studying her face. "I'll wait."

Her throat bobs, and I watch as she takes a long breath then nods. Our separation is a topic neither of us wants to address.

"After we pack, I'll make us dinner. BLTs sound okay?"

I nod. "I can eat bacon all day long. Did you check on June?"

A smile curls her lips. "Yeah. Carl found her a TV and set it up. When I left, she was letting him stand in the doorway of the RV and watch with her."

"He'll win her over in no time," I say. "I'm going to

miss him. I've seen him almost every Sunday for years." I kiss her palm. "How was your day?"

She lets out a breathy laugh. "I've gotten some acceptance emails."

"Oh?"

She nods, that jerky one. "Brooklyn Law, kinda figured that one. Emory in Atlanta, very topnotch, Wake Forest in North Carolina, and Pepperdine in California. All were random shots in the dark when I applied, but they want me."

A lump of cement lands on my chest. "I see. Which one will you pick?"

"I don't know," she says, looking away for a moment before meeting my eyes. "Emory is prestigious and they're offering a scholarship. It's not far from Braxton, and it feels familiar. It's close to Carl and June in case they need something. I mean, I've never had a home, but Georgia feels like home in a weird way. It's the place I've lived the longest. It's where I made friends with Lila and Colette. I met you."

I picture her at a fancy law school. Without me there.

This is her dream, River. *Hers.* You have football; she has this.

"Yeah, that's great. Congratulations. You should pick that one, then."

The truth is, I don't know where I'll be in the fall.

She smiles. "As for the rest of my day, I took exams

and packed for the ski trip. I haven't even napped, and I should be exhausted, but I feel kind of crazy, like I could maybe lift a car with my bare hands. Is that weird? It's just...being with you, this feeling, it's like nothing I've ever had."

That's us, Rainbow.

"It's amazing, isn't it?" I say with wonder in my voice as I pull her between my legs and feel the magic settle around us. She's the center of my storm, my tranquility.

"Yes," she whispers right before I kiss her.

25

Anastasia

"Finally! You're here, bitch! About time!" Lila shouts as I walk in the ski lodge's lobby on White Face Mountain. My Uber just dropped me off after my flight. Excitement curls inside me, and I squeal her name, let go of my suitcase handle, and run for her just as Colette comes around the corner with a drink in her hand, sees us, and joins us, shrieking.

I laugh as we jump up and down.

"So glad classes are over, and we can be together!" Lila calls, whooping as she takes a sip of her cosmo. Much classier than Fireball. I giggle.

"Still wish you were coming home with us, but I get it," Colette adds. "Parents and all that jazz."

"I'll see you in January when the semester starts," I

remind her. I don't want to think about the fact that I *won't* see River in January. "And we have this trip."

"Our flight was so early," Lila complains. "Be glad you got to sleep in."

I nod. I barely slept.

I couldn't.

I'm terrified I'll miss a moment with him.

Last night, we packed his things in record time, took them to the post office, then came back and had dinner. After cleaning, he locked up and we went to my place and crashed. We got in my bed, and in between kissing, we talked. And talked. We couldn't shut up, trying to catch up on the little things about the person you love. He hates food that's green. His favorite color is blue. He doesn't do politics. He wants to have four kids someday. He dreams of living on the same mountain where he grew up. We slept on and off, his body curled around mine protectively, and when he woke me up at two in the morning to get to the airport, he kissed me so long I thought he might miss his flight.

I glance around. It's the evening, and people come and go in the lobby, most of them dressed for dinner. There's a restaurant to my left and an open area to my right that's a bar. Floor-to-ceiling windows line the walls, providing a view of the snow-covered mountains just outside. It's a winter wonderland and my breath hitches. No wonder he loves this place.

We have tonight.

Tomorrow he leaves to be with his family, and I'm staying to be with Lila and Colette then flying home to meet up with my parents.

I don't want to think about not seeing him every day.

I don't want to think about us not being in the same city.

"How are the slopes?" I ask Lila as we head into the lobby, my gaze taking in the elegant interior. "This place is gorgeous." Giant antler chandeliers hang from the ceiling, and a rustic timber and stone fireplace crackles around a luxurious sitting area dotted with dark leather couches and chairs. I spy a few students from Braxton, my eyes drifting as I search for him.

Lila laughs. "Fantastic for people who can ski. I tried the bunny thing, got an instructor, kinda hot looking, but I fell on my ass more times than I can count. Benji skis like a pro, of course. So infuriating. Thank God he left that lizard with Marilyn from the bar. Should I hook up with him?"

"I'm staying out of that one," I murmur as I scan the bar area. I see Kian sipping on a beer. He notices and sends up a hesitant wave.

I snort and wave back.

She follows my gaze and giggles. "I knew he wouldn't work out, but you have to admit, that revenge thing worked for you and River."

I nod. "How's the room?"

Someone breaks away from the bar, and my heart skips a beat. He's tall with broad shoulders, eyes low on me as he stalks our way.

He's wearing jeans, a cream-colored fisherman's sweater, and heavy boots. His hair is mussed, his cheeks flushed. He only has eyes for me as he reaches us and hugs me, his nose in my hair, and I sink into him.

"Oh," Lila murmurs. "Um, I don't think you're staying with us. Or, that's what he told me earlier." She grins at River then at me. "I'm going to grab another drink. See you later? Tomorrow, you're all mine," she adds with a twinkle in her eye.

I nod absently as she and Colette dash for the bar and sit at a table with Benji and a few other Kappas.

River takes my hands. "Surprise. You aren't staying with them. I upgraded to a private room. Honestly, I won't miss crashing with Benji. He snores like a train."

I laugh, a bubbly sound as I touch his face, seeing the pink on his cheeks. "It sounds great. You got some sun. How was the skiing?"

"Beautiful. Going down that mountain makes me happy." He slides his hands into my hair and takes my nape, and I shiver at the ownership I feel in his grasp.

"Everyone's watching us," I murmur, glancing around and seeing the gaze of every Braxton person at the bar.

"Get used to it. I told all the guys who are here that you're with me. Merry Christmas." He grins, looking happy.

"And?"

"They want us to be happy." A rueful expression fills his features. "I'm sure it would be a weird dynamic at the house if I were coming back to school, but I'm not. Guess that's the only positive of me leaving."

I push up a smile. "Yeah."

He tugs me closer and brushes his lips over mine, then gazes down at me, searching my face. "The slopes are open. How do you feel about night skiing? We can get you situated in the room, get geared up, then catch the lift. Just you and me and the snow."

"Sounds like you've put some thought into this."

"Yeah. This is our night."

My heart dips and I have to shove down the anxiety that wants to take over, the knowledge that *this* is it for us.

"Don't think about that," he murmurs quietly.

I nod.

"The view of the stars is incredible," he says. "It's quiet and peaceful, with just the wind in your face and the snow under your feet."

"Lead the way."

I'm in this with him, all the way, no matter how it ends...

26

River

No underwear. Dammit. I drape a fluffy white hotel towel around my waist and open the bathroom door. Anastasia left earlier to pop into Lila and Colette's room. Before that, we spent two hours on the slopes, had dinner in the restaurant, then came back up to the room.

It's one of the penthouse suites with a huge king-sized bed, a living room and fireplace, even a kitchen. I won't get to enjoy it, but I paid for her to stay here while I'm gone.

I blink at the darkness, adjusting my eyes. Water dripping, I make my way to where the light switch is, then pause when I hear "Iris" start playing on the speakers in the room.

I turn around and see her, silhouetted against the big window that overlooks the mountains.

"You're back?" I say inanely. "I mean, yeah, of course you are."

"Mhmm," she says over the soft music.

My chest rises as I take her in, the blood in my veins rushing.

Half in shadow, half lit from the flames in the fireplace, she's wearing my hoodie from the night on the rooftop. Her back is to me as she sways to the music, her hands in her hair as she lifts it up.

My heart catches as she turns around slowly, eyes on me as she slips one shoulder out of the unzipped jacket. She's wearing nothing underneath it, yet my gaze eats up her face, the curve of her cheek, the arch of her eyebrows, the curl of her red lips. I love her. *Her.* It's not about the sex, although that's going to be out of this fucking world; no, it's about who she is.

She knows how to move, this girl. She plays with the collar of the hoodie then releases it with her fingers, slipping her shoulder out of the other arm. She holds it in front of her, easing it down, revealing her breasts, the slope of her hips, the skin of her thighs.

My hands clench.

"Baby..." My voice is gruff, layered in emotion. Never seen her completely naked, and she is drop-dead gorgeous.

"You wanted to look," she says as she drops the hoodie and does a twirl in front of me, and I groan when I see her lush ass, that indentation at the bottom of her spine, the spot where I want to put my tongue.

The song plays softly, and I walk to her, need spiking. I turn her around and cup her face. My thumbs skate over her cheeks, my fingers diving into her hair as I bring her forward and kiss her. It's a dirty kiss, open-mouthed and erotic and deep. I want to consume her, fuck her, *love her*. Her tongue tangles with mine, then her teeth tug on my bottom lip. My hands lift her up and hold her as her legs wrap around my waist.

"That was a short striptease, and I was going to give you a blow job." She laughs against my lips as I fall back onto the bed with her on top of me.

"Later." I flip us over and stare down at her. Her lavender hair splays out behind her, and her green eyes shine in the dim light.

"Hmmm, I thought about surprising you in the shower, but since I wanted to be good, I thought we'd do your fantasy first." She runs her hands through my hair and sighs. Her touch wanders to my face. "I love your hair. Your eyes. These lips. I'm ready for the magic," she murmurs. "Wow me with your vast skills."

I huff out a laugh. "No pressure at all."

We've had the safe sex talk. I'm clean from a football

physical and have always used a condom. She's had a recent checkup and is on the pill.

"Let me touch you like I've been thinking about," I say softly.

I scoot her up to the pillows and hover over her as I whip my towel off and place my knees on either side of her. Long hair, expressive eyes, dark lashes, full breasts with dusky nipples, the long legs, the V between her legs, the one I've already tasted and can't get out of my head.

She laughs nervously. "You're staring."

"You. Are. Beautiful." I graze my fingers over where her heart is. "On the outside. And here. Right here." I trace a heart there.

Her throat moves as she swallows. "I love you."

I don't know if I'll ever get used to how those words make me feel.

"Touch me," she begs.

I hover over her, my bigger body encasing hers. I kiss her forehead, her nose, her chin, then her lips. And I am lost. In the feel of her body against mine, in the smell of her, in the yearning and urgency of her tongue. Pressing her hands out beside her head, I lace our fingers together and kiss her again and again, long and slow and lazy.

"River..." she gasps.

I suck her neck and her body arches into mine.

"Hands to yourself," I whisper as I unlace our fingers and cup her breasts, bringing them to my mouth. "I waited a year for you. I'm going to feast."

She lets out a shuddering breath as I graze my teeth over the tender flesh of her nipple. I suckle until her breasts are pink, until she squirms and reaches for me. I work my way down her body, leaving no piece of her untouched. My lips and teeth and tongue find her collarbone, the side of her waist, her hips, the freckle on her side, her belly button, the inside of her thighs.

I'm on my knees at the end of the bed and she's in front of me, her legs spread. I taste her, my fingers spreading her as I take what's mine. My tongue dances over her as I sink my finger inside.

"So wet for me," I groan against her. "I'm going to fuck you over and over and over..."

She moans and puts her hands in my hair. My pulse pounds as I pump slowly with my fingers, her breathy gasps ramping me higher.

"So expressive, Anastasia..." I say as my finger rubs the top of her channel, the place I touched on the rooftop that sent her over the edge. "You wanna come on my fingers?" I ask gruffy as I look up and hold her eyes. Hers are blown, completely dilated.

"Yes," she breathes as she twists on the bed.

"Hmmm, I'm glad our first time is here, with the

snow and the stars." I suck her pearl into my mouth, my teeth grazing the skin.

She whimpers and tenses, her body tightening.

"That's it," I purr.

"River..." Her hands fling down and grab the comforter, making fists as she arches up and calls my name again. Her core clenches, spasming around my fingers as her body flushes a pink color. Her head tosses from side to side, her lips parted as she tries to breathe.

"Anastasia..." I growl. "Damn. Beautiful."

Her body vibrates, still reverberating from the aftershocks as I take my time, working my hands up her thighs to her waist and her chest.

"Take me. Own me for real," she says.

Easing between her legs, I take her hips and brush my cock over her entrance, then up to her clit, moving through the slickness.

She shudders. "Don't tease me..."

I can't. I want her too bad. That first pump is slow, halfway in, and my heart pounds as I pause and say roughly, "Eyes on me, baby. Never look away. All those days I spent trying to not look at you, I want it all now." I push and slide in deeper, pivoting my hips to twist inside her.

She bites her lip and holds my gaze.

I dip my head to hers, pressing our foreheads

together as I thrust in and out, faster, then harder. My fingers dig into her hips, holding her as she takes it.

Details fly at me: the song on repeat, the smell of her, the sweat between us, the sound she makes when I slide out then push back inside...

Her hands clench my shoulders, her nails digging in, leaving marks. "River..." she calls out as her legs wrap around me.

She's mine, all mine.

"You feel so good..." I sigh as I tilt her hips up to go deeper, our eyes never drifting. I see the future there, don't know how it's going to work out, don't know when I'll get her in my arms like this again, but this, this, give me all of it, every moment.

My thumb brushes circles over her clit as I move inside her.

She digs her heels into my back, arching, wanting more.

"River..."

"I'm there, baby, there, let go, let go..."

She stiffens, shuddering breaths coming from her mouth as she writhes and goes over the edge, and I go with her, roaring her name as I shout my release to the universe.

∿

MUCH LATER, we end up on the floor in front of the crackling fireplace with a quilt underneath us and a fur blanket on top of us. She lies facing me, we can't stop staring, and my arm is around her waist, my leg tucked in between hers. She runs her hands over my face, humming as she traces my eyebrows, the lines of my jaw, my lips. I nip at her with my teeth and she giggles.

"I wasn't bullshitting about sex meaning more when you care about someone. It's never been like that for me," I say quietly.

Color rushes up her face. "Same. Pent-up feelings finally released after a year?"

"Mhmm." After a lingering kiss, I ease up to sitting, grab a pair of underwear, and slide them on.

She arches a brow. "We're done?"

I laugh. "Baby girl, hold your horses. This revenge hottie isn't going far."

She throws a pillow at me and I dodge it, then grab it and throw it back. It pops her in the face. She huffs as she gets up, wraps the blanket around her, and makes a dash for me. She collides into my chest, and I stumble and sail back, hitting the bed with her on top of me. We dissolve into laughter.

"I tackled the football player!" She fist-pumps the air.

I flip her over and tickle her until she's gasping and squirming. "Stop...please... I'm sorry..."

I laugh and lean back. "Okay. Pause for a sec."

"Okay," she says sweetly—and then throws a pillow at my back. I whip around and give her a look.

"You'll pay for that."

She rolls her eyes.

I dig through my suitcase and pull out what I need.

I plop back down on the bed and set the package in front of her with light hands, but inside, nerves fly...

She bites her bottom lip. "This is wrapped in Christmas paper. River... I didn't know we were doing gifts. I didn't have time to get you anything..."

"Nah, it's not about that. I've had part of this for a while anyway." I nudge it toward her. "We won't see each other for a while and..." it's killing me "...I wanted you to have something you could look at over the holidays."

She gives me a lingering look, then opens the rectangular box with careful hands, slowly pulling back the silver string around it. She pulls out the book and flips it over to read the title. "River, oh my gosh...*The Outsiders*...in hardback, too, *and* signed to *me*." Her eyes glitter with emotion.

I lie down next to her. "Mhmm. I figured since you gave me yours, and I kind of wore it out *and* wrote in it, I'd order you a new one off the author's website."

"You've had this?" She clutches it to her chest, her smile huge.

"After I finished the book, I started looking for a new copy for you." I pause. "There's something inside."

She opens it and a piece of paper flutters onto the bed. Dipping her head, she picks it up and scans it, her lashes fluttering against her cheeks. "You wrote a note?"

"Mhmm. I typed it. Can't write worth a damn."

She rolls over to me and fits herself to me, snuggling her back to my chest. My arm goes around her as she reads it.

I know exactly what it says.

I called Lila while Anastasia was in class on Friday, then went to her apartment to see the original note I dictated to Donovan. Lila knew exactly where it was, in her nightstand, and I took a picture of it then went home to get to work. I sat at my desk for two hours, checking my spelling over and over, before she came over to help me pack.

'You should be kissed and often, and by someone who knows how.'

Let me introduce myself. I'm River. I'm your current boyfriend. Cross my heart and hope to die—not really, but you know what I mean.

There are three things about you that caught my attention:

First, you're smart, too smart for me, but for some reason, you don't care.

Two, if you had wings, they'd be the colors of the rainbow.

Three, you touch me, and I have peace. You're a River-whisperer. Dad told me to take care of Mom, be a good brother to Rae, and wait for Anastasia. He somehow knew you were mine.

Where are you from?

Apparently, everywhere. Do you know how cool I think you are? Growing up moving around must have been hard, but it created a woman who looks at someone and sees underneath to the parts others don't.

What are you doing after this?

I hope after this night, in the future, we'll be together, in some city, crazy in love.

Please tell me you're single.

You aren't single, Anastasia. You're mine.

Also... I'm not a serial killer. True.

Or an alien. (People in Walker really dig that stuff.) True.

Or a player. I had my moments.

Or a douchebag. Again, had some moments.

Or a dick. Okay...maybe once or twice.

I'm just the guy in front of you on a snow-covered mountain, baring his soul to the most beautiful girl in the world.

You have dreams and I get it. I'll wait for you forever. No matter how long it takes for us to come back to a place where we can be together for real.

Your first reaction to this note may be to run as far as you can, but you only live once, and we can't lose what we have.

Fate has a way of bringing people together, and, baby girl, we're meant to be.

Kappa Boy AKA River Tate AKA Snake AKA Fake River AKA Anastasia's Man

SHE TURNS TO FACE ME, her eyes bright with unshed tears. "I love it so much." A tear escapes and tracks down her face before she swipes it away. "I've never cried this much in my life." She laughs.

"Glad you like it."

She runs her gaze over it again, then carefully folds it up and tucks it back in the book. "I'll keep it forever."

"I'll take that blow job now," I tease with a grin.

She throws a pillow at me and it bounces off my chest. "Forget that! Your gift is too good, and I don't have anything for you! I can't do better than this!"

"I think this bed has too many pillows," I say on a laugh as she throws another one and I duck. "And you gave me a unicorn pencil."

"It was nothing compared to your note!" She comes at me and swings her legs around, losing her blanket in the melee, then sits on top of me.

"I could get used to this kind of fight," I murmur as my hands span her waist.

"I'm mad you didn't tell me we were doing gifts, but I forgive you," she says in a serious tone. "We're early in the relationship and mishaps will happen, but I need to know about gifts." She pouts. "Yours was so meaningful! I feel terrible!"

"You helped me pack and helped me write that damn paper. I got an A, by the way. I checked online earlier." I chuckle. "I like you riled up though. Reminds me of the elevator."

She sends me a pretend glare.

"Want to do an angry fuck, baby girl?" I purr as I skate my hands up her waist and suck a nipple into my mouth, my eyes on her face.

"Yes." Her breaths are heavy as she pushes me back down. "First, I'm going to lick your python, then make you crazy with a special gift. Payback for not telling me..."

I groan at the heat in her eyes. "Give me your revenge gift, Rainbow."

She moves down my body, a wicked smile on her face.

27

River

"Oh my God! River!" my sister Rae yells as I walk in the door. The floor plan of the house is wide open, a vast den that opens to the modern kitchen. She flies across the room toward me, sidestepping a pile of white gauzy fabric before she jumps at me. "Little brother! Finally! About time you got your ass here!"

My heart swells as I hug her. She's five years older than me, tall like Mom, with the same glossy brown hair and blue eyes. She leans back to take me in, running her eyes over me in that direct way she also got from Mom. "You look good. Relaxed. Which is good. I need things. We jumpstarted the whole thing, so it's nuts. I have to go to the alterations place today, like right now, for my last fitting, Jason needs you to hit the tux shop this afternoon before four, the flowers are terrible, and the caterer needs to know how many people are coming and I honest to God don't know. I've called everyone, or I tried, but it's the holidays and everyone has plans, so we may have a thousand shrimp that no one eats and I'm not sure we can decorate around the giant tree we put up and Callie is everywhere because school is out and we leave for Hawaii after the wedding—that was fun at the last minute—and I hate that we won't be here, like a real holiday, but it's for the best and then I'll be back—" She stops and takes air in. "I won't even get started on the decorations. I wanted some tulle and fairy lights draped from the ceiling, but we don't have the electrical outlets and the wedding planner is losing her damn mind. I mean, it's to be expected. This is all so last minute—"

My sister can *talk*. Well, we both can. I interrupt her before she passes out. "I've missed you, and yes, you can order me around to do your wedding things, but, Mom—"

She gives me a wan smile and a kiss on the cheek. "Right. She's out on the sunporch, waiting for you." She grabs my arm before I turn that way. "Hey, I'm glad you're here, for real." Her eyes water. "It must have been hard to leave Braxton, but this means a lot..." Her voice trails off. "River, it's so uncertain. This wedding...me moving out...it's what she wants. I wanted to go back and forth between here and New York, but she wants me to get on with my life..."

"And your life is going to be great."

She nods, then takes a deep breath. "I have to run out, but I have to go put that dress on, then pick up the dog at the groomer..." She hugs me again, pressing her face to my neck. "I'll be back, 'kay? I'll grab us takeout. The house is a wreck, so..."

She dashes out the door, and I'm heading through the house when Callie rushes at me from the den, and I swing her up. She plants a kiss on my face. "River, River, River, lemme tell you about it."

"What?"

"Christmas play. That's what. I was an elf and Mama and Nana said I was the best one! I didn't mess up, not much, maybe a tiny bit, but I got to give gifts to the babies' class! They let me! Me! I'm a big girl, like really, really big." She moves her hands apart dramatically. "Can you tell I growed?"

"You're almost as tall as me!" I swing her around and she squeals.

I set her down after promising to play a game with her later. She dashes for her room to find what she wants to play, and I take a long breath as I run my eyes over the house, taking it in, feeling that *Ah, yes, this is home* I've been missing so much. I pass by the framed photo of me, Dad, Rae, and Mom and brush my fingers over it.

I step out to the sunporch, a big addition Dad put in when I was a kid. Heated with comfy furniture and a big-screen TV, the windows face the west, the sun shining in. The view is of snow-covered hills.

She's asleep on one of the couches, a blanket tucked around her shoulders. I settle down on the end, being quiet and moving her legs so they rest in my lap. Her face is pale and thin, but there's a peace about her.

"You little devil," she murmurs groggily as she stirs and opens her eyes.

"Yep. I have arrived," I say grandly, sweeping my arms out. "The favorite son. Goldfish killer, skunk lover, and all-around troublemaker."

She sits up and scoots closer to me, pulling the blanket around her. Her gaze runs over my face, searchingly. "You skied. Your face..." Her voice is full of wonder. "Thank you."

"I've barely slept the past few days." I grin.

"How was last night?"

I feel a slow blush rising up my cheeks. "Um...good?"

"I won't ask for the details." She laughs, the sound so free it hits me right in the gut.

I ease my arm around her shoulders and tug her against me.

"I want to meet her," she murmurs.

"You'll adore her." My mind goes back to this morning when I left Anastasia in our bed. Walking out of that room and away from her wore me out mentally. It took the three-hour drive here in a rental car to get my head together, and even then, I only barely managed it. I could have asked her to come with me, I could have, but it wasn't fair to take her away from Lila and Colette, plus she has to get back to her parents, and between the wedding and the holidays, the logistics wouldn't have worked out.

Take care of your mom, be good to your sister, wait for Anastasia...

I'm doing it...

But Anastasia's face when I left?

Devastated.

I mean, she didn't say it—she wouldn't, because she's brave for me—but...

"She's flying back after the ski trip to see her folks."

"When will you see her again?"

I don't know, and I hate it.

"We're taking it day by day."

"Because you want to be with me." She bites her lip.

"For you, for football, for me. School was not my thing, Mom. You gonna get huffy on me?"

She looks out at the hills, and I see a glimmer of tears in her lashes. "No, my huffy vanished the moment I opened my eyes and saw you. I'm *glad* you're here to stay." Her shoulders hunch, a vulnerable bent to them as she faces me. "I just wanted things to be normal, but they aren't. I've missed you so much. My spirit needs you, it does, and I haven't seen you in months, and now you're here and just seeing you in person..." She stops, her throat moving. "I need your three things to keep me going, son, every day."

I hug her closer, and she presses her face to my chest and weeps.

"I'm here, Mom. Not leaving," I murmur softly.

A few minutes later, she pulls away and takes my hand. Hers is thin, the veins blue and stark against her skin, the bones sharp. She laces our fingers together. "Tell me about her."

"I will, I will, but first you tell me about how you are—"

"You are just like your daddy."

"Mom, you have it wrong. He wasn't stubborn. You are, and I'm just like you." I chuckle through the tightness in my chest.

She smiles. "I have news. I spoke with my doctor today. There's a clinical trial at Johns Hopkins in Baltimore. It's not a sure thing, I need tests, but..."

Hope springs inside my chest. "When?"

"After Christmas. I don't want to get my hopes up, but..." She pauses and squeezes my hand. "What do you see when you look at me?"

My eyes mist. "A fighter."

"Damn straight. I'm a kickass bitch."

I burst out with a laugh.

She smiles, then gets serious. "I have too much to let go, River—you and Rae and Callie, and even Anastasia. How on earth would I ever rest in peace knowing you haven't given me a grandkid yet? I wouldn't! I'd be pissed off, and God or the devil—it's up for debate—would beg me to leave. I'm not going anywhere, not now, not now, not even when I'm at my lowest do I let myself consider it..." A tear drips down her cheek, but she's smiling. "And I've got you home! I... It means so much to me, River, thank you so much..." She leans her head on my shoulder, and I hold her.

28

Anastasia

"Where do I set this sweet potato casserole?" my mom asks breezily as she turns around from the oven inside Carl's kitchen. "The counters are covered, sunshine." She hums. "Here!" She sets it on the small island in the middle. "Next to the rolls. What a feast! Thank goodness you're a good cook."

I cooked the turkey, mashed potatoes, and the casserole. She made the rolls. I laugh.

"I made that apple salad thing!" Carl calls out as he and Dad work at the table, placing Carl's white, worn dishes next to the silverware and paper napkins. It's such a stark difference from the table settings at Donovan's this past summer that I blink. Wow, this is so much better.

"Yes, you did!" I say to him. He put too much mayo in the Waldorf salad, but I never said a word.

They go back to discussing football, which my dad knows zero about, but he nods in all the right places.

June is curled up in Carl's recliner with Oscar, *Die Hard* on the TV.

She's wary of us, sending us glances every now and then, but content, and having Christmas here with them was better than my apartment. Plus, she can get up and go back to her RV any time she wants.

My mom gives me a side hug and I smile. I picked them up a couple of days ago, and we've spent time together. I even took them to the alien museum. Dad wants to paint a night sky inspired by the newspaper clippings, and Mom declared she's going to design some intergalactic jewelry. It's not the most fascinating place they've visited, but they loved it. We walked through campus and I showed them the main buildings and talked about my favorite classes. We had dinner at The Truth Is Out There.

My phone rings and I make a dash for it, opening the FaceTime call.

"Hey." I breathe out as I take in River's chiseled face, the easy light in his eyes. A long sigh leaves me. He *is* content there, a peacefulness to his features I didn't even realize he possessed. Being with his mom has given him purpose and clarity. I wish I had those same feelings here in Georgia, but I don't. I adore having my parents around and spending the holidays with June and Carl, but a sharp sense of loneliness pierces my heart when I lie down at night. Our time wasn't long enough.

"Baby girl," he says, his gaze roaming over my hair and face. "Merry Christmas."

Carl jumps in. "Miss you, man! Happy holidays!"

Mom and Dad stick their heads in. "River, how was the wedding?" she asks.

"Went off without a hitch," he tells her, then says hi to my dad.

The daily calls are what I live for, sometimes several times a day.

I pan the room for him so he can see our table and June. She scowls at him and he just smiles. He knows she likes him.

I drift out Carl's back door and step outside. "I miss you."

I see an exhalation leave his chest. "Same."

I catch him up on my parents' plans to fly out the day before school starts for an artist festival in Seattle. They intend to live on the houseboat for a few months and save money for their next destination. He tells me about his mom's doctor appointment on the 28th in Baltimore. They're flying out early and spending a couple of days there so Nina can have tests run to see if she can qualify. I considered flying up to meet them before school starts, but I don't have the money. He offered to give it to me, but I also don't want to bail on my parents during the holidays.

Callie gets on and regales me with the pictures her mom has sent her from Hawaii. She thanks me for the stuffed unicorn I sent her for Christmas. I bought it at the ski lodge and shipped it from there.

"I'm meeting with a scout after the New Year," River tells me quietly when he gets back on. "Not Dan, the guy I met at Braxton, but one from the New York Pythons. He heard I was in town and called. We're meeting in Montpelier."

Joy for him rises. "River! That would be perfect for you and your mom!"

"Don't get excited. It doesn't mean anything. Anything can happen at the draft."

"Houston isn't your first choice."

"No. I'd rather stay close to home and Mom. You still stuck on Emory?" His voice is quiet, his eyes intense.

My throat tightens. "I can't turn down the scholarship."

"Right. You shouldn't. It's your dream." He nods, then frowns as he looks away for a moment. "I miss you, baby, so bad. I wish this were easier, but..."

Yeah. It's not.

～

"HAPPY NEW YEAR, BABY GIRL," River murmurs to me. "It's officially midnight."

I kiss the screen of the phone. "You too."

"Wish I were there, really kissing you," he says, holding my gaze.

My eyes close at the need I see in his face.

This empty feeling is only getting bigger and bigger.

Everyone around me is happy—and I'm not.

My mom dances around my den, waving Christmas garland, then lands in my dad's arms and they kiss.

River laughs, but it sounds forced. "I see where you get it. Smoke any pot?"

I push a smile up. "Lila and Colette are still in Ellijay. Mom smoked one from Lila's stash. I'm sure Lila would love her."

He nods. "Hey, I'm headed to Indianapolis the last weekend in February for the combine. Scouts and agents will be checking me out. It's about a ten-hour drive for you, and I thought, maybe, you could come. I mean, I won't be able to visit much...we spend most of our time on the football field..." His voice trails off.

I shake my head. "I'm supposed to meet with my Emory advisor that Friday morning. It's a group thing to meet the faculty and my cohorts. Afterward, I may scout some neighborhoods for a place to live." I sigh, feeling anxious. "Spring break is the first week of March."

"Mom and I are going to Baltimore that week. Her clinical trial starts then."

"I'm so glad she got in." I smile widely. He told me yesterday that she was admitted but I didn't know the dates.

"It could be a gamechanger, Anastasia."

I see the hope on his face and my heart clenches. I send up a silent prayer, *Please let it work.*

He sighs. "The draft is in late April, but maybe we can carve out a weekend earlier in the month? I could fly in to see you. A lot of it depends on Mom and her schedule. Everything's just...up in the air, baby. I thought about maybe flying to see you in mid-January, but Rae and Jason are moving then, and I don't think I can swing it."

My throat tightens. "Of course. We'll circle back to April when you know more. I graduate May 15th."

Four and a half months away...

"No matter what happens, I'll watch you walk."

"This is hard," I whisper, searching his face. There's more I could say: *I'm missing you so much it's a physical blow, I can't stop thinking about us skiing, us making love, or the way your face looked when you walked away...*

I can't because I don't want to pile guilt on him for leaving, don't want that at all. His mom needs him, and I get it, I get it...

He exhales as he watches me, *seeing* me. "I feel it too, but I'm here. Waiting for you."

I HUG my parents outside the airport on January 5th.

Dad gives me a kiss and wheels their luggage inside while Mom hangs back. She takes my hands and gives me a tremulous smile. "Thank you for the gift of your company these last few weeks. I am so incredibly proud of you, sunshine. River seems wonderful. The way he talks to you..."

I smile wanly.

"Dad's waving for you to come on," I say on a laugh after she keeps staring, not letting go of my hands.

She blows him a kiss then looks back at me. "Listen, when you like a flower, you pluck it. When you love a flower, you water it daily, hold it close, tell it your secrets, and watch it bloom and grow strong. You grow strong with it."

"Buddha."

She shrugs. "Sorta. I kind of mashed it up with my own thing."

I shift around, fidgeting. "What are you trying to tell me? Is this about River?"

Her head cocks. "You're very sad, Anastasia. It

worries me. I've never seen you like this. You seem...lost."

I bite my lip. "I'm sorry, I tried to be—"

"No, no, don't apologize for your feelings. I know my little girl and when she's hurting." She cups my face. "Just...if he's *it*, hold him close. Everything else will come."

I pause. "Everything?"

She nods. "Love is first, sunshine. It's rare to find your *person*. Water it."

THE NEXT DAY, I'm trudging up the steps of the Wyler building, my class schedule clasped tight in my hand. Sixth floor. Dr. Miles. A Study of the Romantic Poets. Right up my alley. *Welcome to the first day of class.*

So why is there a hollow feeling in my stomach?

Cold wind brushes my hair as a text comes in. **Have a good first day. I'm on my way to meet with the scout. Miss you. Love you.**

That empty pit inside me gets a little bigger. With the miles between us, it almost feels as if we never happened.

I'm missing him seeing the little things you have to experience in person.

The moment Carl rushed up to me at the bar and

told me June came in his house and cooked dinner for them.

River wasn't there the night she told me about Roland, her son. We sat in her RV and she poured out her story, the struggles of raising a son without his father, the loss of a job and their home, then the shelter fire.

He missed seeing Benji show up at the bar last night with Spike. The lizard got spooked by something and leaped over the table and landed on Parker's head. Then bit his ear. Okay, not funny. He's okay. Lila chasing Spike across the bar? Now that was hilarious. She tossed a metal bowl on top of him then danced around like it was an everyday thing. Later, I went outside to toss some trash and watched Benji and Lila as they kissed next to his truck.

He didn't experience any of those things.

And I'm here.

Alone.

I step into the elevator, and my heart pounds, wishing, hoping for a man who isn't going to suddenly appear. He can't. He has commitments, real ones that are lifechanging.

A guy gets on, an ATO. He smiles at me then pushes the button for his floor, and I wince. I always slapped it for me and River.

"You alright?" he asks.

I blink rapidly, realizing he must have asked me something.

"Um, what floor?" he inquires.

"Oh, sixth."

He pushes it. And he's not him, not him, not him.

I'm in a daze when I walk into the classroom, the same one from last semester. It makes me gasp. I didn't even notice it on my schedule.

Benji waves at me, and I head his way and sit next to him.

"I can't believe you talked me into adding this at the last minute," he grumbles. "At this rate, I could be an English major."

I push out a laugh. He's been in and out of my apartment for the past couple of days—with Lila. I'm happy for them, I am, but...

I miss River so much.

The professor starts the lecture, and I try to focus as she runs through the syllabus.

I'm not listening. I've racked my brain for a way to fit me into his life, and I can't see it.

If I knew *where* he was going to end up, I might take a stab at finding a law school there, but most universities have already closed their admissions for the fall.

Benji leans in. "Hey, he told me to give you this, said he wanted you to have something the first day. He dictated and I wrote it. Dude is a poet if you ask me.

Never knew that about him." He slides a note over, and I take it with trembling fingers.

ANASTASIA,

I wake up every day and my first thought is, I wonder what skirt you're wearing. Then, I go to sleep and dream of you. Happy times we'll have. They'll come true someday.

My three things for you today: live with no regrets; breathe, baby, just breathe; and like your mom said, a jug fills drop by drop, and soon ours will be full.

It just takes time. Don't give up on us.

I feel you. Even from here, I feel you, and I love you.

I STAND up at my desk, my chest rising. He's killing me with this.

He left and I get it, I do, but what am *I* doing? I don't want to be this lost without him. I don't!

What if...what if I...

"Ana?"

I blink rapidly and look at Benji. "I can't do this."

His eyes flare. "What do you mean? Ana, wait! You need to help me in this class!"

But I'm gone, running out the door, past the professor, past the students. I'm in the elevator, my hands shaking as I run from the only place I've called home, because it isn't anymore, it just isn't.

He told me to live without regrets, to breathe, and to let the jug fill up, but...

I want the jug to be full. Now.

AFTER MEETING with my advisor for an hour, then going to the admissions office and filling out forms, I get in my car and drive the two hours to Atlanta. Once I'm at the airport, my adrenaline has spiked, and I barely recall using my credit card to buy a direct flight to Albany. The flight is a blur.

My mind races as we land. I rush past luggage and get a rental car. Charge it. Who cares?

It's three hours later when I pull up to the two-story white colonial. The address is in my phone; it's where I sent gifts for River and his family for Christmas. A fur blanket for his mom, a unicorn for Callie, a scarf for his sister, a photo of me and River skiing for him.

My phone is dead, and I haven't been able to call him, which is okay, maybe it's for the best. He might have talked me out of it.

His truck is here. Good. His meeting with the scout is over.

Nerves fly at me and I push down my anxiety.

I knock on the door then fidget as I adjust my skirt and purple sweater. The wind blows and I pull his varsity jacket around me, the one he left for me.

A little girl opens it. Callie. She's adorable in person!

She blinks. And blinks. Then smiles. "Wow! It's so pretty!"

She's looking at my hair.

I laugh, then bite my lip. "You are too. It's good to see you, Callie."

"Who's there?" comes a woman's voice, one I recognize from FaceTime.

She comes to the door using a cane to walk. She's wearing leggings with a baggy Pythons sweatshirt, and her hair is soft stubble on top. Her eyes are blue, startling me with the fierceness.

She lets out a surprised gasp, then reaches out and pulls me inside. She doesn't speak, not a word, for an entire minute, just takes me in, her hands on my shoulders, seeing me, reading me. A slow smile crosses her face. "Wow. You did something unexpected, didn't you, Anastasia?"

I nod, feeling the pull of tears in my eyes. "I'm not going back. Just can't go another day. It's not the same anymore. June and Carl are there, but it's not home. I thought it was, but it's not."

"Tell me about it," she murmurs sagely, and it reminds me so much of River that my breath hitches.

Then it all comes out. "My mom said this thing about a flower, and keeping it watered, and I know that's confusing, you'll have to meet her to get it, but I'm wilting without him. I miss him, love him, we only had one night, and I thought I could live on that for a few months, just wait and see, but I can't, and even then, who the heck knows where he'll be, and I don't care where he is really, any city will do. I always wanted a home, but home is him and wherever he is. I'm not going back to Braxton..." I stop and wipe the tears I can't stop from coming.

She laughs under her breath. "Two college dropouts? Insane. Do you have a plan?"

"I don't even have luggage."

"Hotel?"

"No. Do you have some nearby?"

She laughs. "You must stay with us, dear. I insist. What about law school? River says you got into Emory. I don't know much about law, but that's one of the top universities in the country—"

"It's nice to meet you in person, Mrs. Tate—"

"Call me Nina. Please."

"...but you won't talk me out of leaving school and neither will he. I met with my advisor and he agreed to let me wrap up my last few classes online. I can go to any law school. I don't care where it is. Not one iota. I might take a gap year, do some volunteer stuff to beef up my application. He left a note for me, his three things, and it was good, so good, but you know what I need? I need his face." My heart clenches.

She smiles. "He makes the world right."

I nod and wipe the tears from my face. "I need him next to me. So much. I need him not missing the little things. I need him telling me in person my three things. I told him the day of the sunrise that I needed someone to look into my eyes and tell me those, but I don't think he really got that I would give up anything for him. Emory is just a school. River is *him*. He's the kind of guy who *wouldn't* ask me to because he's about this *waiting*, and he has waited—for over a year." I give her a pleading look.

She lets out a soft laugh. "Wow, you can talk."

"You should see me stoned." My voice hitches as I clench my purse tight, my need rising higher and higher. "Do you think I'm crazy?"

"No, dear. I would have done the same thing for my husband. I never liked being away from him. You must love River very much."

My lashes flutter. "So much. Where is he?"

"You mean Uncle River?" asks Callie. She's taken my hand and looks up at me. "He's right there." She points and my eyes follow, finding him to the right standing in the hallway. He's breathing hard, his hair wet from a shower, a towel around his waist.

"Underwear, son," Nina murmurs. "Tsk, tsk. You'd lose your head if it wasn't screwed on."

"Anastasia?" he asks in a low voice, his eyes wide. His throat bobs. "What are you doing...you had class today?"

A strangled sound comes from me as I run for him, straight into his open arms.

"I NEED to make mac and cheese for Callie. I promised," River murmurs to me later. We've been holed up in his bedroom for the past few minutes. Kissing. Making out. He's put on joggers and a workout shirt and we lie in his bed. He leans up on his elbow and twists a strand of my hair around his finger. "You like mac and cheese?"

I gaze up at him, my eyes drinking him in. "I'm starving. Honestly just looking forward to seeing you cook and dote on Callie and your mom."

He dips his head and takes my lips, slanting to reach farther, to go deep. His nose runs up my neck. "Seeing you at my door, hearing those words... I can't explain how much it means to me..." He holds my eyes. "What about Emory?"

"Law school can be anywhere, as long as it's where *you* are. You once said I was too much, too soon..." I exhale. "Are you scared of this? I mean, I'm basically showing up at your door uninvited..."

"Baby. You are always welcome here, but you're giving up Emory for me—"

"There are other places. Are you still waiting, River, because me? I'm not. I know this is sudden, but I need you in my life. I need your mom. Your sister. Callie. People leave me, they do, and I let them go. I wave at my parents and they do their thing, but you, *you are mine*, my flower, like Mom said, and we can't be apart. We just can't," I say earnestly.

His head dips, then he looks up at me, an anguished look on his face. "Walking away from you was the hardest thing I've ever done, and, Jesus, I've missed you so much. You're always in my head. Every second of the day. I've been telling myself everything would be fine, but I was terrified you'd move on without me..."

A tremulous smile comes from me. "I'm here. And I'm not leaving."

Wonder flashes over his face as his arms tighten, and I guess it's finally sinking in. "I can't believe this! Baby, baby, I got you, *I got you*, you're here in my arms and I can't let you leave. I never would have asked you to give up Emory, I wouldn't, but fuck, thank you for coming, thank you, baby..." He stops, a misty look in his eyes.

Emotion slams into me, seeing the love in his gaze.

"Waiting is over," I say breathlessly as I kiss him. "But I need a place to stay. And some clothes. And a job. Is there a bar here where I can wait tables?" A laugh comes from me. "Holy shit, I left my car. Lila has an extra set of keys at least..."

He pulls my chin to him. "We'll get it when we can. Lila will send your stuff, and Rae has some things. You'll stay with us. Mom will put you in a guest room that I can sneak into. She knows we had sex, by the way, so there are no qualms about that if you're worried. She's pretty easygoing about that stuff."

Color floods my face.

River chuckles. "Mom wants you here, and she's going to love you. You'll go to the combine with me, to Baltimore, the draft, and when I move, we move together. We'll try to talk Mom into going with us. You can get a job if you want, but just being here with my mom and me would be great. I have money. Pretty soon, a lot of it. We'll settle and you can go to school. I can help you pay for law—"

"I can get another scholarship."

"My smart girl." His lips hover over mine, his eyes burning with emotion. "Fate put us together. I love you. Please. Just. Never leave me."

My heart fills with joy, for him, for us, with hope for his mom, for our future together. I slide my hands into his hair. "I love you."

We kiss, long and slow.

Life with him is going to be wonderful.

And it was...

EPILOGUE

River

Four years later

"Dude, you bought a Christmas sweater for Spike?" I ask Benji on a laugh. He's sitting across from me at The Truth Is Out There with the lizard in his arms like a baby. The sweater—more of a cape—is lime green with a candy cane and a stocking on the back. How do you even find something like that?

Lila leans in over the table. "No, the real question is... why did he buy himself a matching one? Custom order from Etsy. My boyfriend is deranged."

"Aw, you're jealous I didn't buy you one." Benji gives her a kiss on the cheek.

"Like I would wear it," she grouses, then smiles.

Benji's eyes twinkle as he glances down at his own sweater. "Green is my color. Makes my eyes pop."

"Question," I say. "Does the lizard sleep with you two?"

Lila glares at me. "No."

I burst out laughing. I bet he's in the room though.

Benji, Lila, and Colette live together in Los Angeles. Lila waits tables and writes screenplays, Colette works at an art gallery, and Benji is in graduate school. We see them once or twice a year. This weekend is special. They've flown in for Anastasia's twenty-fifth birthday surprise.

"She's here!" Carl says as he jumps up from our table in the back and peers out the window into the parking lot. He claps his hands at us as he turns around. "Places, people, places! Get behind that corner so she can't see us. Lila, fix that balloon—it looks wonky. Also, it needs to be said, do not pull out your weed. We're in public. Colette, open the cupcakes so she'll see them. June, where did you put my gift? It's a framed picture of us."

"I have it, don't worry," June says as she stands up and follows us as we move to a doorway in the back that hides us from the entrance.

June still lives in Carl's RV and keeps an eye out for spaceships for him. She isn't big on crowds, but her counseling has helped. Anastasia arranged that for her, found someone who'd come to her RV. When Carl asked

June if she wanted to come to the bar for the surprise, she said, *I'd do anything for Anastasia.*

During the offseason, we fly down and hang out at Carl's house for a couple of weeks. Then, we head out to whatever beach destination Crew and Hollis have cooked up for our annual vacay with them. Crew is still a mother hen; Hollis still says his abs are prettier than mine. They aren't.

I glance around at the bar. I miss this place, the Sundays when I'd hang out with my brothers and watch Anastasia. We arrived yesterday, and I went to the Kappa house. I mean, I didn't know any of the new guys, but my photos are still on the wall. They knew *who* I was. A good president. A footballer. Not a king or a god, but a regular guy who cared about his brothers.

After I left Braxton, I was drafted by the New York Pythons. Houston went with the wide receiver from Alabama, leaving the door open for New York, and they scooped me up in the second round. It's a familiar franchise, and several of the staff knew my father. It feels like home, and my jersey number is number three. For Dad.

I didn't get a big payday like a first-round pick does, but in the past few years, I've worked my way up to first string and adjusted my contract.

Wearing a red mini dress and tall boots, Anastasia walks into the bar, my mom next to her. Their heads are tilted close to each other as they laugh about something.

My heart stutters as I take them in. Damn. I'm a lucky man.

Mom's clinical trial and new treatment put a pause on her cancer. She's in remission, takes smaller doses of her medication, and gets regular checkups. Her last scans were clear. She's still here, with us, experiencing my life with Anastasia.

Anastasia smiles, one of her soft ones, and I smile back even though she doesn't see us yet.

She's...

I sigh.

Gorgeous.

Breathtaking.

Kind.

Mine.

Anastasia moved in with us four years ago and the transition was seamless, as if she'd always been part of the family. She helped take care of Mom while I went to training camp after the draft. That fall she picked out an apartment for us in Brooklyn, one close to Brooklyn Law and the stadium. The way things worked out, she didn't have to take a gap year, and I insisted on paying for her tuition. Yeah. That was some good angry sex. I smile to myself.

Mom refused to move with us. Thankfully, by then she was feeling better. We're about five hours from her, and we see her as much as we can, or she comes to stay with us. Her favorite thing is to fly to the away games with Anastasia.

My girl brushes lavender hair out of her face, and I catch the gleam of the amethyst and diamond engagement ring I gave her six months after she moved in. It was summer, right before training camp, and that ring had been burning a hole in my pocket. I was nervous, wondering if she'd think it was too soon. I knew, oh, I knew I wanted her forever. A love like ours only comes around once. It's soulful, consuming, and meant to last.

The plan for the proposal was to go for a walk under the stars at Mom's then get down on one knee, but my ADHD kicked in, and I ended up blurting it out during dinner in front of Mom, Rae, Jason, and Callie.

I know this is fast, okay, it is, but my mom and dad did it fast. When you know, you know, and I get that with us. You have a dream, you're gonna be a kickass lawyer, and I'm gonna play pro, and it's gonna be hard work, but we can do it. We're gold, baby girl, and we're gonna watch all the sunrises and sunsets. I love you and can't go another day without knowing you'll always be mine.

She set down her fork, smiled tremulously, and said yes. Mom cried, Rae giggled, and Callie jumped up and danced. Right there at the table, I got down on one knee and slipped the ring on her finger.

We got married at Mom's a month later. Mom and Rae wanted to do a big shindig, but Anastasia just laughed. She doesn't want fancy things. It was simple, just us and our families. Her parents flew in, and I paid for Carl to come. June wasn't ready for an airplane.

She wore a simple white dress; I wore a suit. Callie was our flower girl. We honeymooned at a bed and breakfast a few hours away, then I left for summer camp.

"She's coming...one, two, three..." Carl whispers as we huddle around the corner of the bar. "And...go!"

"Happy birthday!" we shout as we step into view.

Mom laughs at Anastasia's shocked face. "Surprise, dear. The alien museum was a ruse—although I did enjoy it."

Anastasia looks around, her eyes misting as she takes in the whole crew. Her chest rises, her lashes fluttering. Technically, we celebrated her birthday yesterday at Carl's with Mom and June, so seeing Lila and Colette and Benji is a total surprise.

She runs for me and I catch her in my arms, burying my face in her hair.

"I love you, Rainbow," I whisper in her ear.

She leans back, a huge smile on her face. "Thank you, thank you, for bringing me my favorite people."

I kiss her as Benji hoots. "Keep it clean or I'll have to cover Spike's eyes."

I huff out a laugh and let her go as Lila and Colette huddle around her and they all squeal.

Later, after we've settled at the table, Lila pushes a gift into her hands. "I insist you open mine first."

Sitting next to me, Anastasia opens it, blinks, then laughs at the bound notebook she pulls out. She looks up at her. "*Legally Lavender*? You finished it?"

"Currently shopping it around LA." Lila smirks. "It's gonna be a movie someday."

I drape an arm around my girl. "Is there a revenge pact in there?"

Lila shrugs. "Of course. It was my idea, after all. And yes, I'm in the script as myself. Some names have been changed to protect the innocent." She giggles.

Anastasia hugs it to her chest and laughs.

And...

Damn.

I can't keep my eyes off her, the way her eyebrows arch, the sound of her laugh...

The next day, we walk up the steps of the Wyler building, hand in hand.

"Thank you for humoring me," she says as we breeze past students, ones we don't know.

"I wish I'd thought of it."

"You did think of the library. That was fun, posing for selfies at the table where we met. We got some looks."

I chuckle. "If they only knew the story..."

We wait until the lobby is clear, then step inside the empty elevator. I stand on one side while she stands on the other. She slaps the button for the sixth floor. We pretend to ignore each other, then I turn to her and give her a once-over. She smirks.

I back her against the wall, shove my hands into her hair, and kiss her long and slow.

"You're my air, baby girl," I whisper. "I'm gonna love you forever."

Her eyes hold mine. "Forever."

When the doors open on the sixth floor, she's still in my arms...

DEAR READER,

Thank you for reading the *The Revenge Pact*. I hope you enjoyed River and Anastasia's fated love story.

If you want to keep reading about these football players, you're in luck. The *Kings of Football* series contains two more standalone stories by two other amazing authors. In the next few pages, you can take a peek at Meghan Quinn's *The Romantic Pact* and Adriana Locke's *The Relationship Pact*.

REVIEWS ARE like gold to authors, and I read each and every one. If you have a few moments, please consider leaving a rating or a review for *The Revenge Pact*.

. . .

KEEP READING ALL THE BOOKS.

XOXO,

Ilsa

P.S. SIGN UP below for my newsletter to receive a free **BONUS SCENE** with River and Anastasia. The **BONUS SCENE** will be included in the newsletter on DECEMBER 10th!

You will also receive a FREE Briarwood Academy novella just for joining.

HTTP://WWW.ILSAMADDENMILLS.COM/CONTACT

PLEASE JOIN my FB readers group, Unicorn Girls, to get the latest scoop as well as talk about books, wine, and Netflix:

HTTPS://WWW.FACEBOOK.COM/GROUPS/ILSASUNICORNGIRLS/

EXCERPT 1 - THE ROMANTIC PACT BY MEGHAN QUINN

The Romantic Pact

Crew

"Hazel?" I ask, my heart tripping at the sight of an old friend.

Her warm, caramel-colored eyes snap to mine, her face registering shock. "Crew?" A small smile pulls at her lips. She checks her seat number and then her ticket again and smiles even larger. "Would you look at that? Seems as though we're seatmates."

"Holy shit," I say as she takes a seat and beams at me.

"How are you, Hollywood?"

"Better now." I wrap my arms around her and pull her into a hug.

Hazel Allen.

Born and raised in the neighboring house to Pops's farm, this outgoing ball of sugar and spice was a staple of my childhood ever since I can remember. Her grandpa, Thomas, was best friends with Pops, and she worked on the farm from a very young age. Whenever I visited, she always made fun of me and my latest West Coast style as she strutted around in overalls, a tank top, and rubber boots. Her hair was always tied up on the top of her head, with a rolled-up bandanna around the crown to hold back any stray hairs.

Down to earth, fun, and a jokester, Hazel was one of my best friends growing up.

Pen pals.

Long-distance friends.

And of course, each other's first kiss.

When we pull away, Hazel lifts her hand to my face and presses her palm to my cheek. "God, you just keep getting more and more handsome."

I chuckle.

"And this scruff. Now you're really looking like your DILF of a dad."

"Can you not refer to my dad as a DILF? It really creeps me the fuck out."

"Ahh, but he is a hot piece of dad ass. Sorry." She shrugs, sets her backpack on the floor, then turns in her seat to face me. "When my Grandpa told me about this trip, I had an inkling you might be my traveling partner, but I wasn't sure." She takes my hand in hers. "God, I'm so glad it's you."

"The feeling is mutual, Haze," I say, taking in her rosy, freckled cheeks and the way her hair softly falls over her forehead. *Thank you, Pops.* How easy it will be to travel with one of my best friends.

God, when was the last time I saw her? I think it's been a few years, to be honest. Once college started, I kind of lost contact with everyone. Training, studying game videos, and perfecting my throw took over.

Eyes softening, she asks, "How have you been? I saw your season . . ." She winces.

"Yeah," I huff out, staring down at the way her small hand fits in mine, the callouses on her fingers from all the hard work on the farm reminding me just how different our lives are, despite a lot of the variables being the same. "Wasn't my best show on the field. Just wasn't in it mentally."

"I can understand that." She squeezes my hand and

then says, "But we're not here to talk about all of your interceptions, and I mean all of them . . ." When I glance up at her, she's smiling a Julia Roberts smile. I poke her side and she laughs, her head falling back as she pushes my hand away.

"How have you been, Hazel?" God, I've missed this girl.

"Oh, you know, just living the life out on the farm. Got caught up in some mourning, ate way too much pumpkin pie this past fall. Did you get your fair share of pumpkin spice lattes?" She nudges me. "I know what a basic bitch you are."

I laugh. "Yeah, I had a few."

"A few? I remember senior year in high school when you were drinking one a day. At least, that's what you wrote to me. Then again, it has been three years . . ."

"Has it?" I ask, knowing damn well it's been three years since I've seen her. Three years since . . . hell, three years since I ran from her.

END EXCERPT

Want to find out exactly why Crew ran away from Hazel? Oo, it's a doozy. Keep reading here: https://amzn.to/2HLdH6o

EXCERPT 2 - THE RELATIONSHIP PACT BY ADRIANA LOCKE

The Relationship Pact

Larissa

I reach for the chair in front of me. Instead of finding leather, my fingers brush against something else. Something warmer. Something smoother and rougher all at the same time.

My heart jumps in my chest at the same moment that my head snaps to the side.

452 | Excerpt 2 - The Relationship Pact by Adriana Locke

Oh. Shit.

The most beautiful set of hazel eyes I've ever seen traps my gaze. The warmth of the chocolate brown is cooled by the spring green embedded in the orbs. Gold flecks twinkle as the man slowly withdraws his palm away from mine.

I open my mouth, but I've somehow forgotten how to speak.

"Hey," he says, his southern drawl rippling across my ears. "You can have it."

I shake my head to try to jolt myself out of the haze I'm in. "I ... I can have what?"

His full, pouty lips split into a sexy smirk. "I meant the chair, but if there's something else on your mind, just let me know."

My heart flutters in my chest as a wave of heat courses through my body from head to toe.

A couple of days' scruff peppers a sharp, chiseled jaw. His skin is sun-kissed and imperfect and there's the slightest mole beneath his left eye that gives a bit of softness to his appearance. His body is long, well over six feet, with broad shoulders and a thick chest.

It's one heck of a picture.

Slowly, *oh-so-slowly*, the fog in my brain lifts.

"Can I buy you a drink?" he asks.

A crazy idea pops into my brain. The longer that I

watch the stranger peer at me from under his thick lashes, the more it seems possible.

Crazy, yes, but possible.

"Want to do me a favor instead?" I ask before I can talk myself out of it.

My chest rises and falls in quick succession as he, *and I*, ponder my question. He narrows his eyes as he undoubtedly considers why a woman he just met might need his help.

His heavy brows tug together. "That depends on what it is."

Blood pours through my ears as I realize I'm teetering on the edge of something impetuous. Again. I'm about to do the one thing I told myself I wouldn't do.

Wasn't I going to put the brakes on this kind of thing? Didn't I swear that I was not going to tangle myself up with men? Wasn't I going to save myself time and energy until good men come back into the universe?

I look up and down his long, muscled body.

I bet he's a damn good man.

"Are you going to ask or not?" he asks, killing me softly with a playful quirk of his brow.

Screw it.

I take a quick lungful of air and commit to this insanity. "I'm going to need an answer to two questions."

"Shoot."

"*Quickly.*"

He grins. "I can't answer them if you don't ask them, beautiful."

I steady myself against the term of endearment and stay focused.

"Do you have a girlfriend?" I ask.

His eyes sparkle with mischief. "I like where this is going."

"That's not an answer and we're running out of time."

"No," he says hurriedly. "Hard no. Definitely not. No girlfriend."

"Second question ..." I take another deep breath and then go in for the kill. "Will you be my fake boyfriend for five minutes?"

His grin knocks the breath I'm holding right out of me. "When do we start?"

END EXCERPT

For Hollis and Larissa, starting is the easy part. It's ending their fake relationship that's hard. Fall in love with them here: https://geni.us/Hq6TNb

Keep reading for another excerpt from I Dare You by Ilsa Madden-Mills

EXCERPT 3 - I DARE YOU BY ILSA MADDEN-MILLS

I Dare You

Prologue

Freshman year

Delaney

Welcome to Magnolia, Mississippi, where locusts are as big as your hand and iced tea comes with a double helping of sugar.

It's also home to the best damn annual bonfire party at prestigious Waylon University, which is currently happening right now in the middle of a cotton field.

But...

I shouldn't even be at this party.

It's mostly for Greeks and jocks and popular people, yet here I am, a mere freshman, hanging out with my bubbly redheaded roommate, Skye.

"See?" she says as we take in the bonfire. "Isn't this better than watching cat videos on a Saturday night? What do you want to do first?"

I sigh, feeling nervous. Ever since I moved here from North Carolina, I've been pushing myself to try new things. Might as well put a crazy college party on that list. "Let's get a drink."

She claps and excitedly replies, "Done. Alcohol at two o'clock." We weave through the crowd, headed in that direction, and eventually we reach the bar, which is really just a long collapsible table someone set up. On top are various bottles of alcohol, and I grab the Fireball to pour shots. I've just tossed mine back and set down my cup when a prickling sensation washes over me, giving me goose bumps.

My gaze moves across the crowd, stopping on a tall guy with dark blond hair, broad shoulders, and a cocky smile. *Aha.* He's been staring at me, and now that he's caught, he raises his glass as a half-grin crosses his face.

I blush wildly as I adjust my black cat-eye glasses. I'm not used to such blatant male attention.

Skye—who's followed the trajectory of my gaze—

spits out part of her drink. "Oh my God, do you know who that is?"

"Obviously I should," I say dryly.

Her mouth flops open. "You really need to get out more."

My eyes drift back to him but keep moving as if I'm not staring. "So who is Mr. Hottie McParty Pants?"

"If you don't know him, you don't deserve to know. But, he's H-O-T—like Chris Hemsworth hot. I dare you to flirt with him." She wiggles her eyebrows at me, knowing full well that for some reason, I can't resist a dare. Normally rather reserved, a dare gives me permission to be someone I'm not.

So does Fireball. I sling back another shot.

"I'll bring you a donut every day for a week if you flirt with him," she adds, watching me.

My ears perk up. "The ones with edible glitter?"

She nods, and I toss a quick glance back to him. Our eyes collide again, and a zing of connection fires between us. He has a strong, handsome face and a stance that has masculine written all over it. A smile tips up his full sensuous lips, and—

Two brunettes—twins, no less—approach him, one on either side, and wrap their arms around his waist. He smiles down at them. *Oh. Well then.*

I turn back to Skye and frown. "Player. Not interested."

She waves her hands in my face. "He likes you—I saw it on his face."

I snort. "Probably gas pains. Your dare is not accepted."

We hear our names being called from the other side of the party and turn to take in the helmet-haired Martha approaching us, which is taking some time due to the fact that she's wearing stilettos and a slinky halter dress. She carefully picks her way through the crowd, nudging people out of her way—sometimes rudely—as she focuses on us. *Great.*

"Incoming mean girl," I mutter under my breath.

Like us, Martha Burrows is a freshman and lives on our floor. Rather full of herself, she announced within a week of meeting us that she'd no longer answer to anything but *Muffin*, a nickname she'd given herself.

She eyes us both, a look of superiority on her pretty face. "I didn't know you two were invited to this little shindig. Obviously, I know all the right people, so I'm always invited." Her gaze zeroes in on my outfit and she rears back. "What on earth are you wearing, Nerd Girl?"

"Clothes." I stiffen at her name for me as I tug on my fitted Star Wars shirt and the pleated red miniskirt I made from a man's shirt. My long pale blonde hair is up in curled pigtails, and I went a bit heavy-handed with the shimmery eye shadow and red lipstick. It's not your typical look for WU—which is anything monogrammed—but I'm learning to ignore the raised eyebrows.

Skye, the peacemaker among us three, clears her throat and nods her head at the guy who's been staring. "Delaney has an admirer, but she doesn't know who he is."

Martha-Muffin follows Skye's gaze, eyeballing the mystery man over my shoulder. She gives me an exasperated look. "That's Maverick Monroe, you idiot. He's the biggest football star in Mississippi and the freshman recruit of the year. Word is, though, girls like you aren't his type—not at all." Her hand flicks a stiff honey-colored curl over her shoulder.

My teeth grind together. "Martha, if you think I care what you think about me and whether or not a quasi-famous football player is interested in me, then you are confused."

Her lips tighten. "It's *Muffin* now, and why do you have to use such big words? What does *quasi* even mean?" is her cutting reply.

Skye's eyes get as big as saucers, and I assume it's because Martha-Muffin and I are about to finally have it out. I can't stand her, and she can't stand me. We just...clash.

But that isn't what has Skye in such a titter.

She points over my shoulder, and I get it.

It's the person standing behind me, the one I can't

see. I feel a nervous sneeze coming on and—*thank God*—I somehow push it down.

A husky voice reaches my ears. "*Quasi* means *seemingly* or *supposedly*. What she means is I'm probably not a famous football player but rather one that's been highly touted but is without merit."

Oh, shit. The voice is rich and smooth with just enough southern drawl to make a girl swoon. He also sounds halfway intelligent.

I turn around slowly. Mr. Tall, Blond, and Football is right in front of me wearing a cocky smile.

How in the hell did he get over here so fast?

You know that moment when everything stops and the next breath you take is the first one of the rest of your life? That's what it feels like as Maverick Monroe stares at me with his piercing blue eyes.

I glance down and take in the sculpted chest and hard biceps.

I look back up and see a chiseled jawline that's defined and lined with a slight scruff. I see the thin pink scar that slices through his left eyebrow, and it does nothing to detract from his appeal.

He's perfection.

He's air.

Which I desperately need right now, because I can't breathe.

He smirks, as if reading my mind, and I scramble to

pull myself together. Someone calls his name—it's a girl's voice, probably one of those twins—but he doesn't budge.

His eyes rove over my skirt, glasses, and lips. "The question is...do you even know what makes a good football player?"

"Nice hands?"

His lips twitch. "Hardly."

"A tight end?" I smirk, feeling sassy...which is weird. I don't know who I am right now, but it's like my mouth has a life of its own, saying things I normally wouldn't.

Martha-Muffin chokes on her drink at my remark and Skye watches me with glee, clearly excited that I have the attention of someone who is apparently *very* important at Waylon.

I put my hand on my hip. "The question is...why do I need to know?"

"You don't. All you need to know is I'm the best."

I suck in a little breath at his arrogance.

A guy walks past us and claps him on the shoulder. "Badass game last week, Mav. Rock on."

"Thanks, man." Maverick acknowledges the compliment and lifts his chin, his eyes never straying from mine.

"What position do you play?" I ask. "Quarterback?"

He smirks. "Middle linebacker—defense."

"Sounds fancy."

He laughs.

Skye, who's been eavesdropping unabashedly, sighs with a dreamy expression on her face. "His stats are the best in the country." She clears her throat. "I-I only know that because my brother is a huge fan, I swear."

"Hi, Maverick," Martha-Muffin says as she edges closer to him, nudging me out of the way with her sharp shoulders. "Remember me?"

He focuses on her. "No."

She glowers. "I was in your dorm room with your roommate last week. You said *hello* to me."

He shrugs. "A lot of girls come through. I can't remember them all."

Oh. My. God. He *is* arrogant, but I like how he just shut her down.

Martha-Muffin's face reddens and she mutters something under her breath, flips around, and flounces off. Good riddance.

Out of the corner of my eye, I see Skye is drifting away too, giving me a thumbs-up.

Whatever. I am not going to flirt with this guy...am I?

He's definitely got something about him, something that makes my body buzz. I tilt my chin up, taking in how tall he is. He has to be at least six-four.

His gaze drifts over my face. "You know there's a legend here at Waylon about our famous bonfire party?"

"Oh?"

He smiles, a flash of white on his handsome face. "Legend says the first person you kiss at the party is the one you'll never forget. It might be years later, and still their face is the one you dream about."

"Sounds like hocus-pocus."

He lifts that mesmerizing left eyebrow. "I like to believe in legends—after all, I am one."

I smirk. "Probably a game made up by some frat-boy-slash-jock wanting to kiss all the girls."

He pauses for a moment as if thinking, and then he steps in closer, so close that I can see the varying shades of blue around his pupils. "May I?"

My heart does somersaults.

"May you what?" I ask, my voice low, but I know what he wants. My body is already leaning toward him, wanting it too.

"This." He kisses me, an almost imperceptible touch as he brushes his full lips against mine. The contact of our mouths is electric, sparks of fire skating along my skin.

As if from a distance, I hear someone calling his name. It's a female, and she's pissed.

It's one of the twins probably.

And I'm jealous.

But, I don't look. We pull away, and I stare at him as he stares right back. A stillness settles over the party, although I don't think anything's actually changed. The music is still playing. People are still talking. Beers are being passed around.

Yet...

We're connected.

Two stars in the black velvet sky.

Two ships passing in the night.

Oh, fuck, stop the nonsense, I tell myself.

"What was that?" I ask, my voice breathless.

"That's your first kiss of the bonfire. Now you'll never forget me."

And then, before I can think of a reply, he's gone.

I watch him go back to the twins, frustration coiling inside of me as I exhale.

It would be two years before I kissed him again.

CHAPTER 1

Delaney

It's Valentine's Day evening, and my social life is worse than when I was a brace-faced freshman at William Henry Prep School in Charlotte, North Carolina. At least back then one of the geeks from my math class gave me a tiny heart-shaped box of stale chocolates and a brown teddy bear. All I have this year is a broken heart, a bottle of premium vodka, and an eighties horror movie.

Skye is out having fun, and I'm glad for her. She left

the off-campus house we share earlier for a date with her boyfriend, Tyler, and here I sit...languishing in yoga pants and crying into my popcorn.

I send a longing glance at my phone, waiting for it to buzz with a call or text from someone who cares about me...but it remains silent, mocking me as I press myself into the worn brown leather of the sofa. I hate feeling sorry for myself, but sometimes it gets to me that I don't have any family since my Nana—the person who raised me—passed right before I left for college.

God. I'm lonely.

My nose takes a whiff of the blanket that's pulled up to my face, and I swear I still smell leftover hints of my ex's spicy cologne. Alex is a special teams kicker for the football team at Waylon, and we'd been together since we met in a literature class freshman year. He was my first, the person I thought I'd spend the rest of my life with, and for the past year, part of me half-expected him to propose. Instead, he cheated.

I take a sip of Grey Goose straight from the bottle, eyeing it balefully. At least he had great taste in vodka.

I lift the bottle in the air, toasting. "Happy Valentine's Day, Alex, wherever you are. I hope Martha-Muffin can give you what I couldn't—ideally, the clap."

Yep, my arch nemesis from freshman year slept with my boyfriend, and the worst part was I'd walked in on them in his dorm room.

Feeling that familiar melancholy of being alone creep in, I turn my attention back to the movie. Eerie, spooky music escalates from the surround sound speakers as a girl runs through a forest, her head twisting as she looks to see if she's being followed. Terror is stamped on her face.

It was on Skye's dare that I chose this particular flick, and part of me knows she really just wants me to be preoccupied on a night when I'm alone.

The popcorn is still warm from the microwave as I pop some in my mouth and chew rather furiously, watching as the heroine on the screen is suddenly accosted by a burly figure with a mask. I scream—even though I knew it was coming—sending fluffy white kernels flying. Han Solo, my cat, stands and hisses at me, his black and white fur sticking straight out. I've upended him from his comfy position on the couch.

"Sorry, little man."

Screw the dare. I'll take her punishment, which would no doubt be inventive. The last time I lost, she made me stand on a table in the cafeteria and call out, "My milkshake brings all the boys to the yard."

I scramble for the remote and mute it, wondering if it counts if I watch without the sound on. I *am* watching it, just minus all the bloodcurdling screams and spine-tingling music.

"Give me *Sixteen Candles* or *The Goonies* any

freaking day—those are the best of the eighties," I mutter under my breath as I stare down at Han. "You agree?"

His head cocks ever so slightly. He gets me. I know he does.

I exhale and sit back down, tucking my legs underneath me as I lean my head back against the couch.

Ping!

My phone goes off with a text and I straighten up to retrieve it from the table.

My brow furrows at the unknown number. Usually those are telemarketers or scammers...but it's a local prefix.

I read the text. **Hey, sexy. I'm glad I have a library card because I was checking you out today. Do you have a Band-Aid? Because I scraped my knee falling for you.**

Two things happen at once: I half-giggle and half-snort, causing a coughing fit I quickly recover from. I *was* in the library this morning before my upper level psychology class to work on a paper, but I didn't notice anyone staring at me. Must be my bestie pulling a prank on me with someone else's phone.

I quickly type a response. **Skye? What happened to your date with Tyler?**

It's entirely possible she's feeling sorry for me, has skipped out for a minute to check on me, and is using

Tyler's phone. Any minute now she's going to ask if I'm still watching Michael Myers.

Another text comes in. **I'm not on a date and I don't know a Skye. Is she as hot as you?**

Stop messing around, I send. **I've had a tiny bit of vodka...okay, a lot.**

I'm a dude. Swear to baby Jesus.

My brow wrinkles. Is it possible this isn't Skye? But then who is it?

How did you get this number? I type out.

You put up a listing on the Help Wanted board in the student center a while back. I saw you and got the number. I saw you again today at the library so it must be a sign for us to get together. Wanna hook up, babe?

Babe?

Hook up?

What an assuming ass, I think as mortification shoots through me. No one has answered the listing I put up looking for a male partner to take a salsa class with me. Thankfully, the posting didn't have my name on it (*so embarrassing*), just my phone number, and I've been meaning to take it down, but between working at the library and class, I haven't found the time. I was in a weak place when the idea struck, and now, looking back, it reeks of desperation from a girl who'd recently been cheated on and was lonely.

I glare at the phone as if the jerkwad on the other

side can actually see me.

I'm not your personal Tinder, I reply, my fingers flying across the screen. **Go find someone else to harass.**

Nothing comes through for the next fifteen minutes as I stare blindly at the television, not really seeing anything, just fuming, my mind racing through possibilities of who saw me posting the ad. Hundreds of students pass through every day, and it could have been anyone. I think back to my morning study session today at the library, trying to recall if anyone was watching me, but I was hyper-focused (as usual) and kept my head down.

I should probably block this number.

A new text pings.

Hey, look, I'm sorry. This isn't the person with the horrible pick-up lines and offer of sex who first texted you. Those messages were from my asshole friend who took my phone and texted you without my knowledge. I have it back now so we're cool, right? Sorry for the inconvenience and I hope you find a salsa partner. Later.

Finally, a polite text—except for the goodbye part, because I wasn't done talking. I still want to know who these two people are. Part of me wonders if it's Alex, feeling me out, maybe seeing if I've moved on. He has been texting me, trying to engage me in a dialogue, but I've ignored him. This doesn't seem like his style though.

Hold your horses, stalker. Who are you?

Seconds tick by and I can see the dots on the screen indicating he's replying. I'm picturing a loser at a frat house, the first one to fall asleep, and instead of drawing a giant dick on his forehead, they stole his phone and texted random girls.

My name is Inigo Montoya. You killed my father. Prepare to die.

I laugh under my breath at the iconic movie reference and part of me relaxes. **Good one,** I text.

You're a fan of *The Princess Bride*?

One of my favorites. I even have a t-shirt with Buttercup and Westley on it, I type, referring to the two main characters.

I'll remember that.

Is that why you're texting me on Valentine's Day? To talk about *The Princess Bride*? Are you lonely? My fingers move quickly, feeling comforted that I'm not the only one who's a romance dud on the holiday of love.

I'm texting you because my friend was a jerk. He doesn't mean to be; he just thinks we should hook up.

Not going to touch that comment.

So where are you right now? Dorm? Frat party? Off-campus strip club? My detective cap is on and I'm determined to figure out who this guy is. My mind goes back to a rather geeky, thin guy who hangs out in the romance section at the library. He's given me a few lingering glances when I happen to walk past him.

I'm in bed, he says.

Alone? I'm being bolder than usual.

Yes. You?

I'm hesitant about responding. After all, he could be a serial killer, but I don't get that vibe, and I trust my instincts.

Just me and my cat, a scary movie, and a bottle of vodka—hell of a way to spend V-Day.

At least two minutes go by—a damn long time in the world of texting—and I wonder if he's left or grown bored of me. Chewing on my bottom lip, I'm in the middle of chastising myself for revealing as much as I have when a new message comes in.

Is it crazy and weird that we're talking and you don't know who I am?

Do you know who I am? I ask, adjusting my cat-eye glasses on my nose. If he saw me put up the ad, he probably does. Waylon is small, with an enrollment of around six thousand, so it's likely we've seen each other or even had a class together.

You're Delaney, a junior from North Carolina.

My pulse kicks up as I feel my heart beating in my chest, but those are basic facts he could have gotten off my social media.

He sends another text. **Truth: I think you're gorgeous. We also know each other...sorta.**

He thinks I'm gorgeous? My bruised ego is flattered,

and I shoot a look at Han. "Did it just get a little hot in here or is that the vodka talking?" He rolls his eyes and flounces off to the kitchen. "Are you saying I've had too much?" I call after him, but he pointedly ignores me by not turning around.

I stare down at my phone, wondering what else to say. I should probably end this, but I feel an odd connection with my new texting partner.

I could talk to a random guy.

I want to.

Do it, Delaney. I mentally dare myself.

Are you still there? he says. **Did I go too far? I tend to do that. I should just apologize in advance for anything I'm about to say or do.**

He hasn't gone too far. My interest is piqued. **So who are you?**

I'm a badass athlete.

I roll my eyes. **So you play a sport here at Waylon?**

Yes.

Crap. My heart does a little sputter and takes a nose-dive—it's likely he knows Alex. The athletic dorm is situated on the west side of campus, and most of the players reside there. Football, baseball, and wrestling take up one side of Byrd Hall, while soccer, volleyball, tennis, and the minor sports occupy the other.

I purse my lips. **Which sport? I've sworn off football for the moment.**

Let's keep that a secret, but if you need a name, you can call me He-Man.

And I'll be She-Ra?

His reply is swift. **Hell no—they were siblings. Pick another name, something that suits you.**

Does He-Man suit you? I type. **Do you live at Castle Grayskull? Are you fighting Skeletor?**

Damn straight. I kick his ass every day.

I grin. **You're very serious about this. I'm starting to wonder if you might be crazy.**

Just pick.

Princess Leia.

Perfect, he replies. **I'm picturing you with cinnamon buns on your head.**

I giggle. **I'm picturing you as a muscled blond dude with a brain the size of a walnut.**

Don't be fooled by the dumb jock stereotypes.

And you shouldn't be fooled by my nerdy, quiet girl status. I'm a red-blooded woman with needs. *God.* I can't believe I just typed that. I take another sip of vodka. **What I MEANT to say is I don't do athletes anymore, specifically football players.** *Okay, that sounded stupid.* Clearly, I need to stop texting.

Nothing comes back from him, and my mind wanders.

Is he a football player? That might explain why he's not telling me his name. The guys on the team have a serious bro code when it comes to not messing with the exes of the other players.

I decide to change the subject. **My roommate dared me to watch a scary movie tonight—alone. I was terrified.**

Do you like dares? he texts.

Yes. It forces me to put myself out there. It feels silly to say, but it's easy to tell him because I don't *know* him. I'm beginning to see why anonymity is attractive.

I hear Han meowing at the back door. He has a litter box in the laundry room, but he's rather manly and likes to go out for an occasional romp around the yard to mark his territory. I like to go with him since my last cat disappeared on me a year ago, leaving me devastated.

Hey, I need to go, I tell my mystery man. **My cat needs me.**

Wait, you said you take dares, right?

Yes.

I dare you to dream about me tonight.

What? Why? I ask, my heart rate picking up a beat.

Because I'll dream about you.

Oh. I bite my lip and chew on it. **Like a sexy dream?**

Is that what you want?

Yes.

My body comes alive, every sense on alert. It feels like forever since someone kissed me or made my stomach feel fluttery inside.

I type out, **I need more details if I want to picture you in my head, especially since I don't know who you are.**

You know I'm an athlete, I'm blond, and I like to swing my sword around.

I giggle. **Where are we in the dream? Give me a setting. I need more.**

A few moments go by before he finally responds. **At a frat party. Everyone else is downstairs and you and I are upstairs in an empty bathroom.**

Seriously?

This is my fantasy, Princess Leia. Just listen.

Fine. What are we doing? The room feels warmer, and my fingers are sweaty as I type the words. I picture myself with a dark shadowy male in a tiny cramped bathroom. His hands cup my face as he stares down at me, his thumb tracing over my lips. He kisses me on the neck, sending lightning bolts of sensation across my skin.

My body heats to the point that I squirm around on the couch, fingers hovering over my phone.

What do you think we're doing? he texts.

Kissing?

More.

Shit. **Second base?**

More.

Home run? I send after a slight pause, feeling lightheaded. This has escalated and I'll probably regret it tomorrow, but for right now, I don't care.

We're going at it against the wall, Princess Leia— hard. I like it hard.

I picture it, the small bathroom hot with our proximity. My body arches toward his and he barely has his jeans shoved down yet he's inside me, sliding in and out as I moan...

Shit. This has gotten totally out of control. The feisty girl-power woman in me is rebelling at the suggestion of him taking me hard, but...*holy smokes*, I like it. My heart thunders.

Are you still there?

I type, **I have to go.**

As you wish.

With a flurry of motion, I turn my phone off and toss it down on the couch. He-Man or Badass Athlete or whatever he calls himself is trouble. I stare at my phone for a few more beats before dashing to the kitchen to drink down a glass of ice-cold water.

END EXCERPT

If you would like to read the rest of Maverick and Delaney's story grab your copy of I Dare You today.

ALSO BY ILSA MADDEN-MILLS

All books are standalone stories with brand new couples and
are currently FREE in Kindle Unlimited.

Briarwood Academy Series

Very Bad Things

Very Wicked Beginnings

Very Wicked Things

Very Twisted Things

British Bad Boys Series

Dirty English

Filthy English

Spider

Fake Fiancée

I Dare You

I Bet You

I Hate You

I Promise You

The Revenge Pact

Boyfriend Bargain

Dear Ava

Not My Romeo

Not My Match (Coming 2021)

The Last Guy (w/Tia Louise)

The Right Stud (w/Tia Louise)

ABOUT THE AUTHOR

#1 Amazon Charts, Wall Street Journal, New York Times, and USA Today best-selling author Ilsa Madden-Mills pens angsty new adult and contemporary romances.

A former high school English teacher and librarian, she adores all things Pride and Prejudice, and of course, Mr. Darcy is her ultimate hero.

She's addicted to frothy coffee beverages, cheesy magnets, and any book featuring unicorns and sword-wielding females. Feel free to stalk her online. ☺

*Please join her FB readers group, Unicorn Girls, to get the latest scoop as well as talk about books, wine, and Netflix:

https://www.facebook.com/groups/ilsasunicorngirls/

You can also find Ilsa at these places:

Website:

http://www.ilsamaddenmills.com

News Letter:

http://www.ilsamaddenmills.com/contact

Book + Main:

https://bookandmainbites.com/ilsamaddenmills

Printed in Great Britain
by Amazon